LAURA NAVARRE

GEMINI WILD

Only I would start my new semester at the dark witch academy with a kidnapping (mine) on dragonback and end the night with a marriage proposal I don't want from the King of the Dark Fae.

My intense and sinister kidnapper.

Suddenly I'm not only Zara Gemini, the celebrity bad girl and wild rebel queen of the witching world. I'm the misfit new student at the Avalon Academy for Promising Royals of the Faerie Court. And the unwilling future bride of Zephyr, the Dark Fae King. He claims our union is his last chance to break this curse that's destroying his realm.

Plus I'm already up to my royal neck in dangerous warlocks who'll kill to rule at my side.

Sounds delish, right?

Not so much. See, the enchanted secret world of Avalon has a dark side, and so does this Hades-Persephone fairytale. Sure, Zephyr's the sexy-pretty hottie every Fae at court is jonesing to shag. Turns out he's also broody, tortured, and twisted, with a shattered heart behind his savage surface.

Let's just call Zephyr… a fixer-upper.

Now I've got a curse to break, a warlock to tame, *and* a kingdom to save.

Plus I've still gotta pass my midterms.

Gemini Wild is a spicy paranormal why-choose romance and the sequel to *Gemini Kings*. This LGBT-friendly adult academy series delivers wolf and dragon shifters, dragon riders, teacher-student forbidden heat, first-time MM, bi awakening, all swords crossed, a confident queen who never has to choose, and flaming fast-burn heat. *Gemini Wild* will whisk you away from your day-to-day and set your schoolgirl skirt on fire!

Content Notes

The *Dark Witch Academy* series contains the following:

- MF, MM, and group encounters (if you don't like MM in the harem or only like a little, this is not the series for you!)
- teacher-student heat (all adults)
- age gap
- past suicide (off page)
- abduction
- grief
- violence
- dirty language (if swearing offends, this is not the series for you!)
- death of a parent
- past death of a sibling (off page)
- light restraint during intercourse
- consensual flogging
- internalized homophobia overcome as part of one hero's journey
- talk of pregnancy
- animal (dragon) in danger

Chapter One
Zara

I'm being hunted.

That's a feeling I know way too well. Even though it doesn't happen on the daily anymore. Not with me squirreled away behind magical wards like a law-abiding freshman here at the Academy.

The average person might think me being hunted like a goddamn fugitive wouldn't happen at all. You know, since I'm the Gemini queen-in-waiting of the whole witching world, just twiddling my thumbs and waiting for my reluctant predecessor to vacate the throne so I can ascend?

Well, that person would be wrong.

I get hunted. All. The. Time.

And yeah, that shit's unsettling as fuck.

Same as always.

The biting wind of a drizzly March whistles past, which definitely makes it hard to hear whatever's hunting me. I'm flying in my dragon form, so a transparent membrane drops over my eyes to protect my peepers from the icy sleet that's hammering my scales. But I still can't see much through the heavy veil of clouds and mist hanging over Icarus Island at twilight.

Puffing out a warning rumble for anything in hearing range, I lash my tail and angle my wings to slice through a cold gray swirl of cumulus.

Now I can't see at all. My six-chambered heart beats harder.

My nostrils flare to search the wind, ears swiveling to catch any out-of-place sound. My dragon shifty senses sort through the damp smells of rain and ozone, laced with the first green hint of an early spring.

An acrid whiff of brimstone eddies past.

Max? I snap my wings tight and spin in a spiral to clear my six, looking for my alpha in my blind spot—which happens to be above and behind me, like it is for any dragon. *You following me, big guy? You ready to apologize maybe, you know, for being a total dick?*

Because, yeah, we're fighting.

Again.

But that mating bond that connects me with Max and all my guys? It's fucking silent.

Thought I was alone up here. The quiet hum in our psychic bond says so.

But that niggling itch running down the back of my long neck like a plucked guitar string is telling me I was wrong.

Tingling with nerves, I beat my wings in a powerful downstroke that propels me through the clouds.

The wet fog parts and swirls away. There's the jagged summit of the dormant volcano right under me, heights crusted with snow and ice, looming against a slate sea. Right now the Icarus Academy, and the Roman ruin of a village that shelters us, are hidden behind the mountain. My whole world is gray with rain and twilight.

Somewhere above and to my left, my eye skips over a vivid flash of venom-green. Definitely out of place in these steely skies.

So totally out of place, I'm not even sure I saw it.

My neck snakes around. The protective membrane over my eyes retracts. The blurred edges of my world turn sharp.

Great. Now I'm seeing shit.

Max has me so spun up with his dragon king bullshit—so pissed at his pigheaded dragon stubbornness—that I'm, like, hallucinating. There's nothing here, showgirl. Nothing to see.

Zero. Zip. Nada.

The fog swirls in a violent eddy, disturbed by a sudden gust of movement.

I'm ghosted by the pungent reek of brimstone.

Max? I bare my teeth in a warning snarl. *If you're not here to apologize—and basically fucking grovel—you need to back the hell off. I swear to fuck, if you're playing games with me, you'll regret it.*

I fire that challenge through our mating bond like a catapult.

Of course, he's not the only winged monster that hunts these skies.

Vasili's a shifter too. His serpentine body can wind through the clouds unseen, like the snake he is. V's the top dog alpha of all the warlocks in my harem.

And I definitely wouldn't put it past my snake to fuck with me.

The resentment that's lurking between Max and me? That's nothing next to the electric charge of sexual tension, spiked with competitive instinct and alpha aggression, that crackles between Max and Vasili.

But V smells like caramel and vetiver. Sweet enough to lick all over. And potent enough to make you drunk.

So it's not him I'm smelling.

And the telepathic bond that connects me and all my guys stays silent.

I growl deep in my chest. The air smells sharp with the metallic tang of ozone. Lightning tastes like tin on my forked tongue. Thunder rumbles in the clouds. Electrical energy flickers and sparks along my scales.

That feeling of being watched? Stalked? Hunted? It's getting worse.

And that pisses me right off.

Well, fuck. I'm done hiding.

You want a piece of me? I'm a pretty strong telepath, and I blast out that APB on all psychic channels. *Whoever you are? Come and get me.*

I angle my neck and plunge beneath the clouds. Fully exposed to whatever's out here, I part my jaws and scream a challenge with the lightning voice. A jagged bolt of purple lightning erupts from my mouth and forks across the darkening skies.

That's me—lightning dragon—saying *here I fucking am.*

Roaring my defiance, I beat my wings hard and soar over the summit. Here's where we held my succession ritual a few weeks back, right here on Mt. Apollo, when I finally stopped rebelling against my fate and embraced this whole ball-and-chain queen gig.

The whole shebang broadcast live across the witching world by WNN.

Behind a curtain of rain, the summit's dark and silent as a slasher film. The dilapidated World War II-era bunker looms like a haunted house. But that's just my nightmares acting up again, given what went down inside with me and Lucius and Max's bitch of a mom, the last dragon queen. Who's now—thankfully—dead.

The circle of standing stones where we played nice for the news cams, all wrapped in mist and shadows, gapes up at me like a ring of broken teeth.

It's not like an *Outlander*-type circle. Still, I'm running on instinct. I tilt my wings and angle my body to avoid flying over that fucker. It's a new moon and spring equinox simultaneously in like two days, which I'm learning from my astrology class is a time for powerful and unpredictable magic.

Cheese on toast. If whoever's fucking with me doesn't wanna come out and play, they can kiss my scaly ass—

Something massive drops from the clouds like an anvil, right the fuck next to me. It plummets toward me like a freight train, green as venom, wind screaming around a streamlined shape.

Every nerve in my body fires in alarm. Adrenaline spurts through every synapse.

Operating on pure reflex, I swerve.

My sudden veer sweeps me back over the summit. The stone circle yawns underneath me like a hungry mouth. I tilt wildly to avoid flying right over it, then twist in midair to bellow a bolt of lightning over my shoulder to fend off whatever's coming at me—which is definitely some kinda dragon. Even though we don't have any of those behind the wards, except for V and Max and me.

Lost in the clouds behind me, lightning slams against… something. Whatever that thing is?

It *screams*.

That shrill scream is nails on a chalkboard. Loud enough to make my ears ring. My back bristles and my skin crawls.

Goddamn it. What's back there? I crane my neck around to stare.

I see heat signatures in infrared, it's a dragon thing, and this apparition's burning and pulsing a sinister red. I glimpse the churn of beating wings, a flash of poison green, some kinda dark figure perched high on the powerful shoulders between those wings wearing… a towering crown of spikes… what the fuck…?

While I'm distracted, my wingtip sails over the stone circle, close enough to graze the monoliths.

Something—like the circle itself—grabs my wing in steel claws and drags me toward it.

Never mind how batshit crazy that sounds.

Right here, right now, it's crazy time.

I'm still new to this whole flying thing. Max has been teaching me, but it's only been a few weeks tops since the first time I shifted. Now I'm thrown way off balance, twisting and tumbling and clawing through the rain-washed gloom, I've lost track of that thing that's maybe a dragon but bigger, more, other, worse. It's something worse that's after me—

My whole body tips over the stone circle.

And suddenly, my whole world *shifts*.

It's like someone just dragged a curtain aside to show me what's lurking behind the everyday world of the Icarus Academy. The shadowy summit of Mt. Apollo, it's gone in an eyeblink. The cold glitter of ice in winter sunlight stabs into my night-blind eyes. A sprinkle of snow whips past my snarling muzzle on a gust of frigid wind. The temperature plunges fifty degrees in a breath.

Again, I react on sheer instinct.

I'm small for a dragon. Max says I'm still a juvenile when I'm shifted.

Which means I'm agile as fuck.

I beat my wings hard to shake free from whatever's got a hold of me. I backwing and twist away from whatever it is I'm seeing. Sure, I'm awkward and uncoordinated, but my sudden maneuver hurls me away from the stone circle.

In a blink, that whole crazy hallucination of biting cold and the blinding dazzle of sun on blue-white ice—it literally vanishes.

Just winks out of sight.

Bellowing with alarm, heart thumping away like a jackhammer, scared and pissed as fuck, I wing away hard from the summit and that freaking circle with everything that's in me. Even though it's hard to fly straight when I'm this off kilter, I roar out a challenge at my hidden attacker and spin end-over-end like a Blue Angel fighter jet to clear my six. I'm pretty desperate to eyeball whatever just drove me into that mindfuck of an ambush.

But the skies are black as pitch. Anything with a heat signature that's up here with me is hidden in the clouds. The rain's getting worse, sleet mixed with pebbles of biting hail that plink against my scaly hide.

Sweet Jesus. That stab of sunlight nailed my night vision. I can't see shit and I can't smell a thing.

My ears swivel like mad, but all I can hear is the desperate flap of my wings under the wind's shrill scream. Fear beats in my blood like a second heartbeat.

And I don't like it.

Okay. Okay. Don't fall apart here, showgirl. You just gotta pull your shit together.

My little pep talk notwithstanding, I'm already winging hard around the mountain. Making a beeline at top dragon speed for the clutter of half-abandoned Roman ruins, dotted with warm electric light, that's scattered along the coast.

To be real specific, I'm making straight for Villa Augustus. That's our *domus*. Our residential college.

That's home.

Home's where my guys are, all five of them, even the one I'm pissed at, even the two that are fighting.

Holy fuck. I gotta get home. Like now.

What in the Sam Hill just happened back there? Whatever went down, only one of my warlocks has a chance in hell of explaining it to me. That's the guy I need to talk to. He also happens to be the guy who makes me feel the safest. Which, right now, turns out to be something else I really need.

Lucius.

Chapter Two
Lucius

My desk in the *domus* library is overflowing with student applications for the fall semester.

Truly, the sheer number of them is nothing short of miraculous. The witching world is, after all, slowly dying. This tragic truth has been our grim reality for centuries. During that time, the four races have grown insular and reclusive—none more so than the shifters, of course. In recent years, we've barely attracted a handful of junior witches and warlocks from any race into each freshman class.

Yet tonight here I am, steadily leafing through dozens of enthusiastic applications, while veering between astonishment and a heady sense of elation. Needless to say, I attribute this sudden windfall to Zara's celebrity student status. Since the infamous night of her television debut, the night she finally stopped rebelling and publicly embraced her royal destiny, every clan in the witching world is eager to forge ties with the future Gemini queen.

Merciful God. If we accept even half those who are now seeking admittance, we'll need to hire more faculty.

Miraculous.

But now is hardly the moment to rest on our laurels. The unwelcome task that currently demands my attention is not the matriculation of my future students, but the crisis of the current student who's pacing before my hearth, quietly furious but grimly resolved, with tears streaking her freckled face.

Mallory McSnicker, as she has just divulged to my startled ears, is pregnant.

Remarkably, hers is the third pregnancy this month to roil the placid waters of our insular Academy. That statistic is nothing less than extraordinary in a student body that numbers fewer than forty.

Apparently, this plague of unplanned pregnancies is what occurs when half the population indulges in a literal orgy of unprotected sex during an unsanctioned party in the basement of Villa Hadrian.

That orgy, too, was Zara's doing.

My unsettled silence finally draws Mallory's gaze. She stops pacing before my hearth like a caged tiger and whirls to face me.

"Look, Master Aries." Despite the flood of tears, my formerly meek and mild-mannered student is positively gritty with resolve. "I know what you're thinking, okay? It's probably the same thing Mistress Agrippina said right out loud when I told her. You're wondering why I didn't take care of business and use birth control from the school clinic like a responsible adult, right?"

Dear God.

Truly, I am singularly ill-equipped for such a conversation with a female student. Not to mention this one I barely know.

"To be entirely honest, Ms. McSnicker," I murmur, "I'm hardly in the habit of pondering the prophylactic choices of my students, I assure you."

Except for Zara's, of course. Lately, I've found myself spending entirely more time than is prudent pondering Zara's prophylactic choices.

But Zara is, undeniably, different.

Zara Gemini is far more than my student. She's one of my precious mates. Never mind that mating her was a shocking indiscretion and a blatant violation of the Academy Codex that nearly got me fired.

I owe my continued employment as headmaster of this residential college to a single bitter truth. These days, the faculty of Icarus Island barely comprise a skeleton staff. I'm the only purebred shifter on the entire faculty, the most gifted at Common Magics, and the only professor qualified to teach History of Witchcraft.

Quite simply, the Dean can't afford to fire me.

Mallory McSnicker is no telepath, as far as I know. Her mother is Kryll and her father a mystery, but I'd wager my own wolf that the poor dear hasn't a single Valyrian chromosome in her entire witchy DNA.

Still, she's an intelligent girl. It's quite likely she can surmise what I'm thinking.

Unexpectedly, Mallory's mouth wobbles into an uncertain smile.

"Ugh, sorry." Clearly self-conscious about her emotional outpour, she wipes away her tears and smooths a hand over the disheveled red curls tumbling over her uniform blazer. "It's all I've been hearing from my stepdad over the landline all day. Along with a tirade about why I won't get rid of it. The baby. Which I won't. I'm just… feeling a little defensive. You know?"

Merciful Christ.

Despite my own embarrassment to find myself thrust into the ill-fitting role of camp counselor for this distressed student, this hapless girl who isn't even a member of my cohort, I can't help feeling sympathetic. Birth rates in the witching world are plummeting. Frankly speaking, we need every witch we can spawn, even the offspring of an admittedly weak witch like Mallory McSnicker.

Needless to say, I don't utter a word of this. Briskly I clear my throat and organize the sea of applications covering my desk into a single tidy pile.

"Your choices are your own, Ms. McSnicker," I say as compassionately as possible, my gaze straying to the open door. For propriety's sake, of course, I wouldn't allow her to close it. I typically conduct office hours from my actual office in the Academy crypt. But this particular student is desperate.

Still, I do find myself wishing I weren't alone with this young lady and her awkward dilemma.

The buttery scent of cheese and garlic wafts down the hall from the kitchen where sweet Neo, who's on kitchen duty tonight, is diligently whipping up a pot of fettuccine alfredo from scratch. Under the clatter and clank of crockery flows the distant murmur of Dez and Racetrack studying in the great room. Still more distant, discernible only with my shifter senses, I pick out the staccato tattoo of Maxim and Ronin sparring with staffs in the basement gym. Maxim is new to combat training (at least in human form) and dogged with determination to master every skill he lacks.

He's particularly determined to master every skill Vasili before him has mastered.

When Maxim (inevitably) grows impatient and frustrated with his own slow progress, well, Ronin knows how to… ease his frustration.

In truth, an hour alone with Ronin when he's feeling amorous is more than enough to ease anyone's frustration—including mine, to be certain. Ronin is more than my student, my lover, even my common-law mate. To my continuing delight, I'm one of his alphas.

A shamelessly carnal heat for him, the first mate I ever bit, pools and pulses in my blood. Firmly contained in the shell of my human skin, my wolf paces and mutters.

Sternly I focus my wandering attention on Mallory, who's pacing again herself. If she keeps this up, her schoolgirl saddle shoes will wear a path in our Turkish carpet.

"I'm terribly sorry for your distress and, well, the obvious difficulty you're experiencing." I hesitate. "Still, if you'll forgive my asking…"

"You're wondering why I'm here, right? Since Aggie's my headmistress and not you?" Again, Mallory manages to surprise me, both with her perception and her directness. "Two reasons. Partly, it's because you're the only shifter on the faculty. And the baby, um, could turn out to be part shifter."

"Could?" My brain hones in on the operative word.

Despite her uncertain paternity, I'm willing to wager Mallory herself hasn't a drop of shifter blood in her lineage. As a Kryll, she's a weather witch (of sorts). Yet she also possesses a delicate, almost fragile physicality that in no way resembles the sturdy Kryll constitution, nor any other race I can categorize.

Carefully I clear my throat. "Child, do pardon the question, but…"

"There's a fifty percent chance this baby's gonna be shifter," Mallory says bluntly, pivoting to face me. Her fair skin warms in embarrassment, but her gray eyes don't waver. Those eyes are not at all Kryll, so pale they're almost silver, framed by russet lashes still spiky with salt. "I was with two guys that night."

She doesn't have to specify the night in question. Just enough time has passed since the night of that infamous orgy for all three of the female students thus affected to discover and report their condition.

The fact that Zara herself is not pregnant, no doubt due to the prophylactic shots she administers diligently to prevent conception, is precisely the reason she and Maxim are currently at odds.

Indeed, Zara's resistance to the entire concept of pregnancy is the reason I myself—

"I was with two guys *together*," Mallory blurts. I must say, this unexpected admission is considerably effective in capturing my full attention. "It is—*was*—all three of us. I mean, they were with each other and with me."

"I see," I murmur. Now the poor girl is blushing in earnest. Indeed, it requires substantial resolve on my part not to do the same. With difficulty, I manage to maintain my professorial composure. "Now I understand why it's I to whom you're appealing."

I'm a private person, even a secretive one, and always have been. But there's simply no concealing, on this remote and insular island, that I'm scandalously entangled in a polyamorous relationship with Zara and all four of the male students in my cohort. This circumstance remains very much the case even if Maxim and I are not fornicating—not yet, perhaps not ever, and certainly not unless he himself expresses a clear interest.

I've made the deliberate choice to give our troubled young dragon his space while he recovers from a lifetime of abuse and settles into our queen's harem.

"Yeah. That's pretty much why." Huddled before the fire in her plaid skirt and argyle socks, looking forlorn and at least three years younger than the respectable twenty I know her to be, Mallory hugs her elbows and gives me a pensive smile. "Sure, it's not the way I planned my junior year, but I know how to deal with being pregnant. I'm staying in school and I'm having the kid. Nurse Lavinia at the clinic's a certified midwife. I checked. I mean, she's gonna be pretty busy, because all of us are planning to have our kids and none of us are planning on leaving. Nurse is gonna ask the Dean for permission to hire an assistant."

I'm endeavoring to grasp the notion that this previously unre-markable student should turn out to be so surprising, when she lifts her unexpectedly stubborn chin and surprises me yet again. "Here's the real reason I'm here. I could use some relationship advice."

"Blood of Christ," I mutter. Wishing passionately that Zara were here and that I myself were anywhere else, I adjust my tie. My wolf, who always prefers me naked, frets and grumbles. "If it's, ah, romantic advice you're seeking, perhaps you'd really rather speak with Zara when she returns. To tell you the truth, Ms. McSnicker, I'm not entirely certain I'm—"

"The right one? You are, though." Her reddish brows rush together with a stubbornness I still don't expect. "Apart from my own guy, you're literally the only male shifter on this island I can go to with this. You think I'd take this to Maxim?" She snorts. "Or Vasili?"

Now it's my turn to snort.

Maxim is full shifter and Vasili is a hybrid who's only recently manifested the ability to shift at all. Yet I can literally think of no males on this entire island who would be less likely to exhibit compassion for an embarrassed female classmate. Vasili has never shown a flicker of interest in any woman who isn't Zara. If this awkward girl presumed to trouble him, he'd crush poor Mallory beneath his designer boot with one of his horrible sneers, and look devastatingly pretty while doing it.

Whereas Maxim—homeschooled, half-starved, distrustful, skittish, desperately alone and isolated from human warmth his entire life— Maxim still struggles to connect with anyone outside the polycule.

"I'll concede I grasp your point," I admit dryly to Mallory's expectant face. I swallow a sigh and steeple my hands on my desk. "Very well then. How can I assist?"

"Of all the witching world races, the shifters are the closest to extinct, right?" She barely waits for my nod. "So you'd think the chance I could be having a part shifter kid would be a good thing, right?"

"In principle, yes, from a racial survival perspective. However, not every young warlock is so altruistic—"

"Yeah, no kidding. My shifter guy's totally opposed to this whole thing. I know he's kind of a bully, but honestly, I think it's just because he's scared. Even though our other guy totally wants it, and me being pregnant, it's making him—I mean, my non-shifter guy—super protective. So now the two of them are, like, at each other's throats. Even though they're also still together."

Christ, what a muddle. This troubled girl is appealing to me as both the island's resident authority on shifters—an area of expertise I'll acknowledge—and the faculty's resident expert on polyamorous relationships.

Given the current state of turmoil that prevails in my own polycule, with Zara and Maxim at odds and everyone else trying not to take sides, this assumption is so unwarranted it's nearly laughable.

To allow myself time to think, I switch on the antique desk lamp. A cone of golden light flares with an electric hum and pushes back the shadows. The rows of embossed volumes on the orderly shelves of grimoires and spell books and witching world histories gleam in the lamplight. But darkness presses close against the windows that overlook the peristyle courtyard of our *domus.*

I glance covertly at my old-fashioned wristwatch and swallow a sigh. In truth, Zara is rather late returning from her twilight flight.

She and Maxim must have quarreled.

Again.

I'm still trying to organize a coherent and at least somewhat helpful response to Mallory's dilemma when a familiar patter of footsteps echoes in the hall.

A flood of roses and vanilla inundates my shifter senses. Whining, my wolf rises on his hind legs and scratches eagerly at my skin.

I'm swamped with an overwhelming flood of anticipation and relief. For Mallory's sake, the intensity of these emotions is a reaction I must conceal, because I work hard to maintain a veneer of civilized propriety before my students.

At least the ones I'm not mating.

Straightening my cuffs, I rise behind my desk and turn gratefully toward the door as Zara bursts into view. Her tiny body is bundled hastily into yoga pants that cling to her mouthwatering curves and one of Neo's oversized Academy sweaters. But her gorgeous Hollywood face is flushed with cold, her marvelous teal curls tumbled down her back in disarray. Her turquoise eyes are enormous with what I instinctively know to be alarm.

My wolf bristles to full alert. We pull in a sharp inhale and sift the air for any threat to our mate. Under her own familiar scent, Zara smells like rain and dragon.

She smells—very faintly, but my nose is keen—like an *unfamiliar* dragon. Without warning, my fangs descend.

It's all I can manage not to snarl.

"Fuck, Lucius, there you are," she gasps. "I've been looking for you everywh—"

Then her gaze lands on Mallory, and my precious girl cuts short whatever startling announcement hovers on her lips. Instead Zara pulls in a startled breath of her own. A bonfire of impatience flares in our mating bond—Zara wants me to herself, urgently, for whatever reason.

Quite possibly she wants to explain that maddening scent of a rival male.

But I sense the instant she registers the telltale trace of tears on her classmate's pensive face. That's when Zara's blazing impatience softens to concern.

"Oh, hey, Mallory." Zara's brow smooths and her voice gentles. "I didn't realize you were here. Sorry to interrupt."

"No, it's okay. You're allowed. I mean, the door was open." Mallory gives her an awkward shrug and an apologetic smile. "This is your *domus*, right?"

"We don't mind visitors," Zara says (rather generously, since in truth we rarely receive them). I'm struggling to retract my fangs and reassure my snarling wolf when my mate glances at me. Her teal brows pucker in a frown. "Lucius, I kinda need to talk to you. It's important. But, uh, it can wait till dinner. I'm sure you wanna finish up here first."

"Thank you, my dear," I manage to say in a civilized tone. Damnation. Between that concerning scent and the barely concealed alarm my girl is projecting, I'm decidedly thrown off balance. Normally, mate or no mate, I call her Ms. Gemini whenever other students are present. "I do believe Ms. McSnicker and I require just a bit more time. Then I'm all yours."

I'm hers in all the ways. Ways any rival male not currently granted a place in our harem had better damned well respect.

Despite her own impatience, Zara flashes me a mischievous glance. I've managed to retract my fangs by force of will, but I'm one of her alphas.

She knows my wolf is rising.

"Okay, no problem." Her perceptive gaze flickers over my overflowing desk and the tweed jacket I wore to teach today and still haven't had time to remove. Then my mate's soft mouth firms with a protective air I've come to recognize. She gives me a stern look and directs her attention to Mallory. "That said, it's after school hours and he doesn't work twenty-four/seven. Even if he'd like to. But, I mean, if you just failed a test or something—"

"I didn't. I'm pregnant." Mallory's sudden announcement makes Zara suck in a breath. Our guest rushes ahead. "I mean, I'm not saying it's his or anything, I just wanted some advice on shifter stuff."

I struggle to contain my horror over the sensationalistic prospect that anyone would believe *me* the father of young Mallory's pup (because, dear God, my reputation, and the only part-shifter in Mallory's cohort is indeed a quite rare and exotic breed of wolf).

Zara stops hovering in the doorway and strides fully into the room, her lovely face a study in chagrin.

"Sweet Jesus. That fucking orgy," my girl mutters. "That was totally my fault, with all the pheromones I was throwing off at that party. I mean, yeah, I was in heat, like full flaming heat, and Max and Ronin were setting me off. It felt like the right thing—literally the only thing—to do at the time. But I never meant to make everyone else so crazy that, like, the whole school would forget about using condoms and now half the school's pregnant—"

"Hey, Zara, stop." Mallory hurries forward to meet her, hands outstretched in entreaty. "This really isn't your fault. I own this. The way things were going with me and Jae and Draco, it was pretty much gonna happen on its own, believe me."

Silently I slot in the identities of both prospective fathers. Goodness. Agrippina must have her hands full with this domestic tempest in her residential college.

Thank God this particular crisis is not mine to manage, although of course I'll assist my fellow headmistress in any way I can.

Mallory reaches Zara's side and gives my mate's shoulders a reassuring squeeze, which makes me warm toward the Hadrian girl. It's not every newly pregnant twenty-year-old who would be selfless enough, in the midst of her own personal crisis, to ease another's distress. I don't believe the two know each other particularly well, with Zara still new to the Academy and mostly sticking close to this *domus* and her mates when she isn't in class.

But I can see Zara warming toward her, Mallory's apologetic awkwardness blunting my precious girl's protective instincts on my behalf.

"Yeah, I hear you. C'mon, take a load off." Zara ushers our guest hospitably toward the wing chair near the fire. "But I'm not letting myself off the hook. If not for that orgy, you would've probably taken care of business before you all hooked up, right?"

Mallory drops into the chair with a sigh. "I was taking care of business. I knew where I wanted things to go. I was on the Pill. It just, you know, didn't work?"

"Oh shit. That happens?" Clearly horrified by the prospect of a failed prophylactic, Zara stops hovering over Mallory and shoots me an alarmed look. "That seriously sucks."

I clamp my jaw tight around any revealing utterance that would betray my own feelings on the polarizing subject of prophylaxis, which is currently a trigger word in this household.

The dangerous truth is this. As a shifter vulnerable to powerful mating instinct, and one who's deeply committed to his mates, my wolf and I would like nothing better than to see Zara's beautiful belly soft and rounded with a litter of pups.

Our pups.

Even now, my heart softens and yearns hopelessly for that impossible dream. Aching for a litter of our own, my wolf whines.

But Zara herself has reacted so strongly against Maxim's own powerful instinct to impregnate her that ours is a yearning I dare not reveal. Lately, between those two, the mere mention of Zara's prophylactic shots is sufficient to spark an argument.

Then Neo takes Zara's side, and Vasili makes horribly cutting remarks that skin the hide off Maxim in bloody strips like a hunting knife, and Ronin tries simultaneously to placate Vasili and defend Maxim, while I try my damnedest to comfort everyone and restore peace before someone shifts—

"Right? I took every pill like clockwork too. I dunno why they didn't work. Neither does Nurse Lavinia." Clearly comforted by Zara's empathy, Mallory sighs and curls her tall frame into the chair, bony knees tucked modestly to one side. "But I figure, hey, the witching world needs witches. Survival of the races, I guess that's my job. The other girls in my boat, we all pretty much feel the same."

Zara, who hasn't failed to notice those recently announced pregnancies, nibbles her lip and looks pensive.

Truly, this flood of intimate disclosure—so painfully close to my own hidden yearning—is more than I can bear. Now that Zara is on the scene, in any event, she'll undoubtedly offer more helpful counsel than I on the complexities of Mallory's ménage relationship. Briskly I tuck my pile of applications into my briefcase and emerge from behind the bastion of my desk.

I'm opening my mouth to make my excuses when Mallory says unexpectedly, "It's kinda funny Nurse Lavinia's BC didn't work either. Though she said in her case, she was taking the shots."

"What?" Zara's voice spirals with a note that's perilously akin to panic. "Shut. Up. You telling me Nurse Lavinia's pregnant too?"

"Yep." Mallory nods. "She and that guy who pilots the Academy jet and drops off our supplies? I saw those two together at the Janus Dance last winter. Kinda figured they were an item, and I guess I was right."

Now my precious girl looks positively haunted. "Pregnant despite taking the shots. Jesus, Lucius."

Clearly Zara is now fixated on the alarming prospect that her own reliable method might fail her.

For my part, I'm suddenly fixated on the unwieldy fact that a highly disproportionate percentage of the sexually active women on this island are with child.

"My dear, I know this is unsettling." I'd like nothing more than to wrap Zara in my arms and comfort her, but Mallory too needs comfort. "I'm just going to step out and ask Neo to make our guest a cup of tea, and perhaps fetch a drop of something stronger for you, Zara. Then I need to telephone the Dean."

Despite her distress, Zara makes a face. "Oh, ugh, why?"

"I know you're not a fan of hers—" I attempt.

"Yeah, because she's not a fan of *mine*—"

"But she's responsible for this entire institution and she needs to know what's happening. In light of recent events…" I hesitate, then press ahead firmly, "…I'm going to recommend the clinic offer a pregnancy test to every sexually active female on this island."

"Whoa. That's not gonna help Mallory at this point. And you're including me, right?" Zara says grimly. Her face flushes with temper, because now we've ventured onto perilous terrain. "Oh hell to the no. *I* didn't get pregnant that night, Lucius. I've had my period since, remember?"

I'm desperately uncomfortable to find myself conducting this intimate discussion in front of another student.

Unfortunately, Zara is leaving me little choice.

I lower my briefcase to the desk and approach my mate with care as she bristles near the hearth. "Truly, my dear, isn't it best to be certain?"

"I know what's going down with my own body." Zara gives Mallory an apologetic grimace for the scene and mouths *Sorry*, then pivots to confront me. "If I had a clutch of dragonets or a litter of pups or a baby warlock incubating in here, I'd fucking know it. No one's giving me—or any other girl on this island—a pregnancy test against our will."

Through the mating bond between us, I'm battered by her anger and, worse, her fear. For my wild child of a mate, the prospect that she could lose control of her own body in this way is deeply upsetting.

My wolf whines and lunges in my skin, desperate to comfort her. I ache to reach for her myself, but she's wary and defensive.

Reluctantly, I alter my trajectory to add wood to the fire. Mallory needs to be kept warm, and this diversion allows Zara her space.

"I know this situation is triggering for you, Zara. Truly, I do." I adjust a flaming log with the poker and work to maintain my most reasonable tone. "No one's forcing anyone to do anything. Mallory's made the choice that works for her. For the sake of others, I'm merely suggesting that we *offer*—"

"What the bloody hell's going on in here?" Ronin bursts into the library without warning, with Maxim hard on his heels. "You're upset as fuck. Felt it all the way downstairs."

Barefoot and barely clad, ripped jeans clinging to his sexy hips and his shirt unbuttoned all the way down his tattooed chest, Ronin strides across the library, his long legs obliterating the distance between them, and beelines straight to Zara.

As the strongest telepath at Icarus, he clearly senses who currently needs him.

And Zara, who won't let me anywhere near her, sighs in relief and wraps her arms around his waist and burrows into Ronin's possessive embrace with a degree of trust I actively work not to envy. They're both my mates; I'm both their alpha. My instinct to scent them and claim them both is powerful.

But I am not my wolf.

I am not an animal.

I can wait.

I replace my poker with a sigh and edge away from the fire's crackling heat.

Nearly hidden from view in the big wing chair, Mallory cuddles into the upholstery and extends her hands to the warmth with a grateful look. Already she appears calmer, and I suspect she'd prefer not to expose her emotional vulnerability before her male peers.

Especially the formidable Maxim, whom she barely knows.

Ronin looms over Zara protectively, silky raven hair spilling down over both of them, almost obscuring the fresh love bite on his neck. He's still sexed up from whatever he and Maxim were just doing in the basement. The brimstone mating scent of Maxim's aroused dragon is rolling off both young males in waves. I'm obliged to make a conscious effort not to respond to our mate's arousal the way my wolf demands.

Ronin meets my gaze over the top of Zara's head with his amber eyes narrowed.

"Easy, loves," he murmurs to all of us, which does manage to soothe the ache in my soul. Under his tough guy persona, he's deeply committed to me, to all of us, and he knows how to give comfort. "Just take a breath and tell us what's going down, yeah?"

"What's going down is, I'm pregnant," Mallory says wryly from her armchair, where she appears to have regained her composure. Ronin's surprised gaze jerks toward her. "Along with half the female population of this island, seems like. Zara's worried she could be too."

The entire *domus* seems to suck in its breath.

My gaze veers to my polycule's resident dragon shifter, standing riveted in the doorway.

Maxim, too, is barely clothed, the ratty black sweats he favors for the gym sliding down his lean hips. His sinewy suntanned frame is shirtless, the silver barbell piercings through his ruddy nipples on prominent display—a visual that makes me swallow. (He and I may not be fornicating, but that doesn't mean I'm blind.) His blond hair has fallen from the sleek *bratva* braid he normally favors to slither around his shoulders in disarray. His kiss-swollen lips are parted, his golden shifter eyes are burning, and his slitted pupils are blown wide.

Of course, it's not the prospect of Mallory's pregnancy that forms his obsession.

"Zara," he breathes, his guttural Russian accent far more pronounced than usual. His ardent gaze devours her. "My mate… are you…?"

"Sorry to burst your bubble, but I'm definitely *not*." Her teal head pops up from Ronin's chest. Thankfully, she's begun to sound more like herself. "I had my period, like, two weeks ago, remember?"

Maxim's eyes flame and his nostrils flare. "I remember."

Of course he does. Maxim is so obsessed with Zara's reproductive cycle I suspect he's timed it to the day.

I clear my throat and step carefully between them. "Come inside, Maxim. Let's all have a seat and we'll fill you both in. Let me just get Mallory a cup of tea first."

"And get Neo while you're at it," Zara says firmly. "Vasili too, if you can manage to find him. They're gonna wanna hear this about everyone falling pregnant, like it's an epidemic or something. Then I've got other news like you wouldn't believe."

Indeed. The rival male.

I say this because I harbor absolutely no doubt that any strange male who's winkled his way past this island's protective wards to turn up on our doorstep now, with Zara the declared queen-in-waiting and deliciously subject to frequent mating heats, is here to make a play for her bed.

Without warning, my jealousy surges and my palate tingles under the threatening press of my fangs. Fortunately, between the charred sweetness of burning applewood and the mingled scents of Zara (roses), Ronin (ambergris), Maxim (brimstone), Mallory (rain), and myself (wolf), that maddening alien male aroma is obscured. Conscious of Mallory's wide eyes, I just manage to keep my fangs retracted.

Still, I'll be quite certain to secure the house tight against any intruder before I return with Mallory's beverage.

"It's okay, Master Aries. I don't need tea, but thanks." Before I can slip out on my errand, Mallory climbs hastily to her feet. "I kinda think I've caused enough disruption in your *domus* for one night. We can talk more later. Anyway, they're expecting me home for dinner."

She edges past Zara and Ronin's entwined bodies with barely a wistful look, which I appreciate. As I recall, this girl (like half the student body) spent her entire freshman year languishing with unrequited love for Ronin. But he's no longer on the market, and thankfully she seems to have gotten over him.

Without lingering, our guest hurries for the door.

Zara turns in Ronin's arms, tucking her back against his chest, to watch Mallory go. Ronin himself is no shifter, but his brow furrows as he loops his arms around her waist and bends to bury his nose in Zara's hair, clearly chasing a whiff of that elusive fragrance himself.

Maxim shifts absently out of Mallory's way, which brings him within touching distance of me. The dragon is still quivering with tension and fixated on Zara with alpha intensity. With him I'm very careful not to press, but I take a chance and lay a deferential hand on his bare shoulder to steady him.

He's a Sagittarius—indeed, he's the prince of that clan—and like any fire sign, he runs hot. The heat of his sleek bare skin burns my palm. An unexpected frisson of awareness arcs through me. My wolf rumbles with interest.

Maxim's gaze snaps toward me and locks on mine.

For a breath, I forget what I'm supposed to be doing (which is grounding a volatile young alpha) and merely stare back. His Slavic features are ruthless with focus, but his mouth softens just a bit under my gaze. His tongue darts out to touch his lower lip.

Entirely unbidden, my grip on his shoulder tightens.

"Hey," Zara calls after Mallory, "it's gonna be okay. It really will. I'll find you tomorrow so we can talk, all right?"

My odd moment of connection with the other alpha shatters. I blink and my hand falls away. Maxim sidles past me with a cautious look. Neither of us are telepaths, so I've no notion what he's thinking or, truly, what's just occurred.

If anything has.

Still, I find myself wondering what he felt when we touched.

"Sure thing." Mallory ducks past us into the hall. "No worries, I know the way out."

The others bid her a polite goodbye, but Maxim never even sees her go. He's stalking across the library toward Zara with a predator's intensity. I hold my breath and wait for the explosion.

He's just passed my desk when he freezes in his tracks and pulls in an audible breath.

"What the everloving fuck?!?" the dragon growls, low and menacing.

"Took the words right out of my blooming mouth, mate," Ronin mutters, equally dangerous. "Zara, love, you smell a bit like someone who's not us."

"Aaaaand that's the thing I've been trying to tell Lucius. But Mallory needed him more. Plus you're all so fucking obsessed with this collective fixation on getting me pregnant that I couldn't get a word in edgewise." Tone crisp with irritation, our girl extracts herself from Ronin's possessive embrace and plants a hand on her hip. "There's a new dragon in town. Green one, I mean venom-green and massive and really not nice, though I just got a glimpse." She hesitates, her teal brows arching. "Only this one's got, like, a rider. Guy wearing some kinda green armor and this tall horned helmet that's like a crown?"

A distant ping of memory hums through my brain. I can't contain a gasp of wonder. Swiftly I pivot toward the bookcase between the windows where I've cataloged our witching world lore.

Truly, though, this mad notion I'm entertaining can't possibly be the explanation—

"No… bloody… way," Ronin rasps. "It… it can't be."

The unexpected grenade of shock and grief that explodes through my mating bond with Ronin—painfully clear and honed by his formidable telepathy to a cutting edge—swings me sharply back around to face him.

Under his tawny skin, Ronin's chiseled face is gray with pain.

"Oh fuck, Ronin," Zara breathes, spinning around to face him. Gently she cradles his drawn face in her hands. "You okay? You know something about this new guy?"

"Something?" Eyes wide and black with shock, Ronin barks out a short wild laugh that holds nothing of humor. "Gods! It literally *can't* be him."

Having both of them in distress proves to be too much for Maxim. The dragon snarls and charges across the room and launches himself at both his mates, wrapping his lean frame around them in a protective hug.

Despite the current rancor between him and Zara, Maxim is still her mate. He's her dragon king, just as I am her wolf king. There's a powerful love between them, which is why their estrangement is so agonizing— for all of us.

Now she unfolds with a sigh to welcome him.

Both of them wrap around Ronin and each other in a tight three-way hug.

Maxim unleashes a positive frenzy of shifter scenting, rumbling and rubbing his face into both their necks to claim them—especially Zara, to obliterate this threatening scent of a rival male.

Both Zara and Ronin are well accustomed to possessive alphas. They accept these insistent attentions with affectionate cuddles and sweet murmurs meant to soothe the savage beast.

It's a moment of profound connection that leaves me isolated and alone on the outside.

Again.

Of course, Maxim bonded with Zara and Ronin first. He mated them first (and together—the very encounter that triggered that fateful orgy at Villa Hadrian). At moments like this, the bond these three share is painfully obvious. Normally at these times, Vasili—who's my own alpha, the only one my wolf has ever tolerated—tends to me. With Vasili hovering over me and so deliciously attentive these days, I never feel left out.

But Vasili isn't here tonight. He has his own method of dealing with the myriad mounting tensions in our polycule.

Alone.

Sighing, I avert my gaze from my mates' scenting and whispering near the fire. Quietly I pad across to the bookcase between the windows and scan the shelf that holds my collection of witching world lore. I'm not looking for history—I've roomsful of witching world history at the church where we hold classes. No. It's the whispered lore of ancient legend that tugs at me tonight.

The fairytales.

My careful finger traces the neatly aligned spines of the ancient volumes until the scrolling gold script of the title I seek leaps out at me.

The Legend of Avalon.

Gently I slip the heavy volume from its niche. A sticky film of dust and cobwebs coats my fingers. Clearly, it's been quite some time since anyone has dusted—or read—this particular volume. A clunky brass lock, green with verdigris, clasps the book shut and guards its secrets. The musky scent of mildew teases my nostrils. The residue of witchcraft makes my fingers tingle. This book is bespelled so that only a powerful witch or warlock can penetrate its secrets. I'll need to conjure it open later with common (or not-so-common) magics.

Behind me, Zara is murmuring questions that Ronin isn't answering, while Maxim is emitting a low dragonish purr to soothe both our mates.

It hurts me to look at their entwined bodies, and I don't wish to intrude. But I don't need to touch Ronin to comfort him.

Gently sweeping the dust from the ancient tome, I reach out to Ronin through our bond.

Are you well, my dear one?

"I'm all right," Ronin says aloud, quite firmly, to all of us. His psychic barriers are soldered in place and there's absolutely no reading him. "No need to make a fuss, yeah? I'm good."

I turn to find him extracting himself from our mates' clinging arms and (somewhat to my regret) buttoning his jeans and shirt. His skin is still pale and there's clearly something troubling him. But, just as clearly, it's nothing he wishes to share.

I'll follow your lead then, I whisper to him without speech. *But know that I'm always here if you'd ever like to discuss… well, anything.*

"Yeah, thanks," he says curtly, without looking at any of us, head bent while he buttons, a curtain of sleek black hair shielding his face.

Respecting his clearly stated desire for privacy, as I must, I ease out of our mating bond. As I withdraw, I glimpse just a flash of memory he's left unguarded. A young girl's familiar face, melancholy amber eyes brooding in fragile features, framed by a silky spill of raven hair.

A name plinks through me, salted with the tide of Ronin's grief. *Gwendolyn.*

I'm looking at Gwendolyn Pendragon.

She's Ronin's twin, the tragic victim of a prolonged and vicious hazing her freshman year.

Ronin's twin, who hanged herself.

Then the door to Ronin's memory slams shut. I'm left stranded on the outside, bereft, while Ronin finishes buttoning himself up and closing himself off.

"Okay, Adam," Zara says softly, falling back on the nickname that's a private endearment between them. "I guess this is your call."

Still, clearly, she isn't satisfied. She never knew Gwendolyn, but surely she's sensing everything I am. Behind his walls, Ronin is hurting.

Zara watches him with puckered brow and shadowed eyes.

Maxim hovers awkwardly between them, his alpha instinct to protect warring against Ronin's obvious desire for distance. Finally Maxim turns his full attention to Zara, wrapping an arm around her waist and tucking her up against his side.

She too needs comfort, and she accepts his (since he's stopped using the dreaded P word). She loops her arms around his waist and turns her head to nuzzle his bare shoulder.

From this angle, the ridged scars that slice across Maxim's narrow back and wrap around his ribs, the relic of decades of abuse, are fully on display. My wolf and I suffer a sudden, violent impulse to nuzzle him too. The young dragon is terribly self-conscious and skittish about his scars, but there's no shame in them.

At least, there's no shame for him.

Not for the first time, I'm viciously, savagely, unrepentantly glad my wolf and I tore out his mother's throat.

As for Ronin, he still looks positively haunted. Now his guarded glance falls on the antique tome I'm cradling. His feral face grows still more shuttered.

"Found yourself a spot of bedtime reading, mate?" he mutters, but doesn't allow me time to answer. "Think you'll find whatever beastie's stalking our girl in a fairytale?"

Zara and Maxim both pivot to see what I've got, and Zara's brows arch in surprise.

"Zara encountered a strange dragon *inside* the island wards," I say simply. "My dears, we're literally smelling him on her. Those wards haven't been lowered in weeks, not since the news crew departed, and they've never been breached. Yet our scaly green intruder has to have come from somewhere." I hesitate, but I'm committed now, and they're listening. "So, yes, I believe the only conceivable explanation may lie between this book's enchanted covers."

"There is no explanation," Maxim growls. He tucks Zara close against his side, his oblong pupils narrowed to slits. "I am the last fully manifested male dragon shifter. I am the only dragon who will mate her."

"Well, except for Vasili," Zara murmurs. Despite her distraction, she leans into Maxim with a hum, giving the young dragon the reassurance he's clearly craving.

"Vasili is more snake than dragon," he says with alpha stubbornness, rubbing his face into Zara's hair to scent her. "Even though he too is mine. I tell you, I am the last of my kind."

I shift into teaching mode, which is my default identity.

"I'm fully aware of your status, Mr. Rasputin." Thoughtfully I glance down at the ancient tome. "I assure you, it's not dragon *shifters* I wish to investigate."

"Bollocks." The curse rips from Ronin's throat, and we all glance toward him in surprise. He's powering straight for the door, his amber eyes burning with a look that dares anyone to stop him. "That tears it. I'm not bloody listening to any more of this bullshit."

"Whoa, Adam, just wait a sec, okay?" Zara's bewilderment and concern ripple through our bond.

"I said *no*, all right?" For once, Ronin is blind and deaf to her concern.

Maxim's cold features acquire the distinctive look of cruelty he acquires whenever anyone threatens one of his precious mates, eyes flaming, lip curled, a dragonish snarl rumbling from his chest. He releases Zara and starts after Ronin. But I manage to catch the young alpha's eye and warn him off with a firm headshake.

Frustrated and reluctant but heeding, the dragon falls back.

I'm equally puzzled and concerned, my wolf lunging and scrabbling to confront the threat, but I keep my beast tightly leashed.

Whatever demon is troubling Ronin is one he clearly isn't prepared to confront.

Ronin has nearly reached the door when Neo emerges from the hall to fill it, his purple curls tousled and his clean-cut features harassed. My sweet boy is wearing a black apron tied over his uniform shirt and trousers that firmly announces *This meat is 100% going in your mouth.*

To avoid running into him, Ronin jerks to a reluctant halt. "Red?"

That's his nickname for Neo, who's adorably prone to blushing.

"Don't even." Neo pushes his stylish spectacles firmly up his nose and folds his brawny arms across his chest. "Look. I dunno what's going on in here with you four, but the pasta's totally *al dente*, and the girls and I are starving. Can we please talk about whatever this is while we eat?"

Chapter Three

Zara

Something's definitely going down with Ronin.

His psychic barriers are sky high and he's withdrawn and cagey as fuck. He hasn't said a goddamn word all through dinner or cleanup after. Of course, he's entitled to his moods and all, we all are. When you live with someone, you gotta give them their space.

But that doesn't mean I have to like it.

Tonight, there's a pretty long fucking list of things I don't like.

"Let me get this straight. Because it's kind of a lot to take in." Neo snuggles in next to me on the Renaissance sofa where we're both tucking into minty, chocolatey mugs of Neo's peppermint cocoa. Comfortably he stretches his stockinged feet toward the central hearth in our great room, where we keep a cozy fire burning.

We really need that fire, we totally rely on it in this house, because that beast of a furnace chugging away in the basement is ancient. Beyond the rain-streaked glass doors that open on the courtyard, the weather hasn't gotten any better. Sleet plinks against the windows and pelts the roof with icy pellets. And the wind's really howling.

If I focus on that wind, under the fire's dry crackle and the furnace's distant hum, the storm's voice sounds like a screaming dragon.

As I look warily past Neo's earnest profile toward the wild night, the electric light in the kitchen flickers.

Yeah, the whole Icarus Island grid is also ancient. I'm betting the power's gonna be down all over the island tonight.

Only this time it won't be my fault (because, you know, lightning witch).

"Oh dear." Gently Lucius extracts himself from Neo's other side (they were holding hands, which is so cute) and pads around the great room, finding matches, lighting candles in the gothic candelabra on the big dining room table. "Neo, sweet boy, I'm listening."

"I'm just trying to wrap my head around what the Dean told you on the phone." Neo deposits our mugs on the end table and draws my own stockinged feet, curled up next to me on the sofa, into his lap for comfort. "If I'm doing the math right, six of the nineteen women on this island are pregnant."

"Six that we know about," I mumble. "Maybe even more. All. Pregnant."

Given those numbers, even I can see the logic in the plan Lucius and the Dean just cooked up over the landline. Pregnancy tests at the clinic tomorrow for every chick on the island who wants one, along with a medical survey of the likely who/where/when the inciting events happened with each woman, for data gathering purposes.

Yeah, sure, I can see the logic.

Still, that intrusive fucking survey is another item on the list of things I don't like.

Hearing me actually say the dreaded P word, Max quivers with a tremor of electric alertness. He's hovering protectively on my other side, one arm wrapped around my shoulders, his warm hand engulfing my cold fingers.

Max runs hot and he feels good next to me. He always feels good. Yeah, we fight, but shit. When it comes to me and our relationship, he's all in. Actually, he's all in on our whole polycule.

Even if my guys aren't all fucking (yet).

And, sweet Jesus, I'm all in on him. It's not just because I'm hot for him either. He totally missed dinner (even though he's always hungry, it's a thing with him after being half-starved his whole life) flying all over the island tonight trying to find that strange dragon. He didn't find shit, but I already know he's going out again later. He doesn't lose focus and he doesn't quit. He's gonna keep hunting till he knows I'm safe.

Sometimes I hate him, but I also love him. He's my dragon.

He's mine.

He feels extra toasty tonight, because the furnace is really struggling to heat this big house, and Max is a classic firedrake under all that sexy.

Anyway, that story I told over our fettuccine about my aerial encounter with the rival dragon is really setting Max off. He's feeling threatened and he's feeling protective. So I'm super patient (for me), even when Max keeps growling and rubbing his face in my hair and neck to scent me.

He's doing it again now, his dragon rumbling and fretting in his skin. My dragon queen gives a little chirp to comfort him—one of those weird bird sounds I'm vocalizing more and more since I started shifting.

"Six outta nineteen women. That's fucked up," Racetrack announces, scowling, from her seat on the rug near the fire. She's making s'mores for her and Dez to go with their cocoa. They're both gripping long skewers dripping with melted marshmallow and sharing a big afghan as they curl up together on the rug.

"What Nurse needs to do is gather the data, yeah? Find out if everyone who's preggo was at the beanfest that night or, you know, how far Zara's pheromones actually spread on the wind? That's what the survey's gonna do. It's a research project," Dez pipes up, sounding way calmer about it than I am.

Of course, it's easier for her to be calm since she doesn't have to worry about a surprise pregnancy. She and Racetrack were together at the orgy, and they're exclusive.

Translation? No bun in the oven for either of them.

"I think that's fine, Nurse can test and survey all she wants, long as it's the patient's choice," I say firmly. "We're not lab rats here. We have rights."

Yeah, I know I'm kinda stuck on this point, but it's important. While I was on the run from my psycho dad all those years, sometimes all I could control was my own body, and I've kinda gotten used to depending on that.

"No one is forcing anyone," Max points out, also calmly, in his careful English.

But he's my alpha and he can't fool me. Just the outside chance that I too could wind up "preggo" has him sexed up as fuck and ready for the two of us (or the three of us, because he's fucking Ronin too, and they both like sharing me) to go at it right here on this couch.

I'm not in heat right now (for once). And, at least theoretically, Max isn't in rut. My next superheat's still a few days off, and that's what sets his dragon off. Still, being this close to Max while he's horny has my nipples tight under my Academy sweater and my pussy slick and ready to rumble.

Wait for it, showgirl, I tell my inner dragon. I'm simultaneously revved up on pheromones and queasy with anticipation. *We can't trust him right now. His breeding instinct's making him psycho.*

His desire is our desire, she whispers in my heart, in her deep dragon hiss. *We need not be in heat to rise. And he need not be in rut to follow.*

Great. One more thing for me to worry about.

My own dragon wants to fuck.

She and I, we haven't gone there yet. Not in dragon form.

"Zara." Max frees my hand (now nicely warmed by his toasty grip) and lays a gentle palm on my tummy. "You should take this test. Only to know. Only to be certain."

Goddamn it.

I don't wanna fight with him again.

A familiar surge of resentment, made worse by the tight chafing vise of entrapment, makes my skin itch. What Max doesn't know is that I already have a preexisting appointment at the clinic after school tomorrow. I'm fucking my guys on the daily, and it's time for my regular BC shot.

And what are the odds Nurse will just give it to me, what with everything going down in half the uteruses… uteri?… on this island, without making me take that goddamn test first?

"Not talking about me right now, Max." Sternly telling my pussy to behave, I nudge his possessive hand away from my nice flat tummy.

Even when what I really want to do is tuck his hand between my legs.

"Truly, I fear we must discuss your role in these events, my dear one," Lucius says tenderly. Returning with a fat lit candle, he carefully positions it on the end table near his elbow, beside that locked book from the *domus* library he hasn't let out of his sight all night. "We can't dismiss the possibility that it is some involuntary manifestation of your potent Gemini witchcraft—your magical and symbolic power, as our queen-in-waiting—that is causing this phenomenon. As we're aware, the queen's strength, fertility, and character profoundly shape the fate of the entire witching world."

"Somehow I knew you were gonna say that." I heave a sigh. "Look, we've talked about this. Queen or no queen, I honestly don't think I have some extra-special power. I'm just not feeling it." Even if I *was* feeling it that night during my superheat—a thought I push firmly to the side. "Anyway, I'm just the understudy. Right now, Messalina has her Aquarius ass parked firmly on the witching world throne."

"Well, she is entitled." Lucius runs a thoughtful hand over his yummy mane of Renaissance curls and tucks a stray tendril tidily into the chestnut knot he ties it all back in. "Being crowned queen is a lifelong commitment."

"Don't remind me," I say glumly. Sure, I might've accepted my ball-and-chain destiny in the last episode and announced it to the whole witching world on WNN, but that's another of those things I don't like. "Right now, I'm not feeling very queenlike. I'm just a freshman trying to pass my classes and get a handle on my shit."

"Your time to reign and to rule is fast approaching. Our first Gemini queen. It's not at all surprising that your powers are rising." My headmaster's whiskey eyes are keen as he searches my face.

Then his stare shifts to Max, who's still scenting me and nuzzling my neck, lips scorching my skin, teeth scraping my pulse. My dragon's all stubbly and the rasp of his tawny whiskers against my neck makes me shiver. Not to mention the leather and brimstone of Max's mating scent has me squirming on the sofa.

Yeah, not gonna lie. All that alpha dragon possessiveness is definitely sexing me up, same as always. It's all I can manage not to grab Max's hand and drag it under my leggings. My girly parts are hot and slick for him. For Dez and RT's sake, at least, I restrain myself.

A tiny frown puckers Lucius' brow.

It's gone so fast I might've imagined it… except for the sudden tingle of Valyrian foresight that tells me there's *something* my wolf shifter headmaster isn't telling me.

Something about Messalina and my reign.

Something Max specifically isn't gonna like. Hence the frown.

Shit.

For Lucius' sake, I try to rein in my Valyrian foresight, which has always been iffy and unreliable as fuck. It comes and goes when it wants, always at the most inconvenient times.

Anyway, Lucius and I have a mating bond too, and he hasn't been as discreet as he imagines about his secret yearning for a litter of pups.

However, to his total credit, he's sensitive to my mixed-up feelings on the whole subject. We all feel his yearning, but he's never said a word out loud about wanting to get me pregnant.

Unlike Max.

Who talks about it, like, constantly.

When Max realizes I'm getting another BC shot, which will fend off his potent dragon spunk from making dragon babies in my fertile uterus for months, we're one hundred percent gonna fight again.

Dragon shifters are a critically endangered species, and he thinks it's our duty to procreate the next generation.

"I mean, don't get me wrong about what's happening on this island." I make a real effort to keep my tone reasonable, because there's no point leaning into that next fight. Believe me, it's gonna happen on its own. "It's like Mallory said. I get that the witching world needs witches. If my Mogadon pheromones and my dragon superheats are, uh, helping out with all that, I don't have a problem—as long as the witches who end up pregnant *want* that to happen."

Neo squeezes my feet between his big strong hands, thumbs kneading the arches in a way that makes me want to moan. His touch always keeps me calm. He's my fated mate, so he knows what I'm thinking without me having to spell it out.

And his loyalty is absolute.

But his worried eyes linger on Ronin, who's pacing back and forth, back and forth, back and forth before the glass doors. Beyond Ronin's broody silhouette, black hair spilling down his back, lightning flashes and sleet plinks against the glass.

Ronin's still not talking. He hasn't said a single fucking word since his mini-meltdown in the library.

And his prolonged silence is really starting to freak me out.

"Lucius could be onto something," Neo says gently, because my fated mate's also a peacemaker. Even when he's equally worried about what's going down with Ronin, who's Neo's boyfriend too. "Our queens do have massive magical and symbolic value for the whole witching world. That's why the fact that Messalina can't have any more kids isn't helping us any, you know, with this whole extinction scenario. And she has to know it. Now that she gets you're serious about the job, maybe she'll think about stepping down."

"Not in any rush to ascend here, baby," I remind him. "I'm just the queen-in-waiting."

And I definitely don't mind the waiting.

"Oh, I wouldn't say Messalina Aquarius is… quite… thinking about stepping down," Lucius says delicately. "Her daughter's death undoubtedly came as a shock, and Zara was the Senate's choice, not Messalina's, to replace Cybelle. But it appears the Aquarius queen may indeed be thinking about… making room?"

I'm puzzled till the exact second I pick up the worried vibe I'm getting from Neo, who's still very diligently kneading my feet. Whatever Lucius is trying to say to me is something he's already confided in Neo.

Near the window, Ronin's head swivels sharply to find us. His amber eyes lock with mine.

Easy, love, he whispers through our bond. *Lucius is only trying to help.*

With a jolt, I realize he's in on it too—whatever this thing is that Lucius is trying to work his way around to telling me.

"What the fuck?" Slowly I pull my feet out of Neo's lap and sit up straight on the sofa. "Something you wanna say to me, Lucius?"

"Ah, this may not be the ideal moment. I intended to ensure everyone was properly… prepared… for this development." Lucius' gaze returns to Max, who's also sitting straight up, bristling and scowling, but generally looking as clueless as I am.

Lucius swallows a small sigh. "Alas, it's entirely likely there is no ideal moment for news like this. Although I do wish Vasili, at least, were present."

Yeah. Me too.

Vasili's not an easy guy to be around right now, with him and Max both fighting and (almost) fucking, and both of them wanting that top-dog status in my harem—which is a one-man gig. But Vasili's part of this, part of *us,* and I have a feeling we're all gonna need him.

"He's coming," Ronin says softly. "But it'll take him a tick."

Which makes us all twitch, because at least Ronin's finally talking out loud again. Ronin and Vasili are super bonded. And Ronin's also clairsentient. So of course Ronin's known where my snake is all along, and Ronin just gave that bond between them a good tug.

Now Ronin stalks over to lurk near the fire, bracing one bare foot on the hearth and folding his arms defensively across his chest.

Goddamn it. Even Dez and Racetrack look implicated in whatever's about to go down. Dez's olive-green eyes are shining, her sorrel skin's all flushed, she's literally brimming with suppressed excitement.

Racetrack rolls her eyes at Lucius with total RT attitude that all but says *I told you so, jackass.*

My skin tingles with nerves and the ends of my hair start rising. That's the electrical energy that gathers when my witchcraft rises.

Beside me, Max's snarl of warning makes my scalp crawl. He doesn't like being ambushed any more than I do. My dragon king's solidly on my side, and yeah, I'm grateful. He's not someone you wanna piss off.

"Someone better start talking," I breathe into the pregnant silence. "And don't everyone start at once."

Everyone looks at Lucius.

"The Dean has received… correspondence from Messalina," Lucius murmurs in a tone that I know is meant to soothe me. "Now that you're legally her heir, my dear, she desires to undertake… marriage negotiations."

I stare at him blankly. "You mean, like, with you guys?"

Because they all stood with me, all five of them, when I gave my future queen acceptance speech on WNN. They're all gonna be my kings, the Gemini kings, and the whole world knows it. Even if we're only mated informally right now, the common law way, we *are* definitely mated.

Period.

"It *is* with you guys, right?" I push into the awkward silence. "She wants a fairytale wedding, not just me shacking up with you five."

Curled up on the rug, Dez hugs herself and sighs over the fairytale wedding concept (I guess). She's full Valyrian and a way stronger precognitive than I am, she's like an actual seer. But she hardly ever talks about what she sees.

Which is inconvenient. Especially now.

Carefully Lucius straightens his cuffs. "I believe the queen has another candidate in mind. A… political candidate."

"A rival male." Max uncoils to his feet and looms over the couch. His slitted pupils are blown wide, his golden irises are flaming, and his dragon lurks in his voice. "Saint Sergius guard us. Zara is mine—*ours*.

What kind of alpha are you, wolf? Do you wish our sovereign to accept *another mate* in our bed?"

"It's not precisely what I would wish, no," Lucius says tightly. His fangs are descending and his eyes shading red, showing all that wolfish possessiveness he's fighting to rein in. "But my wishes in this matter are immaterial—"

"Like hell they are." I shove to my own feet, because this I gotta deal with standing up. "You're my alpha and my mate. If someone wants another guy in our bed, you get a say, Lucius. You all do."

My wolf stays sitting, hands extended in a plea for calm, but I'm already way past that point.

I glance from his apologetic eyes to Neo's guilty expression to Ronin's glower by the hearth. Dez is already wincing in expectation of what I'm gonna say, while Racetrack just looks disgusted with the whole setup.

"Told you this was never gonna work, mate," Ronin says to Lucius with a sigh. "She doesn't like surprises, does she? And she doesn't give a fuck for the politics."

"I'm gonna deal with Messalina and her *political candidate* in a sec," I say. "What I wanna understand first is why you all fucking *knew* about this and kept it from me—"

"I did not know," Max growls. "Now that I do, I will hunt this rival down and I will kill him."

"Aaaaand that would be why no one told you," Racetrack snarks, mushing together a melty s'more with a scowl on her boyish face. "Lucius, no offense, but sometimes you're an idiot. I'm with Ronin on this one. I told you she was gonna react this way, and I'm not even in the harem."

"I simply wanted to manage this discussion in an efficient and productive fashion, without undue emotion." Lucius' red-tinged eyes plead for my understanding. "Zara, my dear, this negotiation lies in the Dean's hands, not mine, but she has requested my involvement. This is the first outreach to you, the first olive branch Messalina has ever extended, the first sign of acceptance of your future role that Messalina has ever shown. What harm could there be in merely listening to—?"

"Lucius. No. Just no." I'm struggling against a sickening sense of betrayal that makes it hard to speak without screaming. Static crackles in my hair and sparks at my fingers.

But me losing my shit's just gonna make this whole thing worse.

I pull in a big gulp of air and repeat as steadily as I can, "I'm sorry, but no. If Messalina wants something from me, especially something as personal as another goddamn guy in our bed when we're already struggling like fuck to make this whole thing work…" Damn, I hate admitting that out loud, but it's true, we all know it, we're struggling in this polycule "…then she's gonna have to talk to me herself. So that's what you tell the Dean."

"And you will tell *me* the name of this rival." Max lurks at my shoulder, guarding my back and glaring at Lucius. "Is it this green dragon?"

I blink, because I've actually forgotten about the Green Menace for a sec in the midst of this latest crisis. Near the hearth, Ronin flinches at the bare mention of that green dragon. Then he huddles into himself like he's bleeding inside.

Shit. He's hurting. He's my love, and he's hurting.

God, his pain makes me crazy. I wanna go to him.

But he warns me off with a violent gesture.

"She has not yet named the candidate." Lucius says through his fangs, which I can tell he's working to retract. Slowly the red light dwindles from his eyes. "Clearly, Mr. Rasputin, this discretion was a prudent caution on her part."

"That dragon has a rider," I remind everyone, though of course Max's dragon would see the dragon himself as the main threat. "And I'm pretty keen to get a look in that book you've been toting around all night, Lucius, if you think it can shed any light on that mess. But first things first.

"We can't have secrets like that in this harem." I glance toward Dez and RT by the fire. "Or this court." (Since the girls are my courtiers, on account of sharing the same roof, even if they're not my lovers.) "I mean it. You can't try to, like, *manage* me, Lucius."

"Or me," Max rumbles. "Zara is not taking another mate. And that is final."

"Uh, that's gonna be up to Zara," Neo pipes up. He's been quiet this whole time, just letting the storm blow over. But he's always on my side. "If she likes this guy or just decides it's a good idea to add him, that's her call. Whether you stay in the harem after that? That's yours."

"Thank you, baby." Despite feeling hurt that even my sweet Neo kept this from me, it's impossible for me to stay mad at him. "But I don't think adding another guy right now is a good idea."

"I agree," Max mutters. "Already you have five of us, and we are plenty."

For once, he and I are in total agreement.

Neo's earnest green eyes blink up at me through his spectacles, then shift to Max, who's started pacing behind me. It's hard to tell by candlelight, but I think Neo might be blushing.

He does that a lot. Especially, lately, around Max. But Vasili's been so possessive about Neo, especially since those two started fucking, that Max has been steering way clear. Even though it's obvious (at least to me) that Neo doesn't want Max steering clear.

Which is another brewing problem in our harem.

"Right now I'm kinda with the big guy," I mutter. That's what I call Max, due to his big black dragon. "We got enough problems to deal with. But I do wanna talk to Messalina directly. I'll find a different way to reciprocate that whole olive branch thing."

In the courtyard, a fork of lightning flashes, blinding bright. A violent boom of thunder makes me jump. The kitchen light goes black and the basement furnace falls silent.

Under the howling wind and the hissing sleet, we all wait for the hum of the backup generator we just installed (because of my lightning magic, we lose power a lot) to kick in.

But we wait in vain.

Shit.

"Bollocks," Ronin mutters.

"Mice musta chewed through the line again." Racetrack is already passing her half-eaten s'more to Dez and climbing to her feet. "It's that, or we're outta diesel. I'll go down and take a look."

"I'll go with you, yeah? You'll need someone to hold the flashlight. Just let me find my shoes." Dez pops the s'more tidily into her own mouth and hops up too.

Lucius pads off to the kitchen to fetch the flashlight for RT, because his wolf sees better in the dark than any of us. Max peels away from guarding my back (which he's been doing all night, I mean whenever he hasn't been out flying and hunting for our intruder) and starts stalking through the house. I know without asking that, with this strange dragon and his strange rider at large, my dragon's checking and double-checking to confirm all the doors and windows are locked.

The girls tromp downstairs with the flashlight and the toolbox to look at the generator. Lucius slips after them into the black scary basement, prowling down the stairs with his quiet wolfish step. I know it's because he's picking up Max's unease and his wolf is rising.

My wolf wants to check out that basement for himself.

Racetrack's grumbling about not needing a police escort just to fix the goddamn generator like she's done six hundred times before when the three of them vanish from sight.

Ronin stays where he is near the fire, watchful and unreadable as a sphinx. Right now I'm not picking up anyfuckingthing through our bond.

Groovy.

Even Neo's weirdly hard to read, like our fated mate bond has gotten all cottony. He curls up around his cocoa and watches me pace around the great room with his eyes all pensive behind his glasses.

Next to him on the end table, that big locked book Lucius has been guarding all night is waiting. Unguarded. Next to it, the candle's tiny flame dances in a rogue breeze. That witchy light flows over the scrolling gold letters stamped on the leather cover.

The Legend of Avalon.

I drift closer to get a better look. Those letters are framing some sort of arched portal that's embossed on the cover, an image too faded to see properly, especially by candlelight.

The heavy brass lock is green with age. Looks like it hasn't been opened in, like, centuries. Still, suddenly, that book is calling me. I mean it, that thing's tugging at me like actual fingers.

Whatever fairytales are hiding inside those covers, they're meant for me to discover.

My whole body tingles in unmistakable warning. My hair floats around my shoulders and the shadows around me turn violet, which means the color's coming from my eyes. My psi fire's rising.

Fuck this Valyrian foresight.

I'm opening that book.

"Um, Zara?" Seeing me all ready to reach for it, Neo's eyes fly wide in alarm. "Don't you think maybe we should wait for Lucius before we mess with that thing?"

"He wouldn't have pulled it out if he didn't mean for us to open it." My voice sounds far away, like it's rising from the bottom of a well.

Like maybe it isn't even my own thought I'm voicing.

I can't feel my fated mate bond with Neo at all anymore. Can't feel Ronin behind me, even though he's the strongest telepath at Icarus. Can't even feel my alpha mating bond with Max, who's stomping around the vestibule in his shitkickers double-checking the locks.

From the basement, the labored chug of the generator kicks in.

Fingers tingling, my hand drifts up all on its own and reaches for the book—

Before I can touch it, that book flies right off the table and swerves abruptly through the air. It sails straight across the room to collide against the far wall with a thud. Then it slams to the floor and lies there lifeless, like the inanimate object it's supposed to be.

"Fucking hell!" Sweet Jesus, I must've leaped five feet in the air.

An ultraviolet flash illuminates the room for a sec, giving me a single freeze frame image of Neo scrambling to his feet and Ronin sprinting toward me.

That electric flash is the little lightning I throw off when I get a scare.

Downstairs, the generator falls ominously silent. Somehow, this time, it feels like a permanent silence. The distant sound of Racetrack swearing drifts up the stairs.

Great.

Thanks for that, little lightning.

I just knocked our backup power source offline and probably fried the circuits permanently.

Now all the decent light's gone bye-bye. All the candles have blown out in a weird random wind. The dim ruddy flicker of the fire makes shadows shift around the empty table.

My heart thunders in my ears.

"Oh crap. Are you okay?" Neo wraps his brawny arms around me (which is a brave thing to do after all that amperage I just gave off) and hugs me tightly to his chest, which I don't resist. "Babe, that's why I told you not to touch that thing."

"Too right." Ronin folds himself around me and both of us from behind, all sinew and heat drenched in the spicy scent of ambergris, and presses a hot kiss to my cold temple. "For fuck's sake."

Still feeling jumpy and guilty and irritated at myself, because I know they're right, I mutter, "Okay, but I actually *didn't*—"

"You really should listen to our Mr. Mercury, darling, *do*. He's First Boy on the Dean's List for a reason."

The frigid purr of a familiar sneer jerks my head up from Neo's broad sheltering shoulder with a gasp. An eerie floating form, slim and deadly as a serpent, is descending through the air from the second-floor landing with lethal grace. A long black coat, heavy and sodden with sleet, swirls around his tall frame. His silver hair is slicked back from his cold pale face and dripping with rain.

Well, no wonder that book went flying. My top-dog alpha does way more than levitate. He's a seriously badass telekinetic.

It's just that, these days, he doesn't usually use that scary magical punch he's packing against *me*.

"Cheese on toast, Vasili, warn a girl next time. Jesus. You can't just hurl ancient artifacts through the air like that." I'm trying to get a grip, but he's unnerving as fuck.

Because that's the effect he has when he's pissed.

You know, the way he clearly is at me right now.

But I'm also unnerved because I can't feel him either. Not a single goddamn hint of his spiky, broody, snaky vibe. Not even through that potent AF psychic bond we forged when he gave me his mating bite.

He alights on the great room floor, combat boots with burgundy soles coming to rest light as angel feathers on the wood. My gaze slides up and up his sinister body to zoom in on the antique gold medallion swinging against his chest. It's way familiar, and not in a good way, because that thing used to hit me in the face whenever my lying backstabbing shit of an ex-boyfriend Xiao fucked me missionary-style. It's a cursed doubloon Xiao stole from a Spanish shipwreck. We recently stole it back from Xiao in Vegas. It's been locked away in the Academy Vault ever since.

For good reason.

That's because it's an enchanted object. A nullifying object, to be super specific. I haven't studied those yet, they're years ahead of me in Senior Seminar, but Vasili has. He's told us all about enchanted objects.

This one's sudden appearance sure as shit explains why all my mating bonds just went dark.

But what it doesn't explain is what the everloving hell my Goblin King is doing, wearing that thing.

"Fuck. Me. Sideways," I say slowly. Damn it. I can't feel *any* of them. Any of my mates. I hate this shit. "For Christ's sake, Vasili. Where the fuck *were* you all night? We've got problems here, like multiple major problems. And what the fuck are you doing wearing that screwed-up medallion?"

Chapter Four
Neo

"Way to make an entrance, you big showboat." I lower my feet to the floor and sit up straight on the sofa so I can cope. "You scared Zara. You're kind of a jerk sometimes, V, you know that?"

There. I sound like my normal responsible self, don't I?

Not like some teenager totally crushing on his horrible bully at this Academy who, for some insane reason, I'm also enthusiastically fucking.

Vasili's wicked stare veers from Zara—who clearly wants an answer about that medallion because she's standing there, hands on hips, head cocked and toes tapping—to me. And, wow, it's completely obvious, even with our fated mate bond all clogged up, that Zara's *not* in a kissing mood.

So that villain idles over to me, while slipping his soaked coat off his shoulders and dropping it carelessly to the floor behind him, where it lands with a splat. My heart starts pounding and my face gets hot and I scramble to stand up so I can confront him, you know, properly.

But he waves an airy hand—his conjuring hand—and gives me a telekinetic push with his way-too-powerful-to-be-fair witchcraft that shoves me right back into the sofa.

Great.

Pinned like a butterfly in a biology lab—which is his favorite way to deal with me, especially when I'm skittish—I heave a resigned sigh.

Then my nemesis at this Academy slithers onto the couch and straddles my immobilized body with serpentine grace.

He's wet and he's cold but, well, I don't completely mind. If I'm being honest, I don't even really mind him pinning me, but I definitely try not to show it. He's Vasili, he's a snake, and we're still definitely frenemies (with benefits). With him, you have to establish boundaries.

Even if I did, sort of, ask for his mating bite.

I make my voice firm, like he's a misbehaving dog I'm getting ready to swat with a rolled-up newspaper. "Hey! You stop pushing me around—"

"First Boy." He makes it an endearment (which for him, I guess it is) and darts in to kiss me like a snakebite.

His lips are icy and his fangs are a menace, they're razor-sharp canines pricking my lip. But his tongue's a slick lick of heat diving deep into my mouth to claim every last bit of me. His cold fingers tweak my still-new earring, the same ear he pierced for me, sort of like foreplay? My piercing's still tender and it's taken its time healing, so that short sharp tug of pain makes me gasp and moan at the same time into his mouth.

He barely lifts his mouth from mine and purrs against my lips, "Mmmm, peppermint cocoa. Where's mine?"

"Make your own," I whisper, meeting his ice-blue stare through my steamed-up glasses.

I wonder if that sounds convincing?

He's wearing like three coats of cobalt mascara that really make his eyes pop, and even with his gilded hair slicked back from his perfect face and glittering with ice, he's so rock-star pretty he's really distracting. He has high cheekbones like a runway model and a sharp jaw like a manga character and a cruel mouth that still manages (totally deceptively) to look delicate.

And did I mention he's still pinning me, telekinetically *and* physically, under his sinuous body? His Academy blazer is all damp with sleet. I'm breathing in lungfuls of his musky caramel mating scent.

His pheromones are making me dizzy and his dominance is making me hard.

Literally the only advantage to him pinning me like this is that I can't rock my hips into him, while he's coiling over me in cobra mode. I can't give everything away. I can hide how hard he's making me.

Hopefully.

"Tut tut, Mercury," he breathes, all purring and sexy. "Whatever's gotten into you? That's no way to address the faculty."

Oh, that's typical Vasili. I let out a huff.

"You're only provisionally *on* the faculty. You're not a real prof." I mean to sound, you know, defiant? But my voice comes out all raspy. "Anyway, what are you going to do about it? Spank me?"

"Oh shit," Zara whispers.

She loves seeing us guys together, and I love to please her. But him spanking me (or anyone else in our bed) would definitely be a first. I just can't make up my mind whether it's something I might actually like.

Even though I can't see past Vasili, I can tell Zara's drifted right up close to watch.

It's been a shitshow around here all night, but we might finally be heading in a good direction.

"Hmmmm," he muses, eyes lidded and deadly as he processes what I *might* (sort of, at some future time) be asking for. "Truly, First Boy, you're full of surprises."

"Yeah, I am." I lick my lips, which are dry all of a sudden. My gaze drops to his parted lips.

Would he even be into… *that*? With me?

Darn it. He's such a sphinx there's no reading him.

Before this can go any further, the thud of Maxim's shitkickers thunders up the short flight of stairs from the vestibule. "Romanov?"

I guess he's smelling and hearing Vasili even if he can't feel him. Maxim's gruff Russian voice holds that tone he only ever uses with V. It's this weird but sexy combo of dominance and pleading.

Vasili's eyes narrow with wicked intent. Instead of turning to acknowledge him, V drags my Academy sweater and shirt off my shoulder and darts in to lick the twin punctures of his mating bite. Those scars are new and still tender. Pleasure snakes down my spine and wraps around my dick.

Lord, he's so terrible.

But, gosh, he makes me so hard.

My dreamy gaze drifts past his shoulder to find Maxim looming over us with his slitted dragon eyes all flaming. He's watching me, watching the look on my face. Which is unusual, because most of the time he totally ignores me.

Knowing he's watching, for whatever reason, and seeing him look so predatory makes me even hotter. Helpless to control any of this, I swallow hard and shiver.

V takes his good old time teasing my bite, while Maxim watches like his eyes are going to light us both on fire. I wish some of that heat was for me (because that dragon is smoking hot). But the only reason Maxim even sees me is because Vasili likes to rub the dragon's sexy face in the fact that it's V and not Max who's screwing me.

When my awful snake of an alpha feels like he's totally established his dominance, he finally slithers out of my lap and uncoils to his feet to rear over Maxim.

Those two are confusing as fuck to be around.

Right now I guess it's the dragon's turn to dominate.

Max wraps a hand around V's sleek head and pulls him down into a short hard kiss.

Their bodies come together like, I dunno, rutting elk or something? Like it's a fight instead of a kiss. A puff of Max's brimstone mating scent mingles with Vasili's butterscotch.

The dragon gets all gruff and rumbly and rubs his face in V's neck to scent him. "Sweetheart, you are soaking. And you are freezing. You should not fly in this weather."

Still standing close, Zara gives a little sigh. We all love when Max calls him *sweetheart.*

"Fortunately, I don't require your permission," Vasili flashes, sharp as a wasp. "You're not the dominant alpha in this *domus.*"

He pivots away before he can see the clench of frustration that tightens Max's jaw and the disappointment that furrows Max's brow.

Ronin gets the next kiss, and he's clearly the one who needs it. Ronin's my boyfriend (he actually lets me call him that, which still makes me giddy!) but something's really been bugging him all night. His face is all stony, but his eyes are haunted. He wraps his arms tight around V in a desperate clutch. He looks like he might actually be shaking.

Our alpha literally engulfs him with his body and kisses him like he's going to crawl down Ronin's throat and devour whatever's hurting him.

When he finally surfaces from being engulfed, Ronin seems a little more himself. His tiger eyes are heavy and his tawny skin is flushed. With a scowl, he flicks the medallion hanging around V's neck. "Why d'you want to wear this bloody thing, love? I don't like it. And neither does our girl."

"Now, darling, don't fret. It's merely an experiment. I thought perhaps we'd all appreciate a few hours of fucking peace from the telepathic bombardment of emotion running amuck twenty-four/seven in this harem." One arm still looped around Ronin's waist in casual possession, V scans the room with his basilisk gaze. "Where the hell's Lucius?"

"Downstairs with the girls. The power's out again, in case you missed it," Zara says dryly. "Where you been all night, bad boy?"

"Grading the most atrocious pile of appallingly written essays you can possibly imagine in my office in the crypt." He smirks and preens, because the Dean's finally given that snake Master Zerxes' old office in the cathedral where our classes are held. That office is prime real estate (even though it's in the crypt). It's an unspoken acknowledgment that, assuming V passes his qualifying exams and graduates like he's supposed to this spring, he'll trade in his provisional faculty status and become a full prof.

Then he'll really be a holy terror.

He's already like the Severus Snape of the Icarus Academy. Only he doesn't need a wand or a special curse to sow mischief.

"Hmm, poor you." Zara finally softens enough to grin at him.

That's Vasili's signal, the one he's been waiting for. With a leer, he hooks his horrible fingers in the hem of her sweater (which is actually my sweater that she's borrowing) and reels her in for a proper kiss.

She drapes her arms around his neck and presses her sexy curves against him and kisses him back in a way that makes him hum with satisfaction. Still, I notice she's super careful not to touch that medallion. She doesn't like what that thing does to our mating bond any more than I do. Even without telepathy, I can tell it bothers her that he's wearing it. It bothers her that V feels like we all need distance. It bothers me too, this whole concept that we'd need some kind of break from the intimacy and churn in our mating bond.

Even though he might actually be right.

The six of us together?

We can be… intense.

Especially now, when we're under so much stress.

"Why'd you do that with the book, Goblin King?" Zara murmurs between kisses, Ronin wrapped around both of them, while Maxim lurks and watches (because those three guys share Zara a lot, and it totally gets them all off). "Lucius seems to think that book's pretty important. We've got this, uh, stray dragon who's turned up…"

"I'm well aware," the snake says dismissively. "Ronin told me hours ago. Through our bond."

This actually isn't surprising, Vasili knows everything that goes on around here, probably in this case including the stuff about Messalina's marriage negotiations. These days, he and Lucius are thick as two thieves. Plus I bet V was lurking upstairs and eavesdropping before he came slithering out.

Lord, he's insufferable.

Zara needs him, we all do, and this is how he reacts?

"Geez Louise, you've known for *hours*?" I'm indignant on my fated mate's behalf. "Why didn't you come right home, you jerk?"

"Because I was in the midst of breaking into the Academy Vault to pinch this magical artifact at the time," he says coldly, tucking Zara under one arm and Ronin under the other while he scowls at me. "An act I undertook in the helpful expectation of giving us all a bit of breathing space. Defeating those defensive wards on the Vault was a rather complex endeavor, even for me. Do pardon me for not rushing, Mercury, but I didn't care to be turned permanently to stone by an ossification spell."

Zara and Ronin both look appalled, and Maxim rumbles his displeasure.

Honestly, I'm pretty appalled myself.

The thought of him taking that kind of risk on a whim, without even consulting anybody, is even more upsetting. We're all supposed to be in a relationship, aren't we?

I suck in a breath to tell him.

Suddenly the hearth fire flares and flutters in a violent gust of wind. With a twist of anxiety that knots my tummy right up, I realize I'm doing it again.

I'm summoning wind.

I don't actually know how to do that, not by choice. I'm just a Kryll and we're not a showy race. I do alchemy and earthquakes and that's pretty much it. But some of us have started manifesting some weird strains of witchcraft—you know, dormant recessives and stuff—since we formed the harem.

But we're all dealing with so much emotionally these days, we're like six horses in the same harness all pulling in different directions and fighting each other, that I haven't wanted to cause even more problems by talking about my witchcraft getting weird.

In fact, I'm hoping like heck no one realizes the wind that blew out those candles a few minutes ago came from me.

I'm concentrating on calming down, because the woo-woo seems to happen whenever I get too excited, when Lucius appears without warning at the head of the stairs.

He moves in total silence, like a hunting wolf.

With our mating bond clogged up, he catches us all by surprise.

"Oh Lucius." Zara looks relieved to see him, but also kind of guilty, because of the book. "I was, uh, just gonna call you. You know, now that the Goblin King's home. What's up with the generator?"

"All's well, except for those damnable mice who keep chewing through the wires. We really ought to adopt a cat… if we could ever agree on that." Our headmaster's perceptive gaze rests on Zara's hopeful face (she loves cats), then scans Vasili, who blows him a kiss. "But Racetrack doesn't want me hovering while she rewires."

"Dear pet," Vasili says in the sex-drenched purr he uses to flirt with Lucius. "Don't tease. You know I loathe felines."

"Well, as I've said, we can't manage to agree on the cat." Lucius' stare zeroes in on the enchanted book on the floor. His face tightens and he pads toward it. "To your other point, I was well aware of Vasili's return."

V looks coyly intrigued. "How could you possibly have known?"

"I sensed a disturbance in the Force," Lucius says wryly, totally immune (for once) to V's snaky charm. "Despite that accursed medallion you're wearing around your pretty neck."

That's Lucius' way of saying he's put magical wards on the house to fend off any uninvited guests, which he did right before dinner. I guess Vasili tripped the wire (magically speaking) when he flew home, in a way that alerted Lucius.

"Hmmmm. So you like my new bauble?" Vasili shows off his stolen trinket and preens.

Lucius bends to gather the book in careful hands and shoots him a narrow look. "Not particularly. I certainly don't like the rash and entirely needless risk you took to acquire it. I also don't happen to believe that walling ourselves off from one another's emotions is a particularly healthy way to deal with the difficulties in this polycule."

That's Lucius' nifty shifty senses at work right there. His wolf could obviously hear Vasili from the basement.

V's dangerous eyes narrow. He watches Lucius return to the fire with that scary-looking book cradled in his arms. Our headmaster has plenty of experience dealing with the Goblin King in a temper. Lucius neither meets V's stare nor avoids it, just returns the book calmly to the end table and lowers himself to the couch.

Our headmaster's a no-drama kind of guy.

I reach out to hold Lucius' hand for comfort. He was my teacher before he was my lover, and now he's both, and his touch really *is* comforting. He spares me a distracted smile, draws my hand into his lap, and gives me a nice firm squeeze.

He always knows what I need.

"Oh fine," Vasili huffs. "Have it your way… for the moment." The villain swoops down on his fallen coat, extracts a lead box from the pocket, plucks the medallion from his neck, and drops it carelessly into the box.

The second he lowers the lid, all the emotion in the room comes flooding back in a rush.

Especially Ronin's.

Ronin's emotions are all tangled in a knot of grief and shame and rage that's way too tight and quivery with strain for me to tease loose.

Zara's worrying about Ronin and uneasy over the sudden appearance of that strange dragon and still borderline annoyed at all of us (especially me, ouch, because I'm supposed to be the loyal one she can always count on, but gosh, I was only trying to help) for keeping secrets.

Max is totally obsessed with the idea that Zara might finally get pregnant and it's making him, like, extra fixated on fucking her ASAP.

Lucius is fretting over what other dangerously enchanted objects Vasili might've pinched from the Academy Vault. Also, how to hide this latest transgression from the Dean so she doesn't fire Vasili from the faculty and/or expel him from the school before he can graduate. Especially since V's already on a faculty improvement plan, which means he's basically still on probation from his last transgression.

And Vasili?

Inside, that rattlesnake of a Romanov isn't all indifferent the way he likes to pretend. He's viciously pissed that Messalina wants to shove some strange guy willy-nilly into our queen's bed. He's feeling over-the-top alphahole possessive toward our queen and every mate in our whole harem (even me!)

And he's secretly plotting to fly his own patrol in shifted form later and kill that enemy dragon and his rider.

"Vasili, my dear," Lucius murmurs. "Your protective instincts are truly impressive. But before you go haring off to hunt our uninvited guest, I suggest we consult this tome you've been hurling about."

"Oh hell to the yeah." Zara's face lights up till she's radiant. "Let's do that."

Before she can leap into action and snatch the book right out of Lucius' hands (or paws), Maxim plants his stubborn body between the two of them.

"Vasili is cold and he is hungry," the dragon says softly. "Let him eat first. And we must warm him."

That's total protective alpha shit, and I wait (honestly, we all do) for Vasili to disembowel him like a velociraptor just for, like, presuming.

But I guess V must actually be cold and hungry and maybe tired or sick or something, because he lets Maxim get away with it. My frenemy just sighs and sinks down to the ottoman by the fire, tugging Zara and Ronin down with him. Zara helps V slip out of his damp blazer and snuggles up next to him, her clever fingers loosening the stylish twist of his tie, while Ronin starts unlacing V's trendy boots and working his feet free.

Maxim drapes V's sodden coat over a chair near the fire to dry, then fixes V a plate of still-warm pasta and brings it over. Max even tosses the linen napkin over Vasili's lap and hovers threateningly over him, looking all scowly and protective, until V finally deigns to accept the fork like a queen granting favors and starts eating.

Whoa. That's classic alpha tending behavior and Vasili's totally allowing it, doesn't even seem to notice it, his gaze veering between Ronin's bowed head and the locked book near Lucius' elbow.

All this really makes me wonder when those two, V and Max I mean, will finally blow past this extended foreplay standoff stage in their relationship and actually start fucking.

"Get a plate for yourself too, big guy," Zara urges. "You definitely need to eat before you go back out there."

Maxim finally stops hovering and gets his own plate. It's heaping over with all the remaining pasta and like three breadsticks balanced on top, because that dragon can really eat. We all wait till he's settled cross-legged on the floor, hunched over his plate like someone might try to take it from him, and wolfing his food ferociously.

"Okay, Lucius." Zara shoots our wolf a wry look. "You ever gonna open that book, or you just plan to tease me with it all night?"

We all look expectantly at Lucius.

Our headmaster releases my hand to draw the heavy volume into his lap and rests a respectful palm on the cover. "This book can't have been opened recently. Not since—" Surprise ripples through him, and Lucius' quiet tone sharpens. "Gwendolyn."

Ronin hunches into himself. He's sitting on the floor next to Vasili's legs, back propped against the ottoman, knees pulled tight to his chest, arms thrown over them. Now Ronin buries his face in his folded arms. This position makes his sleek hair fall down like a silk curtain so none of us can see him.

But I don't feel surprise in our bond.

Only grief.

Vasili sets his plate aside and strokes a hand over Ronin's dark head. With a level of tenderness you'd be amazed to know that snake possesses, he kneads the back of Ronin's bowed neck.

Roughly Ronin shrugs his hand away.

V recovers with reptilian speed and covers it up in a blink. But I can feel his shock.

Hey Ronin? I'm not a telepath, but my boyfriend is. And Gwen's suicide really messed him up for a long time. *You okay?*

Without looking up, Ronin mutters a curse into his folded arms. He doesn't want to let me in right now, but that's okay. I just want him to know I'm here for him. We all are.

"Ronin, my dear one, I'm so terribly sorry," Lucius says gently. "I realize this is all a bit unexpected."

"Tell me about it," Zara murmurs, her face cloudy with worry over Ronin. "Since when are you clairsentient, Lucius? That's a Valyrian trait."

"I'm not, but this book is highly sensitive to arcane energy, and Gwendolyn herself—like our Ronin—was powerfully clairsentient." Lucius frowns. "She was a member of this cohort for such a short while. I never realized Gwendolyn possessed an academic interest in the Fae."

"The *Fae*?" Zara's teal brows draw together and her forehead puckers. "Seriously? Are you talking about, like, fairies?"

I sit up straight and push my glasses up my nose.

"Oh sure. The Light Fae and the Dark Fae—the Seelie and Unseelie—they're in the Witching World Lit curriculum. You'll take that sophomore year," I explain happily to Zara. "It's all legends and fairytales. It's fun."

"Fun." Lucius muses. "Like the legend of Avalon itself, today the Fae are commonly believed to be more legend than history. The mythical fifth race that once ruled the witching world, yet the first to be rendered extinct." He pauses. "It's a closely guarded secret that a few scattered Fae still linger among us."

"Cheese on toast." Zara stares, her eyes round as kaleidoscopes. "You trying to tell me fairies are literally *real*?"

"Not in this realm, no." He hesitates. "At least, not any longer, for the most part. The last remnants of the Light Fae, led by the Seelie queen, chose to remain in this realm. Over the centuries, concealed by a glamor that masks their magic, they've quietly dwindled to near extinction. The Dark Fae… well, they chose a different path."

Lucius' tone is all foreboding. With the furnace down, the cold outside is creeping in. Despite the fire's warmth, a chill skitters down my spine and goosebumps race down my arms.

"C'mon, Lucius. Don't drag this out." Zara's vibrating with impatience. If our headmaster doesn't get a move on, my fated mate's just going to leap up and open that book for him.

Lucius bows his head over the volume. "Led by their own evil king, the Dark Fae withdrew into hiding. Embittered and vengeful, the Unseelie King wrought a potent curse, watered with the blood of murdered witches who opposed him—his own kin—to seal and conceal the Dark Fae's last desperate sanctuary. That sanctuary is the legendary isle of Avalon."

Lucius leans close to the book and whispers a word that's too soft for me to hear. Like an Open Sesame or something.

The whole house holds its breath.

Even Maxim stops noisily scraping his fork over his empty plate to scoop up every last drop of alfredo sauce and leans forward intently to watch.

Whatever Lucius says makes the old brass lock glow and fall open. The heavy cover seems almost to lift itself. The thick parchment pages rustle into motion, falling open to the exact page he's looking for. The dry sweet smell of pressed flowers hits my nose.

I adjust my glasses and lean over Lucius' shoulder to look. The lines of fancy calligraphic script are tricky to read, big swirly capitals all gilded, borders thick with vivid illustrations that look ready to crawl or wiggle or fly right off the page.

"Safe and hidden doth Avalon lie behind magickal Wards, watered with the life's Blood of our betrayers," I read slowly, out loud so everyone can hear. "For one thousand years wilt the Way remain sealed. Then wilt the Magick weaken and the Portal decay. Thus may it open… but only in those Sacred nodes, marked by Standing Stones, where the two Realms converge, when the tide of the Seasons shifts…"

I've reached the end of the page, but it literally turns on its own. The green smell of rain fills my head. Now there's a painted illustration of a sundial all smothered in poison ivy, a mossy old ring of standing stones, and just a few words. I swallow and keep going.

"At Beltane… at Samhain…" I pause, because Ronin's just scraped out a curse. His head hasn't lifted, but his pain pulses through our bond. "At Midwinter… at Equinox—"

I break off and glance up, my gaze locking with Zara's. She's clutching V's thigh for support, and her aqua eyes are huge.

"Oh fuck," she whispers. "Spring equinox. That's in two days! And it's a new moon too. Like an extra witchy time. That's what Aggie was saying in Astrology class."

I know all about the impact of the moon on our witchcraft, because I aced that test, and I open my mouth to tell her.

Before I can get a word out, the page turns with a rustle and an ashy puff of burnt amber.

A flash of poison green snares my gaze.

Now I'm staring at the full-page illustration of a flying green dragon, breathing streamers of curling green fire, scales crossed with a fancy gilded harness. That dragon's got a rider—a scary-looking dude in emerald-green armor. He's wearing a sword and a fancy helmet with two horrible black horns, like dragon horns. The helmet hides his face.

In the shifting firelight, the dragon's wings seem to beat.

A malignant eye glitters at me through that sinister helm. Yikes. Feels like that rider's actually watching me.

"Whoa," I breathe. "This looks like the dude Zara saw. You think maybe there's one of those old portals on Mt. Apollo, up on the summit near the standing stones? You think because the spell's decaying and it's almost the equinox, this guy maybe managed to come through?"

No one says a word. I can't even hear Racetrack swearing and clattering in the basement anymore.

For some reason, my palms are sweating. Discreetly I wipe them on my chinos. My gaze drifts to the caption. "Behold. The King of the Dark Fae cometh."

"Bloody *fuck*." Ronin explodes to his feet and we all jump. He stares around at us wildly. "I can't do this. Thought I could just—push through it—but I can't!"

"That's *enough*." Vasili slices the book a vicious glance and slashes a hand sideways. For the second time tonight, that book lifts up and flies through the air, hits the dining room table with a thud, and skids across the surface.

It slides to a halt before it can fall off the edge. All on its own, the cover flips open and the pages rustle. Even from all the way across the room, I catch the glitter of venom-green dragon scales.

I swear to God, those wings are beating.

My entire body goes all shivery with chills.

"Vasili, my dear," Lucius sighs.

"I said that's enough. Enough from that accused book for one night." Vasili leaps up. He's usually hard as heck to read, but he isn't right now. He clearly wants to hold Ronin.

Ronin, equally clearly, doesn't want to be held.

Maxim's on his feet too, he shoved his plate aside and jumped up from the floor when Ronin did. Now a continuous growl is rumbling from Max's chest that worries me.

Oh Lord. If that dragon loses it and shifts in the *domus,* we're all in big trouble.

"Take it easy, big guy. You too, Adam." That's Zara talking to Ronin, who looks a little (lot) like Adam Driver. She stands slowly, like she doesn't want to spook anyone, and keeps her voice steady. "We're all right here with you. I'm just gonna pour you a drink, okay? Shit, we could probably all use one."

Ronin barks out a harsh laugh. "I fancy it'll take more than a bloody cocktail to fix this nightmare. Bollocks, I don't imagine there *is* any fixing it."

"Let's try anyway," I mumble, because his pain is just too awful and I have to do something.

I hop up and hurry over to the wine rack Lucius keeps stocked with bottles of this and that, just regular deliveries from the supply plane, so Zara doesn't have to wait on us. Ronin's a scotch guy (and he's kind of a snob about it). So I'm looking for the good stuff.

Behind me, under the hiss of sleet against glass, Max is still growling. Zara makes one of her dragon queen crooning sounds, kind of like a trill? I know without looking that she's gone over there to soothe him, her dragon king.

Slowly Maxim's dragonish rumble peeters out. But he's worried as heck over Ronin, we all are.

"Ronin, dear heart," Lucius murmurs. "Can you possibly share what ails you? We can't help if we don't know—"

"There's no blooming help for this, believe me." Ronin's haunted tone pulls me around to look. He's scrubbing his hands over his face, really digging with his fingers, like he wants to peel his own skin off. His psychic doors are shut tight and the windows are dark.

There's no one home.

He's the strongest telepath at Icarus, and there's no peeking allowed inside him right now.

"Darling." V catches our guy's violent hands and draws them firmly away from his tortured face. "You're killing us. Whatever this is, it's destroying you. If you can't tell all of us… can you at least tell Lucius? In private?"

That gives me a real jolt. The whole idea of the great and terrible Vasili, the mighty Scorpio scion, stepping aside for *anyone*… the idea of that snake admitting it might be easier for Ronin to confide in Lucius instead of Vasili…

Wow.

Just wow.

I honestly didn't think V had it in him.

Ronin stares into Vasili's desperate face. At last the words wrench out of him, like they're breaking out against his will.

"Here's what you'll find in that fucking book, okay?" Ronin snarls through bared teeth. "It's like Neo just said. The King of the Dark Fae, the Unseelie King, rides a poison-green dragon." Zara gasps, but Ronin just keeps going. "But that beastie's no shifter. That dragon isn't like Max or Zara or any of you lot when you shift. That thing's a half-mad, flesh-eating monster only the Unseelie King can tame."

Now I'm confused. I abandon my search for alcohol no one seems to want and drift back toward him. "That wasn't in our Witching World Lit class. Did you and Gwen both, like, read Lucius' book?"

Ronin shakes his head violently and tries to twist free, but Vasili won't let him. V's holding onto Ronin like he's dangling off a precipice and only V's grip can save him.

"Fuuuuuck." Ronin's eyes squeeze shut and he lets loose this soul-rending groan that even pulls Lucius to his feet. "Look. Everyone thinks Gwen offed herself freshman year because Cybelle and her clique were bullying Gwen. They bloody well *were*, but that wasn't the only reason she did it.

"By the time we got here, Gwen was already damaged. Fragile. She blamed herself for what *I* bloody did before we ever came to Icarus." He pulls in a ragged breath. His tawny eyes glitter with unshed tears. "For her sake, to protect her, I killed the only man I ever loved… till *you* came along." He lifts his head long enough to shoot Vasili a tortured look.

V looks thunderstruck, so this is obviously a newsflash. It's a newsflash for me too, because I thought he and Ronin already knew everything there is to know about each other.

I creep up beside Lucius. Without looking away from the drama, my headmaster wraps a firm arm around my waist to comfort me. Feeling small and somehow scared, I cuddle up against him and breathe in the familiar scent of wolf.

"I… I don't understand," I say softly to Ronin. "What does all this have to do with the King of the Dark Fae?"

"The Unseelie King has a name, but you won't find it in any book. Because names hold power, and his is secret." Ronin swallows hard and drags in a shaky inhale. "His name's Zephyr. And the reason I'm telling you, even though I swore to keep it secret, is because it can't be him who came through. It *can't* be."

Ronin clears his throat harshly and rasps out the rest. "Because *he's* the man I loved. He's the man I killed."

Chapter Five

Zara

"So, guys, I guess we're just not gonna talk about this. Like, at all?"

I'm sitting at the dressing table in my bedroom, stripped down to my panties and swimming in one of Lucius' starched shirts. I'm also dabbing on some of Vasili's high-end facial goop from Paris in the hope it'll do something about those violet shadows under my eyes.

I want all my guys as close as possible tonight.

But I don't always get what I want.

"Apparently not." Vasili slips into my bedroom (which is now also his bedroom, except when he's brooding and wants his own space). He closes the door behind him with a sigh. "Ronin insists he wants to sleep alone. Nothing I said or did—and, believe me, I tried *everything*—could even begin to persuade him differently."

Usually we lock that door once we're all inside (caution habit). But the Goblin King doesn't lock it now, because half my guys are still out there.

Ronin's alone and hurting down the hall in the solo student bedroom he hardly ever uses, which feels all kinds of wrong. While Max is flying circles over this island in dragon form in another hunt for our intruder. The big guy says he can't sleep while there's a threat to me lurking. Through the thick Roman-era walls, my shifty senses pick up my dragon king's distant bellows of challenge and rage.

If he finds my enemy, he'll kill him.

Or be killed himself.

Just the thought of someone hurting my dragon makes me see red. My inner queen roars with fury. Shit, she wants to rise.

"Yeah, no. I don't like the sound of that." I close the jar of silky pink goop with a decisive twist.

"Maybe Ronin just wants to be alone with his memories," Neo offers. He's already in bed, still wearing his glasses and poring over a book as usual. "We gotta give the guy his space, right, even if we don't like it? What happened to Gwen hit him really hard. They were twins, just super close."

"God, I know he's grieving." Even though he's shutting us out, my heart fucking aches with the psychic echo of Ronin's grief. "And, yeah, he's allowed. But the way I see it, none of us should be alone right now. Look, if it turns out Ronin had some secret boyhood friendship with the King of the Dark Fae… even if the guy was his first love or whatever… I'm obviously not gonna pry into that. You know, unless he invites us."

"Well, I wouldn't hold your breath waiting for *that* invitation. Truly, darlings, I wouldn't." With way more violence than necessary, Vasili shoves the grate aside and hurls more wood into our little fire, because the power's still down. We're probably gonna need an actual electrician by morning.

Just add not freezing to our problem list.

I rub my aching chest. I'm literally, physically aching with Ronin's pain, and it's making me crazy. He needs us.

"Here's the thing." I sigh. "Ronin's more than grieving. Clearly he blames himself for whatever went down with him and the guy back home. He *hates* himself for it. We can all feel that, right?"

Vasili hisses something it's probably best I can't hear.

I keep right on going. "I still don't get the connection between the Faerie King and Gwen. I just can't wrap my head around it. But I definitely don't like the way Ronin's shutting us all out."

Lucius glances up from my desk, where he's belted neatly into his burgundy smoking jacket and PJs, a snifter of Hungarian *palinka* at his elbow, efficiently grading a pile of research papers for our History of Witchcraft class. He looks more like my headmaster tonight than a savage wolf, his whiskey eyes lowered diligently to his work, his elegant Vlad the Impaler features composed, all that gleaming chestnut hair swept into a tidy man-bun.

Shifter hair grows like gangbusters, but none of us want him to cut it. Even Max, who mostly gives Lucius loads of space (too much space, actually, I'd love to see them closer), admits he likes the look.

"If privacy is truly what Ronin desires," Lucius murmurs, "we simply must respect his wishes."

"Yeah, well, that doesn't mean we have to like it," I grumble. "In case anyone's forgetting, we don't do too well in this harem with secrets. If we've all learned anything in this relationship, it's that we gotta talk shit out."

Now, for some reason, the Goblin King slices a sharp glance at Neo in our big medieval bed. In classic bookworm mode, my fated mate's buried nose-deep in a pile of dusty old histories from the downstairs library. It's getting late, but he's still frowning and muttering and scribbling notes in his leather-bound journal.

By mutual consent, we've all agreed to leave that weird Avalon book alone downstairs, locked up in Lucius' study, till morning.

Sure, I took a good look inside first, with Lucius hovering protectively over me and Max growling and pacing the whole time. But I only did that once Ronin locked himself in his room, with Vasili lurking in the hall outside looking like he wanted to blast Ronin's door off its hinges. My snake isn't used to our guy shutting him out, and it's put him in a vile temper.

Anyway.

The book.

I'm still processing some of the freaky shit I read in there. But that *Monster Book of Monsters* thing weirds me out with its random opening and shuffling and those moving illustrations and those schizophrenic smells of seasons and weather and shit. Not to mention the pages are literally alive with violent images of snarling dragons and armored riders that make my inner dragon bate and bugle with every page turn.

Long story short? I can't even think about that enchanted book without my Spidey-senses tingling.

It's definitely not coming into this bedroom.

Especially not while we sleep.

"We can talk about this more over breakfast. I'll make pancakes, even though it isn't Saturday." Looking adorably determined, Neo pushes his glasses up his nose.

I know he's hurt that Ronin's shut him out, but my gentle bookworm is trying so hard to be understanding.

"Ronin simply needs time to work through his feelings. My dears, we must extend him that courtesy." Lucius sounds firm and a little growly. He's Ronin's first alpha, which makes his wolf super-protective. But our headmaster's always the adult in the room.

And I'm not just saying that because he's ten years older. We're getting ready to celebrate his thirtieth birthday. (Even though it's really hard planning a surprise party in a houseful of telepaths.)

What I mean is, he grounds us.

Neo frowns. "One thing I'm seeing from this ley line map is there's a ring of standing stones—a really old one—not far from the Pendragon estate in Wales. That's where Ronin grew up. If he was sneaking out to meet a Fae boyfriend or something, and those standing stones are where the Dark Fae come through, like when the wards weaken, I guess that could explain how they met."

"Fuck. We are *not* talking about this without Ronin being here." Vasili thrusts the fireside poker into its rack with a vicious stab and a clatter that makes us all jump. "We're not talking about him behind his back. And that isn't open to discussion, darlings. I do trust that's clear."

My snake plants a hand on his slim hip and eyes us with his dangerous stare like he's daring us all to defy him.

Then he'll make us suffer.

He's still wearing his uniform trousers, but his tie is loose, cuffs folded back to expose the sinewy grace of his forearms. With his frosted hair all rock-star tousled and his sexy-pretty face all sulky with warning, our alpha's hot as fuck.

And, Sweet Jesus, he knows it.

He totally catches me staring. His sullen mouth curls in a smirk. "See something you like, little queen?"

"Thinking about it, Goblin King," I murmur, low and throaty.

Oh, yeah, I definitely am. With everything that's going down in our *domus*, I need them tonight. I need all five of them losing their minds inside me, inside each other, in all the ways, same as always. Vasili and Neo, especially, they're still a new thing in the polycule. They're still learning to trust each other.

Sparks fly whenever those two fuck.

But I can't stop thinking about all those pregnancies. A fertility epidemic has broken out on this island like a goddamn rash. I'm not in heat and I'm definitely not fertile while I'm taking those shots.

But… what if…?

Buying myself time to think, I grab a bottle of body lotion (not Vasili's, that stuff costs a fortune) and wander over to the window seat that overlooks the windy cobblestone street. Sleet hammers the crumbly abandoned buildings leaning over the narrow road. Ice rimes the leaded glass and makes the view all ripply.

Somewhere in the inky clouds over this island, my dragon king is hunting.

Shivering, I prop my bare leg on the cushioned seat and start smoothing lotion up my shin. The smell of musk and roses mingles with the fragrance of burning applewood and the gamy scent of wolf.

That's Lucius' mating scent. He's lowered his pen to watch me like I'm dinner.

They're all watching me, all three of my guys.

Even my bookworm abandons his book to stare.

In this storm, we will not rise, my dragon queen whispers. Her sibilant hiss slithers through my thoughts. *But that does not mean we do not burn.*

Yeah. No shit, showgirl. My inner dragon and I are super simpatico, at least in that way. Horny as fuck for all our guys, both of us, pretty much twenty-four/seven.

But she wants dragonets.

And I don't.

Not right now. We're too young, all of us (except maybe Lucius. It's not just that he's older than the rest of us. He's totally ready, in all the ways, and he'd be amazing as a dad.)

But we've got enough major problems in this harem.

My unease vibrates through the bond between us like a sine wave. My sweet Neo gives a murmur of distress and pushes up to sit. Vasili's absolutely still, that icy gaze burning into me, watching me rub a fine sheen of lotion over my knee. Breath hitching under his electric stare, I glide my creamy fingers slowly up my thigh.

"My queen," Lucius murmurs, still mannerly as a lord, even with his wolf lurking in his voice. In the wavy reflection, he rises with a predator's silent grace. "No one of us here will ever force you to do anything against your will. Admittedly, we've all experienced… a rather trying day. Tonight we can simply sleep, all of us. If you wish."

Yeah, he'd sound like a perfect Old World gentleman—if his wolf wasn't rising.

Worry or no worry, I'm teasing them.

All three of them.

My wolf king wants to fuck.

They all do, all my guys. And God knows, that's what I want. Not just the physical connection and the cathartic release of climax, but the psychic connection of our witchcraft and the emotional comfort of our mating bond. I crave that. I *need* that. We all do.

I'm not gonna let my own fear stand between me and my guys and anything we all need.

"I'm taking the shots," I breathe into the silence. "In science we trust."

"Only if you're certain," Lucius says softly. "Otherwise, we wait."

My teeth sink into my lower lip. I tilt my knee wide to stroke lotion up my inner thigh. Caressing that sensitive skin makes me shiver. It's chilly near the window, but I'm starting to sweat. Under the silky gusset of my schoolgirl panties, my pussy pulses with heat.

"She's certain." Vasili's cruel voice curls like a whiplash through the silence. "First Boy, go to your queen."

Lucius' wolf growls in his chest, deep and savage. In the glass, his wicked eyes pulse red with need.

Dim and blurry in the glass, Neo scrambles out of bed. He's barefoot in plaid pajama pants and a cotton tee shirt stretched over his broad chest. And he's kinda clumsy with Vasili watching, all snaky and broody and intense.

Still, Neo pushes a hand through his messy purple curls and scowls at V. "You're not the boss of me. I'm doing this because *I* want it. Because Zara wants it, and Lucius. And you do too, you big bully."

Neo's like a defiant puppy barking at a pit bull right now, and I can tell he's totally charmed Vasili. Still, the Goblin King unravels his tie with deliberate menace.

I fucking love when he's like this.

Under my swiftly dampening panties, my cunt unfolds and opens like a flower.

Vasili's voice shreds the air. "Stand at the window. Hands on the glass. No touching her or yourself until I allow it, Mercury. Or I'll make you suffer."

"What. Ever." Neo scowls at Vasili through a fallen comma of magenta hair as he saunters past. But he also adds a cute little bookworm swagger to his hips and peels his tee shirt over his head in a slow reveal that shows off his six-pack and the sexy flex of his biceps.

Vasili smolders after him in a way that makes me want to start shedding clothes myself.

Yowsa.

Neo struts past Lucius, who's a twitch away from pouncing on him, with an adorable bookworm blush. None of my guys (except Max, who tries to pretend he's not interested) can get enough of Neo these days. And I love to watch, especially when my titanium pussy needs a breather from being double-dicked, overstuffed, and ridden hard.

Now Neo locks onto me. In the leaded glass, our eyes meet.

My heartbeat kicks into high gear and my breath quickens. I've still got one leg propped on the window seat, thigh spread wide to expose my damp gusset.

I wonder if Neo's actually gonna disobey one of the Goblin King's royal edicts and touch me without V's permission.

"Hey babe," Neo whispers. His lips curve in a shy smile.

"Hi baby. You're soooo sexy." I lick my own lips like I can taste him.

His PJs are hanging low on his hips in a way that shows off his deep pelvic vee and the lick of copper hair that forms his happy trail. I want to lick my own happy trail down those abs of his so bad I can already taste him.

He fits himself carefully into the empty space next to me and leans over the seat to plant his big hands against the glass.

Without touching me.

Pouting a little with disappointment, I trail my hand up my thigh till I'm teasing the edge of my panties.

"Good boy," Vasili purrs. He undulates up behind us, supple as a sidewinder, unbuttoning his shirt with slow purpose. "Lucius. Be a nice pet and worship our queen. She's already wet for us. Can you smell her?"

"I can." Lucius is guttural with need, fangs descending to distort his refined scholar speech. "Bend for me, my queen."

Oh hell to the yeah.

Slowly I lower my foot to the floor and lean forward to plant my palms on the cushion. Lucius looms behind me, shedding his smoking jacket with brutal efficiency.

Shirtless, he looks the way you'd imagine a wolf shifter alpha should, all rangy and ropy with animal strength, dark hair curling on that powerful chest I love to nuzzle. As Lucius prowls up beside Vasili, the Goblin King reaches to free our wolf's hair with a hard tug. Chestnut curls spill over Lucius' shoulders and down his back.

God, it's getting so long. We really should let him cut it.

But I love Lucius like this, all fangy and messy and primal.

It's pretty obvi that Vasili loves him like this too. V grabs a fistful of those flowing locks and drags Lucius into a hard claiming kiss that makes our wolf growl and our snake hiss.

"Oh, sugar," Neo whispers. His head turns to meet my gaze. He's all flushed and his glasses are starting to steam.

Before I can do anything about that, Lucius surfaces from Vasili's kiss and descends on me. His rough hands hook in my panties and drag them down my thighs.

I start to wiggle out of them, but he growls, "No. Leave them. Feet spread."

When I hesitate a hair too long, just wrapping my head around the mood he's in, he shoves a knee between mine and pushes my legs apart. The panties stretch tight between my spread ankles.

I suck in a breath that's heavy with the dark reek of predator. Lucius skims his hands up the backs of my thighs, over the bare swell of my ass, and pushes up the tail of his starched shirt (which I'm still wearing) to expose me fully to his stare.

Harsh in the silence, he drags in a hoarse breath.

From this angle, he can totally see my ass and probably a peekaboo glimpse of my pussy. I go commando down there, Brazilian-style, and the cool night air teases my wet folds.

I squirm and try to spread wider for him, but the schoolgirl panties stretched between my ankles don't have any more give.

"Want me to take it off, Teach?" I breathe. "The shirt?"

"No," he says gruffly. "I like you wearing my clothes. I like smelling myself on you. I like smelling you on my garments. Your mating scent. Your perfume. Your sex. After I've finished with you tonight, I'll never wash that shirt again."

Holy moly, he's in a mood.

"You gonna fuck me hard then?" Yeah, I'm teasing him. He's still holding back, and I love when he's all undone.

"In time." He punctuates his growl with a stinging slap that makes my ass burn. I gasp and twitch. "Patience is a virtue, Ms. Gemini."

Next to me, Neo whines in sympathy.

And eagerness.

Ever since my bookworm taunted the Goblin King earlier about trying a little spanky-panky, that idea's been lurking in all our minds.

Except Ronin's, I guess. He's locked down so tight none of us has a clue what he's really thinking.

"My, my, Mr. Mercury." Rearing over Neo from behind like a naga, Vasili slips off his shirt and glides his deadly hands up Neo's bare ribs. "Feeling a trifle warm tonight, are we?"

"Yeah. It's hot as heck in here," Neo mumbles defensively, clearly fighting not to squirm under V's touch. It isn't, not really, it's actually kinda nippy near the window. Which makes me wonder if my fated mate's getting ready to go into heat again.

Vasili purrs and Lucius rumbles.

Because of course they're all reading my thoughts.

"I'm not, I can't be, the moon's wrong." Neo pants and twitches as Vasili trails his fingers underneath to Neo's tummy. "V, stop, that tickles!"

"Hmmm." Completely undeterred, the Goblin King slips his fingers under Neo's waistband and starts easing his jammies down his hips. "Maybe you're having another microheat. Wouldn't that be diverting?"

We're all starting to figure out Neo's heats work differently than everyone else's, because of his Kryll DNA. He gets lots of little spikes that sex him up, followed by feel-good dopamine hits that make our bookworm drowsy for a day or so.

Me? I get superheats once a month that last for days.

Cheese on toast. If he spikes tonight, it's gonna take all of us (minus Max, I guess) to ease sweet baby Neo over the hump—

But my focus on Neo skids sideways when Lucius works his hot callused hands under my shirt and palms my tits. From this angle, with me bent over, my curves fill his hands and leave my pierced nipples at the mercy of his ruthless fingers. He twists my little rings and tweaks my swollen nubs till I'm gasping and squirming for real. I rock back into his hips.

Fuck. He's still wearing his pressed *Downton Abbey* pajama pants.

"Behave yourself," he growls in my ear, fangs scraping my lobe and pricking my neck. "I make the rules. I decide when you climax. I want you soaking and desperate. I want you wild. I want you frantic to feel me filling your sweet quim."

That's dirty talk for Lucius, he's kinda old-fashioned. But, shit, he knows how to turn my crank.

"If I get any wetter, you're gonna need a flare and a life jacket," I moan, because my juices are literally trickling down my thighs. "God, Lucius, tease me later. I need to feel you inside me. Fuck me."

He snarls and mouths his way down my neck, all tongue and fangs. When he hits the twin punctures of his mating bite, those tiny scars where my neck meets my shoulder, pleasure streaks through me and lights up my clit and just about launches me into orbit.

But at least he stops tormenting my nipples long enough to fumble his pants open and shove them down his legs.

While Lucius is stripping down, the Goblin King's taking advantage of the fact that he's got Neo all nakey. My bookworm's a *very* obedient boy, and he lives to please. Neo's got his palms firmly planted on the glass, legs spread, head lowered, fair skin all goosebumpy. His monster dick juts stiff and urgent between his muscled thighs, drooling a shining rope of precum on the window seat.

No one's told me *I* can't touch, probably because I'm Neo's first alpha, I gave him his first mating bite, and the guys all respect that. Propping my bent-over weight on one arm, I sneak a hand over to wrap my fist around my bookworm's meaty cock.

That first spark of contact makes him gasp. "Oh, wow, babe…"

"Mmmm, you like this, don't you, baby?" My fingers stretch to span his impressive girth. I give him a few slow pumps that spread precum all down his length. My fated mate's silky and veiny and hard as a freaking steel cable, wound so tight he's ready to snap.

He moans in agreement and pumps his pelvis into my fist in short desperate snaps. When I grip his base to slow him down, his heavy balls swing against my fingers.

"Now, First Boy, don't be naughty. Don't you *dare* come without me." Delicate as a girl with an ice cream cone, V licks his way down Neo's muscly back. "I want you to beg. Beg for my cock in your greedy little hole."

My fated mate works his dick into my fist and leans into his defiant side. I know it embarrasses him when V makes him say the H word. "No. You can't make me."

"Well." Vasili's dangerous eyes narrow. "Let's just see about that, shall we? You know I simply adore a dare."

Neo's tone turns mutinous. "You know something, V? You don't have to be such a bully all the time. You can at least be nice to me in private—"

Neo chokes off with a gasp, because the Goblin King's spreading him wide back there.

"*Nice* to you? Well, let's just try. Let's take a nice look at this pretty hole," Vasili croons, and Neo just about swallows his tongue. "Doesn't our boy have a sweet little pucker, Lucius?"

And my wolf, who's actually taken the time to fold his smoking jacket and pajamas over the chair like a civilized gentleman, pads over naked to take a look.

"Well, he's very eager for you, to be certain," Lucius comments, somehow managing to sound scholarly, even though he's talking through his fully extended fangs. "I can see his hole fluttering. He seems quite desperate to accommodate you."

Poor Neo's face is so red I'm afraid he's gonna burst into flames.

Especially when Vasili sighs, "Alas, our First Boy wants me to be… *nice* to him. I suppose there's no help for it. I'll simply have to rim him properly before I rail him."

Neo whimpers and bites his lip to keep from begging.

Now I'd really like a look back there myself. But that's not happening, because Lucius has refocused all his formidable attention on me. He's looming over me, spanning my hips with his hands.

Guess I'll have to abandon my bookworm to our snake's tender mercies.

With a last pump to keep him interested, I relinquish my grip on Neo's dick. Besides, he really *is* close to losing it, he probably is starting a microheat, and the Goblin King's gonna be pissy as fuck if Neo spends in my hand.

Lucius wraps an arm around my waist and drags my ass hard against his boner. I rise on tiptoe and wiggle against him so I can nestle his thick cock between my ass cheeks. He strokes down my tummy to spread his palm flat over my pelvis.

Like, right over my womb.

Wow.

That's an uber-possessive way to touch me. Max does it a lot with that whole breeding kink he's rocking. But Lucius never has.

Until right now.

"My queen," Lucius whispers into my neck, leaning in to tease my mating bite. "Would you like me to… wear a condom?"

I jerk in surprise. We've never done that in this harem, because we're all clean and we're all exclusive. Obviously the only reason he's offering now is because he knows I'm worried AF about getting pregnant.

But I'm taking the shots. We all fuck like crazy, and the method works. It really does.

I just gotta trust the science.

Besides, he's my alpha. The way my cunt is clenching and aching for him to fill me, the way my dragon queen is thrashing and growling inside me, a condom's not on the menu tonight. I mean, alpha shifter semen is potent stuff. It's laced with biochemicals that my own shifter hormones make me crave.

Long story short? I'm gonna need buckets of alpha shifter spunk dripping out of me.

"No condom, wolf king," I hiss in my queen voice. "I want you to fuck me bare."

My wolf splays a palm against my womb in that possessive way I love. He groans into my neck.

"Your wish." He fumbles between us and rubs his rigid cock against my wet cunt to get himself all slicked up. "My command."

With a single brutal thrust, he buries himself deep in my pussy. Stars explode behind my eyes. I let loose with a yell that makes violet sparks shower from my hands.

At least, you know, the power's already out.

My titanium pussy absorbs the hit like a champion. My channel ripples and pulls him in and clenches hard around his shaft. I'm so drenched it definitely helps, but his cock is major, and right now he's out of his head.

"Oh fuck, Lucius," I moan, feeling myself stretch inside to accommodate his girth. "Fuck. You're so thick."

"Sorry," he mutters, guttural as any beast. "Blood of Christ, Zara. You're so hot. Needy. Wet. *Tight.*"

He underscores every adjective with a thrust that seats him deeper. My cunt is weeping with hunger for him, this, all of it.

Next to me, Neo keens and writhes with need. And we're all linked up so tight, all four of us, that I don't need to look to know what's going down over there.

Vasili's coiling to his knees with serpentine grace.

Neo needs to be filled tonight, just like I do. But the Goblin King's such a snake he's just tonguing Neo's balls and teasing him from behind.

He'll make Neo beg if it kills him.

Meanwhile Lucius grips my hips and rocks me into his every thrust. He's wielding that rod of his like a piston. The rhythmic slap of flesh on flesh fills the air. His wolf snarls with every downstroke and his pace is picking up. When he reaches between my legs to tweak my clit, already hard as a fucking pebble and pulsing with heat, my pussy contracts in a spasm that strangles his length.

I explode and shatter in a climax so strong the room goes white.

Shit. Under my glowing palms, the upholstered cushion on the window seat is crisping and smoking.

But Lucius isn't done.

And, God, neither am I.

That first O with me is always just a warmup.

He came when I did, he came a freaking pint, because I can hear the liquid suck of his jizz with every stroke. I can *feel* his cum leaking out and dripping down my thighs. But he's still rock hard, buried so deep inside me he's hitting my cervix with every snap. I clench around him and whine with need. His desperate pace is building to a frenzy.

"My queen," he grunts, syllables all distorted like the shape of his mouth is changing. "You feel—unreal. I can't—can't stop."

My words rise out of deep inside me, from no place I can name. "Then don't. Don't stop. Fuck me harder. I want to feel your wolf rise."

He barks out a laugh and shoves my face down to the cushion, which raises my ass high in the air. My hands are over my head and the acrid scent of burning upholstery stings my nose, but I'm way past giving a shit. His hips burrow into me and his cock pistons even deeper.

Oh God. This is dangerous.

On some level, I know we're literally playing with lightning. Him and me, we're never done it that way, I mean, with his actual wolf. Though I kinda have a feeling, from some of what I've picked up from Ronin here and there, that maybe he and Lucius… anyway, let's just say I'm pretty sure I shouldn't be taunting him like this.

Because my mannerly headmaster is getting really close to losing it.

He's already more hirsute than any of my guys. Now his chest hair feels coarser, more abundant rubbing against my back, the hair on his thighs more bristly as it scrapes the back of mine. His hot panting breaths in my ear sound more bestial. His nails are longer, his hands are clawed (but at least they're still hands), talons curling into my hips till my skin stings.

"That's right, wolf king," I hiss, and I swear to fuck I don't know where any of this is coming from. "Make me yours. Claim me. Claim your queen!"

His claws dig into my skin until they draw blood. He raises his face to the heavens and bays with hunger. Then his cock kicks and spurts inside me like he's never gonna stop coming. Sweet Jesus, he's flooding my basement like it's hurricane season.

I fling my head back and scream with the lightning voice in total fucking triumph.

He howls like the wolf he is. Then he shreds his shirt (which I'm still wearing) with a single swipe of his claws, wraps a fist in my hair to immobilize me, and lunges to pin me flat against the seat.

I've got nowhere to go. Just a split second to grasp what's about to go down.

Yet, for some damn reason, I don't stop him.

Then it's too late.

His fully extended canines lock over my neck and sink deep into my throat.

Chapter Six
Vasili

Well, darling. Color me surprised.

Lucius is actually giving our little queen a *second* mating bite. He's reinforcing his dominance and staking his claim.

As for *why* that's surprising…

From my dubious grasp of shifter lore, double nipping is a major no-no.

One mating bite is typically more than sufficient to stake a lifelong claim. With anything more, that hormonal shifter roller coaster is considered to be too intense. The possessive impulses. The sexual cravings. The endorphin rushes and adrenaline highs.

And Zara, who projects her own alpha essence, and thus requires extremely careful handling? Well, clearly, our girl has completely lost her mind. She's more than allowing this.

She's instigated this.

She's taunted Lucius and challenged his wolf to rise.

His wolf… who clearly wants to mate.

Which means my girl's powerful mating instinct, whatever she imagines she's doing with those shots, is firmly in the driver's seat.

Lucius is howling. Zara's dragon is roaring. Zara herself is bleeding, twin scarlet ribbons streaking from those fresh punctures to adorn her lovely neck. The window seat, scorched by her witchcraft, is practically in flames.

At least I until I smother the flames with my telekinesis like a blanket.

When my queen's teal head twists back to find me, her eyes burn ultraviolet with psi fire. Her gorgeous Hollywood face is flushed with pleasure and savage with need. The yummy sweetness of her mating scent floods the air.

Mmmmm. Ambrosia.

Lucius stops howling and burrows into her neck to tend that bite he's just given her. His delectable dick is still buried inside her, rivulets of spunk still trickling down her thighs, but now his hips are barely moving. He's rocking gently into her and licking her punctures to stop the bleeding and administer the clotting agent in his saliva.

Gradually, they both sink toward stillness, soothed by this portion of the mating ritual. He rumbles and she croons.

Dear fuck.

Lucius is half-shifted and barely human, a rich chestnut pelt sprouting down his long back and powerful limbs. Thankfully he's still bipedal, but his thick fingers and toes are tipped with curving claws. Blind and heedless with rutting, he's scratched her. But we shifters, even part-shifters like Zara and myself, heal quickly.

It's perhaps best I can't see his face.

Ronin… likes him like this. Sometimes. I know because we've linked while they're fucking. I dare say it adds a certain something to their already inventive intercourse when I watch. But Lucius dominates Ronin, the same way he's dominating Zara now, and I won't allow that with me.

"Vasili?" Neo whispers.

My attention snaps back to him—my own dance partner in this racy romp. I'm still kneeling behind him, my cheek resting against the solid warmth of his derrière.

"Yes, darling?"

He's still braced against the window, naked and trembling. "I need you. I really need you. Will you… will you touch me?"

Truly, I'm a dreadful alpha. He needs me and I'm not tending him.

A blade of contrition knifes through me. "You're such a good boy. So good and so patient. Rest assured, First Boy. I most certainly do intend to touch you."

My cool hands sleek up his lovely bitable calves, tease the hollows of his knees (which, for him, are ticklish), then stroke the sinewy backs of his deliciously muscular thighs. He has lovely skin, the milky white of a natural redhead, and sheets of goosebumps spring up under my touch. The dear boy's so deliciously responsive he sighs and shivers at every caress. I hide a private smile and trace my manicured nails over the succulent globes of his buttocks.

He arches his back and leans into my touch. "Yeah. More of that. I want more of you."

I cup and knead his luscious ass, then lean in to nuzzle that perfect derrière, letting him feel the prick of my horrid incisors. They're tiny compared to Lucius' or Maxim's. But unlike theirs, mine don't retract. Mine are freakish and repulsive.

Never mind the fact that, for some godforsaken reason, all my mates claim to like them.

"They aren't repulsive," Neo whispers. He's no natural telepath, no more than I am, but he's reading me through our mating bond. "Nothing about you is repulsive. You're beautiful. You're so beautiful."

Well, that's hardly true.

My permanent fangs make me a permanent monster.

We're frenemies at best, so being this vulnerable to Neo Mercury is difficult for me to tolerate. Still, I reward him for that innocent little fib by spreading him wide with my hands and licking a long delicate stripe from his perineum over his sweet pink pucker. He mewls like a kitten and his hole twitches with need. Now this, I thoroughly approve. He's absolutely clean, he's made himself perfectly ready for me, despite all his little sulks about my so-called bullying.

As I circle and tease his rim with little swipes and flicks of my tongue, I realize I'm still smiling.

Neo gasps and moans and rocks into me. His tight pucker softens and yields to the prod of my tongue. I lap his pretty rosebud with the flat of my tongue and probe him a bit with the tip. He tastes like bookworm and sex and innocence. He's so deliciously innocent.

Despite everything I've done to ruin him.

Deftly I extract a packet of cherry-flavored lube from my trousers and tear the packet open. The tart sweetness of fruit joins the clean soapy scent of sage that rises from Neo's skin and the potent bouquet of Mogadon pheromones (mine and Zara's) that are making us all high. While he waits with mounting impatience for me to finish the preliminaries, I smooth the glistening fluid around and over and, finally, into his tight strangling hole with a teasing finger, never going very deep, not even when he whimpers and wiggles and presses into me, until his pucker is glistening and soft. My tongue flicks out to taste him, sweet yet tart.

He gasps and quivers with every lick. I hum with satisfaction.

Dear God, he's so trusting. So perfect.

So ready for me.

By now, I'm more than ready myself to free my own delectable dinkey from my uniform trousers and use the rest of that lube to slick my own dick. Neo twists around to watch, all flushed and breathless, purple curls tumbling around his earnest schoolboy face. He's in such delicious disarray, steamed-up glasses sliding down his excited nose.

I do enjoy teasing that sweet boy.

I hold his gaze while I slick my disco stick.

Next door, Lucius finally pulls out of Zara. That impressive cock of his is resting from its labors, poor thing. But clearly, he's far from finished. With a snarl, Lucius drops to his knees beside me.

Merciful fuck, let him not go full wolf while he's reaming her. Truly, for that I am not ready.

Well, I needn't have worried. It turns out our headmaster needs his human hands to scoop those rivulets of wolf jizz running down Zara's inner thighs back into her flooded basement. He even manages to retract his claws, the better to push his cum gently back inside her pretty pussy with his reverent fingers.

Indeed, his behavior is really rather… fascinating. I've never seen him like this. He's absolutely lost in classic mating instinct.

He's consumed with the need to breed.

In fact, I seriously doubt that wolf of his is letting anyone else inside our queen tonight.

Which *could* cause a little problem when our randy dragon returns, surly and spoiling for a fuck.

My girl's lost in her own mating daze, whether she's entirely aware or not. She really ought to be more leery of him, me, all of us, given this remarkable unexplained pregnancy phenomenon. Yet she only murmurs sleepily (she's buzzing on pheromones and feel-good mating hormones, half asleep on her feet) and spreads wider to let Lucius have his messy way with her.

By now, her schoolgirl panties are a shredded scrap, drenched with her juices and spattered with cum, draped around one sexy ankle.

I'll just have to buy her another lingerie box from Paris.

But first things first.

I uncoil to my feet and fit the length of my cool body (because I'm a water sign, darling—like any reptile, I'm practically cold-blooded) to Neo's spectacular muscled heat. He arches his back and shoves his derrière into me and wiggles his pelvis to slot me in his crack. Firmly I grip his nape to pin him in place and rub the head of my cock against his shiny hole. He rocks and bucks into my boner.

I swear it's all I can manage not to dive balls-deep into his ass right now, quite before we're ready.

"Oh, Lord," he pants. "For cripes' sake, V. I'm *so* ready. Would you please…?"

"Darling, I'd love to, but I'm waiting for the words," I manage to say coolly. "I told you quite clearly I intend to hear you say them."

"Fine," he gasps, rotating his hips to work me in, because I've given him just an inch to tease him. "I need to feel your… um, cock… filling my…"

"Filling your what, darling?"

"My h-hole," he manages in a rush, with a strangled tone I can barely hear. My aforementioned cock gives a mighty throb. He's so deliciously embarrassed I can hardly stand it. I grip my base hard to rein myself in.

"What was that, Mr. Mercury? I'm afraid you'll simply have to speak up."

"God, you're such a jerk. You know I'm in heat. And the guy I want breaking it is specifically *you*." He groans from the heart. "I need to feel your freaking cock filling my freaking hole, okay? *Please*. Pretty please."

"Oh, *darling*." Slowly, luxuriously, I sink deep inside him on a long exhale. My own tone plunges two octaves. "Nothing could possibly please me more."

As my cock breaches the tight ring of muscle that guards his channel from my horrible depredations, he sucks in a breathless gasp. But we've done this before, he and I, and he trusts me enough (in this one regard) to let me have my terrible way with him. I croon in his ear and kiss the back of his neck. He shudders and makes a conscious effort to relax for me. This scrumptious yielding he does so well lets me press in deeper.

I lean back just a little so I can properly appreciate the sight of his glistening pink hole swallowing me down, inch by tortuous inch, into his tight sucking heat.

Finally, *finally*, I'm happily buried inside him to my balls.

Damn me, he feels simply heavenly, tight as a corset and fluttering with pleasure. My own breathy moan spills out before I can catch it. I fear I may have just betrayed the profound effect this frenemy of mine inflicts on me.

Which gives him power over me. He isn't the only man in this relationship who's vulnerable.

I go perfectly still, barely even breathing, and pray he hasn't noticed.

"Neo," I breathe on a wisp of air.

"Vasili," he whimpers. His muscled shoulders clench and his back twitches. "Oh Lord. Just gimme a sec, okay?"

"Darling," I murmur. "You truly are a sweet boy. You're *such* a good boy taking my cock like this, aren't you?"

My praise makes him nod and shiver with happiness.

Truly, it's a mystery to me now how I could possibly have despised him and resisted him and, well, I suppose one might say, abused him all those years? Even when we were mortal enemies, I was always drawn to him. If I'd only known the way he'd sigh and submit while he takes my cock, I'd have had him bend for me years ago.

"Okay." He sighs. "I'm ready for you."

In fact, he's very clearly *so* ready for me that I decide (for once) not to prolong his torment. I ease back a few inches, then burrow deep inside him. He groans and clenches around me. Hips rolling and flexing, I set a steady rocking tempo that coaxes him to relax and move with me. In time with the snap of my hips, I reach around him to wrap my hand around his impressive length and milk him in a steady rhythm, from base to tip and back.

Beside us on the window seat, our girl lies limp and boneless, collapsed face down on the singed cushion in a curtain of mermaid hair, watching glossy-eyed through half-mast lids as Neo and I give her the type of show she most enjoys.

Two (or more) of her warlocks locked together and building toward an obliterating climax.

My darling Lucius, still *quite* erect, looms possessively over our queen. Admittedly, one glimpse of his half-shifted face—nostrils flared, eyes red, brow furrowed, jaw elongating toward a cruel muzzle, carnivore's fangs on menacing display—well, let's just say his shifted form makes me a bit shivery myself.

This isn't something I dwell on, but we're all monsters in our own way in this bed.

All of us…

Except Neo.

Neo's head turns to watch our mates, but I'm enough of an alpha myself to want him fully focused on *me*. At least while I'm taking him. I grip his soft curls in my fist and push his face gently (for me) into the glass. His lovely beast of a cock jerks and throbs in my fist. Mmmm, now this is more like it. He's pumping out enough precum to make my fingers slick. As I jack him, every downstroke is audible over the fire's crackle and my own quickening breath.

"Tell me you like what I'm doing to you," I hiss, nipping his shoulder with my loathsome fangs. "And don't even think of lying."

"Like it so much," he gasps, chasing my building rhythm with his own increasing tempo. "I swear, you make me so crazy. Oh V—oh God—like that—"

My hips snap into him with ruthless purpose. As he fucks into my fist, I add a twist at the end of my upstroke that works him to a foaming frenzy. In the state he's in, that's more than enough stimulation to make him spill with a shout all over my hand and his belly and the cushion. His dick kicks in my grip, hot jets of semen spurting over my fingers.

I purr with satisfaction and stroke him through his pleasure to prolong his delicious climax.

But I'm not nearly done with him.

I groan through my bared teeth and forcibly rein in my own driving rhythm before I lose what little self-control I still command. While Neo sags into the cushion, limp and blissful and swaying from our exertions, breath loud and shaky in the stillness, I grip his hips to steady him. Pumping into him slowly, I take a moment to lift my gaze from his gorgeously muscled, sweat-slicked spine to find Lucius lurking beside me.

He's watching us, watching me please our boy as he's just pleased our girl, his bestial face savage with satisfaction.

I love doing this with him.

Love being his co-alpha in our queen's harem. Love standing shoulder to shoulder with him and Max to protect all of us against the whole world, the way an alpha should.

Silently, I tell him this through our mating bond.

Lucius gives me a wolfish grin, then gathers Zara's limp body into his powerful arms and carries her to the big curtained bed, cradling her against his broad chest. She's limp and sleepy in his fiendish clutches, her lightning-blue head drooping against his shoulder.

He's just settled her gently into a sea of pillows when the door behind us flies open so hard it slams into the wall.

Hissing with outrage over this fucking interruption—just when I was ready to claim my own hard-earned climax—I pull out of Neo and twist around. I sweep up my casting hand, ready to hurl whatever wretched fool has just dared intrude on my magic moment across the upstairs corridor through the opposite wall.

Barely in time, I recognize Ronin swaying in the doorway, barefooted and bare-chested in a pair of distressed jeans he hasn't even bothered to zip. That cursed Spanish medallion dangles against his chest.

Which certainly explains why I didn't sense his approach.

Ronin explodes into the room and slams the door behind him, golden skin glistening with sweat, midnight hair swirling around him, eyes blazing with tawny fire. I don't need to be linked with my boyfriend to know he's not entirely present.

He's lost his everloving mind.

"No bloody use barricading myself behind locked doors with the four of you carrying on like this, is there?" he snarls like a psycho. His dragon tattoo spews black flames across his chest. "You have the first damn clue we can hear you shagging all over this blooming house?"

Still sluggish with afterglow, Zara murmurs and struggles up to sit.

"Ronin, my dear, I'm terribly sorry—" Lucius attempts through his fangs, sounding (justifiably) startled.

"Well, I'm not kipping down to sleep tonight, am I?" Ronin doesn't even let him finish. He shoves his jeans down his lean hips, climbs out of them, and strides naked toward the bed. "Might as well join the frolic and get a spot of fun myself."

Clearly he can't sleep and his head's a train wreck, but I'm admittedly having a difficult time focusing on anything beyond his pierced and fully erect dick, jutting before him as he advances on the bed like a battering ram. Truly, that Prince Albert of his has *such* a ravishing effect.

Hastily Lucius drags a clawed hand through his wild mane. "If you'll just, ah, give me a moment—"

"No, I bloody won't. Don't you dare shift back," Ronin grates. "That's what I want. You like that." His burning eyes shift to rivet me. "You too. You at your worst. Want you to make me feel it. Both of you together."

Oh, is *that* the mood we're in?

This is one ultimatum that will be my positive pleasure to indulge.

Although I can't feel a thing through our mating bond, due to that accursed medallion Ronin insists upon wearing around his sexy neck, Lucius is all too visibly self-conscious over his own half-shifted state. Never mind whatever naughty little kinks he and Ronin get up to when it's the two of them alone. He's never shifted by a whisker when I'm fucking him. Now my wolf's furtive gaze shifts to me, still lurking menacingly over a spent and blinking Neo like my Goblin King namesake in the movie *Labyrinth*.

Even with my shifter senses, it's a tad difficult to register through the shadow of whiskers darkening his slanting cheekbones.

But I do believe our gentlemanly headmaster is blushing.

Neo crowds up behind me, chest nestling up against my back, chin coming to rest on my shoulder, to watch the show. He's cool to the touch, which means his heat's broken. Without looking, I reach over my shoulder to nudge his glasses up his nose.

"Ronin," Lucius mumbles through his fangs, looking positively shamefaced. "This is… that is to say… like this, I'm… simply too much…"

"There is no part of you that's too much for us," I tell our wolf clearly, so he'll be certain to understand. "No part of you we don't love."

Of course, that's easy for me to say.

I'm not the one he's about to fuck like that.

But I won't utter a syllable to stop him.

Ronin's psychic barriers may be sky high, but at least he's come to us. He's here with us. He's telling us what he needs.

"Go ahead, pet." I spare a smile for Lucius' worried face. "Why don't you take care of our man?"

"Oh, it's not just him I fancy, mate." Naked as sin and twice as sexy, Ronin crawls sinuously onto the bed and straddles Zara with supple grace. "But it looks like our girl's done in, and so's our boy Red."

"Mmmm." Zara winds her arms around Ronin's neck and returns his kiss with languid pleasure and a lazy lick of tongue. "Good to see you, Adam."

But I don't need telepathy to know Ronin's right.

That dear girl's stuffed to her sternum with wolf spunk and shifter biochemicals. Plus she's high as a kite from breathing in my pheromones. What she needs right now is not the punishing, pounding, make-me-forget fuck Ronin's clearly craving.

Not to mention the fact that Lucius's wolf is still lurking possessively over our bed, claiming exclusive alpha rights over our queen's ravishing cunt. While Ronin crouches over Zara with his fully erect cock on proud display, Lucius' wolf rumbles with a guttural growl.

Our headmaster's fangs lengthen still further. He crouches as though he's prepared to pounce.

"Now behave yourself, pet, *do*," I warn his wolf softly. "Or I'll put you on a leash. Our queen fucks whom she pleases."

That principle is more than the working rule in our harem. It's enshrined in witching world law. Our queens are polyamorous. The more they fuck, the more happily they fuck, the better it is for the entire race. The fact that Zara strictly limits herself to just the five of us is already a rather uncommon degree of restraint for a royal.

Of course, Lucius knows this as well as I do. He used to teach our Witching World Law course before I took up the duty.

Here, now, his mating instinct is nothing to be trifled with.

Yet it's equally obvious to all of us that Ronin, in his current mood, gives literally zero fucks.

Tonight Ronin needs his own brutal rogering. In fact, he's taunting Lucius to make him snap. Which, truly, might not be as rewarding as it sounds. There's an odd and rather unsettling energy crackling in the air tonight.

Bless her witchy heart, that's a peril our queen clearly senses.

With a thoughtful glance at our wolf, Zara unwraps herself from Ronin and sinks back to the mattress. Stifling a yawn behind her hand, she murmurs, "You go ahead with him this time, why don't you, Teach? I'm just gonna cheer from the sidelines."

"Not just him." Ronin's head snaps sideways to find me. His burning gaze zeroes in on my boner, already slick and glistening with lube, thanks to my extracurricular endeavors with our apple-polishing

First Boy. "I fancy two alpha dicks inside me tonight. I want a blooming orgasm so strong it takes my fucking head off. Think you and Lucius can oblige me, love?"

Despite the oddly fraught currents swirling in our polycule tonight, my cruelly abandoned cock throbs with renewed interest.

After all, I haven't come at all yet tonight.

I'm well overdue for an orgasm.

I take a moment to coax Neo out from behind me and give him a gentle push toward the bed. Obedient in his blissed-out state, he stumbles groggily over to the mattress and topples in. Happily our bookworm nuzzles Ronin's cheek, then cuddles up next to Zara. She snuggles into her fated mate, tucking her wild mermaid head against his sturdy shoulder with a sigh.

Thanks to me, our Neo's been rather well-ridden himself tonight. His drowsy green eyes are already closing, even before Lucius lifts our bookworm's spectacles from his nose and tucks them safely into their case on the nightstand.

I prowl across the bedroom at my leisure and sift through the stash of lube in our bedside drawer. With five warlocks in this harem (every one of us bisexual) and a gloriously insatiable queen, we burn through enough lube in a month to keep our favorite supplier financially afloat. Truly, we should buy stock in the company. With Ronin watching expectantly and Lucius already getting hard, I sort through the various flavors, select a tube of candied apple (Ronin's current favorite), and toss it in my boyfriend's direction. Ronin snatches it out of the air, triumph flashing in his savage gaze.

In the shifting flicker of firelight, that dead Spanish king swinging on his tattooed chest looks like he's winking at me.

If I'm being honest, I'm beginning to wish I'd left that magical artifact locked safely away in the Academy Vault. I'm positively starting to despise that Spanish royal. But what I truly hate is what that medallion does to the bond between me and all my darlings.

Without the clarity of our mating bond, Ronin's a fucking sphinx. Something major is definitely still amiss.

But, all too clearly, that citadel of privacy is what my boyfriend demands.

Under my frowning stare, he pops the lid with his teeth and upends a squirt of the stuff carelessly into his palm.

"Don't be bashful with that product," I murmur. (Not that he's ever bashful.) "You're going to need plenty of it if you intend to accommodate Lucius and me together in that deliciously tight ass of yours tonight. I'll warn you now, I'm the only person in this room who still hasn't climaxed."

"Best start with you then, love." Holding my gaze, Ronin arches his lithe body and slicks himself up behind. His deltoids flex and his abs ripple. As he works himself open, his eyes go hooded and hot, his brow furrows with focus, and his teeth sink into his lower lip.

While he lubes his own hole under Lucius' heated stare and mine, that climax I've been barely holding off all night tightens my balls and makes my dick ache. I snake out a hand to wind around Lucius' and draw him close. Except for those claws of his (which I rather like), his slim scholar's hand feels familiar.

Even if his heavily furred body does not.

"Will it offend you?" Even with my sharp shifter senses, Lucius' guttural whisper barely reaches my ear. "Or disgust you? To share him with me… while I am… thus?"

For a heartbeat, my gaze shifts from the riveting sight of my boyfriend sexing himself up and prepping himself for both of us. Behind his bestial, half-shifted features, that anxious expression is all Lucius.

"You could never disgust me, pet." Gently I lift his hand and graze his cruel fingers with a tender kiss. "How could you? You're going to give our Ronin exactly what he needs tonight."

"Fuck, yeah, you will," Ronin rasps. He's already lubed and erect and extremely ready for us. Both of us. Holding our stare, he fists his pierced dick and gives himself a few rough pumps.

"No holding back tonight, you feel me?" he says gruffly, eyes fierce with buried pain. "I need to… suffer for what I did. Need you to punish me for my… sins." This he says directly to Lucius, naughtily playing on our wolf's overdeveloped Roman Catholic guilt and atonement kink.

Lucius snarls in primal response.

Ronin's gaze veers to mine. "Then I need you, love, to make me forget. Will you do that for me?"

I'm heartless and practically soulless, just ask anyone, but what little of either I do possess emphatically belongs to him.

"There's nothing I won't do for you, darling," I breathe. "Always."

Then Lucius pounces on the bed like a proper monster and attacks.

Chapter Seven

Ronin

I'm deliberately baiting both my alphas. But I fancied it'd be Vasili, always so impatient, who'd snatch the lure I'm dangling.

Turns out it's Lucius who pounces first.

I've barely time to brace before he brings me down like a wolf with a buck. His hard body collides with mine and pins me sprawling to my back across the mattress. His clawed hands grapple to shove my thighs open and force my knees up. Those twin daggers he calls teeth are already at my throat, sharp as scalpels, scraping the scars of his mating bite.

The imminent threat of having my throat torn out sends a welcome thrill of danger shooting down my spine. That adrenaline rush electrifies every nerve in my wound-tight body.

Bloody fuck, I need this.

He's brutally hard for me, despite having been buried balls deep in our luscious Zara half the night. Her creamy mating scent mingles with the gamy reek of wolf. His boner thrusts roughly against my exposed arse, prods my well-lubed hole, then drives deep. I let loose with a surprised yell.

Guess he's taking me at my word.

Good.

He's got what I need.

With no mucking about in the preliminaries, the fiery burn of his thick cock reaming my ass takes hold. Bollocks, that's a relief—the immediacy of it, the tangible physical need—after the elusive bee-sting burn of regret and guilt and grief that's been driving me bonkers all night.

I grip his mane of curls in one hand, fist the sheets in the other, and writhe in mingled pain and pleasure under his savage thrusts.

On every brutal downstroke, Lucius snarls with satisfaction. The way he's got me pinned flat on my back under his weight, with my arse in the air and my knees shoved up till they're practically in my ears, while he pounds into me with heartless force…

Gods, yeah, he's exactly what I need.

With him reaming me like an animal, I've got no more bandwidth in my brain for the what-ifs or should-bes or might-have-beens.

Nope.

I'm all about the here-and-now.

My cock's pinned between us, but I'm getting plenty of friction. When I shift my hips to get more, Lucius growls and burrows deeper, pegging my prostate with every vicious thrust.

I've got just enough wit left in my noggin to anchor myself in place so he doesn't fuck me right over Zara and Neo's entranced bodies (because nobody's sleeping through what's going down in this bed, believe me) onto that hard floor. I catch a wild glimpse of those two sitting up to watch, wrapped in each other's arms, Zara intrigued and sultry with sex, Red all flushed and goggle-eyed and probably wanting his glasses.

Still on his feet, Vasili rears over our rutting bodies like a blooming rattlesnake. He's slicking his dick with candied apple lube and his cold face is fucking ruthless. We've got to make room for him to join, I mean Lucius and me.

But the moment I try to shift, our wolf pins me harder and fucks into me like he's ruining me.

Good gods, that rod of his can rail me like nobody's business. He's splitting me wide open. This complete physical crisis punches every button I've got and shoves all my needles to the red.

Which is exactly what I need.

In my sexed-up state, that extra friction hurls me hard over the edge. I'm plummeting in free fall, that hornets' nest of memories that's been stinging me all night swept away and buried under the avalanche of climax. I rock my cock into the hard flexing plane of Lucius' abs and explode all over him with a shout.

He throws back his head and howls at the moon.

His dick kicks and floods my burning hole. That hit of shifter biochemicals from my well-satisfied alpha makes the room revolve madly round me.

"Ronin," he rasps in my ear, shaking and panting. He collapses across my body. "My dear one. That was… discourteous of me."

I chuff out a breathless laugh. "Such a Lucius thing to say."

His wolfish face lifts to find me. He's still red-eyed and fangy, but his scholarly brow's all furrowed. "I'm being serious. I was brutal. Forgive me."

"Nothing to forgive." He's heavy as fuck and I fight to breathe. "I bloody needed that."

I'm drenched in sweat and semen, mine and his, his fur's a mess, and apparently he's clipped me with those claws of his, because the tinny tang of blood lurks in my nose.

But that infernal blooming buzz in the back of my brain, that stinging swarm of memories, they're still hovering.

Gwendolyn.

Me.

Zephyr.

Both of them dead. Gwen by her own hand. And Zeph… oh gods… I thrust that blade myself—

Lucius growls in my ear. He can't read me, and that's by design, thanks to good King Ferdinand's medallion wrapped round my throat. But clearly my headmaster senses that persistent buzz of tension I can't seem to shake. His wolf sees it as a threat.

"Well, darlings, that was quite the diverting first act." At exactly the right moment, Vasili slithers onto the bed and uncoils his gorgeously naked self across the mattress. "Let's skip the intermission. I've waited long enough. Come here and ride my cock, Ronin."

"Bloody fuck, yeah." My voice is all gravel with sex and relief. My guy knows I'm hurting. Knows just what I need.

Lucius rolls off me with a sigh, his dick slipping free, along with a warm trickle of spunk. Knowing Vasili's going to give me a proper shagging, with me all messy from Lucius' spend… well, let's just say that gives all of us a proper kick.

Aching and burning in all the right ways, I'm crawling over the rumpled sea of blankets when Vasili's gaze sharpens.

"Lose that medallion," he hisses. And with him, it's never a request.

"I won't have that accursed thing thumping me in the chest while we're fucking."

I hesitate a tick, because I donned this blooming artifact for a reason. But it'll still do its thing—protect those shameful secrets I'm nowhere near ready to spill—if it's close enough. Reluctantly I fish the medallion off my neck and lean over Zara and Neo to drop the bauble in a pile on the nightstand.

While I'm poised over the pair of them, Neo heaves a happy sigh and rubs his drowsy face affectionately against my shoulder.

Zara winds a lazy arm round my neck to kiss me.

"You doing okay, Adam?" she whispers against my lips. My spent dick tingles with interest and my balls flood with heat. Fuck, she always makes me hot. Her soft mouth tastes like cinnamon toothpaste. Or maybe that's the taste of her dragon.

I suck her hot tongue into my mouth for a proper snogging.

Clearly wise to my tricks, she nips my lower lip. "Lucius rode you pretty hard. You okay?"

That's not the actual reason she's worried. She knows I love a hard shag. But she's respecting my boundaries, which is just one of the reasons I love the fuck out of her.

Someday, somewhere, somehow, I'll tell her.

She deserves to know. Then she'll know the worst. The absolute worst. The worst thing I've ever done to anyone.

And to think I did it to the man I loved.

"Yeah, I'm good." I pull back, but ruffle Neo's soft curls to reassure him.

That's a royal whopper and clearly our girl knows it. I'm nowhere close to good. I'm in free fall.

Zara's teal brows pucker, but she lets me wriggle off the hook.

For now.

"No more dawdling, darling." The buried menace in Vasili's silky purr gives me a shiver. "I'm waiting."

Huffing out a chuckle, I roll over to straddle him and tease his rigid cock with my hole. I'm already tender as fuck from Lucius, and I already know Vasili will be ruthless. Still, my junk stiffens and swells with heat. The heavy ring of my Prince Albert swings from my cockhead.

"You eager to get inside me then, love?" I rotate my soaked hole against his swollen shaft. "You eager to ream this?"

"Hmmmm." His velvety tenor licks me like a tongue. "Eager doesn't begin to describe it."

Our eyes meet, and my heart gives a donkey kick.

He's so bloody beautiful, yet so fucking lethal. That's the paradox with him. Face sharp and hard as diamonds, eyes cruel and cutting as ice, lashes like a supermodel and legs that go on for miles (especially when he's wearing heels), all that beauty topped off with layers of frosted rock star hair. He's slim and sinuous as a sea snake, lean hips bracketed between my thighs, but his witchcraft's so powerful he's practically a god.

That's how I've always fancied my men. Pretty as girls but venomous as vipers. Those are the ones I'll bend for. One look at Zeph, that first night he came to me, and I was fucking nuts for him. But it's our shared fucking tragedy that it was only Gwen who—

Vasili's narrow hands lock round my waist. His hips thrust up to spear me. With zero fucking foreplay, he sheathes himself deep inside me.

This time I don't yell, but I definitely gasp.

He's got more inches than Lucius, even though Vasili's not as thick. Still, I'm used to accommodating Max's complicated dick, and I'm still slick and dripping with wolf jizz. So Vasili glides in easy, with an audible squelch.

He exhales a soft moan. "Are you tender, darling?"

I swallow hard. "Yeah."

His dangerous eyes narrow. "Good."

He locks me in place between his hands and pistons into me, hard enough to rip a groan from my throat.

"Fuuuck." I focus on breathing through the burn, one hand braced on his smooth chest, the other wrapped round my own aching dick. "You're fucking wicked."

"I've barely begun, I assure you." Artifact or no artifact, he knows when I'm not focused, and it makes him vicious. His gaze veers to Lucius. "Lube up well, pet. There's plenty of room here for you."

"Oh, shit." I've already come once tonight, but I'm pumping out precum like a garden hose. My hand's all slick and shiny with it. Way past shameless, I jack my own dick and thrust into my fist, my piercing bumping my fingers with every thrust.

As Lucius lubes his dick, the crisp sweetness of candied apple floats through the air to mingle with the caramel essence of Vasili's mating scent and the animal reek of wolf. Smells like a blooming circus, and I adore it. My guy's really making me ride him, taking him deeper inside me with every hammering downstroke. Sweat slicks my skin and drips in my eyes and makes my long hair stick to my back. Finally, Vasili grabs a thick fistful of my locks and uses the anchor to drag my head back, arching my spine, giving his shaft a deeper glide and a sharper angle.

My free hand curls to claw his chest. He hisses and yanks my hair to subdue me, so brutal that I let out a yelp. The sting makes my eyes water. Fire spreads over my scalp to match the fiery burn of my ass. Savage grunts wrench out of me with every thrust.

I'm already soaked with Lucius' cum, and now Vasili's precum, so a rhythmic sucking sound keeps pace with every stroke. Our wolf's already given my prostate a workout, but Vasili's really giving my P-spot a proper pegging.

And, gods of the grove, I need it. I take everything he's giving me and beg for more.

I'm the one who found her.

I found my own sister hanging from her favorite tree in the forest. That primitive forest that lurks right on our doorstep here at Icarus. That secret refuge where my twin liked first to study, then later to hide.

I'm the one who's never stopped grieving her—

Lucius' warm weight settles behind me to straddle Vasili's hips. My headmaster's closeness dispels the stinging swarm of memories.

My eyes close in relief.

He's shifted back, he's fully human, probably out of deference to Vasili's sensibilities, he knows V won't tolerate another alpha domming him on top. Lucius grips my hip to still me, Vasili's dick buried deep inside me, and fits his own slick cockhead against my well-prepped hole.

"Gods, yeah," I groan. Even while my aching passage pulses and anticipates the pain. "Don't be gentle."

Drenched with lube and semen, his rigid shaft probes my hole, then presses in with a stretching burn.

Bloody fuck.

I'm no Christian, but this is literal heaven.

As their cocks align inside me, Vasili lets loose a good moan. His gaze shifts to Lucius and his face goes soft.

"My dears," Lucius sighs on a long exhale. He kisses the scars from

my mating nip, his breath hot, the fruity bite of his *palinka* teasing my nose.

I fucking love them like this, both my alphas buried to the balls inside me, getting off on each other as much as me, closer and more intimate than my own heartbeat. Love having Zara and Neo so close to us too, slowly getting sexed up watching, especially when Neo spoons behind our girl. Can't be certain under the blankets, not with my telepathy all fogged up from that bauble, but I think our bookworm's copping a good feel of her irresistible snatch. Our girl's all rosy and her breath's getting quicker.

I'm missing Max, and I'm definitely missing that ruthless dragon cock he's rocking.

But I know he's close, circling in the clouds, keeping us all safe.

Lucius grips my waist to steady me and eases into a rhythm, pelvis rocking in short sharp thrusts that give all three of us a workout. Vasili sets up the same tempo, pushing into me when Lucius is on the recoil, all of us gasping and grunting with the friction and the deliciously tight fit. I brace between them and hold still as I can.

Vasili pushes up to sit, which gives him more leverage, and knocks my hand aside to take the pilot's seat in that hand job I'm rocking. I wrap one arm round his waist and reach back to twine the other about Lucius' neck.

Now this I thoroughly approve. I'm the mutton in a warlock sandwich.

Lucius leans forward, pumping strongly. Over my shoulder, his mouth sears Vasili's in a fiery kiss.

Tucked tight against Zara from behind, Neo gives a breathless little whimper. He's so fucking sweet he's getting off just from watching and feeling Zara cream all over his fingers. Our girl arches into him, those lush lips parting in a way that makes me fantasize about the way they'll feel later wrapped round my boner. Our gazes meet, hers and mine, in a flash of perfect understanding.

"Go ahead, Adam," she murmurs. "They're waiting for you to spill all over them."

That's all it takes, honestly, for me to lose my blooming mind.

I let out a sound between a snarl and a shout and erupt into Vasili's pumping hand like I'm a gods-damned geyser and I'll never stop coming.

My big O sets off Lucius like a tripped landmine. He barks out a yell and spurts into my ass while I clench and pulse and grip him. Zara writhes and cries out and loses it for Neo, who presses up against her and gasps, "Oh, sugar" in the cutest fucking way.

Vasili holds out till the end like a blooming champ, pumping me through my climax, giving Lucius the rhythm he needs to finish. All before V claims my breathless mouth with one of his snakebite kisses and finally gives me the gift of his own release.

Limbs entwined, sweating and panting, we all collapse into each other. We hold each other up. Limp and wrung out with exertion and emotion, I sag between the two of them and just fucking tremble.

I'm wrecked.

I'm ruined.

Exactly the way I crave.

I've been stretched literally to capacity. I'm pumped so full of alpha cum I'll be feeling the two of them for days. I'm really hoping Max won't be too disgruntled when he pitches up later all randy, the way he does most nights, only to find Lucius gone full alpha guarding Zara's pussy, and my ass totally out of commission for that barbed dragon dick.

In general, despite my worry over Max, I'm filled to bursting with the warm sleepy afterglow of this endless love I feel for all five of them. All my mates, whether we make it official anytime soon according to witching world law or not.

I'm theirs. They're mine.

And yet.

Deep down inside, in the fucking black pit of my past, yawning in my psyche like a bomb crater, in that secret grave hidden deep in my heart, where all those ugly memories of mine have been exhumed and shocked back to life like Frankenstein…

I'm alone.

I'm so alone.

And I'm empty.

I'm so. Achingly. Empty.

Chapter Eight
Maxim

I am on fire.

I am burning.

It is possible I am dying.

Moving with care, I turn off the shower in the Roman-style *thermae* that resides in the basement of our *domus*. The spray of cool water chokes to a drip over my tortured body. I have been scrupulous to rinse away every drop of that enemy dragon's acid breath. But the damage is already done.

I am scalded all down one side from my armpit to my hip.

I am only thankful I managed to protect my face. If that green bastard had managed to strike me headfirst as he intended, that acid he sprayed would surely have blinded me.

As it stands, well, I have survived worse.

Hissing with pain, I towel off, although I can barely tolerate the cloth. Very clearly, I need a numbing potion, but I could not find any, fumbling in the dark through the first aid kit in the kitchen. I have not been living beneath this roof for long, I do not know where else Lucius would keep such a thing.

And I do not wish to wake my mates to ask.

All too clearly, clothing is out of the question. I cannot bear the thought of fabric chafing my scalded skin.

Nor can I roam naked through the *domus* with Dez and Racetrack somewhere beneath this roof. They do not care for men in a sexual way, but I do not wish my nakedness to offend. I settle for knotting the damp towel gingerly around my waist. At last, I take up the candle I have left burning on the ledge for light.

Outside, the icy fall of sleet has petered out. Still, all over this island, the power is out.

As I creep through the pitch-black basement and up the stairs, I am dizzy with pain.

And I am sick with shame.

I fought the monster who attacked my mate. I found him and I fought him. But I could not kill him.

The great room is not so stygian, with embers still glowing in the central hearth. Outside, a weak wash of starlight spills over the courtyard and the turquoise rectangle of the heated pool. But the moon is dark.

Always, the darkness has been my ally in the hunt.

Tonight, the darkness was my enemy.

Of course, I am not accustomed to fighting a dragon with a rider. Behind that scaled armor and that fearsome helm, the master of that green demon wields his own terrible witchcraft. How could I triumph, when the very wind beneath my wings betrayed me—?

But no. That is no excuse. Here is the simple truth.

I am the dragon king, and I have failed my sovereign. I have failed in my duty as her mate.

Truly, if I cannot protect her—my precious mate, my love, my Zara, she who will give birth to my offspring and restore our dying race—then I do not deserve to live.

Head hanging, I trudge up to the second story and down the hall, past the closed door where Dez and Racetrack sleep, past the open door of Ronin's empty room. That is a welcome sign, because he was brooding alone in there when I left. My steps quicken, even though my injured side burns and throbs with every stride.

By the time I reach the room where my queen and our mates are sleeping, I am lightheaded with pain.

Now I move slowly, pausing when I must, so that I will not faint.

Still, I have endured worse. Many times. When I disobeyed her, my Lady Mother would scourge me to the bone, then scour my wounds with salt.

This time too, surely, I will heal.

If not, I deserve this pain.

It is the punishment I deserve for my failure.

I blow out my candle and slink into Zara's room, skulking and furtive as a rat. By the dim glow of the banked coals, in the curtained bulk of her medieval bed, they sleep. All my mates.

Zara is safe. That is the first and most important truth.

My tight chest unclenches in a sigh of relief.

Zara and Ronin and Lucius and Neo sleep naked in a pile like wolf pups, with the wolf himself sprawled snoring on top. Tonight Lucius is literally his wolf, muzzle resting on his crossed paws, eyes closed and tail drooping. That is his way of protecting them, which is an instinct I thoroughly approve.

May he be more successful when that green dragon and his rider come for Zara, as they will surely do, than I have been myself.

Shoulders slumped in shameful defeat, I abandon my candle, let the towel fall where it will, and creep to the bed.

Vasili lies alone, apart from the others, and it is straight to him I go. With every step, these flagstone floors, steeped in the chill of centuries, shock my bare feet. I am shivering. Slowly, through the fog of pain, the knowledge surfaces.

I am feverish.

Clearly, like my brothers who are wyverns, that green dragon's acid breath is also poison.

Clenching my jaw to keep my teeth from chattering, I climb carefully into our bed, using the little rolling stair we leave for Zara (who is tiny) to mount the high platform. Any sort of jump or scramble is currently beyond me, and I do not wish to wake my mates.

Despite my care, I cannot smother a teakettle hiss of pain.

Vasili twitches in his sleep. Thankfully, he does not wake.

Normally, my love sleeps like a sphinx. Tonight he is restless and muttering in a twisted tangle of sheets, breath hitching and lashes fluttering with obvious nightmare. I cannot sense his thoughts, because he has not yet permitted my mating bite. And, truly, I am no telepath.

But he is uneasy.

I would comfort him.

Only now, while he sleeps, will he permit me to protect him.

Carefully I ease my agonized body over his. I angle my injured side toward the canopied roof of our bed. The butterscotch of his mating scent, laced with Ronin's seductive ambergris and the dark musk of semen, makes my skin tingle.

Gently I stroke Vasili's pale hair, soft and treacherous as cobwebs, away from my love's pinched brow. I smooth one finger over his perfectly groomed eyebrows until the line between them eases.

With a trusting sigh that pierces my heart like an arrow, he turns his face into my neck and breathes deep of my scent.

Comforted by my familiar presence, he falls quiet. His troubled breaths turn deep and regular.

Tenderly now, while he sleeps, I cradle him. My dragon rumbles over him with brooding affection. My heart aches with all the love for him that Vasili will not allow me to express.

With every particle of my being, I am his alpha.

I am the only man who will ever master him.

But mine is a claim he continues, most violently, to reject.

Someday soon, I will have you, Vasili. I whisper my promise in Russian, the mother tongue we share, through the mating bond I am trying to build with him. *It can be our secret. I will never shame you. But in this, I will not fail. You are mine.*

As though he can hear my vow, he hisses in a breath. "Rasputin?"

Even half asleep, his tone is sharp as a surgeon's scalpel.

"Hush, they are sleeping," I whisper. I stroke his pretty hair to soothe him.

He catches my wrist to trap me, fingers cold and hard as manacles.

The roughness of the motion sends a stab of pain tearing through my injured hide. I bite back a cry but, lying on top of him as I am, I cannot hide my flinch.

"What the hell was that?" His voice acquires a suspicious edge.

"It is nothing, sweetheart." I lie very still to help the pain subside, but I try to sound comforting. "Go back to sleep."

His head lifts from the pillow to scrutinize my naked body in the dark. "The hell it's nothing. Show me."

Truly, there is no hiding anything from a warlock like him.

"Apparently there is no guarding my shame from you," I mutter, sounding surly even to my own ears. My face burns in the darkness worse than my scalded skin.

As casually as I can manage, I gesture toward my injury. Surely in this poor light, there will be little for him to see.

But he is part shifter, and his senses are keen.

"What the fuck." His sudden spike of concern for my welfare would be deeply gratifying if I were not so embarrassed. "Are you... *burned?*"

Carefully I sit. "Some breeds of dragon can spray poisonous acid. This one is no different than my brothers in the lair, they are only wyverns, but—"

"The fuck it's no different." Vasili slithers out from under me to sit. His determined hand finds my unwilling brow. "Christ. You're burning up."

"Max?" Zara's whisper twists me around to find her, smothered in wolf, eyes wide and fearless in the dark. "Are you okay?"

"Yes," I say firmly.

"No." Rudely Vasili cuts me short. He uncoils to his feet and drags on his sleeping pants. "That fucking Fae bastard and that fucking dragon hurt him. Get up, Rasputin. You need paracetamol and a numbing potion."

Sounding fretful, Ronin mumbles in his sleep. Alertly, the wolf's ears twitch.

I am desperate to prevent them all from witnessing my shame, but apparently there is no way to avoid this. I cannot even reach Zara or Ronin through our mating bond, which means that accursed artifact— that medallion from the Academy Vault—must still be somewhere near.

Despite the artifact, Zara seems to sense what I need. Deftly she wiggles out from under the wolf and settles Ronin's restless arm around the animal's shaggy bulk. Ronin hugs the wolf, Neo snuggles into Ronin, and the three warlocks sink back to dreaming.

If only Zara and Vasili would do the same.

Fully alert, Zara scrambles out of bed and wraps herself hastily in Lucius' smoking jacket. I descend from the bed more slowly, wincing and using the little stair, then wrap the discarded towel once more around my hips, because I still cannot bear the thought of pants.

None of us speak until we reach the dark corridor and shut the bedroom door behind us to keep the heat in.

Then Vasili says curtly, "The numbing potion's in Neo's room."

He stalks away and does not wait for me to follow.

By this, I discern he is disgruntled to have woken with me sprawled possessively on top of him. He is overly sensitive to any hint of admission that I am his alpha.

Even though I am.

"C'mon, big guy." From my uninjured side, Zara slips a purposeful arm around my waist and steers me firmly where she wishes me to go. "Let's get you all patched up, okay?"

It is not okay. I do not wish to burden her. It is my responsibility to protect her. Still, I am beguiled by the soft feel of her curves pressed into my side, the roses-and-cream sweetness of her scent, the energizing tingle of psychic connection as the artifact falls away behind us and our mating bond sparks to life.

"My sovereign, I have failed you." My wretched confession spills out in the open, to lie ugly and exposed for her judgment. "I hunted your enemy and I found him. But I could not kill him."

"Whoa." Her mouth pops open and her eyes narrow to slits. "Looks to me like you just about freaking killed yourself to protect me. You call that *failing*?"

"Well, yes." For some reason I cannot grasp, she is indignant rather than disapproving. I scowl in return. "Obviously. Yes."

My queen heaves a sigh and rolls her eyes. "Cheese on toast. Sometimes you're a very foolish dragon."

"I should have attacked with more guile." Although I scarcely wish to elaborate all the ways I have failed her, still I feel compelled to explain. "I did not realize the rider too would be a threat. Truly, he is a warlock with witchcraft like none other I have known. I gave way to my pride, I challenged him to combat when I should simply have ambushed—"

"Max. Stop. Just stop." Far more gently than I deserve, she ushers me into Neo's vacant bedroom. Vasili has already slipped into Neo's *ensuite* bathroom. He stoops to light a fat candle on the sink, and his tall graceful silhouette leaps to life against the wall.

Doggedly I trudge after him. "I failed to protect you. I failed to protect *all* of you. I failed to protect my mates. Christ, I did not even manage to blood him! He is still at large, still a threat to you. And that is my shame—"

"Like hell it is." Halfway through the bedroom, Zara tugs me gently to a halt. By the spill of starlight through the leaded glass doors, my queen's lovely face is fierce. "Listen, Max. I faced the guy myself and didn't manage to take him out. He's way bigger than me and he caught me off guard. Long story short? I fucking ran away. I wasn't ready and I got scared and I ran away. And now you're hurt. Hurt trying to finish the job I couldn't. Is that something *I* should be ashamed of?"

"Of course not," I say stoutly. "You are our queen. You must never feel shame. It is our place to protect you."

Already she is shaking her head, teal curls tumbling wildly around her face. She folds her arms and cocks her hip.

"Look, I don't need you guys protecting me like I'm some porcelain princess. I've been protecting myself my whole life and doing a pretty damn decent job, most of the time. The way I see it, as queen? It's my job to protect *you*. You and all our mates. And all my, uh, subjects."

I try to interject, but she is having none of it.

"If these Dark Fae are trying to break free of their alternate world or whatever and do some kind of damage in this one," she announces, "I figure it's my job to stop that. If this Fae tries to fuck with us—the way he just fucking *did* by trying to kill you—then it's gonna be *my* job to kill *him*."

Ferocious with resolve, she begins to pace.

No doubt the pain of my injuries has slowed my wits. I can only seem to gape at this outlandish and topsy-turvy notion that she, who is half my size and will be the precious mother of my dragonets, would protect *me*—her dragon king.

Vasili looms in the bathroom door, juggling his candle, a vial of tablets, and (I am relieved to see) a familiar pot of numbing potion.

"Are you *ever* coming in here, Rasputin, or must I come to you?" he says shortly.

This querulous demand puts an abrupt end to my queen's fretful pacing and muttering about how no one ever fucking touches us—*any* of us—and how now there is this Dark Fae she must kill.

"You just mosey on over here with that candle and that potion, Goblin King," Zara says in her queen voice, with which there can be no arguing. "Max, you lie down on Neo's bed. You'll be more comfortable here than in that mildewy bathroom."

Briefly I am distracted from my various discomforts and Zara's menacing promises of bloody retribution against the Fae by the prurient thought of lying all but naked in Neo Mercury's bed. Even if Neo does not currently lie here himself. Now that he is recalled to my thoughts, I realize the clean sage and lavender of his soap lingers in the air.

His scent is not displeasing (far from it), but Vasili is his alpha and I am not, so I try to be discreet as I take an appreciative whiff.

We share the same roof, the same table, the same mates, the same bed. But Neo Mercury is First Boy on the Dean's List, always happily buried in a book, excelling at every task he ever undertakes, praised and petted and adored by Zara and our entire harem and indeed the whole Academy. My own grades are (to put it mildly) unimpressive. I am self-educated. Until I came to Icarus, I could barely even read. In short, I am nothing special in the classroom, I trail in every class, and the students in the other cohorts mock me for my stupidity.

As for Neo Mercury, he does not even seem to notice me.

I notice him.

How I notice him.

But out of deference to this damnably complicated dynamic between me and Vasili, who is rabidly possessive of Neo, I must pretend I do not.

Now, this accursed injury has given me an unexpected opportunity to get close to the elusive First Boy in the only way I can.

Striving not to appear too eager, I lower myself carefully to the bed. It is perfectly made, as though someone might grade him for the chore, although the duvet is dusty with disuse.

But the pillows still smell like *him*.

Neo.

While Vasili is distracted with the candle and the medicine, I turn my hot face into the cool pillow and breathe in deep the clean soothing aromas of sage and books and innocence.

Even though my side is throbbing, under the concealing towel, my cock heats and rises with interest.

Rudely Vasili interrupts my reverie. "Well, dragon, I'm certainly not going to stand here all night. I'm not your valet. Do you want the paracetamol or not?"

"He wants it." Zara hops onto the bed beside me and claims the tablets from Vasili's unhelpful grip. "Uh, and maybe a glass of water, Goblin King?"

"That is not necessary," I say hastily, before Vasili can flay the remaining hide from my carcass with more of his cutting comments.

I extract two tablets from Zara's grip and swallow them dry.

"That should help with your fever, anyway. Now let's have that numbing potion." Zara straddles my legs and settles me between her silky naked thighs.

This is a proceeding which commands both my immediate interest and Vasili's.

Deftly she unknots the towel around my hips. She is about to lay me (and my considerable erection) matter-of-factly bare for Vasili's scathing scrutiny when her gaze meets mine.

Our mating bond is strong, for I have thoroughly bitten her and claimed her. Now she is swift to sense my embarrassment—and the reason.

You and Neo, huh? she whispers through our bond. *Wow. I really like the sound of that, Max.*

There is nothing between us, I grumble sourly. *He does not even know I am alive. And Vasili cannot know.*

Comprehension parts her lips and sharpens her gaze.

She chuckles under her breath and shakes her head wryly. "You sure about all that, big guy? I mean, obviously I know we've got issues we're all working through. But I guess there are more of them than I thought."

"Well, how rude." Vasili pouts. Our queen is growing very skilled at guarding her thoughts and everyone else's privacy, but of course he senses she is doing it. "Perhaps I'll just leave the two of you alone for your little *tête-à-tête.*"

"Stay." My own plea—because it is a plea, a naked plea, a plea I did not mean to voice—should embarrass me. But I do not want either of them to leave. "Stay with me, sweetheart. Both of you."

Zara breathes that same wistful sigh she always breathes when I call Vasili sweetheart. Clearly. she is hoping we can somehow resolve our troubled courtship and all our attendant disruptions before she must (inevitably) ask me to leave her harem. Vasili is her Goblin King, they are deeply in love, and she is the first and the only woman he has ever wanted.

As for him, he utters a very Vasili-like huff that vibrates with impatience. But he slides onto the bed beside me and opens the pot of numbing potion. Biting her lip, Zara eases my towel aside to bare my scalded hip, but leaves a fold draped modestly over the inconvenient bulge between my legs.

The first cool stroke of Vasili's long fingers up my side brings instant relief. It is a weakness to show it, but I moan softly with pleasure.

"Oh, go ahead and moan, it's not unmanly," Vasili says with less than his usual venom. "Neo makes the most potent numbing potion at Icarus. Lucius says our boy is the first warlock to ace Honors Alchemy in a century, even though he's only a junior."

This revelation only reminds me again how completely unattainable the brilliant First Boy is, and will forever be, to a hopeless Remedial Magics idiot like me. But it is better to focus on Vasili's hands on my body, delicately smoothing ointment over my scalded side. Zara scoops out a few fingers of the magical substance, which smells like sage and lavender and Neo, and gently anoints my burned hip. Her inner dragon utters soft croons to soothe me.

My own dragon rumbles and purrs in reply.

Beneath my mates' well-synchronized attentions, the waves of pain battering my sandblasted nerves finally begin to dull and recede. For the first time in hours, my breath slows and my tension eases. Cautiously I allow myself to enjoy the sensation of having both of them take care of me.

Even though I do not deserve it.

"Hmmm." Vasili hums over his work, long lashes lowered, delicate lips parted with focus so that the tips of his cruel fangs are exposed (which would horrify him if he knew). "Rather a lot going on in our polycule these days, darlings. Even beyond the apparent advent of the Dark Fae King and his horrid little monster."

"What more is going on?" I say gruffly, just to keep him talking. His voice comforts me and distracts me from the pain.

"He's talking about Lucius." Zara's face turns thoughtful. Her hand drifts absently to touch her lower belly. "Who's always possessive, that's just part of being alpha. But he's usually really good—too good, honestly—at hiding it. Or just, you know, managing it."

"But tonight, he was not?" I have the visual from our mating bond in a heartbeat. Saint Sergius defend me, the thought of that wolf pumping our queen full of his potent seed, pushing his spend back inside her with his fingers, then guarding her succulent cunt so no other male can breed her…

He is exhibiting classic breeding behavior.

His wolf wants her pregnant.

My dragon bates his wings and trumpets with blind rage.

Intellectually, I know, this is a dangerous instinct I must contain. Of course, Lucius wants pups, he is purebred shifter the same as I, and wolf shifters—like all shifters in modern times—are so rare they face extinction.

I am willing to help raise his pups with her, when they come, as well as though they were mine. I will protect them and hunt for them and kill for them.

But first, I want Zara to bear *my* offspring.

It is only when my queen murmurs, "Easy there, big guy," that I realize I am growling.

"Breeding instinct," Vasili declares, looking bemused. "Dear fuck."

Of course, being Vasili, he sweeps my towel heartlessly aside to expose my barbed dragon cock, stiff and swollen with blatant need. A dragon's cock is like a devil's thick forked tail, and both my mates like the sight of mine. In fact, that sight makes Vasili purr a little himself, which only worsens my plight. He will never admit it, he is sly as a snake about any true feeling, but my dragon cock intrigues him. Just the thought of those all-too-rare moments when I have persuaded him to wrap his pretty lips around my shaft…

Oh Christ.

The mere thought of him taking me anywhere inside his endlessly alluring body makes my dick swell and my barb stiffen and droplets of glistening fluid appear at my tip.

When I am well pleased, that barb locks into place to seal me snug and tight inside my mate, so I can pump my chosen one full to overflowing with my potent seed without wasting a single drop.

With Vasili and Zara and Ronin, all three of them, the thought of mating them makes my barb bristle and my dick ache to lock into them.

The fact that only Zara can actually conceive does not diminish my need. I swear I would sire offspring on all three of them if I could. (This is a thought I am extremely careful never to reveal to Vasili. One glimmer of that filthy fantasy, and Vasili will be so deeply offended he will never let me or my intriguing but relentlessly impregnating cock anywhere near him ever again.) Thank God that when my telepathic mate Ronin glimpsed this mpreg erotic obsession taking up residence in my brain—

the two of us locked and fucking at the time, his ass strangling my shaft as though he was born and bred for nothing else—Ronin only laughed like a loon. In the end, he became titillated over the kink, and even more amorous for our coupling.

Still, the soul-deep certainty that someday, in actual truth, Zara will bear my dragonets adds a special intensity to my need for her.

That is no mere fantasy. It is fated.

"Breeding instinct," I agree in a voice like gravel.

Zara's lapels are falling open and her lush breasts and pert pierced nipples are spilling into view. My gaze drops to her luscious thighs, spread wide to bracket mine, exposed under the rucked-up hem of Lucius' burgundy smoking jacket.

My queen is temptation incarnate.

My hands rise of their own accord to skate up her outer thighs. Her limbs are satin, her golden Red Sea suntan mostly faded after her first Icarus Island winter. Her skin now is flawless ivory, glowing with health and youth. Her curls are thick and shining, her face flushed and dewy, her eyes shimmering with periwinkle fire.

Surely, oh surely, if she would only cease those accursed shots, she would be instantly fertile.

When my thumbs graze the hot damp folds of her slit, her breath hitches. She squirms under my touch. The night air floods with a sudden potent kick of her Mogadon pheromones.

"Behave yourself, big guy," she says, low and languid. "You're injured."

"But I feel so much better," I declare earnestly. And it is true. Neo's numbing potion has worked miracles, and the paracetamol has broken my fever. "Already I am healing, as Neo would say, shifty-swifty."

"That's good, Max. That's real good. We'll get you all checked out at the clinic first thing tomorrow to be totally sure you're okay, but I'm really glad." She smiles at me, but her brow is creased and her gorgeous Hollywood face is clouded.

When my palms glide over the junction of her inner thighs, where her skin is so soft, where she smells so good, where she tastes so salty-sweet, her capable hands close gently but firmly over mine. "No offense, but I'm hanging out the No Vacancy sign on my hoochie tonight, okay?"

My face falls, and our mating bond gives a painful ping.

Though I strive mightily not to show it, I am bitterly disappointed. But of course, she senses it. She raises my battle-hardened hands to her sweet mouth and tenderly kisses my scarred knuckles one by one.

"I'm just gonna respect whatever this thing is that's going on with Lucius for one night," she murmurs against my skin. "He gives so much to all of us, all the time. He never asks anything for himself."

Beyond any doubt, she is speaking the truth.

If our cobbled-together family of misfit witches and warlocks and wolf and snake and dragon shifters works at all, with all of us so young and wild and willful, the cornerstone of our family is Lucius.

Wondrously wise, endlessly patient, utterly selfless, fiercely protective Lucius.

Still, my single-minded dragon does not like this denial. He wants to fuck, he wants to mate, he wants to breed.

And so do I.

Especially with half the women on this island falling pregnant…

"Thank fuck *I'm* not afflicted with this pernicious need to breed." Vasili sneers. His pretty eyes linger on my rigid dick in a way that is absolutely not helping. "Having you and Lucius both inexplicably craving playpens and pacifiers and midnight diaper duty is certainly sufficient for one harem. However, I'm willing to play along with all this… under one condition." His perfect face hardens. "Zara fucks who she wants to fuck. That's always been our cardinal rule. Even if who she wants is not one of us."

Zara stiffens in my lap and fires right back, "I sure as hell don't wanna fuck anyone else, bad boy. We've got enough issues going on with the six of us, in case you haven't noticed. Like major issues we're working on. Believe me, having five hot bi warlocks in my bed is *palenty*. At this point, our bed is literally full."

"Hmmmm." Looking positively wicked, Vasili taps his chin and ponders. "There's always room for one more. You know Ronin's getting *much* more precognitive since all our witchcraft's started evolving. He doesn't think you're done, darling. Admittedly, I'm inclined to agree."

Her head tilts and her eyes narrow. "Well, shit. Is it, or is it not, *my* pussy?"

Vasili waves an airy hand in cavalier dismissal of her objection. "Our darling Lucius, when he's in his proper scholarly mind and not senseless and bestial with rutting, adamantly insists it's symbolically and magically crucial for the fate of the four races that you always feel free to choose. As for yours truly, well, I certainly wouldn't mind another scrumptious warlock bending for me from time to time. Neither will Ronin. And Neo wants whatever you want." He lifts one shoulder in a careless shrug. "I dare say even our dragon here would agree. Eventually. If you ask him nicely."

His smooth tenor drops two octaves in a way that strokes my cock like a hand. Predictably, my dick reacts to him the same way as always. It sits straight up and begs for him like a bitch in heat.

"Yeah, that's all fine, but I'm *not* asking. We clear about that?" Zara demands.

Whatever she might say, I am her alpha, and she cannot resist me when I am hard. For her, I am a genetic imperative. Slowly Zara's hand steals out and wraps around my dick, fingers skimming over the twin barbs which are so sensitive to her touch.

Briefly I worry that she will numb *that*, but Neo's witchcraft is far too clever. The magic in that potion is triggered by intent.

I groan and close my eyes and arch my hips into her exquisite touch.

With my rational mind, I want to say, if she does ask, it will be Zara's choice whom she mates. But my dragon emphatically does not agree. He wants Zara and Vasili and Ronin for himself. And Neo, yes, him too, even though Neo does not want me. Oh, very well, even Lucius, although we are not lovers, I cannot deny there is a part of me that feels… distinctly territorial… over whom he is fucking as well.

"Another guy in our bed isn't anything I want. Or another girl, emby, or anyone else either," she adds firmly. Her warm breath teases my dick, and my eyes fly open. Christ, my two mates are both hovering over me, their heads close together, one teal, the other silver. Their faces are so close that their lips nearly brush my aching tip.

"But, just for the sake of… research," she teases, "if there ever was… someone else… would this be asking you nicely enough, big guy?"

In a lick of electric heat, Vasili's mouth meets Zara's over my dick. And every objection sprouting in my head turns to smoke.

In the end, if this is them asking, they ask me very nicely indeed.

When they ask me like that, I will agree to anything.

But, although we are all half playing, my agreement is not lightly given. I have sworn to them both that I will love them until the world ends, and a dragon does not lie.

Zara is more than my mate.

She is my sovereign. She is the Gemini queen. She is precious and unique. There is none other such as she in all the world.

Our queens are always polyamorous. And I want what is best for her, for our mates, for all of us. For all my race, and all us shifters, and the whole witching world.

This is why I agree that I would accept what Zara believes she does not want.

In the end, they work together to please me to the point of frenzy, all hot mouths and sleek tongues and soft hands, while taking care not to aggravate my well-numbed injuries, and also while respecting as sacrosanct this so-called No Vacancy sign that Zara says she has temporarily hung, for Lucius' sake, over her irresistible dragon queen pussy.

It is nearly dawn and the sky beyond our windows is lightening to silver when we three tiptoe back down the hall, our fingers laced, sated and drowsy, to our room and all our mates to sleep.

Later, when I wake with a start, my Zara is gone.

Chapter Nine
Zara

I'm pissed as fuck.

That's why I take off. Way before the Monday morning alarm goes off to announce the start of another school week.

Even though normally, I'm the exact opposite of a yippy-skippy morning person.

Before I was a lightning witch, I was a cat burglar. This morning, I put the mad skills from those times to good use. All my warlocks are still sleeping off our fuckfest when I wiggle my way out from between Max and Lucius (who's fully human again, this close to dawn), shimmy into the first clothes I can find in the dark (which turn out to be my leggings and Neo's sweater, judging by the scent) and ghost into the hall like nobody's biz.

As I pad down the hall in my fur-lined Academy slippers and creep down the stairs, I don't bother with the candle. I don't need it. My nifty shifty senses have gotten super acute. I can see pretty decent in anything less than pitch dark, even though I only see heat signatures in infrared when I'm in dragon form. I can hear the automatic coffee pot muttering and purling in the kitchen (which means the power's back, yay) and the wind moaning around the eaves.

It's gonna be freaking cold out there. But I'm way past giving a shit.

My rage will keep me nice and toasty.

The only reason I'm not already going medieval on that dragonrider's trespassing ass is because Max is healing up at shifty-speed. I checked him out good before we slept.

But that first gut-wrenching sight of those nasty burns of his… and, God, feeling him in pain like that and trying to hide it for my sake? Seeing his beautiful golden eyes avoiding mine, out of some misplaced sense of shame?

That fucking Fae bastard hurt my dragon.

For that, I will absolutely make that fucker *bleed*.

The acrid scent of coffee pulls me into the kitchen to grab a cup of the stuff that's sludgy black, the first pour from the pot before it fills. It's scalding hot and extra caffeinated (not that I need caffeine when I'm already this much on edge). I sip the bitter brew, black as vengeance, as I hunt through the vestibule for my Academy peacoat.

And the lock pick from my burgling kit that I stashed in my coat pocket last night before I crashed.

Lucius has locked that enchanted book in his bedroom. But I'm Zara fucking Gemini and I am a witch on a mission.

No lock's gonna keep me out.

Parking my mug on the floor outside my headmaster's door, I hunker down and jimmy the mechanism. And whaddaya know?

I've got that lock popped before you can say *Open Sesame*.

Inside the orderly confines of Lucius' bedroom, smelling like patchouli and wolf and a little like Vasili's mating scent (because he and Lucius are definitely a thing), the fat book lies on the writing desk, between a neat stack of graded essays and Lucius' oxblood briefcase. In the pewter dawn that leaks through a seam in the heavy curtains, glittering gold letters in antique script squirm across the cover.

The Legend of Avalon.

My palms tingle and my scalp crawls. Yeah, no. I really don't wanna touch the *Monster Book of Monsters*, especially without Lucius being here. But I'm in a hurry and I need to do my thing. The green brass lock catches my eye, and I'm ready to put my pick to work.

But before I can even touch it, the clasp pops and the cover lifts.

"Shit!" I jump like a scalded cat and spill coffee all over my hand. Not to mention Lucius' bearskin rug.

Sweet Jesus, I'm jumpy.

Hissing with pain and promising myself I'll help with the cleanup later, I approach the desk (wary as fuck) and decide to read standing up.

There's one particular thing I'm looking for.

And I whisper to that book what it is.

"Show me how to kill the Dark Fae."

The shadowy room seems to suck in its breath. Suddenly, I'm wishing I took the time to hit the light.

The thick parchment pages start to rustle and flip, without any physical assist from me. What. So. Ever.

The pages settle open on an exquisite full-page illustration. I'm eyeing a slender male with a graceful swirl of moss-green hair, sprawled face-down in a spreading pool of blood. On the opposite page, the crimson script seems to writhe across the parchment.

Deadly Weapons to Slaye the Fae.

For some reason, my throat is dry. It's hard to look away from that striking image to focus on the words. I gulp down a swallow of grainy coffee and force my gaze away from the visual so I can decipher the ornate script.

Whoa. Now we're in business.

We don't have any ash wood in the *domus* that I know about, so that one's interesting, but out for now.

Fire could definitely come in handy, though it'd be tricky to carry when I'm flying.

But…

Cold iron.

The antique iron poker from the great room fits right into my school backpack (even though a good six inches stick out the top) along with my catsuit and boots and the stiletto I packed last night. My knife is plain steel, not cold iron, but it's a good knife, and I'll feel better having a blade on me. I toss in a lighter, plus one of the insta-burn fire starter logs Lucius uses when our wood's wet and our human fire starter (a.k.a. Ronin, who's wicked with the psi fire) is MIA. I add a box of matches for good measure, then zip the backpack with a buzz.

It's bulging and awkward to lift with that poker sticking out. But I'll manage.

Gulping the last of my cooling coffee, I back away from the book, gratefully leave that scary-ass thing on Lucius' desk precisely where I found it, and use the pick to lock his door again behind me.

Now that I'm not hyper-focused on the book, which kinda blots out everything else around me, my shifty senses are picking up mumbles and stirrings from the girls' room upstairs. My pulse kicks up and my back starts to sweat.

Fuck. I gotta pick up the pace.

Once my guys start waking up, I'll never get out of here.

They'll think they have to protect me.

They don't get that it's *my* job to protect *them*.

I make a quick pit stop to leave my mug in the kitchen sink for later, when it's my turn on cleanup duty. Then I trot back up, scurry down the hall past the bedrooms with my heart in my throat, and scuttle up the steep narrow servants' stair to the dusty third-floor attic Lucius uses for storage.

The dry scent of dust and mothballs makes me sneeze. Blinking in the near-total darkness, I swing the heavy backpack I've been hauling across my shoulders. Then I ghost my way through the obstacle course of cobwebby crates and the spooky shrouded bulk of abandoned furniture, past an antique armoire that gives off major vibes from *The Lion, the Witch, and the Wardrobe*.

Finally, I crawl nimbly on all fours up the ladder through the trapdoor to the roof.

Thankfully that whole sleet-and-hail thing tapered off during the night. But, fuck me, it's wicked cold up here. The wind bites into my exposed face and hands without mercy and makes me shiver.

With my teeth chattering together in my skull and my skin all shivery and goosebumpy, it takes real willpower to strip out of Neo's soft sage-scented sweater, peel off my leggings, and toe out of my nice warm slippers.

But I do it in record time.

I leave everything piled safely on the top rung of the ladder, then lower the trapdoor quietly on top, to keep everything inside dry and handy for when I need it later.

Also, when the guys put out an APB and search the house for my missing ass, they'll find the clothes and know where I went.

Which definitely means they're gonna come after me.

At least the ones who fly.

I don't know how to stop that. And I'm not such a pure idiot that I don't realize I could end up over my head, cold iron and Fae-burning flame notwithstanding, and need the assist.

Now I'm butt-ass naked and freezing in the biting wind. You better believe I waste zero time shifting.

My entire body tingles with warmth as the shift sweeps over me, limbs thickening, spine stretching, neck lengthening, tail sprouting. Teal scales plate my exposed skin. The world sharpens to precision clarity, like my eyes are telescopes and someone's just adjusted the focus. My pupils slit wide to absorb the tiny details of crumbling plaster and weathered stone from the ruins that surround the *domus*. My nostrils flare and my jaws part to taste the crisp smell of hail, mingled with the sweet bite of applewood smoke and the briny tang of the sea.

My ears swivel on my dragon head. The muffed glug of a toilet flushes behind thick walls two stories down.

I wrap my taloned forelegs around the backpack, use my powerful hind legs to spring into the air, and beat my wings hard to gain altitude. The *domus* falls away beneath me. The crumbling ruins of the village spread below, tumbling downhill to the silver sea.

As I climb toward the clouds, the familiar headrush of elation sweeps through me. I haven't been shifting long, flying never gets old, and the thrill takes the edge off that simmering rage that's been chewing at my gut like ground glass since Max got hurt.

Sure, I pretended for his sake last night that I'm fine.

But I'm really fucking *not*.

This whole queen gig isn't anything I ever asked for, and it definitely isn't anything I used to want. But I've finally embraced my fate. The way I see it, saving the witching world from extinction is taking way too long, even before this Dark Fae and his acid-breathing monster showed up and hurt my dragon. I fucking *hate* this passive waiting and waiting.

I always feel better, stronger, more in command when I seize the initiative.

This so-called king showed up here on Icarus for a reason. He attacked me for a reason. Now he's hanging around for a reason.

I don't know what that reason is, but I'm sure as shit not waiting around a minute longer to find out.

Wherever that Fae bastard is lurking and hiding, I don't doubt for a hot second that the sight of me, alone and unguarded in Icarus airspace, is gonna do the trick.

I'm just the bait we need to lure him and his closet monster out into the open.

But I'm not facing him down empty handed. I'm the Gemini queen. I'm a lightning witch, I pack a wicked wallop even on my worst day, and right now I'm loaded for bear.

I let loose with a bellow of defiance and challenge that's edged in the brassy echo of the lightning voice. In the sullen bank of clouds, thunder growls and lightning forks. As the first red sliver of the rising sun hoists its way over the horizon, I tilt away from the Academy and angle my flight toward the wooded hills and the barren mountain that looms over the island.

Up there on the summit at the standing stones, it's showtime.

And I've got a ringside seat.

Chapter Ten
Neo

I wake up when Maxim rolls out of bed.

I like to snuggle up with him (secretly) while he's sleeping, since that's literally the only time he ever lets me close. I know it's pathetic, I mean me crushing on the guy like this, when he so very obviously isn't into me.

Still, when he moves away, I feel a pang of loss.

Lordy, I've got it *so* bad for this guy. I'm so thankful he isn't a telepath.

That's my only hope of hiding how I feel.

When he slips out of bed, like super stealthy, he triggers my curiosity. I lie really still, with everyone else sprawled in a pile behind me and V emitting cute little snores (he has no idea he snores, and none of us will ever tell him), and watch Maxim pull what looks like Ronin's discarded leather pants over his own lean hips.

Dragon in leather.

Oh my Lord, yum.

Maxim keeps a drawer full of clothes in here, we all do, but this morning he seems to be in some major rush. He's favoring his side a little, so something must've happened overnight, but he always heals up fast like any shifter, so I'm not too worried. When he powers for the door, he's still barefoot and shirtless.

The second he darts into the hall and closes the door behind him, I sit up and reach for my glasses.

That's when I suddenly realize Zara's not part of the naked sleep heap next to me. My fated mate is always the last to rise, and the bathroom door's wide open, so I know she's not in there.

My tummy knots in a twist of alarm. My heart bumps against my sternum in the jittery rhythm of dread.

It's kinda weird that she's gone. And none of us are into weird right now, at all, not after that strange dragon and his rider attacked her.

Of course, it's possible Zara's just showering in the basement *thermae*. It's not typical, her getting up before the alarm, but it's possible.

I understand, with perfect clarity, why Maxim just lit out of here like his tail's on fire.

I throw back the blankets and leap out of bed into the chilly air. I shove my arms and legs into my tee shirt and boxers and flannel pajama pants at warp speed while I'm already shuffling for the door. The flagstone floor is freezing, so I pause just long enough to jam my feet into my loafers. I need to put some distance between me and Ronin's medallion so I can feel Zara again in our mating bond.

I burst into the hall just in time to spot Maxim vanishing up the narrow servants' stair that leads to the attic.

That wouldn't be my first choice of where to look, because that dusty old attic really creeps me out. But I figure Max is using his shifty senses to track Zara's scent.

I trot up the stairs after him, which puts distance between me and Ronin's medallion. But I'm still not sensing my fated mate.

Which means she's not in the *domus*.

By the time I rush into the attic, I've put two and two together. And, yeah, this situation is just what I was afraid of. Across the room, the trapdoor in the ceiling is wide open, spilling pearly light down the ladder into the spooky space.

A truckload of adrenaline spurts through my system.

My sudden worry for Zara is matched only by my desperation to catch that dragon before he takes wing and leaves me behind.

I gallop across the attic at a dead run. I barely pause long enough to snatch up the leather-straps-and-buckles contraption we stow up here that I cobbled together a while ago for Ronin when he asked, so he can fly with the dragons in our harem. I'm handy at cobbling things together, whether it's an alchemical formula or a physical gadget. Now I'm extra thankful for my tinkering skills. I drag the heavy harness after me up the ladder and explode onto the roof.

Literally just in time to see Max bend over and peel out of Ronin's leather pants.

Despite my near-panic, I jolt to a stop and whisper, *"Whoa."*

You might think I'd be used to seeing that dragon naked since, you know, we're in a polycule together? But I'm normally super careful not to stare at him like a creeper, since I know he's not into me.

This means the traffic-stopping sight of Maxim Rasputin bent over naked, with cords of sinew standing out down the backs of his thighs and glutes flexing under an expanse of golden Black Sea suntan, just about gives me a heart attack.

Hearing me gasp, he straightens in a hurry and twists around to eye me, with those golden orbs flaming in his ruthless face and a good foot of buttery blond hair swirling around his naked shoulders.

"Um," I say lamely.

"She has gone after that Fae and his dragon." His guttural voice brings me back to my senses. "Tell Lucius I have gone to bring her back. Tell Vasili he must come."

He's already turning away, clearly ready to shift right in front of me, even though Lucius has told him repeatedly not to shift on the roof.

"Wait!" Desperate, I rush forward, the harness dragging at my heels. "We have to get you into this."

Over one sinewy shoulder, he spares the harness a dismissive glance. "There is no time to wake Ronin."

"It's not for Ronin." I suck in a breath to steady my jackhammering heart. "It's for me."

"You?" He turns all the way around to stare. Doggedly I keep my eyes on his startled face and definitely *not* below the waist, even though his barbed dragon dick is an object of fascination. "Neo Mercury, you are afraid of heights."

I swallow past my suddenly dry throat. "I know. But I'll manage."

The wind is whipping his hair around his face, and he sleeks it back with an impatient hand. His oblong pupils narrow to suspicious slits. "What if you cannot? I will not have time to set you down."

"I said I'll manage." Oh crap, I'm not convincing him, and in another few seconds he'll be gone. I clutch the harness to my chest and lock onto his gaze. "Please, Maxim. Don't leave me behind. Please?"

Something flickers in his hard face. I can't tell if it's pity or contempt.

His gaze falls to my bare arms, biceps straining my short sleeves, my fair skin already pebbled with goosebumps. A frown skates across his lips. "You are not dressed for this weather. You will freeze."

I dump the harness at his feet, dive back through the trapdoor for my Academy sweater which Zara left draped over the ladder, and shove it over my head as I spin back toward him with words of reassurance already spilling from my mouth.

"This is good enough, okay, Max? I'll just—"

A blinding flash of light dries the words in my throat. When my vision clears, Max's big black dragon—huge as houses—is standing on the roof.

Right where Lucius has begged him not to stand.

Zara's smaller in dragon form, she's just a juvenile, but Max is no-shit massive. Our *domus* is solidly built, but I know Lucius is afraid of that dragon crashing through the roof.

He's a real monster, with black horns curving back from an evil face, jaws parted around rows of alarmingly serrated teeth, and steam leaking from his nostrils (because he's the classic fire-breathing kind of dragon). Add to that his cruel, clawed forelegs like a tyrannosaur and that spiky crest running down his back between scales like obsidian slabs, with glints of poison-green and indigo in the seams.

In either form, that forked dragon dick between his legs is exactly the same, like a devil's forked tail.

Except, you know, bigger.

The dragon's head snakes toward me. I wave a flustered hand to direct him and he hunkers obediently down, which at least gets my eyes off his junk. Fiery-blushing and praying he didn't catch me looking, I dart between his forelegs to gather up the harness and toss the girth strap over his muscled shoulders.

I've helped Ronin with this harness lots of times, so I know what I'm doing. And it definitely helps that Max is cooperating, lifting his wing so I can scramble under him to fasten the girth, cinching it good and tight.

He lets out a deep rumbly snort, and I shoot him an apologetic look. "Sorry! Is it too tight?"

His long muzzle snakes around to eye me, dragon orbs flaming with impatience.

Better too tight than too loose, that look seems to say.

Right.

I stuff Ronin's leather pants in the saddlebag I've rigged into the harness, because Max will need pants wherever he shifts back, and it might not be here. Then I double- and triple-check my buckles, following the same system I always use to make sure Ronin's safe. This part of the process runs on autopilot, and I try not to think about what comes next.

Maxim extends a foreleg, just like he does for Ronin. I plant a hand on his scales, which radiate heat like a furnace, and try to calm my racing pulse. Shoot, my hand is shaking.

His nostrils flare and he chuffs at me in an obvious command to hurry.

I suck in a breath and scramble up, the way I've watched Ronin do a dozen times, always with sinuous grace and a grin of anticipation lighting his feral face.

But this time, with me, it's different.

It's so different.

Because Max is right. I'm totally acrophobic. I don't even like airplanes. I'm so scared of flying on his back that I'm ready to pee my pants.

But Zara. She needs me. She really does.

Max is a great ally to have at your back in a fight, but he's kind of a hothead and he doesn't always think clearly, especially once his breeding instinct kicks in.

Whereas me? Thinking is what I'm good at.

Anyway, I won't be left behind.

Not this time.

I won't be left out while the rest of our mates keep Zara safe.

My tummy feels hollow and my chest feels tight. Still, I climb awkwardly over Maxim's scaly shoulder and settle between two of the Godzilla-like plates that march down his spine. My hands are cold, but my palms are sweating. I buckle the harness over my thighs good and tight, then give everything a hard tug to double-check.

Max twists his long neck around to give me a narrow look. My heart's pounding so hard I feel lightheaded, but I grip the spiky crest in front of me and clear my throat.

"Okay," I whisper.

His eyes get narrower. You wouldn't think a dragon could look skeptical, but somehow this one manages.

I suck in a breath and yell, "I said okay!"

Max swings his muzzle toward the sky and voices a trumpeting bellow so fierce I can feel his sides vibrate under my butt. Then he launches into the air with a lurch that leaves my tummy back on the roof.

Oh my Lord. I'm going to die.

The dragon's big black wings beat in powerful strokes that propel us into the air. The *domus* and the sloped streets with their crooked stairs fall away beneath us with dizzying speed. I whimper and squeeze my eyes shut tight.

Between my knees, that powerful dragon body labors. His vast ribs expand and contract with his huffing dragon breaths. He's radiating a fiery heat that I find comforting, especially with the sharp wind whistling past my ears and biting into my exposed hands and face. My sweater and flannel pajama pants really aren't much help, but they're better than nothing, and I'm really glad I'm not barefoot.

I huddle into Max as close as I can, asking for reassurance as much as warmth. In response, he pushes out a low rumble and doesn't show off any of the tricks in his aerial maneuvers playbook.

Clearly he knows I'm not Ronin, who digs that daredevil stuff.

Max is totally into Ronin. The way I wish he was totally into me.

But he's tolerating me on his back this once, for Zara's sake.

She's the important thing.

After a little while, when we don't crash and I don't fall off, I work up the courage to sneak a quick peek. The wooded hills outside the village are *way* below, which makes me yelp and squeeze my eyes shut again right away. My tummy turns over in a slow queasy flip and I pray like anything that I won't throw up all over this guy I'm secretly crushing on.

He might not ever like me.

But I'd really like it if he could at least respect me.

After my stomach settles, I risk another look. Now Mt. Apollo is looming dead ahead. I flush with excitement all over my whole body. Max roars and labors to gain altitude, winging hard for the summit and the stone circle where Zara and that Fae had their last encounter.

The air crackles with the familiar charge of lightning.

I sit up straight and start looking for my fated mate. Max hasn't let me fall, and he's not going to. Besides, finding Zara's way more important than coddling my fraidy-cat fear of heights.

We soar over the summit. The circle of crooked gray stones rises into view. A familiar tug of connection and awareness tingles through me and makes me yell with relief and triumph.

That's my Zara!

Max bugles, which tells me he's feeling her too, through their mating bond.

Then I see her.

She's stalking around the edges of the circle without going inside (which is probably a prudent move) all kitted out in her catsuit and boots, hair twisted in a thick teal rope that swings to her waist. She's gripping a flaming torch in one hand and what looks like an iron poker in the other in a way that means business.

When she locks onto us, my cherished one's alarm flashes through our bond like a bolt of lightning.

Guys, go back, go back, go back! Her warning blasts through my head, even as she waves her torch madly to signal us away. *He's here, I'm luring him, I* planned *this, go back—*

Max trumpets in outraged protest.

Yeah, what he said.

Whatever this reckless plan of hers is supposed to be, using her sweet precious self as the bait, I don't like it one bit.

Where is he, babe? I crane to look behind and above me, which I know is Max's blind spot, but I'm seeing nothing. *C'mon, let us help you.*

Max wings toward her, toward the circle, in vast determined strokes. The wind stings my face and hands, though my nose and fingers are already numb. But Zara waves her torch and poker in a big sweeping X, like some sort of demented ground crew at JFK, to warn us away.

"No, don't!" she screams, her voice edged in the brassy rumble of the lightning voice. "Don't cross the circle!"

Something rises over the crest behind her and sweeps toward her, low and deadly, barely skimming the rocky ground like a wicked poison-green locomotive, wings spreading wide to frame her. Between those massive wings, a horned figure crouches, all encased in glittering green armor. A moss-green cloak snaps and billows in his wake like a second set of wings.

Max bellows and dives to her rescue. My stomach drops through the bottom of my feet and my gorge pushes through the top of my head but, please God, now is not the time for me to puke.

"He's behind you!" I shout to my fated mate, verbally and mentally broadcasting on all channels.

Alertness flashes across her face. She crouches and spins, weapons sweeping high, still controlled, still following whatever plan she's got. I can feel the lightning coiling in the air, the power of the lightning voice gathering in her throat—

That green dragon hits her like a freight train, both forelegs outstretched, and sweeps her right off the ground. The impact sends her torch flying, but somehow she manages to hang on to the poker. With a savage yell, she buries her point deep in the dragon's scaly chest, so deep, oh Jesus she means business. She's just speared that monster right under the throat, exactly where the heart is on a dragon.

She isn't playing.

She means to kill that dragon.

The thing screams like a woman. Zara screams too—a scream of raw triumph. A jagged bolt of lightning forks from the sky.

The injured dragon veers wildly, his rider moving with him, fluid as a spill of green ink. Zara's still gripped between the thing's front legs, but she's freaking fearless. She's pulling back her poker like Zeus hurling lightning so she can spear the monster again. This time, I can see, she's aiming right for the throat.

Thanks to the dragon's desperate swerve, her aim's thrown off, but she keeps her head in the game. I can feel her fierce determination as she zeroes in again on her target.

The dragon just manages to avoid her next bolt of lightning by a whisker. And thank God for that, because that bolt could've fried Zara.

The lightning slams into the ground like Thor's hammer.

The crash of thunder makes my ears ring.

But the dragon's momentum carries all three of them—dragon, rider, Zara—into the open air above the circle. The air ripples around them like a mirage.

In an eyeblink, they vanish.

They vanish with our Zara.

Max roars in a blind fury that sprays gouts of crimson fire through the air like a flamethrower on steroids.

I howl in complete and total despair that shreds my throat like paper. *"Zaaaaraaaa…"*

Cold wind screams past as Max dives and charges into the air above the circle. Our girl was literally… just… *there*.

Now the air ripples around *us*.

In a heartbeat, the mountain and the circle and the whole island disappear. The familiar world we know is gone. A sudden violent wrench cuts the harness into my thighs and almost snaps my neck. I catch a wild glimpse of blinding white, a vast terrain of jagged ice, sliced by flying snow blowing sideways under gusts of arctic wind. Max's wings are churning, his mighty body laboring to stay aloft, buffeted from every direction by fierce howling winds.

Still, somehow, we're falling.

Chapter Eleven

Zara

Sweet Jesus, I'm freezing.

When the fuck are we gonna get an actual working furnace in this *domus*?

And who the hell left all the windows wide open? There's like a gale-force wind blowing right over this bed.

Indignant as hell, my eyes pop open.

That's when it finally dawns on me that I'm not actually in bed.

I'm straddling some kinda medieval jousting saddle, like something from the Renaissance Faire, all gilded green leather trimmed in gold. Between my knees, a labored chuff of breath expands and contracts like a bellows. A snaky green dragon neck stretches in front of me, leading to a wicked dragon head whose vicious black horns are also tipped with gold. Puffs of vapor stream back on the wind with every exhale. But those breaths are all ragged and uneven.

That dragon's hurting.

And I'm the reason why.

My memory returns in a jumbled urgent rush that makes me gasp.

My inner dragon bates and bugles in alarm.

Slow down, showgirl, I tell both of us. *Just gimme a sec to catch my breath.*

Which is pretty hard to do when I'm about 1.5 degrees shy of freezing to death.

Gusts of snow-laced wind have completely numbed out my exposed hands and face. My catsuit is totally inadequate to keep me from shivering.

The only parts of me that are warm are my inner knees, because they're pressed against those steamy dragon sides. Plus my whole back, since I'm reclining against something hard and sleek and supple that's warm as a furnace.

Something tightens around my waist. I glance down to find an arm—a fucking arm!—wrapped around me. It's a lean arm, all sinewy with muscle, sporting a green leather gauntlet worked with (more) gold that's gripping a fistful of reins. The rest of that arm is encased in scaly green armor that flexes with every movement.

I shoot straight up at a velocity that would topple me right out of this saddle, except for the fighting straps buckled around my thighs that hold me in. From this improved vantage, I get a good gander of the vast white expanse we're flying over. Looks like the ice planet Hoth in *The Empire Strikes Back*.

Toto, we're not in Kansas anymore.

"Cheese on toast!" The words explode from my numb lips on a frosty cloud. I twist to get a visual behind me that confirms my every fucking fear.

I'm sharing this saddle with the green knight in the horned helmet. Thanks to those horns and the twin sword hilts jutting over his shoulders, this guy towers over me. With the faceplate down, I can't see a hint of his face.

But I can feel him watching me.

Correction.

Judging by the silent intensity and total fucking fury that emanate from this guy's perfectly still frame like a forcefield, he's actually glaring at me.

I guess that's maybe because, yeah, I hurt his dragon. Shit, I would've killed his dragon for what that thing did to Max. First chance I get, I intend to finish the job.

And I'm betting this guy can smell it on me.

My homicidal intent.

Too bad my iron poker's nowhere to be found. And I already know without looking that my pack was left behind. Plus my stiletto's gone from my boot.

Not that any of that's gonna stop me from hurling lightning like Thor son of Odin as soon as I'm off this thing.

I need a proper look-see at my new reality. But I seem to be locked in a staring contest with Mr. Green back there.

Fuck if I'll be the first to blink.

Holding the potent stare I sense burning through me behind that scary helm, I pitch my voice to carry over the howling wind. "I dunno how the law works around here. But where I'm from? Kidnapping's a felony offense."

He doesn't even blink (as far as I can tell).

If anything, the sense of fulminating wrath that's beating out at me from this dude's unmoving frame gets worse.

Driven by the brutal headwind, my braid whips forward to lash my face. I catch it and tuck it back without breaking that stare of his I can sense if not see. "But maybe the law doesn't apply to you, huh? If you're the Dark Fae King?"

Still no answer, except for the flex of his arm around my waist as he does something with those reins he's gripping. He's actually gripping those reins in both fists. The way we're situated, I'm basically in his arms. That's typically not a situation I'll tolerate—like, *at all*—but my options are kinda limited while we're airborne, and apparently he needs to be holding those reins to steer or something.

Regardless, this whole brooding silence routine is really starting to piss me off.

He kidnapped *me*, right?

If anyone on this dragon has the right to be furious, that would be me.

Which is boatloads better than being scared, which I very easily could be, if I let myself. My situation here is fairly alarming.

There's no sign of Max or Neo, which is something else that really worries me. My mates and their safety. God, where are they? I must've passed out after this guy grabbed me, and I'm not really sure how much time I've lost.

What I do know is this. It's been long enough that I'm freezing. Ice crystals are clumping on my eyelashes, I can't feel my face, and I'm shivering so hard Mr. Silent Treatment has to feel the tremors.

"Look." I heave a breath that explodes white from my lips. "I bet that armor keeps you all nice and toasty, but I'm freezing my ass off in this catsuit. I'm gonna go hypothermic pretty quick." Silence. "Oh, for fuck's sake. Do you even speak my language, or am I wasting my breath here?"

Finally, the guy reacts.

But he still doesn't speak.

He just transfers the reins to one fist and reaches behind him to grip the wind-whipped cloak that's billowing from his shoulders. With a single graceful sweep, abrupt as hell, he tosses a thick fold around my shoulders.

Guess he does speak my language. Or at least understand it. I really gotta wonder if he's the guy Ronin knew. The guy Ronin thinks he's killed.

But this doesn't seem like the time to ask.

Not that this dude would answer anyway.

I'd really like to reject the warmth he's offering so begrudgingly, especially since I gotta get even closer to Mr. Taciturn to take advantage. But I really am freezing, the heavy cloak is lined with rich sable fur that's already warm with his body heat, and I've got a pretty robust survival sense.

Even while my brain's busy debating and my pride's busy rebelling, my body decides on its own to tuck all that soft sleek warmth around me. I turn away from him to make it less awkward and intimate that we're sharing a cloak like this. But I also reach back with my free hand to grab another thick fold for my uncovered side and I wrap that around me too.

This whole maneuver brings me way closer to him than I like, with his arms and his cloak around me and my back tucked up against his chest. Now that we're this close, I realize he's actually not very big, not much bigger than I am, under that horned helm and those double swords and all that impressive armor. He's just such a… *presence*… that he feels massive. He holds himself all rigid, totally still and contained inside that scaly green rig that encases him like a dragon's hide. He's obviously not liking our cozy arrangement any more than I do.

But at least he's not copping a feel.

That horrible concept makes my whole body heat up.

Gosh, that would be just terrible, him feeling me up with those tooled leather gauntlets, running those graceful fingers that handle the reins so nimbly over the curves under my catsuit.

I bury my cold face in the fur. A warm spicy scent, like burnt amber and nutmeg, twines into my nose. His essence tastes sweet and hot, like a clove cigarette, on my tingling lips.

Without thinking, I lick my lips and breathe in deep. The aroma's unusual and it kinda reminds me of my guys' mating scents. But maybe that's normal for him, you know, just your average elf scenting away. He's gotta be a totally different species.

For absolutely no logical reason, breathing him in like this, tasting him on my tongue, my stupid heart starts pounding.

My inner dragon is rumbling, watchful, she's kinda checking this whole scene out. I feel like maybe she's checking out Mr. Green and his mean machine.

Yeah, no. *That's* not happening.

This isn't gonna be some Hades-Persephone scenario where the big bad abducts me and carries me off to Hell in his dark chariot and we fall madly in love and fuck like rutting dragons. For one thing, he doesn't exactly present like an amorous suitor. It's not like he showed up on my doorstep with flowers and chocolate.

And I'm sure as shit not some flowery spring virgin.

I'm pretty much the exact opposite.

Anyway, I gotta get back to my guys. Holy moly, they're gonna lose their minds over this whole missing queen situation. Soon as Mr. Green lands this thing, I'm summoning lightning. Then I'm gonna shift and fly right back home.

I sit up straight to put as much distance as I can between me and the bad guy, then take a good look around to orient myself for the return trip. It's definitely like *Ice Planet Barbarians* down there, a jumbled landscape of ice and snow that's gonna be hard to navigate, rimmed all the way around by a glacial blue sea. Off to the left looms a big-ass mountain, an actual volcano that looks seriously active, with smoke streaming out the top and a few skinny ribbons of fiery lava snaking down the sides.

Okay.

When I fly back, that volcano goes on the right.

Dead ahead, there's the frigid sea, dotted with jagged icebergs like scattered teeth. There's a city of some kind right on the shore, it's like Tolkien's city of Gondor down there, dominated by this palatial structure with wedding cake tiers, bristling with pointy spires and turrets like a rococo cathedral. In fact, the whole geography reminds me a little of Mt. Apollo and the Academy back at Icarus, if our island was in Greenland instead of the Med.

A flash of rusty brown, totally out of place against the blizzardy sky, twists my head up. At the exact same moment, the green dragon dives and lets loose one of those godawful screams that sounds like the shrieking mandrake in *Harry Potter*. Behind me, an electric quiver of tension runs through the Fae.

My heart gives a lurch of alarm. That flash of rust is a new dragon, a brown one, plummeting straight down on us from above.

This new one doesn't have a rider. But what he does have are extended talons on all four legs like an eagle stooping for the kill. They're razor sharp and longer than the apex carnivore's in *Jurassic World*.

My inner dragon trumpets a challenge.

"What the fuck?" I yelp.

The Fae dives forward, crushing me against his chest, and reels in a gauntlet full of reins. He shouts something (so he does talk), just a single word I don't understand, like the sound of water hissing over rock. The green dragon swerves to one side, twists his wicked neck, and sprays a torrent of steaming acid right in the brown's flight path.

The brown screeches and veers, wings churning, to avoid the acid. But he's so close. Jesus, I can see his evil red eyes fixed on us with unswerving focus, his serrated jaws parted in a sharky grin. He's in rough shape, all skin and bones, and his hide's all scarred and his wings are tattered. But those nasty-ass talons extend as he swerves right after us in hot pursuit.

That's hunting behavior.

"He's still coming," I yell, just in case this extremely relevant fact has escaped anyone's notice.

I hum to summon the lightning and rev up my witchcraft. For some reason, to my alarm, all that comes out of my throat is a harmless-sounding buzz.

Deftly the Fae shifts the reins to one hand and sweeps his free arm overhead in a graceful circle.

Out of absolutely nowhere, a vicious crosswind swirls around us, building in strength as it twists past, and slams into the enemy dragon. Propelled by that cylindrical funnel of wind, the brown nightmare goes tumbling backward end-over-end through the air, screaming the whole time.

Well, dayum.

That's some nifty witchcraft right there. Color me khaki with envy.

We don't have anything like the ability to summon and direct tornado-force winds, at least that I know about, in our bag of tricks at Icarus.

In a continuum of effortless motion, the Fae crouches forward (pressing me right back against his chest) and unspools the reins in a liquid parabola to give the green his head. His dragon extends and flies like blazes for the city by the sea, wingbeats still ragged from when I harpooned him.

I crane to look over the Fae's shoulder, but that brown dragon's clearly had enough. He's in full retreat, flying in a scrambling panic for the volcano. We're close enough to Mt. Vesuvius over there to see the sides pitted with caves, both large and small, many with steam curling from their mouths. The brown darts into one of the big ones and disappears inside.

I'm used to dragon shifters, but I don't think the green can shift, and clearly the Fae needs those reins to control him. But at least the green seems, like, domesticated.

That brown was nothing tame and nothing human.

"Sweet Jesus," I breathe. "Guess you got feral dragons on this island, huh?"

Of course, there's no answer. But now I know this guy can talk when he wants, I'm ready to be persistent.

In fact, I'm ready to be a goddamn nuisance.

"Why'd that brown attack us?" Hearing nothing but the wind and a whole lot of silence, I twist around to give him the stink eye. "Oh, c'mon, seriously? I know you can understand me and I know you can talk. That cat's totally out of the bag. So you might as well answer. Why'd that brown come after us like that? I mean, what was he after?"

Through the helm, the guy's completely inscrutable. But I know he's watching. I can feel him watching.

The feel of him watching makes me sweat.

At last, he unbends enough to give me a single word, sliced by an accent sharp as a razor, spoken in a voice like gray silk.

"Dinner."

Ho-ly shit.

Yup. Definitely not in Kansas anymore, Dorothy.

Apparently, in this reality, the dragons eat you.

The sooner I figure out how to ditch this guy, click my heels together three times, and fly back home to my warlocks, the happier—and the safer—I'm gonna be.

Chapter Twelve
Maxim

"Neo?" I clear my throat and try again. "Neo Mercury. Can you hear me?"

Worry gnaws at me like a wyvern gnawing on a bone. Worry for Neo lying senseless on the ground. Worry for Zara and her unknown fate. Worry for our mates left behind to wait. Worry for my own depleted state.

If I do not control this worry, I will spiral into useless panic.

To prevent this, I focus all my attention on Neo. He is the only problem I can currently do anything to solve.

Although that is only if I am lucky.

Restless and flushed with fever, my sovereign's fated mate lies unconscious, as he has done now for hours without waking. He is huddled, defenseless on his side, on the floor of this cave I was fortunate to find.

We have taken shelter in the flank of this volcanic mountain, in a cave that is dry and snug and small enough to prevent the feral and hostile dragons who inhabit this strange island from entering.

Clearly we are not the first people who have ever sheltered here. There is a pile of dusty furs, half decayed but still usable, that I have carefully arranged into a nest for Neo. Mineral water trickles over rock into a pool in the rear, warm and sulfurous, but drinkable. The steamy air blunts the worst of this bitter cold, for which neither of us are suitably dressed.

But the most obvious sign of prior human habitation is the cloudy white crystal I have found in a niche which flares into cool white light at my touch. That crystal is still glowing, emitting a soft but steady light— a magical light, though this is a strange magic I do not know—that pushes back the shadows as darkness falls.

By this pale light, I take stock of our situation.

In a word, it is grim.

Truly, Neo is not well.

Bitterly I curse myself for yet another failure. My curses echo against these rocky walls, dense with painted cave art that moves and breathes in this witchy light.

These painted walls are alive with dragons. Dragons diving, dragons flaming, dragons rending. Black dragons breathing fire, brown dragons tearing flesh, green dragons spewing acid.

My newly healed side throbs with remembered agony.

There are even blue dragons breathing lightning, they are lightning dragons like my sovereign. At home they are rare, but here they seem common. My chest clenches with desperate worry for my Zara. My skin itches and my senses sing with the need for *haste, haste, haste…*

And yet.

I will go nowhere without Neo.

I will not abandon him while he is helpless.

Saint Sergius guard me. I should never have yielded to Neo's plea and brought him. During our desperate flight through the portal, through the blizzard, through all those dangerous hours when that flight of feral brown dragons hunted us through the snows with ruthless persistence, I was forced to extremes of flight that left poor Neo clinging miserably to my crest, heaving until his belly was empty, too sick even to scream.

By the time I found this shelter, shifted to my human form, and carried him inside, he was limp and boneless in my arms as a corpse.

Now I have dragged these old furs close to the hot spring for warmth and arranged Neo with care among them. For he is not dressed to survive these frigid temperatures. I should have insisted he bring a coat. Boots. Gloves. Hat.

In all ways, I have failed him.

He is precious. He is cherished. He is adored by all our mates. He is sweetness and love and innocence.

I have not protected him as he deserves.

In truth, I am in little better state than he, although at least I am conscious and ambulatory. I am hungry and weary and cold. I bless Neo's foresight and his thoughtfulness for stowing Ronin's leather pants in my saddlebag, or I would be bare-assed in this chill. I even found one of

Ronin's discarded button-downs, rumpled with half the buttons missing, forgotten in the bottom of this saddlebag. It offers little warmth, but it is far better than going shirtless, exposing the shame of my scarred back to whatever we encounter here. So I have gratefully claimed this garment.

The familiar aromas of Ronin's ambergris fragrance and Vasili's butterscotch mating scent waft from the silky fabric. These enticing scents make me all the more frantic to return to my mates.

But there will be no leaving this strange land until we find Zara.

No leaving until she leaves with us.

No leaving until we can determine exactly how we blundered into this strange realm, and exactly how we can leave.

And none of that will be possible until Neo has roused from his stupor.

"Neo Mercury? Are you well?" I hunker on my heels and lay a careful hand on his broad shoulder. Fever seeps through his tee shirt to warm my palm.

Still, he does not wake.

Frowning, I uncoil to my feet and stalk to the mouth of the cave. The icy wind curls around me like a whip. It cuts into my unprotected skin and lashes my long hair in stinging tendrils against my face.

I twist my hair into a hasty braid, then hug myself tight for warmth.

No matter if I am freezing. I am Russian. We do not fear the cold.

We have sheltered high above this island, and the earlier blizzard has passed. Now I stand sentinel above an icy tundra, like the frozen steppes of my lonely youth, a landscape that glows blue and violet under icy stars whose constellations look nothing like those we are learning from Mistress Agrippina in Astrology class.

Above the inky sea, a full moon is rising.

In its fullness, the sight of that swollen silvery orb strikes me like a blow. For the moon is dark at Icarus.

In this place, even the skies are foreign.

The sight stirs in me a deep disquiet. This landscape is bleak, but it is not lifeless. An aurora of pale lights, like the one in our cave, glows and pulses near the midnight coast. That is where I will find that stark alabaster city with its sharp shining spires that I glimpsed from the skies.

Tomorrow, when we have rested, we must go there.

I know in my bones that city is where I will find my Zara.

The distant scream of a hunting dragon makes my own beast snarl and slither beneath my skin. This is not the long shrill cry that sounds like a woman's scream from those brown nuisances with their tearing claws, but the nails-on-chalkboard squeal I have heard once before.

That is the cry of the green dragon, back on Icarus, before he sprayed me with his acid.

I have seen many feral greens from a distance. Very likely, this is another, and not the one I seek. Still, my pulse hammers with urgency and my senses scream with fear for my sovereign, alone in this terrible place.

Stones cut into my bare feet as I hurry into the cave to kneel again at Neo's side. His clean-cut face is flushed with fever, fair skin glistening with sweat, soft curls tangled from the wind.

While he is awake, I would never touch him. Vasili is his alpha, and he is jealous and possessive of this one to the point of violence. (At least where I am concerned.) He shares Neo with all the others.

I alone am forbidden to touch.

In this unresolved business between Vasili and me, this armed standoff of alpha loving alpha, neither of us able to yield, the strained distance that yawns between Neo and me has become a dangerous casualty. One that may still prove fatal.

But Vasili is not here now.

This once, I will permit myself to touch.

Gently I stroke those soft curls away from Neo's damp brow, then trail my fingers over his flushed cheek. His jaw is sandpaper bristly, for of course he has not shaved. I tell myself I am checking his temperature, which is true.

But also, I am touching him for comfort.

His comfort.

And my comfort.

He sighs in his sleep and turns his hot face into my rough palm, as he would never do while awake. With all his generous heart and his yielding body, he loves all the others. But to me, he is indifferent. My chest aches with yearning.

Rubbing my aching chest absently with my free hand, I try to form a plan. Here we have shelter and water, but no food. We are strong, a day without food will not kill us. But tomorrow without fail, I must hunt or steal to fill our bellies. I am no thief, I am the Sagittarius prince, and my pride rebels at the notion of sinking to thievery.

Still, there is no doubt we will need all our strength to survive this hostile place. Our sovereign needs my strength, not my pride, to save her.

Despite the hot spring that radiates warmth, this night air is crisp. I tuck the old fur around Neo's shoulders, but he pushes it fretfully away.

I offer him water from the spring, which I have collected in a discarded plastic bottle I found crumpled with Ronin's shirt. Without drinking, Neo mumbles and turns his face away.

There is nothing more I can do for him. Except pray for mercy to the Russian saints and the Orthodox God in whose pitiless faith I was raised.

"Please wake up, Neo," I whisper, wretched with worry, slipping into my native tongue. "*Diy Bog, pozhalusta,* do not take him."

The moon crawls into view, framed in the cave's deep mouth. As the cold light spills across his face, Neo pushes the furs down around his hips and starts plucking restlessly at his shirt. His brow furrows and he mumbles, "Hot… *off…*"

Clearly, he is overheated. But this cave is too cold to undress him.

"Neo, I am here." I grip his hands to quiet him. "I am here."

He breathes a deep sigh, as though my words soothe him. The next moment, one restless hand twists free from my grasp and fumbles down his stomach to wrap around his dick.

My gaze veers from his flushed and fretful face to the considerable bulge he is cupping, outlined beneath his pajama pants. Then my stare shoots to the full moon.

That moon was full on Icarus when Zara first bit him.

Neo moans, long and low.

But this is not a moan of illness.

He kneads his dick through his pants and arches into his fist. My inner dragon stirs and rumbles with interest.

He is appealing, yes? my dragon hisses, in that way only I can hear. *You desire this one. You know a better way than words to wake him.*

"Now is not the time," I mutter. "He is no Sleeping Beauty. And I am not that kind of prince. I do not wake enchanted sleepers with a kiss. Besides, I am nothing he wants. He is Vasili's—"

Without warning, Neo gasps. His eyes flash open, vivid green in the moonlight. Blurry and unfocused (because I have removed his glasses), his gaze darts over the lurid paintings that flicker around us, lingers on the odd glowing crystal in its niche, then flies to my worried face.

"Slava Bogu," I say fervently. Glory to God. "Neo, you are safe. We are alone and you are safe. Tomorrow, without fail, we will find Zara. Now I will bring you water."

His gaze moves over my face, from my anxious eyes to my parted lips. Then he studies my chest, half-exposed due to the missing buttons in Ronin's shirt. My nipple piercings gleam in the witchy light.

His hips rise and his powerful frame arches and he grinds his dick into his own tight grip. His reddish brows draw together and he bites his lip. Color rushes into his face.

This is no fever. He is blushing.

"Um," he whispers, still clutching my hand so I cannot move away. "Wow. Hi, Max."

"Neo." I struggle to put words together in a way he will understand. At times like these, I wish my English could be less labored. "The moon…"

His body writhes under the furs until he kicks them free. Even as he bucks into his own fist, jacking himself through his pants, his intelligent eyes are apologetic.

"I think I'm having a microheat," Neo says meekly.

I stare. Clearly he does not understand what is happening, but I do. Christ.

I am alpha, and he is in need, and I have long harbored… feelings for him. My own skin is heating, my groin is tingling, my barbed dragon cock is rising to push against these leather pants that encase me.

Suddenly, these pants are far too tight.

"This is no microheat." Struggling to think, my brain slots the pieces into place. He was bitten by two shifters less than a month ago, and the moon in this place is full. "Your first superheat is starting."

His eyes cloud in confusion and he nibbles at his lower lip. "But… but I don't have superheats."

"Neo Mercury, you are Kryll. And multiple shifters have bitten you. No one knows what you will have. If your superheat is starting, there is no preventing it." Desperate, I glance toward the cave mouth. "We must… we must bring you to Zara. Wherever she may be, we must find her."

I try to rise, but he clings to my hand.

"We can't get to her in time," he says miserably. "What I'm feeling, it's, well, intense. I can't wait. If I can't break this heat on my own, if I'm not, uh, serviced… will I die?"

Damn this wretched alpha rivalry between me and Vasili. Our mate is in need. What Neo needs specifically is the biochemical hit of my alpha shifter semen to shatter his mating heat.

Clearly, tonight, what he needs is me.

A sudden rush of purpose makes my skin tingle. The air floods with the scorched smell of brimstone.

That is my mating scent.

"You will not die." My dragon lurks in my voice. "I will break your heat myself."

His jaw drops and heat rushes into his face until he is blushing to his hairline. Then his eyes flash with a look of injured pride. That is a look I recognize.

"You? But… Maxim… you don't even *like* me." His tone manages to be both belligerent and plaintive.

I close my eyes and mutter, "Saints of the northern steppes, grant me patience. I… I like you well enough."

In truth, I like him far too much. But that is a secret I will never share.

Or I will trigger Vasili's rage.

Neo releases my hand and pushes me away. His voice acquires a note of stubbornness. "Well, I mean, you don't like me that way. I'm not some charity case, you know? I don't need, like, a sympathy fuck." His voice hardens. "I'll just take care of it myself… *ooooh*…"

The last word unravels on a long sexy groan. My eyes fly open to find he has shoved a hand under his waistband to knead his naked length.

Under Ronin's pants, my barbs shoot out to hook into the leather.

Mother of God.

I want this boy so badly, I have wanted him so long, my dragon cock will not even wait until I am inside him to engage.

When I am well pleased, those barbs lock me tight inside my mate for hours.

Beyond any doubt, this one will please me.

No force under Heaven will keep him from me.

I struggle to articulate this, to tell him what he needs to know. "Neo, I am alpha. I am the only alpha here, but I am what you need. It is only… if you will allow this… I will not be quick. You have seen me when our mates are in heat, have you not?"

"Yeah. I've seen you with Zara and Ronin when you, um, hook in?" He licks his lips. "Would you hook into me like that?"

"Yes," I say ruthlessly. "I will mount you from behind, and my barbed dragon cock will lock inside you. Then we will be… inseparable… for many hours. All night long, in the moonlight, we will rut. Sometimes we will sleep, but still my barb will not release you. Again and again, I will pump into you and pleasure you and fill you to overflowing with my dragon seed. Finally, when I have given you many orgasms, when you are drowsy with pleasure, when you are limp and dripping with your spend and mine, this will break your superheat."

"Wow." His lips part and he blinks up at me. He looks dazed at the prospect. In his needing, his leaf-green eyes pulse with heat. "That's… a lot. A lot to wrap my head around. And it's a lot to ask from you, Max. Especially when you don't even like me."

"Well." Discreetly I adjust my anatomy down below. "I do not… dislike you. Much." He seems unconvinced, so I rush ahead. "It will be no great hardship. Believe me."

Still, to my intense frustration, he digs in his heels. "So this would just be some pity fuck? Tell me the truth."

How can I explain to him, this is anything but pity? I need him as badly as he needs me. His heat has already sent my dragon spiraling into rut.

We are mad with wanting him.

But this, I cannot confess.

Surely, if our joining is nothing more than biology, if I am nothing more to him than some random alpha, conveniently placed to service his superheat, Vasili will forgive.

Even if Vasili is not normally the forgiving sort.

Firmly I grip Neo's masturbating hand to stop him from spilling in his only pair of pants. I lock onto his stare—embarrassed but defiant— and give my alpha free rein.

"Neo Theodophilus Mercury, will you stop arguing and asking questions. It is time to take off your pants."

Chapter Thirteen
Zara

I don't get another word from Mr. Taciturn behind me till we get to where we're going.

And believe me, it's not because I haven't tried.

By the time we're winging our way over Unseelie City down there and our dragon starts his descent from cruising altitude, darkness is dropping like a shroud. Cold blue lights glow from a hundred windows, between cruel towers sharp as spears, set in glittery white walls with harsh angles that look chiseled from ice.

"Through dangers untold and hardships unnumbered," I mumble, because there's nothing like a few lines from David Bowie's *Labyrinth* for comfort when I'm missing my guys, "I have fought my way here to the castle beyond the goblin city…"

Mr. Green back there doesn't answer (big surprise). By now I'm fucking hoarse from shouting questions into this shrieking wind. His dragon's labored breaths are getting louder, and I'd almost feel bad for that thing, if he hadn't tried to off Maxim.

When Mr. Green leans back on the reins, the dragon's head arrows down. We plummet from the sky like a stone.

I barely manage to throttle back a scream, because I'm not gonna give this jerk the goddamn satisfaction. But my inner dragon lets loose with a good bellow that ricochets around my soul and lights me up like a pinball machine.

Yeah, not so much. Guess she's a control freak like me.

She doesn't like flying when she's not the pilot.

The wind rakes my face and screams in my ears as we plunge

straight toward a quiver of pointy spires and witch's hat towers, bracketed by slanty rooftops with ridgepoles sharp as razors. Sweet Jesus, we're gonna splatter like watermelons when we hit. They're gonna have to scrape us off that roof with a trowel—

At the literal last second, the green veers and wings toward a terrace the size of a helicopter landing pad. He lands heavily, all clumsy with exhaustion and probably blood loss, clearly woozy from when he and I went at it. In fact, he stumbles and almost falls, then just stands swaying, slumped and heaving for air.

Between my knees, I can actually feel that dragon trembling.

This time I can't suppress a twinge of pity.

Shit.

We've barely stopped moving before the Fae uncoils from our shared dragon saddle and springs to the ground.

That's when I realize, this whole time, the guy hasn't even been strapped in. This throne-slash-saddle thing only has one set of fighting straps.

And he's buckled those around me.

My stupid heart gives another stupid ping. But I'm not gonna be an idiot about this. He's probably keeping me alive to torture me or something.

Even encased in that scaly green armor, the Fae moves like a whirlwind, unbuckling his heavy fur cloak and letting it fall carelessly to the flagstones as he sweeps past. He's one hundred percent focused on his dragon.

His injured dragon.

An injury I inflicted.

Damn it, I'm *so* not gonna feel bad about this. That thing could've blinded Max.

Jesus, what even happened to Max? And Neo?

The Fae strips off his green leather gauntlets and lets them fall. His naked hand, slender and graceful as a girl's, glides over the dragon's scaly shoulder in a way that looks comforting as he circles around to the front.

Right before this flying Godzilla blocks my view, the Fae pulls off his scary-ass helmet.

But, shit, the way this dragon's parked, I can't see a thing. Even given that blue-white glow that looks electrical, but probably isn't, seeping from the big cavern in front of us.

I give myself a good shake and start working on the buckles that strap me into this saddle.

A low word that sounds like a Fae curse floats back from up front. The dragon flinches and lets out a low keening moan.

"Ash!" the Fae bellows.

Shit. Is that a curse or a name? I work faster on those buckles. Especially when my shifty senses pick up the distant thud of running feet.

Someone's definitely coming.

I pick up the pace and rip the buckles open. The last one's stubborn as fuck. Muttering my own curse, I shift my gaze from the cavern to focus on my task.

That's when I realize I'm wearing something funky. Thick silver bracelets, one on each wrist, forged in this interlocking vines-and-thorns setup. They're really pretty. Heck, they're actually exquisite.

But it's like the things are soldered shut around my wrists. I can't see an escape hatch.

I take one look and my inner dragon hisses. The word explodes in my brain from nowhere.

Handcuffs.

Panic detonates in my heart like a grenade.

If there's one goddamn thing I hate, it's being locked down against my will, while someone else makes my choices for me. Which means Mr. Silent up there's pushing every single one of my buttons—

"For moon's sake," the Fae mutters, still hidden from view by his dragon. *"Ash!"*

The green dragon keens for emphasis. Inside the cavern, a door slams. Then booted steps are pounding across the floor and bouncing off the cavern walls in sharp rocky echoes.

Whatever's coming sounds… huge.

Jesus. I shake free of my daze, rip the last buckle open, swing my leg across the saddle, and leap down to the terrace like a Marvel Avenger to land in a crouch (because cat burglar).

That's where I'm hanging when the newbie bursts into view.

Sweet.

Fuck.

That's gotta be the biggest fucking male I've ever seen.

He's maybe not quite as tall as Vasili, but this guy's just… *built.*

He's got muscles on top of muscles, flexing delts and bulging biceps and powerful chest, all on impressive display, laced into this gray doeskin leather vest. Slate leather pants cling to sinewy hips and corded thighs in a way that *screams* sex. Fur-trimmed leather boots and a belt with a wicked-looking long knife complete the desired effect.

He's Conan the Barbarian.

Unlike Conan, this guy's got a head of spiky pewter hair and silver eyes that glitter like diamonds. His hard face isn't young, he's got some years on him. But the tips of his ears are definitely pointy. An elaborate tattoo of knotted vines and thorns winds around one thick bicep, complete with drops of crimson that drip from the inky spikes. Those arms of his could snap me in two like a matchstick.

But first, he'll have to catch me.

Showtime, showgirl. Time to vamoose.

I shoot to my feet with adrenaline spurting through every synapse. In my human form, there's nowhere for me to vamoose, because this terrace is perched high above the windy cobblestone streets and rooftops, and somewhere through that cavern looks like the only way to exit stage left.

Lucky for me I don't have to exit stage left on foot—

"Sparrowhawk?" After a single hard look that takes me in from nose to toes and misses nofuckingthing, the newbie's gaze dismisses me and shoots straight to the Fae with the dragon. Whose name, I guess, must be Sparrowhawk. "Nice of you to turn up before I had to send out the posse, kid. Queen's so pissed she's spitting blood—"

"Xhevith is injured." The Fae's precise voice slices through this Ash guy's Midwestern twangy *hi-how-are-ya* like a stropped razor. "Cold iron. Barely missed his heart by a breath. Fetch me a healing potion. Quickly."

The newbie's sharp eyes narrow and the lines carved in that rugged brow dig deeper. He takes one look at whatever's doing up front with that dragon, then pivots on his heel and vanishes into the cavern.

Moving pretty damn quick for a big guy.

Duly noted.

Well, I'm outtie. Time to seize my moment while everyone's all distracted and summon my inner dragon. I spin toward the open air and wait for the sweeping tingle of my shift to sweep over me.

And wait.

And *wait*.

Zara. My dragon queen sounds unusually subdued. Even meek. *I cannot rise.*

What. The. Fuck.

We are wearing charmed silver. It is moon magic. Until it is removed, I cannot rise.

A sudden surge of fury erupts in my chest, so strong it leaves me lightheaded. Heat rushes into my face.

What the actual *fuck*—

"Moon and stars, Ash. Will you *hurry*." The Fae's voice snaps around me and spins me back. I still can't see the guy, just his horned helmet propped upright on the ground.

In a rage, I tear at the bracelets on my wrists. But I can't find the clasp, and they're too tight to slip off.

What do you wanna bet this charmed silver's also fucking with my lightning magic? When I tried summoning lightning to fend off that brown dragon, I barely got a fizzle.

"Sorry to keep you hanging, Your Transcendence." The big guy, whose name is apparently Ash (because it's not like anyone's bothered to make an intro), sounds totally unfazed by his buddy in a towering temper. The newbie reappears with a little silver pot gripped in his capable-looking hands and schlepps it over to the dragon.

The Fae's green-sleeved arm darts into view and snatches the pot.

"Poor Xhev." The big guy—Ash—runs a practiced palm over the dragon's scaly shoulder, and the green whines softly. "Nailed ya a good one, didn't she, buddy?"

Jesus. I refuse to feel bad about this. I'm the wronged party here. I've literally just been kidnapped. Plus that green dragon tried to kill Max.

I'm still tearing at the bracelets, ready to chew off my own hands to get rid of them, when the newbie's diamond-sharp eyes swerve to me. A lotta those big muscly guys aren't too bright, at least that's the stereotype.

But I know right away this one's something else.

He's different.

There's a clever brain behind that shrewd gaze.

"You're gonna wanna take it easy on those bracelets, princess," the big guy drawls. "I made 'em to be comfy for ya. But that can change real easy. And, tell you true, I'm kinda tempted. You've already taken a big piece outta Xhevith and pissed His Radiance right off."

At least this guy's willing to talk. Even if it's only to issue threats.

"Well, isn't that just too bad." I plant my booted legs and brace my hands on my hips. Because the thing to do right now is brazen this out till I'm back in the driver's seat. I'm still wearing my utility belt, which is a positive, and I wonder how thoroughly His, uh, Radiance went through it while I was *non compos mentis*. "Cry me a river, big man."

"This one's got a mouth on her," Ash observes, presumably to the still unseen Sparrowhawk. "Won't that be a change around here."

"Guess His Radiance is used to being deferred to, huh?" I tilt my head. "Well, that sucks. I've got a funny habit of not deferring to guys who fucking kidnap me."

The big guy rubs a weathered hand over his square jaw. If I didn't know better, I'd think he was maybe suppressing a grin. His silver eyes take their time roaming over me, from my messy teal braid to the curves encased in my catsuit to my defiant stance in my platform boots.

Despite the permanent chill in the wind that's still whipping past this terrace, my pulse gets jumpy and my skin heats up.

For no good reason.

What.

So.

Ever.

This guy's already admitted he aided and abetted his buddy in my kidnapping. Plus he's way too old for me. I mean, he's older than Lucius. He's ancient. So it totally does not matter that he's hot.

No, really. It doesn't.

"Yeah, they're not used to your type around here." Now this guy Ash sounds thoughtful. "Lucky for you that healing potion was brewed under a new moon. Iron or no iron, it's gonna patch our boy Xhev right up."

Well, not for long, new moon or blue moon. Busting out of this rat trap's gonna result in some serious collateral damage.

But I've never been afraid of that.

Ash is still watching me, and I really hope he's no telepath. But maybe he can read my face. Because he gives me a slow nod that isn't totally lacking respect. "Queen of the witching world, huh?"

So they do know who I am, but I was already taking that as a given. Whatever's going on around here, my nabbing wasn't a random thing.

I've got a definite feeling the radiant Sparrowhawk up there doesn't do random. And he doesn't do impulsive.

That guy's a stone-cold planner.

"That's me." I agree to the whole identity thing, because why not. I own it. My booted toe taps the pavement. "I'm a little unclear who you are."

"Oh geez, where are my manners?" The big guy's diamond eyes assess me. "I'm Ash."

I wait for more, but I figure I'm lucky to get that much. Names hold power, we learn that first thing in Common Magics class. We use names for Compulsion spells. And I read in the *Monster Book of Monsters* that the Fae keep their true names secret.

Still, I need to keep the info coming. "You're, uh, one of the Dark Fae, right?"

"Nope, I'm Light Fae. Seelie. Born and raised up proper in your world, like the rest of my folks. We're pretty good at blending in with the normals, just your regular average joes. Here, I'm just a guest." His hard face turns canny. "Permanent guest though. Just like you're gonna be, true?"

Yeah, no. Not true. Not planning on it.

"So, what, did His Radiance kidnap you too, big man?" I ask, though somehow that doesn't seem likely.

With literally zero warning, His Radiance slips into view.

Which means suddenly I've got a full frontal of maybe five and a half feet tops of coldly furious Dark Fae dragonrider.

He's no taller than I am, but he's slim and sinewy under that scaly green armor that fits him like dragonhide. Those crossed swords jutting over his shoulders make him seem bigger and way more formidable. A silky curtain of moss-green hair sweeps past his shoulders and swirls around him in the breeze, held back from his cruel face by a couple of skinny braids he's twisted into a coronet. That fashion choice gives me a good eyeful of his wickedly pointy ears and the green eyepatch that slices across his forehead and covers one socket.

His exposed eye, the exact color of creamy jade and the exact temperature of arctic ice, burns into me like frostbite.

He slingshots the words in my direction, with a liquid accent and a sibilant hiss. "I stole him from the Seelie realm. Just as I have stolen you. Whatsoever an Unseelie Fae covets for himself, he steals."

Wow. I try to wrap my head around what he's saying. Like whether that word choice—*covet*—means here what it would in my world. I can't tell because he's weird, there's like a culture gap between us, but he's hard to look away from.

My gaze ping-pongs between these guys.

There's definitely, like, an electric charge in the air. But I'm literally a lightning witch. There's always an electric charge in the air when I'm around.

"Geez Louise." The big guy rolls his eyes at His Radiance and gives a good-natured groan. "Throttle back a little on the melodrama, will ya, kid? You're not some kinda brute who just knocked me upside the noggin and tossed me over your shoulder, are ya?"

Mr. Green's lip curls in a snarl that exposes one sharp little fang. "You fought me."

"Oh yeah, sure, but I wasn't exactly giving it my all, was I?" Ash shrugs his big shoulders. Somehow I get the definite sense they've covered this terrain before.

The Dark Fae's single eye narrows dangerously. "You stabbed me. I still bear the scar."

Ash gives him a wry grimace. "Enough with all the fighting and stabbing. C'mon, Sparrowhawk, you're gonna upset the princess."

Guess that's my cue to get back in the convo.

"Too late." I fold my arms across my chest and cock my hip. "Seriously. I'm already upset—and *don't* call me princess. I mean it. I'm Zara. You're Ash. The dragon's Xhevith. And I guess Mr. Charming here is Sparrowhawk?"

The Dark Fae levels me with a highly suspicious look. Clearly, I'm getting his name over his dead and decomposing but possibly immortal Fae body.

Ash gives an easy chuckle. "Nah, that's just what I call him. Pretty much since he was a tyke. With everyone else, His Resplendence here mostly goes by his title. You know, the formal one."

I wait, but that intel's not forthcoming. "So, what, I'm supposed to be picking that up telepathically or something?"

I guess he doesn't appreciate my snark, because the Dark Fae pivots away with an eloquent grunt and beelines for the cavern. Which gives me a proper look at those slender swords crisscrossed over his rigid shoulders, that silky swirl of moss-green hair that reaches halfway down his narrow back… and the flex of his impressively tight ass.

Whoa. That scaly green armor fits the tight flex of that ass like Underoos.

In fact, I'm so distracted by the view that I almost miss the words. But the dragonrider's glacial voice floats back to me like snow on the wind.

"I am Zephyr. The Unseelie King."

Chapter Fourteen
Neo

Max wants me to take off my pants.

Oh Lord. I just can't seem to get past that statement.

Honestly speaking, this entire so-called rescue mission has been a total nightmare. I've slowed Max down way more than I've helped him.

And now, thanks to my messed-up Kryll hormonal cycle and something Max keeps trying to tell me about the moon, I guess I'm going into heat.

Apparently it's my first superheat.

Normally I'd be, well, over the moon. But given our current situation, my heat is just gonna be one more distraction I'm causing for Max, who already has so much riding on his shoulders.

Yay.

At home, me having a superheat would be so special. Zara would make a major fuss over me that would be totally adorable, and the guys (minus Max, I mean) would be all over me. Here, I'm only getting in the way, and making it harder for Max to help Zara.

"That's it then," I sigh, trying not to look at Max's expectant face as he hovers over me, all resigned to helping me through this mess even though I absolutely don't turn him on. "Max, you better just leave me here. Go find Zara. You can either come back for me later, or I'll catch up to you when I'm, uh, finished…"

My words trail off because one, Max lets out this godawful snarl, and two, my first peak is starting.

You know that moment when you're right on the edge of coming, and your heart is racing and your face is hot and your skin is tingly and your whole body is jacked till you're practically levitating off the bed? That moment when (if you're a guy) your balls draw up tight and every shred of sensation in your entire body rushes to your cock?

So, yeah. I'm totally having that moment.

Right in front of Max.

"Ohmygosh," I gasp, just gripping my base as hard as I can under my pants and hoping like heck I don't spill right in front of him like I'm still a virgin or something. "Max—please—I need privacy—like, *now*!"

"For someone who is First Boy on the Dean's List, tonight you are not so bright." Max's voice lowers to a gravelly growl. "I am going nowhere. Take off your pants."

Good grief.

I'm normally a patient guy, but I'm definitely not feeling patient tonight. This big pigheaded dragon is just too loyal and too stubborn to leave me.

The thing is, in this condition, I'm way too impatient to wait.

He's looming right over me with his hair pulled back in that sleek *bratva* braid that makes him look so ruthless, wearing Ronin's clothes with the shirt unbuttoned to expose his silver nipple piercings and his sexy suntanned chest, and he's pumping out this brimstone-and-cinnamon scent of aggression that makes the situation in my pants even worse.

"Was gonna say I can't do this in front of you," I tell him in a rush, "but I mean it, I can't wait. So it's happening. Can you at least, like, go outside or something?"

I almost never lose my temper, just ask anyone in our polycule.

But honestly, he's literally asking for it.

"I have already said I am going nowhere." Geez, every time I push back, his voice drops another octave. That dragonish growl of his wraps around my throbbing junk and squeezes. "Take off your pants."

My temper goes off like a popped balloon.

"Fine." I shove my pajama pants and briefs down my hips and my junk springs free, all flushed and veiny and swollen with need. He growls again at the sight, like maybe I just offended him or something, but too bad. He asked for it. I kick the hot flannel impatiently down my legs and peel my tee shirt over my head while I'm at it, because there's nothing dorkier than a guy with a hard-on who's only wearing a shirt.

Now, for sure, he'll be outtie.

I mean, sure, we share a bed—Zara's bed—but with all the activity that goes on in that bed on a nightly basis, he pretty much manages to ignore my whole sex life. Right now? Just the thought of how totally he manages to ignore me, and how desperately I wish he wouldn't, is so infuriating.

Not to mention embarrassing as heck.

"There, I'm all nakey. You happy now?" I know I'm being childish, but I'm in heat, for cripes' sake. I glare up at him with my face just flaming.

I'm being so bratty that I guess I'm finally annoying him too. His topaz dragon gaze roams over my naked body with his pupils slitted in this intense and menacing way that just makes me hotter.

Then his gaze lifts to my face and his brow furrows. "You are angry."

"Gosh, you think?" I squeeze my eyes shut tight so I can pretend this is less embarrassing than it is. Somehow I muster one last Herculean effort and manage to let go of my dick.

Just for a sec, so I can think.

"Sorry." I heave a sigh. "Ugh. I know I'm being annoying."

"Annoying?" His startled tone pries my eyes open. He's literally crouching over me, with his face all broody and his shirt slipping off one sinewy shoulder and his golden skin twitching, like his dragon's about to pounce.

"Neo Mercury," he says slowly, "the word I would use is not annoying. No. You are… alluring."

Huh?

Me?

Comprehension rides to my rescue in a rush. Okay, now I get it. He's a total alpha, he's as alpha as they come, which means my heat is triggering his dragon.

That's all this is. Just shifter biology.

It's Genetics of Witchcraft 101.

And I've always been a good student.

I swallow down this stupid sense of disappointment that tastes bitter on my tongue as aspirin.

Still, I manage to man up and say the decent thing, as kindly as I can, even though my heat is raging. "You go on outside, Max. I'm not really who you want. I'll just, um, give a holler or something when I'm finished—"

That's as far as I get before he snarls again and lunges to shut me up with a ferocious kiss.

Wow.

I was totally *not* expecting to be kissed.

I actually kissed him once before, you know, early on, before I realized he wasn't into me? In my defense, that was the first morning we all woke up together in Zara's bed, and we were both half asleep at the time.

This time, we're both wide awake. And his kiss is, like, scorching. His lips are hard and hot and totally relentless. My mouth is open because I'm in the middle of explaining things to him, so his tongue surges right in and finds mine in a long slow lick. He tastes like sulfur and cinnamon and he kisses me like he's claiming me, he's just devouring my mouth and sucking on my tongue and, wow, his fangs are descending in a hurry. Which means he means business.

Or at least, his dragon thinks he does.

But I know better.

This is just biology.

I try to back off so he can pull himself together. Instead, he grips my jaw in his callused hand to deepen the kiss. I give a muffled squeak of surprise and protest.

"Max… please…" I mumble, somewhere between returning his kisses and tonguing his fangs (because OMG, I have a major fang fetish. Gosh, if only he would bite me.) "Trust me on this one… you don't really want this… you only… think you do."

One sharp canine nips my lower lip hard enough to sting and sends an instant pulse of heat through my boner. Even though it's not the mating bite I'm craving, my hips rise right off the furs I'm lying on. I barely manage to reel myself in so I don't come all over him.

"Listen, Max, I mean it—"

"Will you stop trying to send me away," he mutters between kisses, sounding really ornery. "I am exactly where I need to be."

Oh Lordy. He's gone. His super-shifty alpha hormones have totally taken over.

And me? I'm gone too. Even while I'm trying to persuade him to leave, I've got one hand wrapped in his braid and one hand gripping his shirt to pull him in closer.

When I realize he's fumbling with his zipper, my heart starts pounding like I'm running a four-minute mile. My junk's so hard for him I'm afraid I'm going to come just from smelling him and tasting him, before he even touches me down there. And maybe that would be for the best? If I come on my own, if I'm not triggering his alpha, maybe then he won't feel like he needs to—

The buzz of his zipper hits my hormonally heightened senses like a grenade going off.

He's pushing his leather pants down his hips and my hands are just totally operating without any direction from my head to unbutton his shirt and spread my palms over his sleek hot skin. His abs are all tight and ripply and his heart is racing (all those alpha instincts for someone he doesn't even like must be really hard to handle) and there's a lot of mating scent coming off him.

Like, a lot.

This is all honestly more than I can resist. My fingers skim his nipples and give his piercings a careful twist. Because Zara really likes that when I play with hers, and I know from covertly watching him with our mates that he likes it too. He hisses under my touch.

"Is this okay for you?" I mumble, just to check.

"Sweet," he groans into our kiss. "So sweet. You taste… like you smell."

Huh. I guess that means I taste like sage and hand-milled lavender bath soap, which just sounds icky.

But he absolutely does not seem to mind.

His tongue tangles with mine like he can't get enough of the (apparently soapy) way I taste. Finally, he covers me with his whole body the way I'm craving, the way an alpha should. I squirm against him happily, feeling for the first time the hot prick of his barbed cock, like a devil's forked tail, nudging all eager and insistent between my thighs. I let my knees fall open to give him what the alpha side of him wants, which is, basically, my submission.

The instant our cocks touch, my heat takes over. I moan and hump against him with absolutely zero restraint. My orgasm is boiling at the base of my spine. Gosh, when I come, it's gonna be major.

He works a hand between us and wraps his hot fingers around our cocks, lining us up together in a way that makes us both moan. The way his barb scrapes against my shaft totally gives me the shivers, and I know from watching him with our mates that his pointy parts are super sensitive. Right now, goosebumps break out down his arms from the friction.

Okay then.

He's just gonna have to live with this after.

It'll just be a one-time thing.

No biggie.

Even though my idiot heart is already feeling all achy-breaky and doesn't seem to be getting the memo about this being a temporary situation and definitely not the start of a romance.

I push his shirt off his shoulders, but I'm super careful not to touch his scarred back. He's really sensitive there, I mean emotionally, because his mom used to whip him, and so far he's only let Zara and Ronin touch him there. Usually he won't even tolerate Vasili standing behind him (and this is one thing V doesn't push on), but those two still have all that unresolved alpha crap to deal with.

Max burrows between my thighs and I grip his shoulders and my body is absolutely ready if he wants to burrow deeper, my knees coming up, my abs flexing, my hips angling to offer him my hole—

"Neo." He cups my face between his rough palms, even while his hips are pumping and his dick is rubbing against me, and we're both panting and getting all sticky.

Gosh, he's gonna tell me it's time to stop, I just know it.

And I've gotta listen. I've gotta.

I force my reluctant eyes open to meet his stare. We're so close our noses are practically bumping. When our gazes lock, he chuckles.

Which is… unexpected.

"You look, what is the word, mutinous?" He leans in to press a kiss to my furrowed brow. "You are soft but fierce, like a feral kitten."

Oh great.

That's just what any guy wants to hear from the guy he's crushing on.

Whatever look I must be wearing makes his chuckle deepen. He's literally laughing and dry-humping me at the same time.

"Do not worry, *kotyonok*," he murmurs against my mouth. "I am not going to stop. But I am going to fuck you now, and when I do, my cock will lock into you, and I will not be quick. Also, we do not have lube. For all these reasons, I will not take you this way."

Abruptly, he pushes up to kneel.

Oh crap.

He's finally come to his senses.

I'm crushed.

My disappointment is spiraling and I'm in free fall.

That's when he finishes, "I will have you on your knees for me, Neo Mercury. I will have you from behind."

My frustration vanishes with a pop. I gasp and scramble up and flip over on my elbows and knees before he can change his mind. When he doesn't immediately pounce on my offered bottom but just gives one of those dragonish rumbles, I sneak a hopeful peek over my shoulder. He's still kneeling behind me, one hand wrapped around his fascinating dick in a slow pump that slicks precum all down his shaft and over his stiffened barbs.

Wow. His gaze is just riveted.

On me.

He's riveted on the totally shameless display I'm offering back there, with my pucker all ready and my balls hanging down all tingly and hot and tight (because after spending this whole semester in Zara's harem, I do know how to get an alpha's attention).

He's actually so focused it's almost like he wants me for real.

But I'm not gonna make this any more than it is, which is just a really decent alpha getting me through my first superheat as a kindness, like the way you'd feed a stray that shows up on your doorstep starving.

Reminding myself again that we both know what this is and what it isn't, and we're both totally fine with it, I reach between my legs to give my aching and desperately neglected junk a few pumps.

"*Kotyonok*," he says in his growly Russian. "You are a terrible tease."

Now I don't even care if he wants to call me kitten. I just want him to fuck me before I explode. I want him to wreck my hole. I give an impatient wiggle that only makes him chuckle again.

Gosh, I guess me being in heat is just a barrel of laughs.

When I actually whimper with frustration, he stops laughing. His rough hands run up the backs of my thighs in a caress that makes me melt.

Like, literally. He's a fire sign like Ronin, and fire signs always run hot.

His hands keep going, smoothing over my butt, and he purrs with approval, so I guess he likes what he sees and feels. Now I'm really glad I spend all that time in the gym at our *domus*. I do it to please Zara and all our mates.

Oh, God, Zara. I miss her so much. I know she's a total badass and she can definitely handle herself but, gosh, I *really* hope she's okay—

"The sight of you like this," Max breathes in my ear, all rough and raspy, and wow, he's covering my whole back with his lean naked body. "So determined and so desperate… for what only I can give you…"

His accent gets stronger when he's turned on, I noticed that right away watching him with Zara and Ronin, and right now his accent's on steroids. His hands glide over my ribs and rub my chest in a way that somehow manages to be soothing. He's being really careful not to freak me out with his unique peen, but I'm not freaked out, I want him much closer. I push back into him until his barbed junk nudges my butt.

"Hurry," I mumble, burying my hot face in my folded arms.

"Be at ease. I will give you what you need, yes?" Then he nuzzles my shoulder and scrapes my skin with his sharp shifter fangs.

Now it's my turn to get all goosebumpy.

"Yes," I agree. But suddenly it's all I can manage not to demand a mating bite.

Now.

Darn it.

I keep reminding myself this is no big deal, no biggie, no biggie, and I think I've got it all straight in my head until the exact moment he gives his slick dick a few pumps and starts teasing my hole with a wet finger.

Oh sugar.

I'm super sensitive back there, and that frisson of first contact pushes me right over the edge. I throw back my head and yell as the first big O barrels through me. His free hand wraps around my dick and pumps me through it, with me coming buckets all over my own tummy and chest and him crooning in my ear with his sandpapery voice the whole time, plus working his finger into me while I'm all distracted and totally not minding the burn.

I know from being with Zara that her superheats are multi-O affairs, and now it looks like mine will be too.

Because when I finally stop spurting, I'm still hard.

By now Max is inside me to the third knuckle. He pulls back long enough to swipe a hand through the mess I've left all over myself, then starts pushing two fingers, all slick with my own jizz, back into my eager hole.

For a guy who was working really hard to convince himself he was straight until literally a few weeks ago when he first got a look at Ronin (who'd make anyone curious, I swear Ronin's like gateway dick for straight guys), Max is really good at this.

I don't even miss the lube.

"Hurry," I moan again, and this time he actually does. The burn as he pushes in a third finger without real lube is no joke.

Sweat breaks out across my forehead and I bite my lower lip.

"Neo." He stops right away, because he's really focused on me right now. He rubs my back to soothe me and nuzzles the side of my neck. "We can… do this… another way. Without penetration."

My head pops up from my folded arms and I twist around to glare at him. Yeah, sure, the biochemicals in his alpha shifter spunk splashed anywhere on my body will break my heat, even if he doesn't come inside me.

But all too clearly, this is the only time I'm ever gonna get to be with him. If this is our only time, I want to feel him inside me.

I want him to finish inside me.

"No, I'm good." Meeting his worried stare, I soften my voice and manage to summon a smile, because he needs reassurance too. "It's okay. You're not gonna hurt me. Unless, uh, you've changed your mind?"

His brows rush together in a ferocious scowl and his slitted pupils telescope wide.

"I have not changed my mind. You are mine," he growls. He's a man of few words when he's on a mission. "But you understand this will be for… all night. You are ready for me?"

My gaze drops to his dick, which is definitely ready to rumble. Zowie. He's totally rigid, barbs flaring from his tip like a devil's forked tail, a shining tendril of precum drooling from his slit. I know just how that dick of his is going to lock inside me, know he's going to ride me and fuck me and make me come for hours, and know that's exactly what I need. As my gaze finds his, I lick my lip (which stings from me biting it so hard) and give him an earnest nod.

"I'm ready for you," I tell him. "And I trust you."

That's apparently the exact right thing to say, because his fierce expression softens into a kind of awe.

"You are something I do not deserve," he says simply. "But I will strive to be worthy of you. Relax for me now, *kotyonok*."

My chest swells with this achy fullness of all the things I can't say out loud. I want to tell him he deserves everything. Heck, I'd give him the moon if I could. He's so loyal and so devoted and just so committed to Zara and Ronin and all of us, even me, despite his shitty upbringing and his shitty family and the shit way his evil mom always treated him. He's been all in on Zara and, really, our whole polycule (even Vasili, though they had this major love-hate dynamic happening at the time) from Day One.

I only wish Zara could be here with us now.

My heart gives an anxious ping because, gosh, I really miss her. She always loves watching us guys together, she loves that we love each other, loves seeing us happy. She'd love seeing the two of us like this—

Max drags his hand again through the hot mess that splatters my belly, which gets me focused right back on what's happening here and now. Patiently he works more of my own cum into my hole for lube, then slicks himself up back there. I turn my head and peek under my arm to watch. I feel all shivery (in a good way).

Like, with anticipation.

Then he gives my own junk a few exploratory strokes that have me revved up and ready to come all over again.

When I'm gasping and pumping into his fist, he scissors his fingers to open me wider back there, and I'm pretty much past missing the lube at this point. My next big O is building, my balls swelling and drawing up tight, my hole fluttering and pulsing around his fingers.

By the time he pulls out and lines up his amazing dragon dick, his swollen cockhead nudging against my pucker, I'm so totally ready for him to fuck me that I'm way past being polite.

"Sorry to be in such a rush but I can't wait," I get out in a hurry, so that I've sort of warned him. Then I arch my back and pretty much shove myself onto his dick.

The air is drenched with his brimstone mating scent. I know I'll smell like him after, which makes me so happy. I've wanted this with him forever, since that very first morning we woke up together in Zara's bed, that time I kissed him and it felt like he kissed me back.

That was before I realized he wasn't into me.

But, Lord, he's into me now, even if it's just shifter biology and my superheat. His thick dick pushes into me with a stretching burn that makes me yell.

Then his barbs engage and lodge inside me with a plink that throttles my yell into a surprised hiccup.

Buried balls-deep inside me, he bites out a Russian curse and freezes.

"Oh… wow…" I whisper into the silence.

My heart is galloping like a racehorse on Derby Day and there's so much adrenaline flooding my system that I feel ready to levitate right off these furs. I give an experimental wiggle, and his dick hooks deeper. Physically, the sensation of being hooked this way is a whole new thing for me. Emotionally, I love the way this feels, like he's claiming me. Like he'll never let me go.

Right now, I'm his in all the ways, exactly the way I need to be.

If only he'd give me his mating bite.

My eyes squeeze shut and my lips press together to hold in that demand I have zero right to ask him for.

He'd only want to bite me if he loved me.

I mean, if he loved me for real.

His harsh breath is hot on my shoulder and his lean body is damp with sweat. He presses his lips to my ear and exhales on a wisp of air. "Talk to me, Neo. I cannot read your mind."

Right. Because neither one of us are telepaths and we'll never have a mating bond unless he bites me.

Which he won't.

"This is… really intense for me," I say honestly, because I'm not gonna lie to him, and he needs to know. "But I can handle it, I mean, you. I can handle you." And I can, really, every way except emotionally. "Just go slow at first, okay?"

"Yes." He drags one fang along my earlobe, and I almost spill for him right there. He backs off me a few inches, then pushes deeper. The scrape of his barb inside me sends adrenaline sparking through me, lighting me up like Fourth of July fireworks.

I let out a breathless moan. His breath hitches in my ear.

"You are beautiful, Neo Mercury." His voice is shaking a little, maybe from the effort of holding himself in check. "You are perfect. As perfect as I always knew you would be. The way you yield for me. The way your body accepts mine. The way you take my cock…"

His words dissolve into Russian I can't follow, but my head's already spinning. This is the way he talks to Zara and Ronin, the mates he actually wants, the way he whispers to Vasili late at night while our snake is fast asleep.

He must talk that way to anyone he fucks.

But the combination of those words, all reverent and prayerful, and his careful thrusts inside me, makes all that pent-up heat I'm barely holding at bay come rushing back.

I turn my head to find his surprised mouth in a searing kiss that makes us both groan.

"More… I'm ready for more," I mumble into his burnt cinnamon kiss. "I think I'm gonna… come again."

Apparently, the thought of me coming while he's buried deep inside me is a good thing, because his dick swells and gets even harder. He shoves my head gently into my folded arms and holds me down, my hips tilted at exactly the right angle, while he deepens his thrusts and picks up the pace and really starts working me.

As my body softens for him, accommodating his barb and his length and his urgency, pretty much the whole shebang, my hole starts to clench and flutter and grip him, holding him inside me at every downstroke, like my body's afraid of losing him before we both finish. He grips my hip nice and firm to brace me and hammers into me, all while keeping my face pushed down into my arms. It's a subservient kind of posture. But I've never had a problem submitting to my mates.

"Gosh, I'm gonna come so hard for you," I gasp, just to sorta warn him. I work a hand between my legs to find my throbbing junk.

"Yes—No—I—need to feel you." He nudges my hand aside and takes over the job himself, pumping me with hard rhythmic strokes that bliss me out bigtime. Every time his dick hammers into me, his downstroke pushes me closer to the edge.

"Do I please you like this?" he says roughly into my neck.

"Wow… yeah… more of that…"

Without thinking, I angle my head to the side to offer him the place where my neck meets my shoulder, which is prime real estate for a mating bite. I've already got Vasili's neat twin punctures on that side, and Zara's pretty half-moon scar on the other, but Max definitely doesn't seem to mind.

He licks the scars from Vasili's bite, which is another classic alpha thing, at least for the alphas in our harem, who all like each other. They tend each other's bites. I'm uber-sensitive there, right under the hot slick of his tongue, and for this one time, I can pretend they're all *my* alphas for real—V and Max and Lucius, right along with Zara. My cock kicks in his grip and I shiver and, gosh, I'm making *so* much noise, we both are. But there's no one around to hear.

Clearly liking the way this is going, Max growls my name and starts chewing on my neck, almost hard enough to break the skin.

That totally shoves me right over the edge.

"Max… yeah, like that… ah… ohmygod—" My words dissolve into basic gibberish. Pleasure spirals through me and shoots up my shaft. My sac draws up tight and my hole clenches around his dick. A wordless shout punches from my throat.

I come a lot during my heats—I'm not kidding, it's a *lot*—and this time, with him, I'm like Old Faithful. My whole body shudders and I spurt all over his pumping hand and my chest and thighs and the furs bunched up beneath me.

The floor lurches and bucks under my hands and knees in the sharp concussive jerks of one of my really strong earthquakes. Which is probably not the best thing to do to a place with an active volcano.

But I'm way past caring.

Because Max is coming too, he's roaring my name with his dragon lurking in his voice, his amazing dick is kicking and spurting jets of hot jizz deep inside me. He shoves my face into the furs and clamps the side of my throat under his fangs and pounds into me in this relentless hammering rhythm like he'll never stop.

And I love that I'm pleasing him. Love that he's like this. Love that he's taking care of me.

"Max—God—I love—" Barely in time, I reel the words in.

Geez, that would just be a totally disastrous sentence for me to finish.

Still, as his pounding rhythm stutters and slows, as he tucks me up tight against him and rolls us both sideways (avoiding the big wet spot) on the furs, as he spoons around me with his barb still engaged and his hips still rocking into me and our bodies still locked together, I finish my sentence anyway, deep inside my soul where no one else can hear.

I love…

You.

I've been into you forever.

And it's not like a brotherly love either. I'm pretty sure I just fell in love with the only guy in our polycule who doesn't actually want me falling in love with him.

And he'll only feel bad if I tell him, because he can't return the feeling. As amazing as he is, as amazing as he makes me feel, as amazing as I know he's gonna keep making me feel all night long until he breaks my heat, because we're definitely not done yet… he's *not* my new boyfriend. He's just a really great guy doing a solid for someone in a jam.

Here's what that means.

It means I can't wear my heart on my sleeve and my thoughts on my face the way I usually do.

Somehow, I've gotta keep the way I feel about him secret.

Chapter Fifteen
Zara

I'm still standing on the Unseelie King's terrace, freezing my ass off in my catsuit and staring after Zephyr—the guy with the same name as Ronin's supposedly dead boyfriend, who's apparently *not* dead, and I honestly don't know if that newsflash is gonna comfort Ronin or kill him, since Ronin never told me their whole story—when I feel the stone ledge under my feet tremble.

That tremor's gotta be either an underground subway or an earthquake.

I'm putting my money on Option B.

I didn't see much in the way of mechanized transport down here when we were incoming. And there sure as shit isn't any King of the Dark Fae Porsche or Maserati action happening on this ledge or in the big cavern next door.

In fact, that cavern's pretty basic except for a wide platform, bathed in cool white light from crystals mounted in the walls, that looks like a dragon bed.

The Unseelie's in there now, totally unfazed by the tremors, unbuckling the harness from his green menace with a lithe efficiency that tells me they're both pretty used to this whole routine.

Looks like this Zephyr's a tend-your-own-dragon kind of guy. And I'm guessing Xhevith is his only form of transport.

Which means we really are having an earthquake.

That shake-and-quake really makes me miss my fated mate. The earth moves just like this back home when Neo has a good strong climax.

Sweet Jesus. Neo. I really hope you and Max are okay.

And not only for your sake. I got a feeling Ronin's gonna need all of us for support when he finds out this little shit who used to be his boyfriend's still breathing.

Hugging myself against the biting wind that seems to be a constant in this place, I navigate the shake, rattle, and roll and manage to stay upright. When the shaking subsides, I make my way to the terrace's unguarded edge. Over the shiny spires and slanty roofs around me, that active volcano is looming, its upper cone streaked with ribbons of lava glowing orange against the night.

The sulfurous reek of cinder and brimstone is strong enough to sting my sinuses.

"Welcome to Avalon." Ash's baritone rumble in my ear makes me twitch like a startled cat. I know he's still out here, but Jesus. For such a big guy, the dude walks like a cat. Anyway, thanks to him, at least I've put a name to the place.

"Avalon, huh?" I sigh. "Guess it's more than just a legend. Or a book."

"Yep. You'll find this place is all too real. Not gonna try anything stupid, are ya?" he asks, all casual.

"What, you mean like siting a whole Fae city at the foot of an active volcano?" I snipe. "That kind of stupid, or another kind?"

If the guy thinks I'm gonna throw myself off this ledge in a suicide plunge like some kinda ninny, he really doesn't know me very well.

They're not getting rid of me that easy.

I'll leave when I'm good and ready.

On my own terms.

Now this Ash is lurking behind me, every bit as dangerous to my immediate welfare as his kidnapping accomplice or that erupting volcano. With my enhanced shifty senses, he's close enough to smell. Actually, he smells kinda bracing, like the ocean on a diving day when the whitecaps are all choppy and the wind's screaming in your hair. In fact, his closeness makes my skin itch.

But fuck if I'm gonna show it.

I keep staring at that smoking volcano (which does tend to draw the eye). You don't see that shit every day. But I widen my feet and shift my stance.

You know, in case I need to fight.

"You say that about this city like you think they got a choice. Think they got anywhere else to go?" His tone is easy, all folksy and twangy, but I'm not buying it. This guy's had an issue with me ever since I took a hunk out of their scaly household pet.

Well, join the club, big man. That feeling of aversion is *so* fucking mutual.

"The way I heard, the Dark Fae chose to come here—to Avalon—after a *really* nasty parting of the ways with your Light Fae buddies. Guess maybe they shouldn't have burned that bridge, huh?"

"Ancient history." His words close the door pretty hard on that line of convo. So I can't ask about that shit I read in the book, like the Unseelie using the blood of their Seelie enemies to open the portal to Avalon and slam it shut behind them for a thousand years.

"Just water under the bridge? That's pretty forgiving." I pause, but he only grunts. "Anyway, guess they just gotta live with the choice they made."

And, fuck, apparently so do I.

Right now, I need to scope out the sitch. Get the lay of the land. So I lean into the bitter headwind that's stinging my face and pushing my body. I scan the twisted tangle of streets below.

This goblin city's all hilly and stairstepped like the village around the Academy back home. It's hard to see much in the dark, and there's zero intel in terms of inhabitants. Only a few of the tall arched windows around me are lit with that cold starry light.

Maybe there aren't many Dark Fae left in this place.

Just like there aren't many witches and warlocks left in the witching world.

Behind me, Ash shifts his big body like a snow lion getting ready to pounce. "Sure, the Dark Fae chose these digs and built this city. The way they tell it, that was pre-volcano, before this endless winter. Now most of 'em can't leave, even if they'd like to."

He bends low to finish. "Must be nice being a casino czar's kid. You ever been trapped anywhere you didn't wanna be, princess?"

My pulse spikes with anger, which makes my tone sharp. I slant him a look over my shoulder that tells him to back the fuck off. He's twice my size, for Chrissake. "You mean, aside from the way the two of you are trying to trap me right now? Or the five years I spent trapped and hiding in one shithole after the next while dear old dad the casino king kept raising the bounty for my head?"

His jaw drops in surprise and his mouth opens. But I don't give him space to answer.

"Basically, you don't know a single goddamn thing about me," I tell him. "You think I'm some spoiled rich bitch, all raised with a silver spoon? That's gonna be too bad for you, big man."

Because yeah, this isn't my first rodeo, I've been kidnapped before.

Like any good cat burglar, I always land on my feet.

Now he can get a word in edgewise, the guy's all quiet, maybe recalibrating a few factoids about his abductee instead of feeling the need to formulate some snappy comeback. This is a Fae who thinks before he talks. And sure, maybe I shoulda just kept my mouth shut and let these guys underestimate me.

But it's been a long day, and they're under my skin—both of them—in a way I typically don't allow.

Now there's a restless itch in that same skin that drives me to pace the ledge, working off my anger, trying to make a plan, looking for God knows what. There's no way off this terrace except the cavern that green dragon lumbered into. Nothing to see out here except the moon, a swollen white orb rising over the midnight sea.

The moon's reflection streaks silver over the inky waves.

For some reason, the sight of that full moon makes my itch worse. Maybe because it's not supposed to be full. Moon's dark right now back at Icarus.

I can feel this moon's gravitational pull tugging at my lower belly like an umbilical cord.

Chafing my arms with my icy hands, I shoot another irritated look at Ash, who doesn't even seem bothered by the frigid wind nipping his bare tattooed arms. He's staring up at the volcano with booted legs spread and big hands clasped loosely at the small of his back.

Right over his impressive ass.

Sure, I have a thing for leather, but shit. The man is built. He's just a massive male, all powerful shoulders and corded back and bulging quads. He's also got a second long knife strapped to his thigh to back up the one thrust through his belt.

I'm good with a knife. If I had his, I could use it.

Bet there's no charmed bracelet to guard against that.

He's brutal and blunt. He's strength without refinement. He's basically a total contrast to that lean wicked Zephyr with his viper's tongue.

But I bet he still bleeds.

The sound of a slamming door spins me away from my stabby fantasies. Now the dragon harness is hanging neatly on the wall, the dragon himself is noisily slurping water from a cistern in the rear…

And the Dark Fae King has just totally vamoosed.

"Cheese on toast!" I burst out. "You telling me that Unseelie asshole kidnaps me and then just walks off and leaves me standing on his doorstep like a stray dog or something? What kinda kidnappers are you people, anyway?"

Ash keeps staring at the volcano, all pensive, moonlight shining like a crown in his spiky pewter hair. But his voice gets grim. "The desperate kind. Being cursed with a slow death sentence kinda makes ya that way, you feel me?"

Now, of course, I can't help thinking about the slow extinction event that's overtaking the witching world. If these Fae are the last remnant of a supposedly extinct witching race, the way Lucius said, they gotta have the same problem.

Along with a bunch of unique ones, like a massively erupting volcano and really extreme climate change.

"Just to be clear, what kinda slow death sentence are we talking about?" I cock my hip and fold my arms across my chest.

All deliberate, Ash turns to face me. His silver gaze slides over my expectant body in a slow sweep that heats me up, like, with anger. Yeah. Anger. There's not gonna be any Stockholm Syndrome situation going on in this abduction.

Softly he says, "This city and all its people are cursed."

My heart gives a good hard thump. We don't study curses in Common Magics 101, because we're only freshmen. But I've snuck a few peeks at the curses in Vasili's Senior Seminar grimoire, and they all look pretty nasty.

I clear my throat. "Cursed, huh? How'd that happen?"

Ash chuffs out a grunt. "Reckon I said enough about all that. Any rate, that was before my time."

His sudden taciturnity gives my Valyrian foresight a tweak that makes my skin tingle.

My whole job when I ascend the throne is to reverse the witching world's decline and halt the extinction of the four races. That's a role I resisted like fuck at first, but now I'm all in.

I mean, it's not like the world's gonna save itself, right?

If these Dark Fae are some estranged part of the witching world and they're dying too, maybe my sudden appearance in Avalon isn't a totally unrelated thing.

Maybe there's something here I need to do.

I tilt my head and drill the guy with a hard look. "You maybe wanna tell me what I'm doing here, Ash?"

His gaze sparks with appreciation for the connection I clearly just made. Too bad my flash of insight doesn't loosen his sexy lips. "You wanna know why you're here, princess? That yarn's for Sparrowhawk to spin ya."

"Fine. Then I'll ask him. And don't call me princess." I pivot on my booted heel and stride right into the cavern like I know where I'm going.

At least that move gets me out of the wind, and it's warmer in here too. Those crystals embedded in the rocky walls do more than emit light. They're actually giving off some badly needed warmth.

Plus that dragon himself is kicking out BTUs like a goddamn furnace. As I beeline across his digs, the green stops slurping water and twists his wary head around to eye me. That gash I ripped in his chest has clotted over, looks like that healing potion might be doing the guy some good.

Not like I'm relieved or anything.

That dragon hurt my Max.

"Yeah, you just stay put," I tell the dragon. "Go eat or something. I'll be outta your hair in a sec."

For all I know, him eating involves hunting down random Fae in the streets and dismembering them before he dines on their bloody entrails, but right now that doesn't sound so bad to me. You know, assuming those Fae in the streets are like the ones I have to deal with in here.

The dragon snorts like he can understand me. My inner queen voices an audible chirp, just telling him what's what, even if right now she can't rise.

That's a situation we're gonna change.

I'm headed for the closed door, which looks like the only option off this ledge while I'm wearing these fucking bracelets. Ash ambles along behind me. Ignoring the guy for now, I pull the door open and march down and down a winding spiral of stairs, lit by more of those glowing white crystals set at intervals in the wall.

Those crystals and the lack of mechanized transport make me wonder if the Avalon wards do more than fuck with electronics, the way the magical wards do on Icarus. Maybe this place isn't even electrified.

Which would definitely make the weather a problem.

Ash follows at his own pace, feet silent on the stairs. Which means I can't backtrack, even if I wanted to.

But retreat's not what I'm looking for.

Right now, I'm spoiling for a fight.

I spiral down those stairs till I finally reach the bottom, then push open another door and sashay through like I'm the queen of this world too. A good-sized room opens around me, kinda like the great room back at Icarus, with a central hearth and twisty Art Nouveau furniture scattered around, a row of tall arched windows over a frozen courtyard, then the moon-washed sea.

I'm all the way inside before I register the Unseelie King standing quietly by the hearth with his back to me, peeling out of his scaly green armor. His swords and gauntlets are lying neatly on a delicate fainting couch that looks like it's swooning under their weight. A jumble of crystal slags and a weird white fire blaze silently in the big hearth.

In front of that witchy fire, the Unseelie's already stripped down to his waist. He's literally wearing nothing above the ass except that swirl of moss-green hair that blankets his shoulders and slides against his olive-toned skin.

The guy's whippet-slim and, honestly, not any taller than me—and I'm downright petite. But he's built like Bruce Lee, not a pinch of fat on him, just trim cords of lethal muscle flexing in his narrow back and knotted deltoids as he unbuckles the utility belt at his waist with spare, efficient movements.

I jerk to a dead halt and stare at the guy, with my pulse jumping and my skin heating in a way that's fairly alarming. Usually, when I insta-heat like I'm having a hot flash or something, that means my mating heat is starting.

My gaze shoots from the electrifying sight of my half-naked abductor to the full moon floating over that inky sea.

Sweet Jesus.

That goddamn moon.

I better not be starting some off-cycle mating heat.

Here, without my guys? That scenario would *not* be good.

While I'm standing there sussing out the sitch going down with my body, that guy Zephyr just keeps stripping. He coils his heavy belt with a single vicious snap and drops the leather loop on that spindly fainting couch with the rest of his gear, which just about makes the thing collapse.

Then he toes out of his boots with a couple of supple twists.

Clearly this is something he does on the daily, peeling in and out of that armor. And he doesn't seem to be wearing a stitch of clothing underneath.

The way I barged in, I wasn't exactly stealthy. But maybe somehow he didn't hear me?

Just in case, I clear my throat.

Neatly he lines his boots beside the fainting couch. Without sparing me a glance, he starts working the scaly armor down his hips.

"Yikes, Sparrowhawk." Ash's amused voice behind me makes me jump. "We got company here. The princess doesn't need to be mooned by your bare ass before she's even had her supper."

The thought of supper is instantly appealing, seeing as how I've missed breakfast and lunch. But right now, I've got more immediate issues on my mind.

"I've seen worse," I fire back. Then, hearing the way that sounds, I almost swallow my tongue. "I mean, I've seen shit that's a lot more shocking than some Fae's skinny ass."

"There you have it," Zephyr says briefly, apparently to Ash. Then he just bends over right in front of me and drops trou.

Oh.

My.

God.

I'm telling you, he's got an ass for the *ages*. Because of course he does. All sleek skin and drum-tight glutes and a flash of sac between his sinewy thighs—

Whoa. I hastily avert my eyes.

Still, the incendiary sight of him naked is seared onto my cerebral cortex. I mean, that ass of his would give my guys *major* ideas. I'm willing to bet V or Max (or both) would be railing him before he got his legs out of his armor.

What's worse, my dragon queen—who's been one hundred percent content until this exact minute fucking our five current mates—lets out a sibilant hiss of interest like a teakettle set to boil.

I gaze steadily at the full moon and feel the first pulse of heat down below like a second sun.

Fuck. I am in *so* much trouble.

"For the last time," I say weakly into the riveted silence, "don't call me princess."

"Okay, Zara." Ash's voice is warm with amusement and maybe something more, but I don't know him well enough to be sure. Still, that gives me a little thrill of triumph, because it's the first time either one of these guys has actually used my name. "Guess you earned that one, the way he's been jerking your chain. Sparrow, you stay put by that fire and lemme getcha some pants."

"Great idea," I mutter.

"Fine." Sparrow—Zephyr—sinks gracefully to sit cross-legged on a silky rug that's all green and silver by the fire. Then he lifts his arms to unwind the skinny braid wound around his head that holds his hair back.

Still with his back to me. Since I walked in here, that fucker hasn't even done me the courtesy of looking at me.

Which is pissing me right off.

"Okie-dokie." Ash ducks through a door next to the stairs and disappears.

Leaving in his wake a whole lot of awkward.

To ease the tight silence, I stroll over to the wall of windows and look out. That puts me in front of His Radiance, who can now deal with *my* backside. It would serve the Fae bastard right if I stripped down to the skin myself.

But that might give him the wrong idea.

Besides, it's cold as fuck in here. Never thought I'd say this, but I actually miss the geriatric furnace in our *domus*.

Not much to see out there in the dark, but I can definitely feel him watching.

Just looking at the rising moon makes my skin tingle. Because it's definitely the moon and *not* the heat of his glare, I mean, that's affecting me.

I pivot away from that dangerous moon so fast it sets my braid swinging and march over to the fire's feeble warmth. With the blaze and the flue set squarely between us, I can't see much of the Fae.

Which suits me fine.

Considering he's sitting there naked.

"Handy kinda fire you got here." I extend my cold hands to the flickering white flames, which definitely do emit some heat, though not as much as an actual fire.

Actual fire can kill the Fae, according to that book in Lucius' library. I wonder if I still have that lighter in my utility belt.

"Witchfire," the Fae says briefly, startling the fuck out of me, because when I talk, he typically doesn't say shit. "From the crystals."

"Witchfire, huh?"

Trying out the word, I lean sideways to peek at him around the flames… and catch him leaning sideways to do the same. Our stares lock for a blink—his single eye wide and wary, eyepatch gleaming emerald in the witchy light—before we both suck in a breath and jerk back to put the fire between us.

Still, that instant of contact sears me to the bone.

I stare blindly into the so-called witchfire, but that glimpse of him dances before my eyes. He's pretty enough to be one of my warlocks for sure, all sharp cheekbones and delicate jaw in a fierce face, framed in that silky spill of pine-green hair. The eyepatch makes him wicked, but his startled eye and parted lips, with just the tips of his fangs showing, make him look… vulnerable.

With all that pretty he's rocking, too bad he's such a dick.

"Zephyr," I say softly. His name feels funny on my lips. Intimate. In a way I don't expect. I swear I can sense him twitch in response. "Why am I here?"

Silence opens up between us, long enough that I figure this is one more question he doesn't intend to answer.

Then his liquid voice trickles through the fire between us. "Didn't your queen regnant tell you?"

"You mean Messalina?" I snort. "Newsflash. Her and me? We're not exactly on speaking terms. I wasn't her choice of successor. When her daughter died, she needed an heir pretty quick, and the Senate basically forced me down her throat."

Another pause, while I guess he absorbs that.

"Pity," he murmurs, sounding totally indifferent. "I imagined you'd know. That she'd do that much, at least, for Avalon."

I hate being kept in the dark, so my voice spikes with annoyance. "Well, I don't. And she didn't. So cough it up."

"Very well." Geez, he sounds so distant, like he's light years away. "You've been summoned here to attend a wedding."

Instant alarm bristles through me. Now I'm way more on guard, if that's even possible. My mind shoots back to that convo with Lucius and the guys before I left. Straight to the subject of Messalina's outreach to the Dean.

"Oh yeah?" My voice goes spiky with suspicion. "What wedding?"

"A royal wedding. A king's wedding." His words fall slowly, like a sprinkle of raindrops in a silver voice, just taking his sweet time till I want to march around this fire and wring the truth out of him. "To be precise, you've been summoned here to attend… my wedding."

He doesn't sound happy about it (like, *at all*) and that makes two of us. Really, the thoughts I'm thinking are too horrible to be voiced.

I fold my arms across my chest like that's gonna fend off this truckload of fuckery bearing down on me and I scowl at him through the fire. "Well, congrats, I guess."

"I don't require your felicitations." The air between us turns broody, like storm clouds condensing under the ceiling. "My pending nuptials are hardly a love match."

My foresight gives another ping. Something about the way he's talking makes me wonder if maybe he's in love with someone else.

Someone he can't actually marry.

Well, cry me a river.

"No fairytale wedding for you then. Even though you're a Faerie." Ha ha. "Who's the lucky lady?" My gaze sneaks toward the door where Ash vanished. "Or, uh, gent?"

Of course, predictably, he clams up again. It's Ash who pipes up from the doorway, where he's toting an armful of green clothes.

And thank fuck for that.

I need that Fae to have clothes on.

"The real Q you wanna ask is *why*, princess." Ash moseys over to the naked Fae and drops the clothes gently in his lap. "Why he's getting hitched, when otherwise he wouldn't wanna. He's doing it to break the curse."

"Ash." Sharp with annoyance, Mr. Naked uncoils to his feet with a snap. I look away fast to avoid getting the full frontal. But not before glimpsing a flash of drum-tight abs, a narrow tongue of moss-green pubic hair… and unambiguous evidence that the Fae male is extremely well endowed.

My inner dragon croons with approval. Shit. I'm warm all over and my face is scorching.

Please fuck, let me not be going into heat.

"You gotta tell her, Sparrow. She's part of this whether you want her to be or not. You tell her or I will." Ash positions himself where he can see both of us, so I can see the determination stamped all over his rugged face.

Zephyr wrestles the pants over his hips (which is totally a good thing, I mean it) and maintains his stubborn silence.

Ash heaves a sigh. "Okay then, I'll start. You two are the only two that can do it. He needs you to end this shitshow."

"Me?" I hurl the word at him like lightning. "Whatever problems you've got here feel like they're totally your doing. What do I have to do with some Dark Fae curse?"

The big male sucks in a breath to tell me.

"That is quite enough." Suddenly Zephyr's all up in his grille, barely dressed in a pair of juniper-green breeches that cling to his sinewy body like he's naked. He bristles up at his much larger buddy, every twitch and quiver of him infused with quiet rage. That liquid Unseelie voice pours low and deadly through the hush. "Utter another syllable of this matter to that woman and I vow, by the moon, you'll regret it."

Ash ducks his head and eyes Zephyr under his silvery brows. A dangerous light sparks in the Seelie's pale gaze and turns his irises to mercury. The two Fae smolder at each other until the air between them crackles electric with tension.

I realize I'm holding my breath.

"Aw, shit, Your Resplendence," the big male drawls, all husky with challenge. "Guess you're just gonna have to take it out of my hide, ain'tcha?" An energy zings between them that's potent as fuck. Until Ash's shimmery gaze shifts to me. "Here's the real reason he nabbed ya, princess. His subjects are dying."

My breath rushes out on a gasp.

"All of 'em." Ash gives me a grim nod. "That's on account of your world, your witching world, and something your bitch of a queen did twenty-some years ago while she was over here."

Zephyr pivots away with a muttered oath and a look of absolute wrath and stalks around the fire to snatch up his shirt. He's hard to ignore, but I manage to stay locked on Ash, the one who's actually talking.

"Messalina again." I give a hard nod back. "Can't say I'm all that surprised. What'd she do this time?"

Ash rubs a big hand over his square jaw and says flatly, "She stole his queen. Sparrowhawk's. The one he was fated to mate. When his queen was just a baby. She stole his queen—and the kid died."

"Oh, shit. That sucks. I—I'm really sorry." And I am. Every innocent death is a tragedy. That little kid didn't do squat to deserve whatever happened to her. "That's what triggered the curse?"

Ash's head dips. "Yup."

That effing Messalina. Her and me, we're really gonna need a convo. That's, like, the first thing I'm gonna do when I bust out of here.

And it's not like I can't see where this whole train wreck is heading, because I didn't just fall off the turnip truck.

Still, I need him to spell this shit out.

I level the big male with a grim look. "And I'm involved in this how?"

Across the room, Zephyr fights his way into his shirt in a silent fury. It's this gossamer white thing that laces at the neck, and he's really pretty in it, with his green hair and his pointy ears and his feral beauty, even when he's hissing and baring his sharp little fangs at Ash.

But this Ash? He's a real steady Eddie. He just fixes his eyes on me and keeps talking. "Our queens have symbolic and magical value for the whole realm. Just like yours, you feel me?" He waits for my nod. "To make things right? To break the curse? Sparrow needs the thief to return something of equal value to Avalon. That's you—and only you. He needs *you*."

Well, great.

With exaggerated interest, I spread my arms and look all around me. "Well, I'm here now. And judging by the erupting volcano and the arctic weather, me just being here isn't doing shit. So what specifically does His Resplendence need me to do?"

"He needs you to marry him, princess," Ash says, nice and easy, like he's not totally turning my world upside down. "Whether that's what he actually wants or not. Ceremony's all set to go down at moonrise tomorrow, at the equinox, before the portal shuts for good. Then, uh…"

For the first time, watching me and whatever he sees in my face, the big man seems to lose his nerve. Maybe it's because my dragon queen is stirring (even if she can't rise) and my braid is floating around my shoulders and the shadows are turning violet with the psi fire that's pooling in my eyes.

Maybe I can't shift or hurl lightning with these fucking charmed bracelets on, and sure, those are my major magics, the ones we know about. But I've got a salad of witching world DNA from all four races. I'm rocking all sorts of dormant recessives that have never even been switched on. Till now, I've had my hands pretty full with my lightning and my shifting and my warlocks and all our issues.

Now, all of a sudden, I'm super motivated to figure that dormant recessive shit out.

Ash shifts his substantial weight and clears his throat. "Then…"

"Then *what*?" I demand, with my dragon lurking in my voice.

Zephyr glares at both of us in a white-lipped rage, his jade-green eye incandescent.

But the Dark Fae doesn't say a thing. Clearly he knows he can't stop whatever big reveal's about to go down.

The big Seelie male pins me with a look I can't escape. "Then, at moonrise, he needs you to fuck him. That's what'll break the curse."

Chapter Sixteen
Lucius

Dear God, my head is pounding.

I've been devouring the contents of every book on Avalon and the Dark Fae in the Icarus Academy library for so long my eyes feel scoured with sand.

In fact, I've been hunched over these ancient histories and fairytales until I've lost all track of time. Beyond the stained-glass windows of the choir loft in this gothic cathedral where we house the Academy library, all the outdoor light has faded.

I'm relying on my wolf's keen eyes to read in the dark.

But, for all my determined effort, I've found nothing to alter the monstrous suspicion that sprang to life, fully formed in my brain, the instant I woke this morning to find Zara missing.

That suspicion has lurked and skulked in my psyche all day, because I know Zara.

I know my queen. I know what she's capable of.

Indeed, my suspicion has only worsened since I found that damnable book of Avalon legends in my study, lying open to that dreadful page—

"You'll ruin your eyesight reading in the dark." Vasili's murmur wakes my wolf, who's finally fallen into an exhausted sleep after pacing and growling in my skin all day. "Besides, that headache you're cultivating so diligently is one whisper away from a migraine, darling."

My wolf stirs with an anxious whine. As my mating bond tingles to life, my weary gaze lifts from the pile of volumes spread across the table to find my alpha's blade-slim body looming over me.

I'm vaguely startled to realize the shadows in this loft have grown so thick I can barely see him, even with my keen shifter senses.

"I… I don't suffer migraines, typically." With a sigh, I roll my knotted shoulders to loosen them, then reach to switch on the table lamp. "But I suppose you're right about the light."

The dim electric glow, tinged green and amber from the Edwardian lampshade, pushes back the shadows. Around us, the overstuffed shelves of spell books and grimoires and bestiaries and genealogies spring to vivid life. The light spills over Vasili's disheveled Academy uniform—tie loose, cuffs undone, blazer unbuttoned—and turns his tousled shag of hair to lavender.

In fact, my alpha's state of dishevelment is rather uncharacteristic. One look at the drawn and haggard cast to his sharp face, paired with the exhaustion that seeps through our mating bond, has me leaping to my feet in alarm.

"Vasili, my dear." Gently I take his arm to steady him and lead him toward the cluster of wing chairs near the dying fire. Under my touch, he's quivering with fatigue. "You'd best sit down yourself before you fall."

With none of his usual grace, he drops into the chair I offer.

Indeed, he all but collapses into it.

"Don't hover, pet. You're dead on your feet yourself." With a wan smile that doesn't reach his shadowed eyes, he tugs me into his lap.

Admittedly, I'm so weary myself I barely resist. Of course, I'm larger than he is, big-boned and rangy, while he's slim and deadly as a saber. But he's never had any difficulty at all handling my body. Now our tangled limbs overflow the confines of this high-backed wing chair until the furniture groans in protest.

I inhale the scent of rain and spices (which is the way Vasili smells after flying) and settle my weary bones into the familiar shelter of his arms… my colleague, my student, my lover… with a sigh.

I too am in desperate need of comfort.

His barely-there murmur is gray with fatigue. "I've overflown this entire island twice. Ronin and RT have canvassed every inch of this village and the surrounding forest on foot."

"Zara missed her appointment with Nurse Lavinia at the clinic," I sigh, "which was surely not by choice. For Zara, a rigorous adherence to that birth control regimen is practically her religion."

I let my aching head sag until it rests against his shoulder, since we're alone here, with no one else to witness my despair.

"And Dez is home manning the landline just in case," he finishes softly, "but of course there's been no news. There's simply no sign of them. Zara, Max, Neo, that damnable green dragon… and his rider. Whoever that rider turns out to be."

Gently I massage the aching bridge of my nose where my headache is gathering. "Well, that settles it. Zara was researching weapons against the Fae in that enchanted book for a reason." I steel myself to say the rest. "You do realize my initial hypothesis is very likely correct. She means to kill the Unseelie King."

Together we breathe in the darkness.

Silently I curse the precious hours I've lost today, teaching History of Witchcraft and Common Magics to an unsuspecting and largely unappreciative student body, insisting my entire cohort sustain a charade of normalcy, pretending Zara and Max and Neo are merely in bed with a bad case of the snuffles. Hoping against hope they'd return before I'm required to report the disappearance of half my cohort to my already disapproving Dean.

Now, it's quite apparent they won't, and I must. Truly, this endless day has been a nightmare.

And it isn't over yet.

Vasili's smoky lashes flutter with realization. His eye makeup is smudged and his lip gloss is long gone. Given the trauma we're experiencing, clearly, my relentlessly vain and fashion-forward alpha has neglected his daily preening.

Now he pulls in a long breath. "I suppose that means our little queen has done it again, hasn't she? Gone off on one of her daredevil crusades and left half of us behind." His delicate features are inscrutable, but I know him. "Only this time, she took Neo… and left me."

"That's rather a large assumption, my dear. No doubt, she means to return as soon as she can." With careful fingers, I graze his pale cheek.

As dreadfully as he behaves, as difficult and prickly and broody as this holy terror of a warlock may be to live with, as complicated and tangled and sensitive as I find our teacher/student/colleague/lover/co-alpha dynamic to be, the simple truth is this.

He's easy for me to love.

In fact, he's impossible for me not to love.

The key to understanding Vasili is understanding his deep-rooted and extremely well-hidden fear of abandonment.

This is precisely the fear that Zara and Neo and Maxim——all three of them his lovers—have now triggered.

"Stop worrying about my fragile psyche, Lucius. I won't break," he says sharply. His body bristles with sudden annoyance.

Indeed, he snarls and all but shoves me out of his lap. I loop an apologetic arm around his waist and cling to him like a burr.

With a huff and an ill grace, he subsides in a sulk. "Obviously, I doubt the three of them left this island by choice. Zara clearly meant to slay the creature and be back before breakfast, while Neo and Max rushed off half-cocked to protect her, probably without her consent. Then the entire beastly affair proved to be more than the three of them could handle. And now the Unseelie has them."

Hearing the entire disaster stated so plainly makes my headache worse. Christ, it's as though someone is attacking my temples with a pickax.

I barely manage to swallow a groan.

When I can speak through the pain, I whisper, "I can delay no longer. Our queen-in-waiting is missing, along with Senator Mercury's precious son and the witching world's last surviving fully manifested male dragon shifter. I simply *must* inform the Dean. And this is no discussion to entrust to the landline. I'll go directly to the Dean's Tower."

In truth, this is one discussion I'm positively dreading. And not merely because my superior will be gravely concerned for our missing queen and the others and bitterly disappointed in me.

I must also take into account the alarming contents of that note I found in my faculty mailbox this morning, written in the Dean's copperplate script, which has been weighing upon me so heavily all day.

In my currently depleted state, my impossible alpha snatches the memory from my mind in a flash.

"Dear fuck. That royal bitch Messalina's coming *here*?" Clearly appalled, he rears back in our chair to eye me. "What the hell, Lucius?"

My headache administers a vicious stab that spears into the tender nexus between my eyebrows. The pain is so intense my wolf whines and my eyes water.

"She's coming here tomorrow for the mating ceremony," I mumble through the agony. "The very ceremony Zara herself has yet to agree to. In all fairness, Messalina hasn't a clue that Zara's opposed, because I haven't had a spare moment between crises to inform the Dean. Christ, what a mess."

His cool fingers brush my throbbing brow. The contact affords me a merciful flicker of relief. In the shell of my skin, my restless wolf whimpers and sinks to his haunches.

With a frown, Vasili probes my no-doubt-tortured features with his penetrating stare.

"The Dean will simply have to inform Messalina—and presumably the amorous bridegroom—not to come," he says shortly at last. "The enormous distraction of the queen's arrival… and that bitch specializes in distraction, believe me… is the very last thing we need here now. If nothing else, the fact that the presumptive bride is missing offers the perfect excuse for putting them both off."

"You're very likely correct." Reluctantly, I gather myself to rise. "I'll suggest it to her. Now I'd best take myself to the Tower, before the Dean retires for the night. She's hardly a night owl, and this isn't the sort of news that improves with age."

"You'll go nowhere until I fetch a generous dose of Neo's headache potion for your head from my office in the crypt." Vasili scowls and tightens his grip at my waist to restrain me. "Besides, darling, I need to open the Vault. This time, I rather thought I'd ask for your help."

"The Vault?" Fuzzy with pain, I blink at him. "Well, thank you for asking this time, at least."

Despite all our troubles, my wry tone makes him smirk.

"What magical object are you pilfering this time?" Admittedly, I'm rather afraid to ask.

He waves away my fears with an airy hand. "Oh, it's not for me, I assure you. It's for Ronin. He's been turning the entire *domus* upside down looking for a scrying mirror."

"A scrying mirror?" A dart of surprise pings through me. "For far-sight, do you mean? But Ronin doesn't scry. None of us do. That's an extinct gift, mostly, although Mistress Agrippina seems to think Mallory McSnicker might have some aptitude…"

"I don't need to tell you Ronin isn't taking this well," he says sharply. "Not any of it. Not this political marriage Zara's supposed to make, not the disappearance of three of our mates—which Ronin imagines he should have anticipated, with his newly enhanced Valyrian foresight. And certainly not these painful reminders of his twin's suicide and whatever happened in his past with that Unseelie bastard, which he still refuses to discuss." Vasili shrugs over the Unseelie, but his glacial gaze is icy with menace. "When it comes to that Unseelie and this scrying mirror, I'd rather like to indulge our mate."

"Very well." Too heartsore and distracted to pursue the matter, I sigh and disentangle myself from Vasili's lap. "What harm can it do? We'll go to the Vault."

"As soon as we collect your headache potion," he says firmly.

Together we climb to our feet. With care, I gather my various notes and papers into my oxblood briefcase, while my impatient alpha waits and broods in the shadows.

Despite my gnawing worry for Zara and Neo and even that reprobate Maxim, I'm grateful beyond measure that Vasili is here, that I'm not alone, that his razor-sharp intellect and terrifying gifts are my allies in this particular fight.

As I snap shut my briefcase and switch off the lamp, I realize I never expected to trust him the way that I now do.

Because of that trust, I choose to confide in him my latest concern.

"When I inform the Dean about this debacle," I venture softly as we slip through the darkness, "I can't be certain how she'll react. Our august administrator has never been one to tolerate failure from the students— and even less so from the faculty."

"Oh, my, I'm simply quaking in my Doc Martens." Dripping with disdain for the Dean's authority, Vasili ushers me before him into the narrow stairwell. "Truly, pet, let her fume. What can the old witch possibly do? She needs you in your post far too badly to fire you."

"If you're asking me to guess how she'll punish me," I mutter, "she'll probably insist, at minimum, that I be the one to explain this entire wretched affair to Messalina."

Chapter Seventeen

Zara

I gotta get off this enchanted rock of an island.

I gotta.

Like, tonight.

I've already been gone from Icarus a whole day. God, my guys have to be worried sick. And I just know the Dean's gonna blame Lucius, because he's my headmaster, that I'm MIA.

But, yeah, me getting off this rock tonight is gonna be a problem, seeing how I'm locked into some fancy guest room in the Unseelie King's quarters, apparently for the night. A feat that bastard managed to finagle smooth as a goddamn con man, just by ushering me into these digs so I could use the loo (which I hated to ask him for, but desperately needed), then locking the fucking door behind me.

Now I'm done in the medieval-looking john (which does have piped water and kind of a gravity-flush toilet) and I'm finished with the whole scenario of pounding and swearing and demanding to be let the fuck out while no one answers. I've muttered and paced around this exotic-looking bedroom with its mint-and-teal mosaic floors and its oceany friezes of waves and krakens and sea dragons and mermaids. I've checked out this delicate twisty furniture that looks like someone twisted or magicked it into shape from bleached driftwood. I've poked and squinted at the apparently self-sustaining witchfire burning in a jumble of crystals in the hearth

I've unlatched a door of ripply volcanic glass that opens on a balcony perched high over a jumble of jagged rocks and night-black sea.

But it's way too high to jump, and it's cold as fuck out there, seriously, so I don't linger.

I hesitate a good long while over the bowl of pale blue apples I find next to the bed, with a wheel of green cheese, a loaf of crusty bread, and a carafe of pink wine. There's some Greek myth about kidnapped Persephone in the underworld that gives me heartburn over the thought of eating. She eats pomegranate seeds or some shit, which traps her to spend half of every year down there with Hades, lord of the underworld.

But I'm no Persephone.

I'm no innocent spring virgin (to put it *really* mildly).

And I'm starving. For real.

So I eat, like, everything. Two tart apples and half the nutty-tasting bread and a fat wedge of creamy cheese, all washed down with a big pewter goblet of crisp wine so light it practically evaporates right off my tongue.

I mean, a girl's gotta eat, right?

I'm so hungry I eat standing up, ignoring the linen napkin and the cheese knife (which is definitely the only kind of knife my jailer is giving me), just wolfing my meal with my bare hands.

Finally, when my tummy stops grumbling and I'm feeling nice and sated, I pilfer a silk cushion from the bed. That bed is major, big enough for me and at least three of my guys, and rocking a fat overstuffed mattress smothered in a duvet that looks like swan feathers sewed together, all snowy white with a rainbow shimmer. Giving that whole fuck platform a hard no, because I'm just not feeling that comfy, I plop my cushion down on the stone ledge of a window seat to protect my ass from the cold, then cram myself into the seat and brood.

Sweet Jesus. That fucking Messalina.

This guy Zephyr might be Mr. Taciturn, but it's pretty obvi he doesn't want me here, any more than I wanna be here myself. He's, like, a *very* reluctant Hades in this whole Greek drama we're enacting.

But I don't need him doing my math for me.

I can put two plus two together on my own.

Clearly he's the political marriage Messalina wants me to make. He's in it to help his people out, I guess, which makes me respect him a tiny bit and get why he's doing it, even though I still hate his guts for the way he went after Max and the way he just takes without asking and his pissy temper and that autocratic sense of entitlement I find so infuriating.

If the guy just came to me on his own at Icarus, explained the sitch, and asked for my help?

Whole other story. I'd have tried to help.

Not saying I'd marry the guy or anything, but we'd have thought of something. I bet Lucius and Neo, in particular, would have wanted to help. They'd have come up with all kinds of ideas.

But the way things stand now? No way in hell I'm staying here on Fantasy Island with His La-Dee-Dah Radiance forever, while my warlocks wonder what the hell ever happened to me, and the witching world keeps marching toward extinction with that worse-than-useless Messalina's ass warming my throne.

Especially when I'm wondering whether Messalina negotiated this whole Avalon arrangement just to get me offstage so I'm no threat to her reign.

I'm getting chilly and stiff, all scrunched up in this window seat, and I'm starting to eye that comfy-looking bed despite myself, when a pulse of heat floods through me. Like I've just opened the oven door or something.

Heat races over the surface of my skin and pools in my tummy. My pores open and I start to sweat.

My gaze shoots to the full moon that's floating over that Faerie sea. A dark winged silhouette, clearly some kind of dragon at a distance, flits past the swollen orb. Just looking at that moon and that dragon makes things worse down below. My cunt clenches and my crotch gets slick.

Oh fuck.

That's definitely my mating heat.

I jump up and beeline over to the carafe and quaff a hefty gulp of that chilled wine, which is crisply delicious but totally doesn't help. Then I nip into the bathroom and peer into the oval mirror above the sink, lit by another of those glowing crystals. My face is all flushed and dewy, my eyes are heavy-lidded and shimmery, and that fresh mating bite Lucius gave me last night (which has kinda slipped my mind given all the other shit going down right now) looks ouchy and inflamed. Because with me stuck here, obviously, Lucius can't tend it.

Add that to the list of problems, I guess.

Without an alpha to tend that bite and pump me full of bio-chemically enhanced shifter spunk, I could be at risk of developing mating fever, which can happen when a mating bite goes untended.

Because that shit can be lethal.

I unzip my catsuit to the waist—you know, just to cool down—and my tits spill out. They're looking fuller than usual, the areolae puffy and swollen, everything's feeling tender, and my nipples are extra sensitive.

I mean, if I'm going into heat, that has to mean at least I'm not pregnant, right? That right there's the silver lining in this oh-shit scenario.

But I really don't know for sure. I'm still a total newbie with this shifty stuff.

What I do know, really clearly, is I need a fuck.

My hands drift up on their own to cup my tits. I'm all tingly and warm. When I tease my nipples, twin arcs of pleasure streak through me, shooting straight to my clit.

My throaty moan fills the room. My sharp incisors sink into my lower lip.

Which just makes me think of Zephyr with his wicked little fangs.

I don't know shit about Fae mating customs. Where's my sweet bookworm Neo and his encyclopedic knowledge of Faerie lore when I need him, right? That thought makes me miss him even more, if that's possible. But right now, my inner dragon really wants to give that Dark Fae King a mating bite and then fuck him till he breaks our heat.

I mean, that's the plan anyway, right?

At least as far as he's concerned?

Shit, he was practically begging for it, the way he stripped down and bent over right in front of me—

"Nope," I announce, popping the P, right out loud so my libido can't miss it. "No go, showgirl. That right there's your hormones going haywire. You hate that guy."

He is ours, Zara, my dragon hisses. *I have seen him. And the other, the Seelie, already he desires you. We shall have them both!*

"Um, no, that's a negative," I say firmly.

At least as firmly as anyone can who's feeling herself up in the mirror, tweaking a nipple with one hand, while the other dips inside my catsuit and under my panties to find the slick heat between my legs.

At the first purposeful touch on my clit, another moan spills out of me. I circle the hard pulsing nub with a shaky finger. My pelvis flexes and my hips roll into my touch.

Wow.

I'm already super close to coming.

I'm just gonna have to get myself off. And maybe get creative to see if there's anything decent in my jail cell I can use as a dildo—

The faint echo of a yell is so distant it barely registers, even with my shifty senses. But that cry is so charged with pain and, God, all these other emotions I can't even put into words that it gooses me like an electric current.

I freeze and stare into my own startled gaze.

Sweet Jesus, I look obscene, with my catsuit all the way unzipped and slipping off my shoulders, while I knead my tit and rub my clit like I'm shooting porn or something. If any of my warlocks saw me like this, my guys would have me stuffed with dick in every orifice before you could say *triple penetration.*

Another cry drifts into the loo.

Hell.

That's definitely a guy shouting in pain.

I yank my hand out of my catsuit and zip up so fast I almost catch a nipple in the zipper. The musky scent of my own slick floats around me as I shoot out of the loo across the bedroom to the balcony. I unlatch and swing the door open as quietly as possible, because I don't see any major need to draw attention to myself till I figure out what's happening.

The raw groan of agony that hits my eardrums has me poking my head right into the bitter cold.

Toward that balcony like mine I saw earlier, one room over and a floor down. That's where those sounds are coming from. I noticed the setup when I did my recon. And, sure, I'm a reformed cat burglar with zero fear of heights, but there's so much I don't know about this place and the layout that I originally opted not to make a blind jump.

Now, with those sounds leaking out, like someone down there's getting tortured?

Whole new story.

I ghost outside and measure the distance to the next balcony with a practiced eye. I can clear ten feet in training with a running start, but I won't have that here.

Still, I'm in my catsuit, and my boots have great traction.

The wind whips my braid forward over my shoulder to lash my face—and that's what decides me. That wind's fierce as fuck.

But it'll be at my back when I jump.

I take a few secs to clear the ice and snow off my balcony rail, then nimbly climb the thing till I'm crouched on top. Again I measure the distance to my landing pad, looks like about 8.5 feet over and down, give or take a few inches. Plenty of moonlight to see by, plus a dim spill of light seeping through the volcanic glass below.

Here's the bottom line.

That lower balcony's big enough and sturdy enough to handle my weight. I just gotta clear the rail (which is all iced over and snowy like mine just was, natch). And I need to land clean, without breaking an ankle or alerting the fun parade down there they've got company.

Easy, right?

I pull in a few long breaths of air so cold it burns my lungs. Just to settle myself and focus. What I definitely *don't* do is look down at those big jagged boulders way below, with white curls of sea foaming at their base.

I deepen my crouch till my quads sing with strain, fix my gaze where I wanna land, and push myself hard into open air.

Faster than thought, the lower balcony rushes toward me. I shoot out my arms, palms locking around the icy rail—and slip.

One arm flails around and finds nothing. I lock my other hand hard around that rail and cling like Velcro. The hard jerk of my full weight tears through my weight-bearing arm and shoulder. I barely bite back a cry of pain.

Shit. I'm dangling by one hand over a whole lotta nothing.

And my grip is slipping.

You better believe I waste zero time flinging up my other arm to lock a second hand around the rail. That gives me the leverage I need to stabilize my swinging body, lock my grip, and arrest the skid.

Then, gently, without looking down, I rock my body side to side till I can flex my abs and hook one boot on the ledge. Then it's just a matter of using my core and upper body strength to drag myself onto the rim and crawl over the rail.

I land on the balcony with a soft hiss and drop to a crouch behind a driftwood chair piled high with snow.

For a while, I just focus on breathing till my hands stop shaking. A truckload of adrenaline is coursing through my system and making me lightheaded. But I gotta admit it feels good to use my skills again, the ones I actually trained for.

Feels good to know I've still got it.

And the affirmation reminds me I'm not without resources in this place, even if I can't shift or summon lightning while I'm wearing these fucking bracelets.

A hiss and a *crack!* siss through a gap in the balcony doors, followed by another drawn-out groan. This cry's all raspy, like the yeller is losing his voice from all that yelling. I poke my head around the chair, but the glass doors are frosty and I can't see shit. On the plus side, that frost hopefully also means whoever's on the other side can't see *me*.

I suck in a breath, slide out from cover, sidle right up to the opaque glass, and press my eye to the gap.

Once my brain absorbs what I'm seeing, all the breath explodes from my lungs in a big frosty whoosh.

Like someone just punched me in the gut.

It's inky dark in there, ominous dark, except for the harsh spotlight effect a couple of those crystals create, just an island of pale light floating in the darkness. That cold witchlight gleams on the heavy industrial-strength links of silver chain suspended from a hook in the ceiling and cuffed around a pair of brawny male wrists. The guy wearing the cuffs is totally naked, chained in place with his muscled arms overhead and his broad back to me.

And, sweet Jesus, what a back it is.

My eyes sweep up the corded length of those bulging calves and thighs, over an ass that's so hard and so perfect it looks sculpted from rock by Michelangelo's chisel, then over a powerful back that's inked shoulder to shoulder with an intricate, dazzling, sinister tattoo of dark angel wings.

The same intricate ink winds around one of those massive arms in an ivy-and-thorns motif, accented with drops of crimson. That's ink I've seen before.

Like, recently.

I recognize that bloody thorn tattoo the same way I recognize that head of spiky pewter hair, the mighty span of those muscled shoulders, the sheer size and power of that giant frame.

It's Ash.

Of course it's Ash.

Chained up and dangling from that hook like he's the nameless next victim in the *Texas Chainsaw Massacre*.

Ash, with his shoulders and back crossed with narrow red slashes, thin ribbons of glistening crimson seeping from the lashes to paint those gorgeous angel's wings in freshly spilled blood.

When I suck in a shaky breath, my heart hammering so hard I can practically hear it, the metallic scent of sorrow mingles with the tinny smell of snow.

And that whippet-slim guy with the flogger, every sinew vibrating with quiet intensity that's as striking as a shout, leather strips slithering against the stone floor and slapping against his boot as he prowls around his much larger prey like a leopard, with a mane of moss-green hair spilling down his back?

That's Zephyr.

That absolute fuck of a Fae.

When recognition sinks in, the red flood of fury that erupts through my body like lava exploding from a volcano just about takes the top of my head off.

I'm literally murderous with rage.

The strength of my reaction totally catches me off guard. Sure, I don't know Ash all that well, but it's pretty fucking obvi he's completely devoted to Zephyr.

And that Unseelie bastard is *hurting* him.

I'm shaking with outrage, poised on the verge of doing something really idiotic like busting in there to rescue the guy, when the Unseelie's liquid voice trickles through the gap in the door and freezes my boots to the ground.

"If you wish to beg for my forgiveness, Seelie Prince," he murmurs, "I will now hear you."

The Light Fae chuffs out a breath. "Now why'd I wanna go and do a thing like that? You're enjoying yourself back there, ain'tcha?"

Somehow Ash's drawl manages to sound simultaneously pained and amused. Just the way you'd imagine a Seelie Prince (another royal, who knew?) would sound under torture.

"There is perilous little enjoyment to be found in Avalon in these dark days. Not least in this betrayal of my hard-won trust by my closest and best-loved ally." Zephyr slaps the flogger against his own boot. The snap makes Ash flinch. "I warned you, Seelie Prince, did I not?"

Another crack of the lash against leather, this one sharp enough to make even me flinch. "I warned you to say naught to the Gemini queen."

My mouth drops open in outrage.

Now wait just a goddamn minute.

Is that little tyrant punishing Ash for clueing me in on my own allegedly upcoming wedding, the way Zephyr himself was too chicken-shit to do?

"Admit it, Your Transcendence," Ash pants while he hangs there bleeding. "You dig it when I defy your imperial orders, don'tcha? Cuz then I give you an excuse to do *this*."

He flexes his flogged shoulders, even though the movement makes him hiss.

"I hardly require an excuse. And you are yet unrepentant." Zephyr clasps his hands behind his back and tilts his head like he's admiring his handiwork. "Admittedly, the sight of you is… not displeasing."

Somehow Ash manages to chuckle, even with the blood dripping down his back. The chained Seelie pivots around some to look behind him, arms twisting overhead, which gives me… whoa… a profound profile view of a really colossal and fully erect cock.

Everything I thought I knew about this scene going down in front of me gets turned inside out.

Without warning, that snarky comment Ash made to the guy earlier whispers through my brain. *Guess you're just gonna have to take it outta my hide, ain'tcha, Your Resplendence?*

Well, dayum.

Ash and that boner he's rocking just gave that *closest and best-loved ally* monicker a whole new meaning.

"Worth it then," Ash says huskily. "To please you. Just go ahead and swing that flogger a little harder, why don'tcha? You know I've taken worse."

Jesus, this is fucked up. This whole dynamic between the two of them. It's one thing they're captor and captive from two enemy races and probably fucking the shit out of each other. I mean, who am I to judge how these two get their jollies? I get the whole enemies-to-lovers appeal.

But that raw flash of blazing heat in the Seelie's gaze as he smolders down at Zephyr—who's still got his back to me—while Ash bleeds on the floor…

Knowing it's maybe like a consensual thing?

All that mating heat, which my concern for this guy's welfare shoved temporarily under wraps, comes roaring back.

I wait, holding my breath, for the little pissant to swing that flogger again. But Zephyr only strolls around to face his captive and drapes the horrible implement of punishment around Ash's powerful neck in a slow sliding caress that makes the big man gasp and shiver.

Honestly speaking, the sight and sound of his obvious pleasure makes me shiver too. The spellbinding scene of that massive brute of a male so totally in the thrall of this slender, delicate, pretty-faced Fae who's barely any bigger than I am, who controls the giant Seelie Prince so effortlessly…

Shit.

Maybe it's just my mating heat—but I honestly don't think so.

Together, those two are absolutely riveting.

"When it comes to that spoiled upstart queen, 'tis true, I would rather you'd kept your silence." Barely speaking above a whisper, Zephyr rises on tiptoe, grips one end of the flogger in either hand, and draws Ash's silver head down toward him. "If I must wed where I do not love, if I must forever forswear my heart's true yearning for cold duty's sake, if I can control nothing else in this fate I must suffer—then at least I will control the manner of the telling."

It's awkward for Ash to bend, the way he's shackled, and moving at all has to hurt. But he strains down and Zephyr lunges up and their mouths fuse together with a desperate groan like they're both starving.

Ash pours his whole body and heart and soul into that kiss. He kisses Zephyr like he's just begging the guy to love him. And that Unseelie asshole meets him kiss for kiss and totally brands the guy with his mouth in an unmistakable stamp of ownership.

When Zephyr lowers one hand to wrap around Ash's cock, I feel that searing contact like a hand cupping my cunt. My body responds with a flood of Mogadon pheromones and a rush of musky vanilla mating scent I'm helpless to control.

And, all too clearly, that touch rocks Ash's world.

The Seelie's brow furrows and his eyes squeeze shut. He arches his back and shoves into his tormentor's commanding grip.

"You're being so very good for me. You know so very well how to please me, don't you?" the Unseelie croons, in that voice like water trickling over rock. "Shall I give you the release you're begging for?"

"Not unless you're gonna go first… and let me watch." Ash's breath goes harsh and he pumps into Zephyr's fist. "I swear to fuck, Sparrow, I just wanna… watch your gorgeous face… when you come for me."

Zephyr's breath hisses in. I squeeze my thighs together and feel myself getting damp. Oh God, are they really going to—?

Then, to my total fucking disappointment, the Unseelie releases his guy's fabulously thick and priapic dick and steps deliberately back till he's totally out of reach.

What. The fuck.

I mean, *come on.*

They both *so* very obviously want each other. And, Christ, I so very obviously want to watch—

"You know I dare not," the Unseelie says, with obvious regret, and for a sec it's like he's talking to both of us. "The mating ceremony looms on the morrow. I'll require every erg of repressed sexual energy I can possibly command to fuel my witchcraft and break the curse when I mate my unwanted mate."

Well, isn't that a bucket of cold water poured right over my goddamn head?

Since I'm the unwanted mate he's got lined up to do the bump-and-grind?

That metaphorical cold shower makes me realize I'm literally freezing to death out here on this balcony.

Fortunately, my resurging anger rides to my rescue like the Lone Ranger and heats my blood to a boil. While I glare at him through the gap, Zephyr retrieves his flogger from around Ash's neck in a single deft flourish, pivots on his heel, and strides right out of the room with the bloodstained leather strips trailing on the stone in his wake.

Guess I'm not the only one who's lost that lovin' feeling, thanks to that preview of coming attractions.

Ash watches him go in silence till the shadows swallow him up. The gentle snick of the door closing rings sharp in the fraught silence.

Then, to my dismay, Ash's spiky pewter head swivels in my direction.

"Might as well c'mon in, princess," he says calmly, "before you freeze to death out there."

My heart almost stops beating.

Then I straighten my cold-stiffened limbs out of my crouch with a sigh of resignation.

"Cheese on toast," I grouse, pushing the door wide. "How'd you even know I'm out here?"

"Easy-peasey," he says patiently, apparently unperturbed by the fact that he's totally naked *and* he's got an audience. "You got the moon behind ya, isn't that right, cat burglar?"

"Fuck," I mutter in disgust, getting out of the biting wind as quick as I can and pulling the door shut behind me. "Guess I'm out of practice."

Actually, I'm pretty sure my professional cat burgling days are behind me, what with being the next queen and all. Still, they're useful skills and I intend to keep them sharp.

"To be fair, you don't cast much of a shadow, little thing like you. Probably woulda missed ya." His conversational tone deepens. "But I can kinda smell ya. Starting your heat, ain'tcha?"

Which is all kinds of awkward.

Hell. My first instinct is to totally deny it.

But why bother? It's basic biology, just what happens when you take mating bites from three separate shifters like I have. And he already said he can smell it on me.

Apparently, that's just one more thing he already knows about me.

And whatever he knows, I'm gonna assume Zephyr knows too.

Anyway, I need to stop focusing on how exposed and vulnerable that whole concept is making me feel. Right now, I've got way more immediate issues on my mind.

Like the state of Ash's poor flogged back.

"Never mind about me. That's not why I'm here." I march straight over there and make a swiveling motion with my finger for him to turn. Looking bemused, the guy actually does it—pivots away to show me his back. He actually follows my lead.

Then again, I guess he's good at that.

"I can't believe he just walks out and leaves you chained to the ceiling *bleeding*," I announce, my indignation mounting with every furious step. "I mean, hasn't His Radiance ever heard of aftercare? What kind of dom just walks away and *leaves* somebody… what…?"

My flood of outraged words trickles off to a sputtery drip. By now I'm right behind him, ready to assess the damage… and the cruel stripes from that vicious flogging are barely there, fading even as I watch. Just leaving streaks of dried blood to mar the pretty feathers of his angel's wing tattoo.

"Whoa." I breathe. "Your back. It's, like, healing?"

"Oh, sure," he says easily over his shoulder. "That's Seelie witch-craft for ya right there. We heal lickety split from just about anything. Except fire and iron, the standard stuff."

Wow. That nifty swifty healing he's rocking sure puts that scene I just saw go down in here in a whole other light. Because of course Zephyr's gotta know the way Ash heals up.

The same way he'd have to be brain-dead not to know how much Ash clearly gets off submitting to him.

That spectacular boner's one hell of a tell.

"That healing magic of yours sure must come in handy." As gently as I can, so I don't hurt him worse, I lay a hand on his back. He's sleek and hot and smooth to the touch.

Mmmmm.

His skin's velvety soft. Soft as though every downy feather on his inked-on wings is real.

A shiver works over his skin and goosebumps rise all along his shoulders. Suddenly, I'm super aware that he's completely naked and close enough to feel that heat rising off his skin. That spectacular ass of his is just inches away.

And we're touching.

Lightly I skim my fingers over his shoulders. His breath quickens in the hush. The clean invigorating scent of the ocean rises from his skin, mingled with the spice of Zephyr's burnt amber.

I breathe them in deep. Both of them. God.

Now that I know that shit I saw was consensual?

Those two were hot as fuck together.

"Does this still hurt?" I whisper.

"Feels good." By now his baritone's gone so rumbly I can feel it in my bones. "Don't stop."

My mating heat pools and pulses between my thighs till the gusset of my panties (which freeze-dried out on that balcony) is drenched. Again. My throat is dry and my heart is pounding.

No matter what he's asking for, I really need to stop touching him.

Or at least, if I have to touch him, I need to let him down from that hook.

But I can't seem to stop tracing the outline of those tattooed angel wings spread across his shoulders. I swear that ink's so good they're almost three dimensional, like those wings are gonna break free of his back and spread.

I clear my throat, but fuck, my voice still comes out wrong. I'm all sexed-up and throaty. "I, uh, guess you must really hate me, huh?"

His winged back swells in a long inhale.

"Nah, I don't hate ya, princess. And that's the God's honest. What's going down here with you and him, you're not to blame for any of it, true?" He pauses. "Sure, I maybe resent ya for it a little, that it's gonna be you and not me who marries him. But that ain't the same thing as hatred."

I shake my head, even though he can't see me behind him, because nothing like that's going down with me and Zephyr.

Still, the Unseelie is very clearly committed to his course. He obviously feels bound by it, whether I'm on board or not.

That has to be painful for Ash.

My voice softens to a scrap of breath. "How could you not hate me? If it wasn't for me, Zephyr could marry you. The one he actually loves."

"Me?" He chuffs out a dry snort. "Nah, I'm just the consolation prize, you feel me? He's still in love with your guy. The telepath."

The word hits me like a kick to the chest. I mean, it literally knocks the wind out of me. "My guy? You mean *Ronin*?"

"Yup. Ronin Pendragon. That's the guy he'd marry if he could." He pauses. "Even after Ronin betrayed him."

I honestly don't know why I'm so shocked to hear any of this. I already know Ronin and Zephyr have major history. That whatever went down between them tore Ronin apart. And given all that history, I'm not at all surprised Zephyr's had a hard time forgetting him.

Because, with Ronin?

Out of all the guys in my harem, Ronin's the one everyone falls for and no one forgets.

Still, it didn't look to me like Zephyr was thinking about somebody else while he was working Ash over. That Unseelie sadist was fully present in the moment.

And I definitely don't like the casual self-deprecation I'm picking up from this guy in front of me.

I let my roaming hands drop. I circle around so I can look Ash in the eye. "Don't sell yourself short, big man. I mean, sure, I know those two had a thing once upon a time. But it's totally obvi now your guy's in love with—"

Oh sweet fuck.

Somehow, with Ronin and his spectacularly failed boyhood fling with His Radiance dominating my mind, I managed momentarily to forget about the full frontal.

Now that I'm experiencing it up close and personal, I'm pretty sure there's gonna be no more forgetting it.

Ever.

"—you." I finish my sentence faintly (that *was* what I was gonna say, wasn't it?) and lick my suddenly dry lips.

Because that Seelie's got the thickest, meatiest cock I've ever seen, springing from a thatch of pewter curls. Proportional to the rest of him, wider at the base but nice and fat at the tip, still flushed and slick with precum from that hand job I witnessed, coupled with a ballsack that would take both my hands to handle.

Not that I'm planning to handle him or anything.

But he's got more going on down there to draw the eye than size. The thick ridge underneath his dick is studded with a double row of silver piercings.

That's a total Jacob's ladder.

I've never fucked a guy with a Jacob's ladder.

And we're not starting now, showgirl, I remind both myself and my very intrigued and excited dragon. *He's not why we're here.*

Except why am I taking this exact moment to remember that convo I had with my guys the night before I split? That convo about me not being done and them expecting me to take more mates and everyone consulted being more or less okay with it—?

"First time you seen a pierced dick, princess?" Ash's voice, warm with humor, hits my ears. "Guess I shoulda warned ya, huh?"

My gaze veers from the object of my obsession to find his craggy face creased in a lazy grin. Like he totally doesn't mind me staring rudely at his package.

But his mercury gaze shimmers with hidden heat.

Zara, he is ours, my dragon queen whispers. *We should claim him.*

"Yeah, no. This isn't about me," I say as firmly as I can. For everyone's sake. "And stop trying to change the subject. First things first. We need to get you unchained from the ceiling and, uh, dressed before we continue with the conversating, okay?"

Ash's silver eyes flick toward the door Zephyr vanished through and his face turns thoughtful.

"Not gonna say no to that," he sighs at last, chains clinking as his shoulders shift. "I ain't as young as I used to be, and that's a fact."

"Right. Let's make it happen." I exert my willpower and manage to turn away from the way-too-compelling sight of this massive, erect, and very naked Fae male to look around for a chair or something.

But this room's tiny and pretty bare, except for a couple of tall mirrors angled to reflect whoever's hanging from this hook and a nice little collection of floggers and crops and other *Fifty Shades* accessories hanging neatly on the wall.

The Unseelie apparently uses this funhouse exclusively for his little games with Ash… and, you know, anyone else His Radiance chooses to torture/fool around with.

It definitely crosses my mind to wonder if His Radiance is planning to fool around with me that way, especially since he seems pretty hostile to the whole concept of mating me. I don't think I'd be into being hung from a hook like a slab of beef.

Still, the thought of all that intensity and focus and tightly contained control, exquisitely trained on me…

Honest to fuck, I don't even know how to feel about that idea. Zephyr's a dick, but I can't deny (at least to myself) that something about him and his situation here kinda compels me.

With me going into heat, I can definitely see all that repressed passion of his working out in my favor—

Behind me, Ash sighs and his chains clink. "Why don'tcha just leave me, princess? Sparrow will be back after a bit. He's got a spell that'll open these cuffs."

My gaze shoots from my own conflicted reflection to his. The way these mirrors are set up, I can see the guy from the chest up (since I'm standing right in front of him). That fantastic physique of his looks incredible, all spotlit and stretched out on display. A fine sheen of sweat from his recent activities glitters on every powerful flex and ripple.

But that pose isn't meant for comfort, and he's already said he wouldn't mind me getting him down. I mean, the guy might be built like Vin Diesel, but he's no spring chicken.

He's gotta be pushing like forty or something.

I pivot to face him, being *very* careful to keep my gaze diligently trained above the waist. "I'm one of those 'do now, think later' kinda girls. We're not waiting around till Zephyr's in the mood. You, uh, mind if I get a little closer? I'm gonna have to touch you for this."

His own gaze slides down my body in a slow caress that heats me up (given my whole hormonal situation) like an actual caress.

"Not at all, princess," he drawls. "How close do you wanna get?"

My dragon purrs for him, but I manage to swallow the sexy sound before it rises from my throat. "Pretty close. Stand as firm as you can for me."

A spark of appreciation flares in his eyes. He spreads his feet and takes a good strong stance.

Without letting myself overthink the situation, I launch myself at him, plant my hands on his broad shoulders, and scramble up his body like a monkey, then strap my legs around his taut waist. I wrap my arms around his neck to anchor myself in place.

That move slots his impressive woodie right up against my crotch. But that's not the reason I'm doing this.

No, really. It's not.

My eyes lock with his gleaming gaze. When we're this close, his eyes are so silver they're almost metallic. A girl could get seriously lost in those eyes.

Not to mention the raw strength that thrums like electric voltage through his bulging deltoids and impressive pecs and rock-hard abs. Every inch of all that strength is pressed against me.

"I'm gonna do this the old-fashioned way." Shit, I sound breathless. And not from the exercise.

"Works for me." Pressed against him like this, I can literally feel the words rumble from his chest. "I'm an old-fashioned kinda guy."

I'm already perspiring under my catsuit. And fighting not to sink into his shimmering stare. I don't even mind that he's so much older than me, even older than Lucius. He wears it really well. All those years give him a rock-solid steadiness and a quiet kind of confidence that make me feel steadier and more confident myself.

"Okay, princess," he breathes, low and rumbly. "So what happens next?"

Next we claim him, my dragon pipes up decisively.

Now I definitely need a distraction.

Somehow I wrench my gaze away from his to check out the heavy links of chain looped over that hook in the ceiling.

"You just hang tight and stand still for me. I'll have you down in a sec." I shift my weight, and his cock slots against my pussy through my catsuit like we were goddamned made for this. I swear I can feel every individual stud of his Jacob's ladder sparking friction down my slit.

A little moan spills out of me before I can bite it back.

Color darkens his rugged face and his voice goes all guttural. "Or you could just stay here."

"I don't think His Radiance would like that very much," I breathe. "Me macking on his guy."

"You think he'd mind?" He gives a husky laugh. "Guess you haven't been hanging around this place long enough to see how we roll. Avalon's just a distorted mirror of your Icarus Island. That's how the Unseelie got the portal open. Sure, Fae royals only marry once, but there's no royal wedding on my to-do list. And Sparrow… he likes to watch."

Now that's a nice fat nugget of Avalon Island lore… not to mention Ash-and-Zephyr context… that I'm definitely tucking away to think about later. Right now, I've gotta focus on the present. I clear my throat, grip his shoulders, and give that chain another assessing look as I plan out my approach.

"So you're one of the Light Fae, their prince or something?" I scoot a little higher up his torso to give myself some purchase.

"Or something," he agrees. "Not a daughter, so I'll never rule, and I ain't jonesing for that crown either."

"Did you and Zephyr meet at the Faerie ball or something?" I use my upper body strength to inch higher up his frame. This entire maneuver is mashing my tits against his chest in a way I'm pretty sure he doesn't mind.

But at least my crotch is no longer frotting his cock.

"Or something," he says again. "The Light Fae and the Dark, we usually don't mingle. Cuz of all that bad blood from the past. But Sparrow's mom—that's Maeve, the dowager queen, you'll meet her—

she wanted her kid to know the enemy. So she started sending him through the portal for tutoring by a Seelie royal. That's how we met."

"You were his *tutor*?" I wait for his nod. Geez, that makes me so hot. They're just like me and Lucius. Which makes me miss my wolf shifter headmaster even more.

I swallow down the ache in my chest. "Cute meet then, huh?"

"Yeah, real cute," he says dryly. "He was just a kid at the time, and he wasn't there by choice. He was a regular little shit. Fair to say we didn't hit it off back then."

"Sounds like he hasn't changed much." I get a good grip on his shoulders to push myself higher.

"Oh, he's changed all right. Him getting the hots for me came after—" He breaks off with a hiss.

Because I've just levered myself up with my arms, and I'm carrying almost my full weight on my braced palms.

My legs are dangling free. And my tits are pressed against his face.

An image streaks through my brain like a comet. An image of him unzipping my catsuit with his teeth.

"Geez Louise, princess," he mutters, voice muffled by my catsuit. "Warn a guy next time."

Which really makes me hope the Fae aren't telepaths.

"Now where's the fun in that?" I pant, inching to one side like a gymnast balanced on her hands. I gotta make room now on his shoulder for my knee. "You were saying? About you and Zephyr?"

I'm actually surprised by how much I want to hear the rest of this story.

"I was saying," he says patiently into my chest, "him getting the hots for me came after your Ronin betrayed him. Your guy broke him into a million jagged pieces. I put him back together again. Sparrow was all grown up by then. That's when I finally wised up and figured out I was pretty hard into the kid myself."

"So how did Ronin… betray him?" I feel like holding my breath, but right now I need all the oxygen I can get. I'm using my core to curl up my body and get a knee on Ash's shoulder, all without losing my balance, and I'm hoping like fuck I don't pull a groin muscle.

Ash holds super-still for my unrehearsed acrobatics and says flatly, "Ronin was the one who took Sparrow's eye."

Hearing those words is such a shock I almost fall off the guy. Somehow I manage to get one knee up, and then the other, instead. Now I'm kneeling on his shoulders and gripping the chain for balance.

"Fuck. Me. Sideways," I whisper. "Ronin would never… I mean, sure, he can be brutal. He's trained to kill. But he would never do *that*. He loved the guy."

"Ronin woulda killed him, but Sparrow got away—and came to me." His voice roughens. "It was me that patched him up. Physically— and in other ways."

I grip the chain, which has plenty of slack and isn't actually bearing his weight, in both hands to steady myself. Now I've got a bird's-eye view of that thorns-and-blood tattoo inked around his giant bicep, and suddenly I know who he's wearing it for. Ash's face is wedged between my thighs, and my heart is pounding with way more than exertion.

What I don't know is what to think. Or how to feel. About any of this.

Zephyr and Ash.

Zephyr and Ronin.

Zephyr and me.

Because the way I'm starting to get emotionally sucked into this whole shitstorm saga?

I'm fucked.

"Then Zephyr kidnapped you." I push out the words and barely wait for his grunt. "Same way he kidnapped me. Because he takes what he wants without asking."

"Yeah, sure. It's kinda tradition." Under my knees, his shoulders twitch in a miniscule shrug. "That's just the way these Unseelie operate."

"Some tradition." Now it's my turn to grunt. I infuse as much skepticism into that short utterance as I can manage.

"Wanna know why I'm telling you all this?" Ash turns his face into my catsuit-clad thigh, which definitely kicks up my heart rate. "So you'll maybe cut the kid a break, princess. He's one of the good guys, he really is, you feel me?"

What I feel is the way his mouth moves against my inner thigh. What I feel is things I shouldn't. What I feel is why he's dangerous.

And not only because I'm in heat.

"Yeah, I feel you," I say roughly. "And I feel like you're way more forgiving than I am. Too bad your so-called good guy didn't ask before he took me. So any break I cut anyone? It's gonna be for you."

I stretch my arms overhead, unloop the heavy chain around the ceiling hook, and let it fall behind him. The heavy links rattle to the floor, his muscled arms come down, and his hands close around me to steady me.

Those strong hands of his engulf my waist, and man, he's so big his two hands nearly touch. In a single swift move, he lowers me down his body in a long unbroken sweep that lights me up like a Roman candle. My pulse is thundering in my ears and pounding between my legs. Every inch of my skin is hot and tingling.

The air floods with a sweet rush of my Mogadon pheromones that gooses both our vitals.

Now he holds me suspended, my boots dangling in the air, my face level with his. His cheeks are flushed and his eyes are lidded, irises burning with platinum fire.

I clutch his powerful shoulders. "Listen, Ash—"

"Zara," he grates. "Fuck."

I think he's still swearing when our mouths meet in a blazing kiss.

Chapter Eighteen
Zephyr

I've just finished cleaning my love's precious blood off my second favorite flogger when I receive the ill-timed honor of an unannounced visit by the dowager queen.

Queen Maeve.

My moon-fucked mother.

She arrives on dragonback, of course, which is the only way a Dark Fae royal travels anywhere. For this reason, I have the slim advantage of an early warning to tuck away my flogger out of sight. I am warned because my green Xhevith despises my mother and that moon-cursed monster she rides in equal measure. Xhev's unease at housing her beast in his lair ripples through our bond.

In my great room, the dowager queen is waiting.

I steel myself for the encounter and smooth my face to the impassive mask she expects from me, this king and heir she tolerates (as I am her only offspring) but whom she will never love. Then I stride into the gauntlet of her presence and acknowledge her, as one does, with the twitch of a smile I am far from feeling.

"Your Moonstruck Magnificence, what an unexpected honor," I say coolly. "The hour is late, but I am at your disposal."

There is a trick to dealing with her which I learned years ago, because a Fae cannot lie, but she is ruthless with any truth. The trick is to show her impeccable courtesy, reveal nothing of yourself that matters, and spend as little time as possible in her presence.

She turns slowly from the window where she towers, slim and sharp as an icicle, glittering in armor of frost-white dragonscale. Hair the pale blue of a glacier sweeps high above her pointed ears and spills down her rigid spine. Her arctic stare rakes over my casual-night-at-home attire and lingers, as always, on the eyepatch that mars my beauty.

"Of course," she murmurs. Of course her presence is an honor, of course the hour is late, of course my time is hers to waste. "Fear not, for I shall not linger. You tarried long in the mortal world, my son. I had grown… concerned."

I greet that understatement with a politely lifted brow. According to Ash, she's been in a towering rage because I left without telling her and acted without consulting her. One glance from this queen in a towering rage breaks mirrors and shatters steel.

When she is truly wrathful, she unleashes her dragon.

When she is truly wrathful, people die.

I was absent from Avalon for two days.

By now, she will have reduced the entire court to a state of sweating terror.

"My business required more time to conduct than I anticipated, but all is well," I say, a statement that is vague enough to be no lie. "Within these walls, I hold the Gemini queen."

In my mother's smooth brow, a tiny line appears. "This was not the arrangement to which Messalina agreed when we negotiated your marriage treaty. She will be displeased that you have stolen the girl."

To this, I give a shrug of supreme indifference. "She may be displeased, but she should not be surprised. After the damage she wrought here, when she took the royal babe from Avalon, I would not make the mistake of trusting Messalina to honor any arrangement." I pause. "Besides which, stealing whatsoever we desire is the Unseelie way."

"In their world, our ways are long forgotten. If Messalina's babe had survived, matters might have been otherwise." My mother's eyes go lidded. "As for the Gemini queen, until this very moment, you have not given any indication at all that you desire her."

I am about to agree that I do not. But my throat closes around the words.

That the Fae do not lie has nothing to do with hackneyed mortal virtues. In this, the lore that is written of my race in your fairytales speaks true.

We Fae are physically incapable of uttering an untruth.

In this moment, in this matter, I am incapable of disparaging this willful, wrathful, impossible witch I have stolen.

Without warning, a vivid image of Zara Gemini flares to life in my mind, her lush curves encased in that wildly inappropriate catsuit, her turquoise eyes blazing with power in an angel's face, every particle of her being infused with righteous fury. That was how she looked when she screamed defiance and buried cold iron in poor Xhevith's chest.

In the heat of battle, fighting on foot and alone against a flying dragon, she missed his heart and a killing blow by less than a handspan.

In truth, she is nothing at all that I expected.

"She is… not a conventional queen," I say carefully. "In any sense. But she has the strength to survive here in Avalon and the wit to rule at my side. For now, that is all I require."

"Oh, surely not *all*," my mother murmurs. "The longer this cruel winter endures, the swifter our people perish of cold and sickness and despair. With our women rendered barren and our males rendered sterile by this moon-damned curse, we can no longer replenish our failing race." Her voice gains resonance, a battle horn blown over arctic tundra. "To complete the ritual and shatter the curse, you must find more than strength and wit to commend this Gemini queen. You must desire her. As a man desires a woman."

She gives way to a delicate pause. "My son, this is not your typical inclination."

Carefully I control my face to reveal nothing, not so much as a flicker of the truth. True it may be that I have never lain with a woman as I have lain with a man.

Still, on occasion, there has been the rare woman I desire.

With measured steps, I advance on the witchfire and extend my hands to the subtle warmth. "This Gemini queen is… not displeasing to behold. Have no fear. When the time comes, I will contrive to manage the deed."

"Ah, now I see you are eager to bed her. Of course, a life of unbroken celibacy will do that to a man," my mother says complacently. Her booted heels strike a measured tempo on the stone. She crosses to stand by the witchfire at my side.

Because I sense the shrewd glitter of her sidelong gaze, I am in no way deceived.

Her show of complacency is her own deception.

In plain fact, I have not always been celibate, no matter what the Merlin prophesied would be required of me to break the curse. But this truth is one my mother need not know. She has always been deeply suspicious of my attachment to my Seelie tutor Ash—an attachment she believes to be platonic. Thankfully, she has never thought to suspect my boyhood friendship with Ronin. In her mind, Ronin Pendragon is nothing more than an insignificant mortal, even if he is a powerful warlock and the scion of his clan. One day he will lead that fiery Leo clan of his, but my mother could never conceive of the truth.

That insignificant mortal is the reason I am no virgin.

I smooth my face and give her a neutral response. At least, I am as neutral as any man can be when discussing the particulars of his sexual history (or, in my case, its virtual nonexistence, except for Ronin) with his mother.

Inevitably, this entire line of discourse reminds me of Ash, still chained to the ceiling and waiting patiently in my dungeon. One would never know it to look at him, but my love is well past forty. I know the unrelenting Avalon cold troubles his joints.

Privately I resolve to say whatever I must to be rid of my unwanted guest. Once I dismiss my mother, I will free my love.

Unfortunately, Queen Maeve is not so easily dismissed. Her brow arches in a skeptical half-moon. "They say the girl is willful."

"That's putting it rather mildly," I mutter, recalling Zara Gemini's stubbornly persistent questions on dragonback. Indeed, she interrogated and provoked and challenged me with a rare and reckless determination. I found myself hard-pressed not to respond in kind.

Even now, the heated words that could have flown between us hover on my lips. No doubt we have a royal confrontation looming, that untamed girl and I.

In truth, I suspect she is more than untamed.

This Gemini queen is entirely wild.

"Willfulness is not an attractive quality in a future queen." My mother's thin mouth turns down in a frown. "Messalina's willfulness, when she was wedded to my brother Oberon, cost Avalon their royal daughter's life. Just as the willfulness of Gwendolyn Pendragon, who should have been your queen but for her own selfish obstinacy, cost Avalon hers."

Gwendolyn was never the Pendragon I meant to marry, so it was not her obstinacy alone that formed the fatal obstacle to our union.

But the need for spilling that secret is long past.

I make of my silence an armor that the spear of my mother's anger cannot pierce.

Delicately she adjusts one dragonscale gauntlet. "For the girl's willfulness, fortunately, I possess the perfect antidote. You must enroll Zarina Gemini at once in my finishing school."

I stiffen and immediately curse myself for the betrayal, which I know (since she misses nothing) my mother has marked. She considers herself a great patron of education and the arts. As such, it suits her fancy to style herself headmistress of the Avalon Academy for Promising Royals of the Court.

As a survivor of the Avalon Academy myself, I experience a violent qualm of misgiving at the thought of the volatile and headstrong young Gemini installed in that cheerless and often lethal institution. I may never love the girl, but her strength has earned my respect.

Once she has played her part to save my people, I can afford to show her a measure of mercy.

Even if I will never free her.

"My respected mother," I say lightly. (I cannot call her *dear*, which would be lying.) "*Must* is a word that is not used with kings."

"Except by queens," she says smoothly, "whom all kings honor."

According to Unseelie law, she and I are co-equals. Since I gained my majority, neither of us may rule without the other. If Zarina is ever crowned (an act I have not proposed, and which my mother has not suggested), we three would rule as equals.

"Even so, I am not entirely certain that enrolling Zarina Gemini in the Avalon Academy is a sound notion." I struggle to articulate a logical and unsentimental reason my mother will accept. "She has no ability to summon elemental Fae magic, just her own Gemini witchcraft. Hers is a power which, without those charmed bracelets, you would have no hope of containing."

My mother's arctic eyes brighten with a spark of challenge.

With a smile that makes my blood run cold, she spreads her gauntleted hands. "All the more reason to ensure this queen is properly educated so her loyalty to you, to us, to our people, is absolute.

Presumably, with suitable instruction, the creature *is* capable of comprehending Fae custom and courtesy and proper deportment. Even if she is mortal."

My misgivings are growing worse. But if I sustain this protest, my mother will grow suspicious. She'll believe I'm growing attached to the Gemini queen. And she will see any such attachment as a disastrous vulnerability.

This, I cannot afford her to perceive.

"Very well," I say coolly. "I'll bring her to the Academy in the morning. You can ascertain for yourself whether she is capable of benefiting from your instruction."

My tone is acrid, barely a whisper short of sarcasm. My mother's deadly eyes go narrow and dangerous.

"Oh, my boy, never think of bringing her yourself," she croons, "given your many important duties. Merely have her sent. As headmistress, fear not, I shall attend to the rest."

That is precisely what I do fear. But there is no advantage in showing it.

I pivot on my heel, stride to the sideboard, and pour a generous snifter of mortal Tennessee whiskey for Ash. That is the refreshment he always prefers after one of our little sessions.

Pointedly, I offer nothing to my mother.

Keeping my back to her, I announce, "Zarina Gemini will attend the day school only. As my queen, she will naturally lodge with me."

This much, at least, I will do to spare this girl I have stolen from her home to save mine. By the moon, the day school is bad enough. Lodging Zara with the other boarders, the last of the Fae to be born before the curse—all members of the poisonous Fae nobility who angle to share my bed—while the girl's witchcraft is disabled?

Lodging her defenseless in that vipers' pit would kill her.

"Indeed?" Surprise ripples through my mother's brittle voice. "You do apprehend you are under no obligation to bed the creature more than once, merely to complete the ritual and lift the curse. I have assumed that you and your Seelie paramour—"

"Who is a prince in his own right, and no paramour." My words flow without impedance, since my passion for Ash is unconsummated. Technically, my statement is no lie.

This time, my reminder carries an edge my mother cannot pretend to miss.

Without waiting for another of her provocations, I stride for the spiral staircase that leads to the dungeon where Ash is waiting and no doubt cursing my tardiness. "Your Moonstruck Magnificence, I must beg your indulgence. The hour has grown late. I fear your Yersinia's presence is keeping my Xhevith from his well-earned rest."

Just as you are keeping me from mine, I finish in a silence that I mean her, this time, to penetrate.

"Then we shall take our leave." Choosing for once to tolerate my dismissal, my mother glides toward the stairs herself, since Xhev's lair and her own pestilential monster wait for her above.

I contain a sigh of relief that I shall finally be rid of her, at least for one night, and begin my own descent.

"Rest you well tonight for the equinox, my son," she calls, sweet as poison, to my rapidly departing back. "So you may perform your royal duty with this wild Gemini tomorrow and break this pernicious curse. Before it destroys us all."

Chapter Nineteen
Zara

Ash's mouth meets mine like the ocean crashing on the shore. I'm cold from my balcony recon, but his mouth is so warm. He tastes like sunlight and something tangy and sweet, like Florida grapefruit. He smells bracing like the sea before I dive.

And he kisses with an older guy's confidence.

Before I've even made up my mind to do it, my lips are parting and I'm opening to his kiss. My tongue meets his in a hot lick that makes us both moan.

He's still gripping my waist with those big hands of his and holding me like a foot off the ground, so our heights are equal. I slick my hands over his massive shoulders to feel all that strength he's holding in check. His powerful muscles quiver under my palms and his relentless boner nudges the seam between my thighs.

Every nudge of his cock, every sweep of his tongue, every slow thrust of his hips against mine stokes that mating heat pulsing in my slick core to a bonfire. That bonfire between us will burn the world down.

For shit's sake, I barely know the guy.

But I swear to fuck, this male is mine.

"Ash," I breathe into his kiss. I cradle his craggy face and thread my fingers through his spiky hair and try to think. "Listen. You and me? If we do this, it's gonna get complicated."

His silver eyes flash open and crinkle in a smile. "No worries, princess. I can do this standing up."

My dragon purrs with approval for him, because she's more than on board with that whole plan. I make a sound somewhere between a laugh and a groan, then pull back from his kiss to try again. "I mean, you're not leaving this place, you're like a prisoner of love. And I'm definitely not staying, so…"

"You think not, huh?" He leans in to find my mouth in another rain of slow kisses that literally melts my brain. "Could be you'll like it here. Sparrow can be a pretty persuasive guy. Me too, when I set my mind to it."

He lets me slide down his big body, inch by inch, which lets me feel all that swollen length of him scorching me through my catsuit.

I guess that's him setting his mind to it. I gotta admit, the technique is effective.

By the time my feet hit the floor, my resistance is unraveling and I'm ruined.

"Ash," I breathe. "I'm trying to be real about what's happening here." I loop my arms around his neck and lick down his corded throat and his muscled chest. I taste sweat and heat and amber.

Burnt amber. That's Zephyr's scent.

God, Zephyr must've been all over him while Ash was chained to that ceiling.

That thought makes me sink my teeth hard into my lower lip. The sting clears my head a little. I rake my gaze up my male's gorgeously chiseled, too-sexy-to-be-believed naked body till I meet his watchful stare.

I like that he's waiting for me to say what's on my mind. I like that he's letting me set the pace for whatever goes down between us. And I really like the thought of undoing all that careful patience and lighting that slow fuse till he ignites.

"Go ahead," he murmurs. "I'm listening."

"Okay." I pull in a big breath. "Like I said, I'm not staying and you're not leaving. So here's the only way this works."

"I'm all ears." He ducks his head to meet my conflicted stare and waits.

"We keep it simple," I announce as firmly as possible. "We make this a one-time thing."

His brows draw together and his forehead furrows.

We don't have a mating bond or anything, I'm not even sure if these Fae do that whole telepathy thing like me and my guys. But you don't need to be a mind reader to get that this Seelie Prince isn't used to ultimatums.

Or that he isn't crazy about this one.

"For one thing," I try to explain, "I've already got five mates, and there's still a bunch of shit we're working through. When it comes to adding on, I've kinda got this get-out-of-jail free card because of being queen, it's supposed to help the witching world, like symbolically and magically, when I level up. And my guys are all down with that." A sudden idea makes me suck in my breath. "I dunno, maybe while we're saving the world, that'll help your Seelie back home. I mean, if they need help."

"Yeah, we could use the assist." Ash leans down to nuzzle my ear, which makes me all shivery and goosebumpy. (I'm, like, really into his mouth anywhere on my body right now.) "We're part of the witching world too, even if we don't act like it. We survived by keeping our existence secret, even from the other witching races, for a real long time. By now, we're pretty close to extinct ourselves."

Yes, Zara, thisssss, my dragon whispers in a drawn-out hiss. *He is meant to join us.*

Great.

Now apparently I've got a dragon who predicts the future. I guess while I'm wearing these bracelets and she can't rise, you know, she has to pass the time somehow.

"Right. So I'm gonna fix that. We're gonna save the Seelie. You can help." Starting with him getting these fucking bracelets off me, which I'm damn well gonna ask for. I'm just waiting for my moment.

Because it won't do me much good if I ask and he says no.

"Shoot, Zara." He nuzzles behind my ear, where my pulse beats hard and fast. "You're a force of nature. You're unstoppable. Even in a situation like this one where you got your back to the wall. You're actually kinda amazing."

That makes me feel a warm glow that I really hope isn't Stockholm Syndrome. I'm not gonna be a cliche and fall in love with my kidnappers.

"Don't try to sweet-talk me, big man." I smooth my hands over the hard planes of his chest. "I mean it. You and me, we're a one-hit wonder till I can talk to my warlocks. Even if we do work something out with this living-in-two-different-worlds situation, I'm not taking this thing any further than tonight without having all five of my guys specifically on board, I mean, with the whole idea of you."

"Guess that includes your Ronin, huh?" His muscles knot under my hands and his tone turns stiff. "I'm okay with sharing ya, but I ain't too keen on sharing anything with that guy. Not after what he did to Sparrow."

Silently I add that significant problem to my ever-expanding list. No doubt about it, starting anything up with this Seelie is gonna be hella complicated.

Then my gaze falls on the full moon floating through those glass doors, and I feel a powerful tug in my uterus that reminds me of something else. "Also, uh, there's another problem."

His body's already stiff as fuck against mine, due to the whole Ronin thing. Now a muscle flexes in his jaw, but his tone stays level. "Lay it on me."

I give him a wry look. "I don't carry condoms around with me in this catsuit."

Some of the resistance eases from his jaw. "Shoot, that's not gonna be an issue. I'm clean as a whistle. Anyway, the Fae don't catch mortal bugs and viruses. And you can't catch ours."

I file that useful factoid away and move on to the next major issue. "There's also the fact that, one, I'm running a little late to get my next BC shot—you know, since your boyfriend kidnapped me and all? And, two, this Avalon moon's fucking with my cycle."

"You worried about having a half-Fae kid?" He engulfs my chin with his big hand and strokes my cheek with his thumb. "Don't be. If you wanna conceive in Avalon, you need moon tea to open your womb. There's a whole ritual. I'll tell ya the truth, these days conception's a pretty rare thing for all the Fae, both Seelie and Unseelie. Even before the Unseelie got hit with this infertility curse."

Hearing those words, a tension I didn't realize I was carrying eases its grip on my shoulders. Sure, it sucks for the race that the Fae aren't conceiving. That shit's gotta be concerning for them on a societal level. But when it comes to my own heat, knowing about that moon tea puts me back in the driver's seat. Plus his touch steadies me and grounds me in a way I'm surprised by, above and beyond the verbal reassurance.

And I'm starting to get really curious about that curse (despite the fucked-up way Zephyr's gone about dragging me into it).

But that whole story's gonna have to wait.

At least till I break this effing heat.

"I wanna hear more about that, and I want you to tell me." I lean in to nuzzle his chest and feel his massive body tremble under my mouth. "Later, okay?"

"Whatever you want, princess." His voice rumbles against my kiss. "I mean that. Anything. Long as it doesn't hurt Sparrow. You just tell me what you want."

Hell.

I bet, in his mind, asking him to nix these magic handcuffs falls under the *things that could hurt Sparrow* caveat.

I'll just have to convince Ash otherwise.

And you better believe I can be pretty damn convincing.

"You just tell me." He rocks his pierced boner gently into my tummy. "Tell me what your body needs."

I gotta admit, I'm starting to see the upside to having a submissive male on his knees for me (metaphorically speaking). Who knew I'd even be into that dominance kink?

Zephyr might be a total dick, but he's really onto something where that one thing is concerned.

"Hmmm." I lick over Ash's nipple and watch it contract. Then I graze it with my teeth, which makes him gasp and tighten his grip on my hips and push his cock harder into my tummy.

I already know pain gets him off, obvi, but I'm not about to start working him over with one of those crops or floggers or the other kinky shit Zephyr's got hanging on his wall.

I bite him a little harder though, with my shifty-sharp incisors, just to see what he'll do.

"Oh fuck, Zara," Ash whimpers, such a soft sound coming from such a big guy. Honestly speaking, it makes me go a little crazy. I bite harder, almost hard enough to break the skin. He grips my ass and grinds hard against me.

I give a low purr, that's my dragon vocalizing, and suck his nipple into my mouth. Not all guys like nipple play, but this one definitely seems into it.

Yet I'm still holding back because, given that whole *we're gonna keep it simple* rule I just laid down, I don't want to give this guy a mating bite by mistake.

It would be no mistake, Zara, my dragon hisses. *He is ours!*

"Quiet," I mutter against Ash's skin.

I'm talking to her, but he traps another whimper behind his teeth like he's trying to obey me.

Which makes me feel powerful as fuck, even while I'm a captive here myself. I rake my nails lightly down his chest to see if he likes that too (which he does, bigtime). Then I do what I've wanted to do since the minute I walked in here. I stroke my hand down his rock-hard abs, follow that lick of happy trail down to the pewter-gray bush between his thighs, and finally wrap my hand all the way around his thick dick.

He sucks in a breath and punches his hips into my touch.

I swear to Christ, my fingers barely close around his girth. He's hard as steel, all hot and smooth and veiny, the underside of his shaft studded with that row of barbell piercings. I'm not even sure how he'll fit inside me.

We're just gonna give that the old college try.

By now my cunt is rippling and clenching. I need that dick inside me. I'm gonna guess he needs the same, because he's breathing hard through his nose and clenching his jaw and bucking into my fist.

I reach under him with my free hand to cup his ballsack, so big and tight and swollen he overflows my palm. His head falls back and a low tortured cry rips out of him.

Fuck, he needs to come. And so do I.

I'm seized by a sudden inspiration. "It's okay, you can talk when I do this. Let me hear you."

And boy, does he.

"Goddess," he gasps. "I'm dying here. Not sure how much longer I'm gonna be able to hold out. Just lemme see you naked, and I'll die a happy man."

"Oh, I'm gonna do a lot more than that." I keep up the stroking, up and down his thick length, navigating that double row of studs that's gotta feel freaking amazing anytime he's inside someone. Finding the exact rhythm and pressure that make his breath labor and his face flush and his eyes glow like silver moons.

Under my teasing hand, his balls draw up tight. Sweat breaks out across his tortured brow. His big hands knead my ass, but I know he's waiting for my permission to do more.

With three alpha males in my harem, plus me being kinda alpha myself, that waiting-for-permission angle makes Ash pretty unique. He's so different from all my guys, except maybe Neo who has his own sweetly submissive side (which drives me and all his alphas wild). As a recent virgin, my bookworm Neo's still shy and awkward but very eager, in a way we all adore.

But Ash is a man who knows exactly what he's doing. That means he's holding his own eagerness in check.

"Okay, big man," I breathe. "Go ahead and unzip me."

His gaze locks on mine like he's drowning and I'm all that's keeping him afloat. He sinks to his knees before me and drags down my zipper, from my throat to my navel, in a long slow pull.

With his teeth.

The buzz of the zipper releasing is loud in the charged silence.

"Wow," I whisper. He lifts his head to give me a lazy grin.

Now my catsuit gapes all the way down in a way that exposes all my cleavage but still covers my tits.

Like, barely.

Then he licks back up that vee of exposed skin in a way that melts my knees, so I have to grip his shoulders just to hold myself up. A flood of my flowery Mogadon mating scent juices up the joint. We both inhale a heady hit of pheromones that makes my head spin. When he unbuckles the utility belt around my waist, he fumbles a little, because his strong hands are shaking.

"This okay?" He checks before he lets the belt drop, and I nod to give him permission.

Because I'm not sure I can speak.

By the time my belt hits the floor, my mouth is actually dry with anticipation. My whole body's tingling, my braid is unraveling and floating, and my fingertips feel like they're on fire. The only reason I'm not shooting sparks is because of those bracelets.

He skims his hands up my sides and stops just under my tits.

Which makes me wanna scream with frustration.

He licks his lips and his voice goes all husky. "Now's a good time to tell me to stop if you want that. Cuz once I see you naked, I'm not sure stopping's gonna be an option."

"Yeah, no, not stopping you." I lock onto his heated stare. "I want you to fuck me with that thick dick till you break my heat and we both get off so hard we see flaming comets."

The timbre of his voice drops all the way down to bass. "Now that, I can do."

In a single swift movement, still on his knees, he reaches up and peels the catsuit off my shoulders and down my arms. Now I'm standing there naked to the waist, with my own piercings on parade. My nipples are already tight and tingling and my girls are so full they feel ready to burst.

"Fuck. Me." He growls. It's a sound so savage it shoots straight to my clit.

"That's definitely the idea," I agree, good and throaty.

He gives a low laugh and leans in to envelop my pierced nipple with his mouth in a hot sucking pull.

Then he feasts on me.

He devours me.

He pretty much destroys me.

I mean, he literally can't seem to get enough of me and my girls, which is flattering as fuck. He kneads and licks and nibbles and sucks. He pushes my tits together with his hands so he can suck on both nipples at once, which feels so amazing it makes me cry out. I thread my fingers through his hair to hold him right there and lean into his strength so he's holding me up. Under my catsuit, my pussy weeps.

If I don't come soon, I'm gonna trigger some previously unknown witching world recessive gene and burst into flames.

Clumsily, working one-handed while I jack him off with the other, I shove my catsuit down my hips.

He stops what he's doing with my tits long enough to help, peeling the catsuit down my legs, but leaving my turquoise lace panties in place. They're actually Vasili's panties, and you can bet my snake always looks hot as fuck wearing them, with his perky ass and his long legs, especially when he wears heels (which always makes Max and Lucius lose their minds).

But judging by the way Ash's hot eyes stay glued on my body without even blinking, I don't look too shabby wearing these panties either.

He unzips my boots and cradles each foot in turn to ease me out of the footwear. Next, the catsuit lands on the floor. Then it's just Vasili's lace between Ash and me.

Though I'm pretty sure we're gonna have the actual Vasili between us too, once my Goblin King figures out what's going down here in Avalon.

Sweet Jesus, the thought of my snake going toe to toe with the Unseelie King makes me even wetter (for some reason, not that I'm gonna be into that, because I hate that Unseelie bastard). Still, I'm pumping out pheromones and mating scent by the quart, enough to make the whole house—if not the whole city—horny.

Ash growls again and buries his face between my legs. Through the soaked lace gusset, his mouth closes over the swollen bud of my clit.

I fling back my head and give a sob. My first big O barrels down on me like a freight train with steam pouring from the engine and the whistle blasting. I clutch his head and fuck his mouth through my panties while a rush of slick coats the walls of my snatch and adds the musky smell of my cunt to the sex-drenched air.

When he hooks a finger under the lace to slide between my slick folds, then eases into my soaked and aching hole, my pussy clamps hard around him and we both give a good long moan.

"Princess," he groans against my clit.

The vibration feels so good on my oversensitized girly parts that I grip fistfuls of his hair and grind into his face and ride his finger inside me like I'm Mustang Sally.

It's definitely not my first rodeo, but I'm feeling wetter than usual, considering no one's come inside me yet. I've never been a squirter, but now there's cream drenching my panties and slicking my thighs. Every pump of his finger makes a squishing sound inside me.

In other words, I'm more than ready for the main event.

And he's been ready for me all night.

I manage to stop fucking his face long enough to push the panties down my hips, and he's right there helping. Even though he has to withdraw his amazingly effective finger from inside me to assist.

Somehow we get the scrap of lace down my legs and off me. They're currently my only pair of panties, so I appreciate that he doesn't just shred them.

This whole time, he's eyeing me like a white lion ready to pounce on his next meal, all stalky and dangerous, those miles of muscles sleeked with sweat, his pierced dick jutting straight out.

I gotta admit, it's a good look on him.

My dragon preens under his attention. Shifter or no shifter, she's making it pretty clear she likes the guy.

And just the sight of him has my heat cresting and ready to peak.

"You ready for me, big man?" I purr at him.

His silvery stare slides up my body. "I'm all yours."

For the second time tonight, I launch myself at him and scramble up his extremely naked and aroused body. He chuffs out a surprised breath and catches me, arms closing hard around me to pull me in tight. I wiggle a little higher up his torso to feel the head of his amazing cock nudge the seam between my legs. Finally, I settle down over his shaft and sheathe him deep inside me.

Cheese on toast, he's huge. The way his girth stretches the walls of my snatch. And that Jacob's ladder of his.

I can feel.

Every.

Single.

Stud.

Striking sparks of sensation all down my hoochie.

"Oh, sweet fuck," I gasp on a sharp exhale.

"Zara," he groans through clenched teeth. "Oh Goddess. You always… this tight?"

"Mmmm." That's literally all I can manage to say. My ability to articulate has left the building.

He's filling me so full and, God, the inches just keep on coming.

But I can handle him. I have an industrial-strength pussy.

My head falls back on a long moan. His lips find my throat and he pants against my skin. His strong arms hold me up. I squirm and wiggle down his shaft till he's seated balls-deep inside me.

Despite the fact that his whole body's trembling with desperate need, he holds himself fiercely in check and gives me the time I need to get used to him. I'm so close to coming again that I'm literally afraid to move. I gotta get a little control first and remember my own damn rules.

Keep it simple.

One-time thing.

No mating bites.

And absolutely, positively, no falling in love.

Then he starts moving his hips and pumping his dick inside me. And I'm lost in this, us, him.

I'm totally fucking lost.

Chapter Twenty
Ash

Okay, I'll be the first joe to admit it.

Let's just say, when it comes to dysfunctional relationships, I know a few things.

Falling toes over teakettle in love with my own goddamn student—who also happens to be a pissy prick on his good days, a bloodthirsty savage on his bad ones, *and* the vicious king of our rival race—well, that was never part of the game plan.

Now here I am, for Pete's sake, making the same goddamn mistake all over again.

I'm falling for this wild child royal rebel of a Gemini. The same royal rebel Sparrow's gotta marry and fuck to break the curse. I'm falling for her even though I'm decades too old for her, she's in love with a guy I get off on dreams of killing because of what he did to Sparrow, plus we all know damn well this wild Gemini ain't sticking around Avalon for long.

But it's like they say. The heart wants what it wants.

That's always been my problem.

Shoot, Zara started punching my buttons the minute she landed on our terrace in that Avenger suit and those platform boots, mouthy and fearless and gorgeous as fuck, her with that goddamn Pendragon boyfriend, and Sparrow ready to murder her for stabbing Xhevith.

But when the princess risked her royal neck in that daredevil balcony stunt, just to rescue my sorry ass from this dungeon? And me the guy who put her in those handcuffs?

Me, the guy who usually ends up rescuing every joe in the show who's neck deep in the shit, just got tossed a life preserver myself.

Yep.

That's when I handed the Gemini queen my heart on a plate with a carving knife.

Now I'm all in. Deep in. I'm buried balls-deep in my royal beau's intended bride. And I'm losing more of my gosh-darned mind with every pump.

Bet there's gonna be hell to pay.

Look, I'm no Christian. Us Fae, we're good old-fashioned moon worshippers.

But right now I'm in ten kinds of Heaven.

Zara's wrapped around me like a sexy octopus, all lush curves and soft skin and supple strength, with that face like a Hollywood starlet and that pussy like a sex goddess. I'm a big boy, I'm a lot for any girl to handle, with or without all that metal I'm rocking down below. But this gal's taking me like a champ, gripping my shoulders and digging her heels into my butt and fucking herself senseless on my dick like I'm her favorite dildo.

And sure, she's in heat, that happens with shifters like her. But this one wears her whole soul in her reckless eyes.

Here's the bottom line.

She might think we're a one-time thing.

But I know better.

She's mine.

I wrap my hands around her sweet ass to anchor her, while she fucks into me with these breathy little moans and sighs and wiggles that sex me right up. She's pumping out mating scent and pheromones by the bucket that I ain't exactly immune to, those wild teal curls are spilling out of her braid to stick to her skin and mine, plus she's soaking wet and slippery with sweat and so damn tight I just about lose my mind with every downstroke.

I'm trying to hang onto my head and give my girl the good reaming she needs from me to break her heat. That's when the air in the room gets dense, like it's pressing against my skin.

I know that feeling like my own dick.

That's the way I feel every friggin' time Sparrow walks into a room.

The fact that him and me, we ain't actually bumping uglies despite all our X-rated hanky-panky, even though I'd rail the guy or bend for him myself (either way works for me) in a hot second?

All that untapped sexual charge between him and me makes us both hyper aware of each other. That's how I know he's standing in the doorway, watching the princess and me fuck.

He's watched me tap a lotta ass, all genders depending on his mood, cuz I'm a real equal opportunity kinda guy when it comes to getting Sparrow off. He gets off on watching (and sometimes, you know, directing) since he can't do the bump-and-grind himself right now, on account of he's gotta save himself till he breaks that curse.

But something about him watching me do her…

Zara.

Geez Louise. I swear to fuck, this girl's a goddess. This whole scenario going down with the three of us gets me hotter than a five-alarm fire.

I walk her backward till her spine grazes the wall. Then I brace her good and steady against the surface, still wrapped around me with her feet off the ground, so I can take the lead myself. Now I'm pinning her arms to the wall and pumping strongly into the hot strangling clutch of her divine snatch.

"Ohmygod, Ash," she moans.

Her head falls back against the wall, her eyes close, and her mouth opens. A flush is rising in her face, she's holding her breath for seconds at a time till she has to gasp and suck in another lungful of air, and her hips thrust hard and fast and feverish into mine.

When I angle my pelvis so I can drive in even deeper, working the studs of my Jacob's ladder against that spot she likes so much, she lets loose with a keening cry that shoots straight to my balls.

She's real close to coming.

"Attagirl, princess," I grunt, fucking into her good and hard. I can feel Sparrow's arousal in the heat of his stare burning into my flexing ass. Now I'm determined as hell to get all three of us off, the only way I'm allowed to get Sparrow off—without touching him. Which is why he chains me up when we screw around. "Lemme hear ya."

She's not shy, this Gemini queen, I'll say that for her right off the bat. With a Fae gal, you gotta coax 'em past this modest restraint they're brought up to project.

But Zara Gemini just locks onto my gaze like a lifeline and lets me fuck every last cry and gasp and whimper out of her.

Lemme tell ya, every thrust of our bodies does beautiful things to those amazing tits of hers. With every jiggle, those pink nipples and silver piercings pretty much beg for my attention. When I tongue her tight nipples till they're good and shiny, her cries torque even higher. I'm alternately suckling her and enjoying the sight of her flushed and increasingly frantic face.

That's when her eyes snap open and her gaze darts over my shoulder.

I can tell the exact sec she and Sparrow lock eyes. She sucks in a shocked breath and freezes.

Guess the cat's outta the bag now.

The only Q in my mind's how my new gal's gonna react to discovering we've got company. A Fae chick would play it all coy or pretend to be modest and outraged.

The air thickens against my skin. That's him, my guy back there, getting ready to blow.

That heartbeat of silence is electric.

Energy hums and zips among the three of us like lightning's about to strike.

"Now," Sparrow breathes into the silence, his smooth voice all savage and raw with strain. "Both of you. *Now.*"

I've got a tick to wonder if she's gonna tell him to pound sand.

Then my girl's cunt clenches around my junk like a fist. A hot gush of her honey drenches my dick. Her scent of cream and roses floods the air. As her climax rips through her, she cries out my name in a pitch that could shatter glass. Me, I let out a yell that could wake the dead.

Holy hell. That climax we've both been chasing barrels through me like I'll never stop coming.

And Sparrow's strained, husky, barely audible moan? For me, that's the cherry on top. Since my guy's more than capable of coming, under what passes for normal circumstances in our screwed-up sex life, without making a sound.

Slowly, the ability to string coherent thought together returns to my sexed-out brain. That noise Sparrow just made means he got off too.

He got off bigtime.

Just like she did.

Which means this thing's gonna work out real good for all three of us.

Damn. That was one hell of a climax. I actually feel floaty, like my balance is all hinky. I can't feel the floor under my feet.

Tell you true, that big O was so strong it takes a sec for my vision to clear. That's when I realize the actual reason I'm all floaty and can't feel my feet.

Zara's blissed out. She's so blissed out it's good for this old guy's ego. In fact, she's physically floating (and this isn't a figure of speech, you feel me?) a good two feet off the floor, with her hair swirling and coiling like Medusa snakes around our bodies.

Levitation.

That right there's a Mogadon gift.

A real powerful one.

And not one she's known to have.

Plus there's this. Since the two of us are still locked together in post-coital bliss, I'm levitating right along with her.

I see the instant my girl gets what's going down. Comprehension makes her eyes fly wide. Her hands lock on my shoulders and her legs clamp around my hips.

"Easy there, princess," I murmur, trying not to startle her, even though that horse has clearly left the barn. "You got us up here. Reckon you can get us down?"

Her surprised mouth closes and her brow furrows with focus. A few secs later, in kinda a controlled descent on her part, we bump down together to the ground.

"Cheese on toast," Zara mutters, all raspy from screaming with pleasure I gave her. "I'm gonna go out on a limb. I'm guessing neither you nor Peeping Dom over there's got another set of magic handcuffs on you that's supposed to keep me from doing *that*."

Chapter Twenty-One
Ronin

It's after midnight, and I'm in bed but not sleeping. To be specific, I'm in Zara's big medieval bed, buried and smothered in over-possessive alphas.

I've got Vasili on one side and Lucius on the other, all of us naked but none of us fucking. Those two were just too bloody wrecked, after this blooming day we've all had (what with Zara and our guys still MIA) to do much more than a quick kiss-and-cuddle with me and each other before they both conked out.

Must be nice, mates. Me, I can't sleep a wink.

Lucius is sleeping with his face buried in my neck, so he can nuzzle my mating bite in his sleep. He's fully human, because Vasili's in no state tonight to take Lucius wolfing out in our bed. That's my dirty little kink, taking Lucius half-shifted and all brutal, but it's not one Vasili shares. Just now, Vasili's sprawled pretty much on top of me, his long limbs thrown over Lucius so he's alpha-guarding both of us. Right this moment, Vasili's snuffling those cute little snores none of us will ever tell him about, right in my ear.

Normally, with both of them so attentive, I'd be sleeping like a baby.

Tonight, I'm way too aware of the blasted ache in my chest that comes from missing everyone who's not here. My overprotective dragon Max, who never lets me sleep without first getting me off. My sweet bookworm Neo, who nods off most nights over his homework with his glasses sliding down his nose. And *her*, Zara, our badass queen whose larger-than-life energy lights up the whole *domus* and every room she struts into. She's the snarky, sassy, sexy sun we all revolve around like planets.

Zara.

Zephyr.

Gwen.

Fuck. It's hopeless. I'll never sleep.

My restless stare roams over the shadowy contours of Zara's bedroom, all silver and gray in the moonlight, till I find my girl's desk. That's where I spy the teasing gleam of that trinket Vasili pinched for me from the Academy Vault.

A scrying mirror. A real one. A fair replica of the one Zeph gave me years ago, so I could always reach him when I wanted him.

The one I shattered in a fit of grief and rage after I killed him.

At first I wasn't sure, I tried (and tried) to reach him after, and there was way too much baggage between us for him to ghost me. Anyway, Zeph was all fire and fight. Ghosting was never his style. That's how I finally knew.

I knew he's dead.

He has to be dead.

Admitting it to myself nearly fucking killed me, but he's dead.

Still, that had to be Xhevith, didn't it, that green monster who scalded Max with acid? And Fae dragons, Zeph always said, only ever bond with a single rider.

Fuck.

I push out an exasperated huff, then start the cumbersome process of stealthily squirming out from underneath my warlocks. Vasili's a notoriously light sleeper, he'll wake if you even twitch, and Lucius is lying on my long hair, but somehow I pull off the trick.

What feels like eons later, I've got those two wrapped round each other, I've bundled myself up against that nip in the night air, I'm wearing a pair of Neo's preppy sweats that smell like bookworm and hand-milled soap (which just makes the ache in my chest worse), and I'm wedged cross-legged in the window seat with the scrying mirror cradled in my lap. Cold spring rain whispers against the window.

I'd really fancy a bit more privacy for this stunt I'm about to pull.

But I know there's no bloody way I'm getting that bedroom door open without waking both my guys.

And I'm damn well not about to do this with those two peering over my shoulder. Lucius would be fretting himself sick over this latest slew of whatever rules I'm breaking. While Vasili's already jealous as fuck over the mere notion of Zeph and me. Over the past day, Vasili's gone from casually curious to sharply suspicious and increasingly hard to handle. I guess my flat refusal to discuss Zeph and our history hasn't helped.

If you're wondering, yeah, this is me dragging my feet.

Because for some damn reason, I'm nervous.

Finally, I steel myself and look in the mirror. Gods, that thing looks so innocent, just a round moon of cloudy glass in a charmed silver frame. It's Faerie magic, we witches don't far-see (which is what a scrying mirror's for). But I'm a Valyrian telepath, a strong one, and Zeph taught me to scry when he gave me a glass as a gift.

I haven't looked into one since I shattered mine. Which I only did after weeks of staring into the thing, begging Zeph to answer, till I'd begged myself hoarse.

That's when I stopped hoping against hope and finally admitted to myself I'd killed him. For months after, I was a mess.

Gwen didn't show it at the time, but turns out she was a fair bit worse.

She died blaming herself for my shattered heart.

Now it takes a bit to clear my head, the way Zeph taught me, and peer into the glass till the foggy reflection of myself starts swirling. My face is harder, my eyes are colder, and my hair's lots longer than it was three years ago. It falls on either side to curtain my face and enclose the mirror and me in our own private world.

I lick my dry lips in a totally fucking futile attempt at moisture. I cradle the mirror in one arm and rub that blasted ache in my chest with the other.

"Zeph," I breathe on a wisp of air.

The fog shifts and swirls over my own haggard image. Gods, I look like shit. I've got major shadows under my eyes and I really need a shave.

Of course, the glass is empty. Same as always.

But someone fucking took Zara.

And Max and Neo, they're somewhere.

My brow furrows in the glass and my golden eyes turn savage. "Zeph? You there, mate? If you are, this time you'd best bloody answer."

Nothing.

No. Thing.

As in, nofuckingthing. At all.

Just when I'm about to hurl the mirror through the window in a bitter rage like I did the last one, that infuriating fog thins and clears. My ferocious reflection ripples and blurs.

My pulse thunders in my ears.

Slowly I make out the contours of a new face. A fierce face, so clearly not human, alien yet familiar as my own breath, all blade-sharp cheekbones and delicate nose, divided by a green eyepatch that's new. Lips stretched in a sneer around sharp little fangs. The spill of mossy hair around a pair of pretty pointed ears.

My heart gives a leap and a thump so hard I gasp out loud, shit, before I can swallow the sound so I won't wake my warlocks.

"Zeph," I croak, because I can't bloody breathe. For all I know, I'm having a damn heart attack. They'll wake to find me blue-lipped on the floor. "My gods. You're—not—dead."

No thanks to you. His waspish tone hisses through my head, though I know he's audible to me alone, same way I am for him. *No doubt you thought me dead when I fell from the roof of Pendragon Tower with your blade buried in my face. Now you regret that your knife proved insufficient to finish the job.*

"No." Horrified, I shake my head, back and forth, back and forth, I can't seem to stop doing it. "No! I—never meant to kill you. Fuck, I didn't even want to hurt you. I only threw that knife in the first place to *warn* you—"

Pity about the eye then, warrior. His remaining eye narrows, hard with distrust. *I never before knew your aim to fail.*

Old guilt burrows through my gut like a tapeworm. He's not saying anything I haven't said to myself a million times. Still, I try to explain to him, though I'm pretty sure it's futile, since I can't explain it to myself. "Look, I was a right proper mess that night. Considering what you were doing in the first place in my fucking home without a fucking invite—"

Never before had I needed one. His voice drips acid with suspicion. *After what happened between us the time before, can you truly blame me for believing my presence would be welcome?*

My jaw drops in complete disbelief. "That night was totally different, and you damn well know it!"

Was it indeed? His head tilts in a mocking way. *Tell me, warrior, how precisely was that night different?*

I'm relieved to tears that he's alive, but at least one thing hasn't changed. The two of us together have always been electric.

No surprise that he's already pissing me off.

"Like you bloody have to ask? For one thing," I hiss, "what happened between us on Samhain was fucking *consensual.* Then you came back to Pendragon Tower at solstice to do what you do, you and all your Dark Fae. To steal what you wanted, and devil take the consequences."

It is not stealing to take what is already mine, Ronin Pendragon. His eye smolders at me before his gaze drops, silky lashes fluttering against his cheek. *Or so you led me to believe. Was it all naught but a game for you?*

Gods, this is torture. Does he even know the way it ended for Gwen? She never stopped blaming herself that I killed my own lover in her defense.

The memory makes me savage. I rake back my hair and scowl at him. "A game? Are you mental? For fuck's sake, you had to know I'd *never* be down for—"

Lucius mutters and chuffs in bed, that's the sound his wolf makes when he's waking. Which reminds me that my voice is rising, and I'm operating here on borrowed time. After all, no matter how it ended or who's to blame, what happened back then is ancient history.

I was a kid. Zeph was whole. And Gwen was alive.

I scrub a rough hand over my face and try to focus. "Look, forget about me. Forget about the past—"

I would love nothing more. Unfortunately, you have left me with a permanent memento. His graceful hand gestures at the eyepatch. *I am reminded of you every time I look in the glass.*

Guilt writhes through my chest. I did that to him. I took his bloody eye. Though, gods, I swear I never meant to.

I loved him.

Fuck. I have to stay focused here. Have to. Focused on the ones I can actually help.

Any moment I'll have Lucius breathing down my neck. I'm not Fae, so what I'm doing with this mirror doesn't come easily. To scry, I bloody have to concentrate.

If I'm distracted, I'll lose the link. And if I ring him up again, I rather strongly doubt Zeph will be in any mood to answer.

"Zeph. Listen." I sweep my hair behind one ear and keep my voice low, extremely conscious of my sleeping warlocks. "I need you to tell me the truth."

He mocks me with an elaborate pretense of surprise. *Why, how else should I speak? You know I cannot lie. In this regard, you and I are unalike.*

Focus, chap. Focus.

I hunch over the glass. "You've taken Zara. Haven't you?"

His voice hones sharp and cruel as a throwing knife. *I came to Icarus Island to do what I do, me and all my Dark Fae. To steal what I want, and devil take the consequences.*

He's mocking me, playing my own words back to me, but I don't give a flaming fuck. In his twisty Fae way, he's just admitted to taking Zara.

"Can't imagine she much fancies being taken." That's me making the understatement of the century. My queen would've fought like blazes. Carefully I ask, "Is she… okay?"

He flashes a slip of fangs in a smile that's pure malice. *Oh, rather. Originally, you know, I planned to return her when I'm done with her. But now, I somewhat wonder whether she might prefer to stay.*

As if.

I bark out a scornful laugh. "Yeah, well, you don't know her, mate. And you've got a day tops to get her back here, before your little Unseelie lark causes a major interracial incident between Avalon and the witching world. Then you'll have got that queen bitch Messalina to contend with."

Now he doesn't answer, that's one of his tactics since he can't lie. But his smile turns sly as fuck.

"What about Max and Neo?" I press.

When he just looks quizzical and arches a brow, another of his tricks to avoid lying without telling the truth, my voice torques tight with impatience. "You know, Maxim Rasputin, the world's last fully manifested male dragon shifter? And Neo Mercury, the witching world senator's favorite son? Have you got them locked away in Avalon too? Because if you're not bothered by the notion of Queen Messalina in a royal snit, you'd best be bloody bothered by Senator Mercury when he finds out you've got his boy. That bloke's not one to be trifled with, believe me."

He lowers his head and stays silent so long I'm ready to start swearing. Only the real threat of waking my restless warlocks keeps me quiet.

At long fucking last, his head lifts. That sly smile is back. *Why do you not come to the standing stones and find out for yourself? I have a friend in Avalon who has long yearned to make your acquaintance.*

I open my mouth to take up that challenge head on, but his hand sweeps sharply across the glass. Fog swirls in his wake.

When it clears, he's blooming gone.

"Oh, fucking hell," I groan in complete disgust.

I've just made a bloody mess of that, haven't I? Not to mention, the man's just put my heart through a blender all over again. He's alive, I didn't kill him after all, and Gwen flipping died for nothing, if that guilt's what finally pushed her over the edge. But I've left him scarred and crippled for life, and he hates me.

And he has Zara.

And he probably has Max and Neo.

And, fuck, I need to get them *back*—

The plink of a pebble against the window beside me, sharp over the murmuring rain, makes me sit up with a start.

At the same moment, Lucius jerks upright in bed and mumbles sleepily, "What?"

Of course, Vasili's wide awake (probably has been for ages, damn it) and already crouched beside the bed, gorgeously naked and bloody lethal, with two of his wicked knives in hand, poised to make someone bleed. His dangerous gaze sweeps over me, my furtive expression, and the scrying mirror in my lap.

I clear my throat, lay the mirror aside, and rise to my own feet. "Look, love, before you blow your top—"

"Save your breath, Ronin, *do*, until you're prepared to tell me the full truth. I assure you, my patience with this entire tedious affair of your mysterious ex-lover and your silent treatment is entirely exhausted." The plink of another pebble against the window mercifully snaps Vasili's icy stare away from me. "What the fuck is that?"

He darts past me to the window, because there's no keeping him back, and rakes the night with a single probing stare.

"Dear fuck," he says flatly. "It's Mallory McSnicker."

"At this hour?" Looking befuddled, Lucius bundles his tumbled chestnut curls into a knot at his nape. "What can the girl possibly be thinking? It's well past curfew, and pouring rain."

I crowd up next to Vasili's tall body in the window seat and peer down. In the narrow cobblestone street outside our *domus*, I can just make out Mallory's pale face staring anxiously up at me under the hood of her Academy raincoat.

When she catches sight of me, she gives an excited little hop and gestures frantically.

"It appears she wants you to come down, darling," Vasili says coolly to me. "Since I very much doubt it's *me* she's breaking the Dean's precious curfew to see."

Lucius springs out of bed and reaches for his PJs and smoking jacket. "For Heaven's sake, wave her around to the door, Ronin, and let her in before she wakes the girls or catches a chill. Indeed, we'll all three go down. Who knows? Perhaps she has tidings of some kind about our missing mates."

Actually, the bloke who has tidings about our missing mates is me.

I just can't figure out how to tell Lucius and Vasili who's taken them without spilling the beans about all the rest.

Chapter Twenty-Two
Vasili

"Sorry to come barging in," Mallory McSnicker blurts the moment Ronin ushers her, clumping and graceless in her unfashionable galoshes, into our *domus* great room.

There she stands dripping on our Turkish carpet.

While Lucius murmurs the standard pleasantries, I deploy the lifted Romanov eyebrow, accompanied by an icy glare directed at our guest, until the hopeless creature gets the message. She gulps and shuffles apologetically from the carpet onto the hardwood.

Which is scarcely an improvement.

"I'm so sorry for breaking curfew, Master Aries," she rushes ahead. The girl is clearly nervous and babbling, which I find rather intriguing. "Needless to say, Mistress Aggie doesn't know, and I'd really love if it could stay that way? Anyway, I've gotta hurry right back. My guys don't know I'm gone. If they wake up and I'm not there, it'll get pretty hairy."

"Indeed." Calmly Lucius adds wood to the fire, which provides enough illumination to lift the darkness and give the entire scene an air of coziness I feel entirely certain is unwarranted. "Well, Ms. McSnicker, you've certainly captured our attention. No doubt your business at this hour must be pressing."

Oh, our headmaster looks calm as a Buddha, darling, but don't let him deceive you. His wolf is lurking in his voice.

He's desperate to get Zara back. He's desperate to protect all his precious charges.

Just as I am desperate.

Instead, the Dean has poor Lucius buttonholed into making a series of unpleasant calls on the landline before breakfast to the formidable (but currently oblivious) Senator Mercury and the certain-to-be-irate Messalina.

"Oh, it's pressing all right." Mallory pushes back her rain-soaked hood to reveal her russet hair, twisted into a braid that's absurdly passé. Between that braid and those freckles, good God, she looks like an escaped actor from some geriatric rerun of *Little House on the Prairie*.

"I, uh, I know where Zara is," she announces.

This little bombshell abruptly derails my inner critique of the creature's appalling fashion sense. In the startled silence that follows, an electric jolt of urgency sizzles through me like a bolt of lightning. I hiss in a sibilant breath and barely manage to repress the violent impulse to rush forward and shake that girl until the truth spills out.

Unhindered by my instinct to conceal any shred of honest emotion (because, truly, no one needs that kind of insight into my inner workings), Ronin crosses his muscled arms over his chest and scowls at Mallory. "Oh yeah? Where's that, then?"

Even bundled into Neo's unthreatening sweats, my boyfriend looks and sounds like a belligerent bully. But I know him better than anyone else. He's actually defensive and vulnerable as fuck.

He certainly should be, given that clandestine *tête-à-tête* he conducted through the scrying mirror. (Because, of course, I eavesdropped.)

Pity I could only hear Ronin's half.

So color me interested in Little Miss Mallory's grand reveal.

Mallory licks raindrops off her lips and looks nervous. "She's, uh, in Avalon? That's where the Unseelie—you know, the Dark Fae, we studied them in Witching World Lit?—that's where they live."

"Oh, we're well aware of Avalon," I murmur in a silky tone. (Now don't blame me for sounding suspicious, it's simply my nature.) "The immediate question in my mind is how *you* know, McSnicker—and, indeed, how you're aware that Zara's missing at all, since that information is currently embargoed."

Except for the inhabitants of our *domus*, and now the Dean, no one on Icarus is supposed to know our future queen is missing.

"Yeah, what he said. And thanks, but we already bloody know where Zara is." Ronin shoves into Mallory's space to tower over her. "You got any intel on Max and Neo?"

Of course, he's not at all surprised to hear Zara's whereabouts confirmed, since his ex-boyfriend "Zeph" apparently divulged that information during their cozy lovers' quarrel.

Mallory blinks up at Ronin with her uncanny silver eyes. "Wow, Max and Neo are missing too? Um, does Neo's dad know about that? Because he's about to—"

"Never mind about Senator Mercury just now." Gently Lucius nudges aside the looming Ronin, then slips around behind Mallory to help her out of her dripping raincoat before she completely ruins our floor. "Ronin, my dear one, why don't you brew Ms. McSnicker a nice cup of Dez's masala chai. Our guest is chilled through."

Ronin merely glowers at this laughably transparent ploy to usher his threatening presence offstage.

Finally Mallory (who does look a bit peaked) says meekly, "I don't need any chai. I really can't stay long, or Jae and Draco will wake up."

Lucius carefully conceals the startled reaction I know he's experiencing over this revelation of the sleeping arrangements in Agrippina's supposedly gender-segregated residential college. Apparently the students are residing no more conventionally (or chastely) under Aggie's roof than we are under this one.

Without comment, Lucius slips away to hang Mallory's raincoat over a chair near the fire to dry.

Mallory turns to follow—which offers me a glimpse, above the collar of her baggy House Hadrian tee shirt, of the elaborate tattoo scrolling up the back of her neck. I can't see much, but I certainly know quality ink when I see it, and that piece of body art is exquisite.

At a glance, I appear to be eyeing the feathery tips of a pair of dove-gray wings, like an angel's.

How… fascinating.

"Now." Lucius settles Mallory firmly onto the settee near the fire, where the poor dear can drip-dry. "Is there anything more you're able to share with us concerning Zara's location or welfare?"

"Right." Mallory clutches her bony knees and leans forward to peer up anxiously at Lucius. Then, well, the words simply pour out. "Like I was saying, Zara's in Avalon. You can get there from here, sometimes, by the standing stones. I think she's okay, I mean physically."

My rush of debilitating relief regarding my girl's welfare is something else to be carefully concealed. I stand very still and guard my expression.

Lucius gasps and grips Ronin's shoulder. I watch my mates soften and sag into each other in a sweet little moment of shared comfort.

Mallory barrels along without further urging. "Zara's, uh, with this guy who's the king over there? Probably against her will, so it's totally not her fault? And there's gonna be this whole delegation from Messalina's court and the Senate coming through here tomorrow to get to the same place—"

"Sweet fuck." Since both Lucius and Ronin appear to be rendered speechless (and I suffer no such impediment, believe me), I do what comes naturally. I assume command of this train wreck before we all hurtle over the cliff in this avalanche of revelation. "Let's skip to the end, shall we? As you've heard, we've already tumbled to the same conclusion about Zara, Avalon, and—whatever *was* his name, darling?" I glance inquiringly at Ronin.

"Zephyr," he mutters, glaring at me, because he knows quite well I haven't forgotten. I've simply grown tired of waiting for him to start talking. "King of the Dark Fae."

"Ah, yes, that was it." I meet his sulky glower with a smirk, then narrow my eyes on Mallory. "I'm going to take a blind cognitive leap and conclude that, since Messalina and her entourage are traveling to Avalon, this Dark Fae King is the arranged marriage Messalina wants Zara to make. How am I doing so far?"

Perhaps the McSnicker girl doesn't care for my patronizing tone, because her silver eyes narrow back at me. "Yeah, that's pretty much the nut graf."

I blink. As a Russian, English isn't my native language. But it's extremely rare that I encounter a word I don't know.

Needless to say, I dislike the experience immensely.

And I'm simply astounded that this little mouse of a schoolgirl is daring to push back against my bullying. Because that's precisely what she's doing, in her own understated fashion.

When Zara's here, my girl tends to blunt the keen edge of my reign of terror over the entire student body.

Clearly, I'm out of practice.

With a swift twist of my casting finger, I give Mallory's carroty braid a sharp telekinetic yank to express my displeasure. Although I keep the gesture far too subtle for Lucius to discern that I'm pulling her hair, my victim gasps at the sting until her eyes glisten with a satisfying sheen of tears.

Oh, that's *much* better.

"Ow. Take it easy. The nut graf is like the bottom line in a news article, Vasili, okay?" she mumbles, rubbing her scalp. "It's a journalistic term. I was the editor of my high school newspaper. And I figure the word's appropriate, because Senator Mercury never travels anywhere without a full court press, and he's coming here with Messalina. Their plane lands at noon."

"Fuck," Ronin says for all of us, pacing before the fire like a chained tiger with his tail lashing. "What in blazes is this? Zara's bloody kidnapped, and they trot out the bloody press corps? She never agreed to the fucking marriage. Doesn't she get any say? She's the future queen, for shit's sake."

Lucius bows his head and presses a hand to his brow. "To be fair, her position on the marriage was never communicated to Messalina or anyone else before Zara vanished. The Dean has tasked me to convey this context to the court via landline, which I suppose I'll now be doing in person when the entourage arrives." He sighs. "At this point, Messalina must assume Zara has consented to the marriage. Our girl's presence in Avalon, once that becomes known, could also be perceived as voluntary."

"That's mental." Ronin snorts. "What about Neo and Max? Is their disappearance supposed to be voluntary too? Any rate, I doubt that senator's going to fancy learning no one's seen or heard from his son in days."

"Indeed, there's something else that hasn't been explained, isn't there?" I'm not wearing my heels at this uncivilized hour, but I prowl to the settee in my stockinged feet and glare down from my still impressive height at the fidgety Mallory. "Pray tell us, McSnicker, how precisely *you've* become so privy to all this privileged information about Messalina and the senator's travel plans? And how do you know Zara's in Avalon?"

Now don't say I'm ungrateful, darling. Truly, the McSnickers are an utterly inconsequential witching world family. They're nobodies, with barely a flicker of witchcraft to speak of. They certainly lack the connections to be privy to the particulars of the queen's travel itinerary.

Oh, I don't possess a Valyrian gene in my entire DNA, that's

Ronin's territory. But it hardly requires Valyrian foresight to discern the presence of additional information our Ms. McSnicker isn't divulging.

I abhor secrets.

Unless they're mine.

Under my gimlet gaze, an uncomfortable blush rises in Mallory's pale cheeks (making her look *all* red. Honestly, the only redhead I've ever found alluring is Neo, who's dyed his hair that delicious shade of purple.)

She squirms on the settee, then squares her shoulders and lifts her chin with a bravado I reluctantly admire.

"Um, I've kind of got an inside source. A confidential source," Mallory tacks on firmly, "so don't ask. He's in Avalon. They're expecting the witching world contingent over there by moonrise tomorrow. That's when the mating ritual starts."

"Then that's how much time we've got to prevent it," I say into the startled silence.

"How in blazes are we supposed to do that?" Ronin thrusts an agitated hand through his hair to sweep it back from his ferocious brow. "Zeph's got his mind made up. He wants her. He'd never have nabbed her otherwise."

I glance around at all of them, the circle of worried faces all clearly waiting (whether they'll admit it or not) for this island's dominant alpha (a.k.a. *moi*) to tell them all what to do.

Fortunately, I'm more than equal to the role.

"Mallory will return home to soothe her agitated mates." (I try not to say this too dismissively. But I don't try very hard.) "Lucius, you'll meet Messalina at the airstrip when she lands and explain that our girl's been taken. You'll explain that Zara's adamantly opposed to the match. I rather doubt Messalina will be in the mood to be persuaded to call the whole thing off, but it's certainly worth a shot. Besides, that's what the Dean wants you to do, pet. And you seem to want to retain your professorship in this inane institution."

I wait for Lucius' distracted nod, then turn to my pacing and agitated boyfriend.

"Ronin, darling, you seem to have an inside source in Avalon yourself. So it's straight back to the scrying mirror for you. Do try your damnedest to persuade your pissy ex to delay the ritual, if not cancel it—

and demand that he put Zara on the line. I imagine we'll all feel rather better once we hear from her." I pause. "With any luck, our little queen will know where to find Neo and our dragon."

It troubles me greatly that no one seems to have seen those two, and I know I'm hardly alone in my growing fear. After all, that dragon is Ronin's mate too. And we're all desperately worried about Neo.

Moreover, this course is the safest strategy I can conjure to contain Ronin's dangerously reckless impulses.

I certainly don't want him going to those standing stones alone.

"Right then." Ronin frowns. "Will do. But I promise you, Zeph's not in much of a listening mood. I'll ring him up, but I hardly expect him to answer. He's got his reasons, whatever they are, for going this route. What d'you intend to do yourself, love?"

I sketch an airy shrug and stroll toward the stairs with my sexy hips swaying. "Oh, I'm going straight upstairs to pack my scrumptious Louis Vuitton traveling bag. Or perhaps I'll take the Gucci, because a man only has one chance to make a first impression. I do believe it's past time for me to pay a visit to Avalon myself."

Chapter Twenty-Three
Maxim

This long night has passed and a pale dawn is breaking in this strange land.

I am still buried deep inside Neo.

He sleeps in my arms, a slow healing sleep, in our nest of rumpled furs. His broad back is tucked against my chest, and my arms are wrapped tight around his waist. This sweet and gentle boy always spoons in his sleep.

But tonight is the first time he has ever spooned with me.

Before we slept, I made him climax so hard and so repeatedly that I finally broke the first frenzied peak of his mating heat. He will surely spike again—and soon.

For now, we have earned this brief respite.

I too am utterly spent and deeply sated. My limbs are heavy and my eyes are sandy. My skin is stinging in a dozen places from where he has scratched and bitten me in his passion. I find a pretty crescent in my flesh still throbbing from when this gentle boy went wild and sank his teeth into my biceps. This mark is from the last time I made him come. By then, we were so closely attuned to one another that I made him spurt just by pumping into him, without even touching his dick.

I wear his marks with pride. But I am full shifter and already healing. My barbed cock has finally softened, so I could withdraw now from my mate's body. If I wished.

But I do not wish for that.

In truth, that is the last thing I wish.

Indeed, the mere thought of that physical withdrawal, the emotional separation, and all the inevitable distance between us that will follow, fires through my sated body a spurt of alpha agitation.

Again, my barbs shoot out and lodge in my mate's well-plundered passage.

I know he is tender there, how not, after this epic night we have shared? Still, even sleeping, my mate softens and sighs and pushes his muscled ass into my pelvis. Our mingled scents—his clean-smelling blend of sage and lavender, my dark mating scent of leather and brimstone—drench his skin and make my senses swirl.

Mine.

He is mine.

Even if, I suspect, he does not yet know it.

Beyond all doubt, I have formed a mating bond with this tender-hearted boy. That last time we coupled, it was all I could manage not to give him my mating bite.

Now I bury my face in the side of his neck and rub my stubbly jaw against him. I need a shave and a shower, but there is no hope of that in this uncivilized place. Besides, I know this new mate of mine likes the rasp of my whiskers against the pinprick scars of Vasili's mating bite, which are still pink and sensitive. I know this because Neo shivers every time I do it.

When I lick the scars now to tend the bite, the way we alphas do, cherishing and spoiling the lovers we share in our sovereign's harem, Neo shudders deeply. Over the soft trickle of water from the hot spring, his husky moan fills the cave.

Saints of the northern steppes.

Vasili.

There is no doubt Vasili will be very difficult to manage.

"Max," Neo whispers, sluggish with sleep. His well-ridden hole flutters and clenches around my eager length. "Wow. I literally can't believe you're still inside me. It's almost morning."

"Be at ease. Soon we will rise," I sigh in his pierced ear. That little silver hoop earring is another reminder that he belongs to Vasili. Just as he has always belonged to Zara.

Now he belongs also to me.

By all the saints, this is one claim I will never renounce. He is mine.

I trace his ear with my tongue to make him melt. "I promise I will not hurt you. I will never hurt you. Let me just…"

Carefully I rock into his hot strangling hole. My barbs will not retract now until I make him climax for me again.

He sighs and melts and yields to me so sweetly. "Mmmm. Yeah, okay, do it. One last time. Just… be gentle, okay?"

"*Kotyonok.*" I breathe. He wants me again as I want him. And this is *not* the last time. He is my sweet fearless kitten, he is mine, he is mine.

Gently, so gently, I thrust into his tight heat. The soft sounds of liquid suction whisper through the cave with every careful thrust.

His beautiful hole is slick and drenched and dripping with my seed.

All night long, my barbed cock has trapped my copious essence inside my Neo. My dragon cock does not know we cannot breed him. If we could, after the night we have shared, my mate would surely ripen with my offspring. And I would care for him so tenderly, he would know no fear, he would want for nothing.

A dragon's breeding instincts, they are potent. Already my pace is quickening, my breath growing hoarse and rough, my grip on his willing body turning hard and urgent.

My emotions are knotted in a complicated tangle. I want what I cannot have, to bite him, to breed him, to show the world he is mine. To claim him, this sweetest and gentlest and least complicated of all our mates, as Vasili and all the others have claimed him.

But Neo is only with me in this way because there is no one else.

Because of the driving imperative of his mating heat.

Mercifully, he allows none of this to stop him. He fumbles to find my hand and drags it to the swollen shaft jutting between his thighs. I know he is tender there too, I have used him so ruthlessly and so well. But this evidence that he wants me again makes my dragon roar with satisfied possession.

I stroke his own fluids down his shaft to lubricate him and pump him in time with my thrusts. I am trying to be slow and careful and gentle, all the things he needs. But when he cries out and arches his spine to impale himself on my dick and spurts hot jets of his seed into my fist, I bury my face in his neck and thrust into him until I spill, with a hoarse groan, deep inside him.

My fangs, a dragon's fangs which never descend unless he intends to use them, punch down from my palate to fill my mouth.

In this moment of mindless need, I barely manage to recall that I must ask, I cannot just claim him. I must ask. And he must consent.

Roughly I mutter into his neck, "Neo, my mate, my love, my kitten, will you let me—"

My confession of love is shattered by the distant scream of an enraged dragon. My alarmed gaze swerves to the cave mouth.

Against the jagged oval of silver dawn, a flight of feral dragons flutters across the sky. Black and brown and blue and green, their scales glitter the same hues as those painted so vividly on these cave walls. They seem to be the common colors for dragons here. As I watch, the live dragons outside claw across the lightening heavens until they pass beyond my view.

In my arms, Neo breathes a gentle sigh and presses a kiss into the crook of my elbow.

"I really love when you speak Russian to me," he says shyly. "You and V both. I'm gonna have to learn it so I can understand what you're both saying to me. But, uh, we should really get up now. We have to find Zara."

I am, in all ways, fully on board with finding Zara.

Today, without fail, we must find our sovereign.

Yet I am disgruntled to realize I have just told this boy what he means to me—he is my mate, he is my love, he is mine—and he has not even understood me. He is not able to read my thoughts through our half-formed mating bond because I have not yet bitten him.

But this mention of Vasili. It is awkward but timely.

Truly, I cannot bite Neo until we are all in accord. Zara, his first alpha, must be consulted without fail. There are others who will also be affected, for we all share this sweet boy. This is how we live together in our queen's harem.

We make such choices by mutual consent.

With a sigh, I quiet my impatient dragon. I will my unruly fangs to retract and my softening barb to disengage. Then I withdraw my spent member from my mate's accommodating body. When I do, a flood of my seed trickles out of him. My jealous dragon demands that we push every precious drop back inside our mate.

But this is no time to indulge my breeding instinct.

Neo rolls on his back with a groan, pushes a hand through his tangled curls, and struggles to sit.

"Kotyonok." Gently I grip his shoulder to steady him, then take the liberty of leaning in to steal a tender kiss. "Remain here a little longer. Your heat is not ended, you will peak again. And I am… not easy to accommodate. I know this. Your body requires rest."

His soft lips firm and he shakes his head. "You didn't hurt me. You really didn't. Besides, I can rest after we find Zara. As soon as we all leave Avalon, together I mean, my heat's gonna pass."

"We will find her," I say fiercely, leaning my brow against his. "I swear to you, we will find her."

"I know, Max," he whispers. "We have to. She needs us."

"She does." I straighten with a sigh. "But she needs us strong. At least you must bathe in this warm water. Your body requires this to heal, Neo Mercury. And we must eat today without fail."

"But—"

"There is no *but*. Now I will hunt for us. When we have eaten and you have regained your strength, then we will find her."

Confronted with my insistence, he reaches for his glasses and continues to look stubborn. But he is too intelligent not to recognize the value of my words. When his intense green eyes meet mine through his travel-smudged spectacles, searching my face for reassurance, my heartbeat kicks and quickens.

Already he is responding to me as his alpha.

Even if he does not know it.

I twist my hair into a braid to keep it from my face and give him the reassurance and direction he craves. "Rest. Bathe. Eat. Within the hour, we will be aloft."

His determined gaze flickers toward the brightening sky, then toward the pool, which I know will ease his soreness. Finally, his stubborn jaw softens. "You promise?"

"Yes." In the chilly dawn, I claim his soft sweet lips once more, then release him reluctantly and scramble to my feet. I glance around us to gauge what else he will need, make a few mental notes on supplies I must scavenge or steal to keep him safe, then stride naked toward the ledge.

"My dragon will hunt for you and he will roast your meat," I fire over my shoulder. "Prepare yourself to fly again when I return."

"Right. Great. Flying." Neo's glum tone summons a reluctant grin to my lips.

At the mouth of the cave, I pause to glance back at him. Already he is gathering his clothing and mine, smoothing and folding, creating order in our small shared space.

He is even making our bed, such as it is. Even in this unholy place, he is a model citizen.

"We might need to come back here," he explains, bent over the task so I cannot see his face. "Or someone else might need shelter. I don't want to leave a mess."

"Neo." Patiently I wait until his trusting face looks up at me. "Do not fear. I will take care of you and Zara. I will protect you. I always protect what is mine."

His gaze flutters and falls. He gives our sleeping furs a sad smile and shakes his head. "Don't worry about me, Max. I know exactly what this was and what it wasn't."

Frustration knots my gut and tangles my tongue. *"Kotyonok—"*

"I said don't worry about it, okay?" Neo scowls and pushes to his feet.

His buff build is gloriously naked, abs rippling, quads clenched, ass flexing under miles of smooth fair skin. He is splendid, and the sight of him steals my breath. But I do not like that he is already hastily pulling on his pants, as though he does not wish me to see him naked. Although he puts a brave face on his condition, my sharp eyes can clearly discern it by the gingerly way he is moving. His weary body requires the hot bath I am insisting he take.

Sensing my scrutiny, he pushes his glasses up his nose and furrows his brow at me in a frown. "Relax, Max, I'll wash up after you go, all right? I will. Let's just focus on what matters most. Today we've gotta find Zara."

I am dissatisfied to leave this matter between us so badly unresolved. Already, he is erecting walls to keep me out.

Still, I cannot fault his logic. In this strange and dangerous land, the safety of our precious sovereign must indeed come first.

But I swear this thing between us is not finished.

We are not finished.

Wordlessly I turn away, break into a run, and launch myself into the open air. As I plummet toward the snowy tundra, a tingling warmth rushes through my limbs.

In a blinding flash of light, my human form falls away.

I pull a flood of icy air deep into my mighty lungs, beat my vast wings in a powerful downstroke that arrests my plunge, and roar my deafening challenge to the sunrise.

With every stroke of my wings as I soar high in the Avalon sky, I whisper to the wind the name of my queen. My mate. My soul.

Zara. Zara. Zara.

My sovereign. I am coming.

I am coming to find you.

Chapter Twenty-Four
Zara

I orgasm in my sleep.

It's one of those dreams where you know you're dreaming. Because there's literally no other reason I'd ever let that fucking green-haired Faerie burrow his sinewy body between my knees and bury his wicked mouth between my thighs and fuck me with his long tongue (all sandpapery like a cat's, which definitely adds a certain something, plus the fangs) till I explode in the type of hard shuddering climax that typically summons lightning.

Only I'm still wearing these fucking cuffs, even in my dreams.

So, you know, no fireworks.

Still, I definitely lose it in other ways for the dream ream under Zephyr's magic tongue. In fact, I scream so loud with pleasure my own voice jolts me awake.

When my eyes pop open, I'm plastered against the freaking seafoam *ceiling* of my rent-a-room. With my palms planted on the surface, my nose brushing the stone, and the filmy folds of my un-Zaralike nightgown floating around me.

Sweet Jesus.

I'm levitating.

I levitated when I came.

Which is pretty fucking concerning, amiright?

I spasm against the ceiling and give another yelp.

My yell shatters the spell and unwinds the witchcraft I guess I wove in my sleep. I plummet, thrashing and swearing, a good twelve feet from the ceiling to land on my bed in an undignified heap, with a force that nearly splits the seams on my overstuffed mattress. Around me, the sweet scent of lavender and fresh hay puffs up.

"Shit!" I clutch desperate fistfuls of the feathered duvet that's way too smothery to sleep under, because my mating heats come complete with hot flashes that last till my guys fuck me through them, and my lone magic moment with Ash wasn't anywhere near enough to break this one. "Shit shit shit."

Man, I need Vasili. He's Mogadon, levitation is a Mogadon gift (though not every Mogadon has it), and he flies like freaking Tinkerbell. He can teach me to handle this rogue witchcraft.

Or maybe I just need to get these cuffs off, so my witchcraft can manifest the usual way. You know.

Dragon.

Lightning.

Little mind reading on the side.

Without warning, the bedroom door (which was magically locked behind me for the second time last night by that goddamn Dark Fae, with me snarking and bitching the whole time) flies open. Without any kind of knock, natch. In the milky morning light that's pouring through my window, Zephyr's slender body commands the space.

I swear, this guy's so intense he sucks all the air out of the room. Or maybe, I dunno, the air literally grows denser when he walks in.

Either way, the temp definitely spikes hotter.

He's barefoot and bare chested, breeches dragged hastily over his hips, green hair tumbled around his face with his pointy ears peeking through, grasping a silver sword that hums with lethal witchcraft like a goddamn lightsaber.

He just barges in and invades like the Visigoths sacking Rome, his narrowed gaze raking my bed, the balcony, the closed bathroom door. Like he's looking for enemies to run through with that sword of his. Despite the obvious haste that probably dragged him straight out of bed when I yelled for help, I can't help noticing he took the time to put on his eyepatch. Because I seriously doubt he sleeps wearing that thing.

Which makes me wonder if maybe he's self-conscious about his missing eye. The one flaw in all that beauty.

My heart gives a little ping that feels suspiciously like pity.

Oh hell to the no. I am *not* feeling sorry for that Dark Fae bastard. I'm not gonna be some Stockholm Syndrome poster chick.

Even if he did come charging in here like he's gonna protect me or something.

Awkwardly, I clear my throat and sit up in bed, reluctantly grateful for this filmy nightgown thing someone left for me to wear. It's not exactly modest (or practical). But at least I'm not nakey.

"Uh, you can stand down," I mutter. "False alarm."

He looks at me wildly.

"False alarm," I repeat.

Why am I getting the sense that Avalon might not be the safest place for a girl to crash, even without this whole curse hanging over everyone's head?

His gaze drifts over my body, curls streaming everywhere, nightgown tangled around my thighs, the filmy panel over my tits practically transparent. Slowly, the alarm fades from his face.

Only to be replaced by a different kind of intensity that's even more feral.

After last night, he's definitely seen all of me. And it's pretty obvi he likes what he sees.

Another hot bi warlock.

Actually, two of them (I mean, if I include Ash).

I'm fucked.

I pull my knees to my chest to cover up my boobs and study that lightsaber he's gripping. "Ground Control to Major Zephyr. Abort mission."

"You were screaming." Dark with suspicion, he darts to the bathroom, snatches the door open, and peers in.

I eye the way his half-laced breeches cling to the taut contours of his ass. "I just, uh, I had a nightmare."

A nightmare of him tongue-fucking me till he broke my heat.

Sweet baby Jesus.

My thighs are still slick with my own juices from that little fantasy and, probably, residual warlock spunk from my actual dungeon hookup with Ash. Because once His La-Dee-Dah Radiance locked me back in here last night, I was way too wiped to figure out that whole antiquated gravity-plumbing system that supposedly supplies the shower.

Anyway, probably best to keep this latest levitation incident to myself.

I told those two last night, when I levitated post-climax, was a one-off. Just some freak outbreak of witchcraft from my mixed-up recessives.

If it turns out it's not? If it's more than that? This whole levitation gig could be an advantage I don't wanna reveal to my kidnapper.

"A nightmare." Slowly Zephyr turns toward me and lowers his sword. He sleeks a hand over his hair like he's self-conscious about his own disheveled state. "You screamed as though you were being tortured and dismembered."

"Is that likely to be something I gotta worry about?" I'm half joking to break the tension.

His green gaze narrows. "Yes."

"Whoa." My gut tightens as I wait (and wait) for more. "C'mon, buddy, that's important intel you just spilled. If I gotta worry about somebody jonesing to erase me, you need to tell me so I'm prepared."

As well as I can be, anyway, while I'm wearing these cuffs.

He hisses a word that makes his sword stop glowing. Weapon loose in his grip, he prowls to the balcony door. The guy moves like water, all ripply and fluid, but he's savage as a stalking cheetah. He'd be the smallest of my guys (I mean, if I ever agreed to take him), but also the fiercest and the most feral. He's barely tamed. I don't know if the Fae even have alphas, but he'd be oil and water with Vasili and Max.

Lucius would be fascinated by him.

Neo would be so sweet with him.

But Zephyr's got all this really explosive baggage with Ronin. Not to mention the massive complication of Ash—

From the window where Zephyr stands gazing out, hair spilling down his bare back, his distant voice drifts toward me. "Not all of my Dark Fae kindred believe in the Merlin's prophecy."

"*What* prophecy?" I tilt my head and try my damnedest not to ogle his ass.

"The prophecy that has dominated my entire life. The prophecy that it is a powerful witch from your world, a witch of royal blood, whose marriage to me will save us from our doom."

He lays a palm against the glass and bows his head. Now his voice comes muffled, so I've gotta strain to hear. "There are those who believe I should take a different bride. One who is Fae, from the dwindling Seelie who hide among your mortal race. For my detractors at court—those who argue against me to the dowager queen, my mother—you are a dangerous distraction. To her, you are a threat. One that is best eliminated."

"Seriously?" At his terse mutter, I groan and prop my chin morosely on my knees. "Great. I've only been here, what, one night? And I've already gotta watch my back?"

Slowly he turns to study me. Again his gaze drifts over my half-naked body, my tumbled curls, my bare shoulders, my soft arms, the silver cuffs. Guess I must look pretty defenseless to him.

Even though I'm not.

His pretty lips part so the tips of his fangs are showing. His tongue touches the tip of one fang.

Which just makes me remember the way that tongue of his felt fucking me in my dreams.

Heat ripples across my skin. The back of my neck starts to sweat.

"Never fear," he says softly. "You are precious to me and to all my realm. You are the very key to our survival. Do this thing for me and mine, and I will keep you safer than my own heart." His face turns broody and bitter. "And that is safe indeed."

For some reason, my stupid body gets all tingly. My pulse skyrockets and my tummy somersaults.

I snort to snap myself out of that shit. "Yeah, no. You're the guy who put me in danger in the first place. You worried about my safety? How about you take these cuffs off, Your Resplendence?"

I say it the same way Ash does, all dry and sarcastic. One corner of the Fae's mouth turns up.

If I didn't know better, I'd think Mr. Taciturn over there's fighting a grin.

Then his face turns somber and he shakes his head.

"Until after the ritual, I dare not risk your flight. But after we have broken this curse, if you aid me, if you make yourself my ally instead of my enemy, if you swear yourself loyal to me and mine, then will I set you free."

That promise of freedom definitely gooses my vitals. Especially if, like I read in Lucius' book, the Fae can't lie.

But they're twisty.

Which means I really gotta focus on what this guy's actually saying.

"You mean after we fuck, right? After we tie the knot?" I demand. Because when you're talking to these Fae, you gotta nail shit down. "Assuming I'd agree to that, which I haven't."

"Yes. After we… fuck." Geez, the sound of that word on his pretty lips. Again his gaze drifts over my body in a way that heats my blood. Damn it. "After tonight, I will set you free, but you may not wish to leave. You and I will be bound by oath and by law. By the moon magic we will weave between us and the powerful curse we will shatter. By the way your body will welcome mine."

Not wanna leave?

Welcome his totally non-con fucking?

This guy must be smoking something.

I cock my head. "You sure about all that?"

"Yes, Zara Gemini. After last night, I am sure." This time, his smoldering look makes me shiver *all* over. The fact that Ash and I both got off on Zephyr's say-so is something I'm definitely still processing. "To the Unseelie, the sexual act we will share is sacred. For a Fae, those bonds can never be broken. You will be mine and I will be yours."

He is already ours, my dragon whispers. *I have seen it.*

"The thing is, I've already got five mates," I remind the room in general. "And those are guys I really am bound to."

"Yet you have not married them." Zephyr's liquid voice turns silky. "Perhaps you are not yet certain."

I narrow my eyes in warning. "Oh, I'm certain all right. We're mated the common law way. Which is a totally valid way for the queen to hook up under witching world law. And you better believe I'm gonna marry them all, like, officially." The sooner the better for that, I'm starting to think. "You planning on mating them too, Your Radiance?"

"No." Zephyr's eye darkens from jade to juniper. Menace lurks in his voice. "You may be certain I have no interest whatsoever in mating that motley crew of vicious and untrustworthy males in your harem."

I extend an arm to point at him.

"See that right there? That's gonna be a problem. I'm not a one-horse kinda cowgirl, I'm true poly. In our polycule, we're all together. No one gets left out." Which isn't totally true, since Max (who joined late) is still working through all kinds of complexity with Vasili and Neo and Lucius.

But it will be true. Someday.

On this one, I'm gonna trust my gut.

"When it comes to our lovers, those we choose for pleasure, we Fae royals are polyamorous as well. But my requirements, my tastes, are very…" He hesitates, head tilted. "Specific."

I snort again. "I'll say. You're not bringing that flogger anywhere near me or my guys, believe me."

He prowls toward the bed, which I find alarming but try not to show.

"'Tis true that I enjoy the gift, freely given, of my lovers' submission," he murmurs, in that voice that's like water spilling over stone. "But I do not require pain to achieve pleasure. What you witnessed last night was a… unique accommodation… to the unusual circumstances in which Ash and I find ourselves."

Now he's lurking at the foot of my bed in a way that definitely makes me jittery. He's close enough for me to smell the burnt amber scent of Fae and the leathery musk of dragon.

If he gets any closer, he's gonna meet my foot.

I'm not combat-trained for nothing, and I train with Ronin on the regular to keep my skills sharp.

"What circumstances?" When he says nothing, I shake my head impatiently. "Spill. I mean it. You put me here in a pretty shitty sitch without even asking. Now you want me to fuck you and make all kinds of promises to help you out. You don't get to be all Fae and mysterious and secretive."

When Mr. Taciturn presses his lips together and looks all Fae and mysterious and secretive, I pull in a breath and pray for patience. "What. Circumstances."

His breath spills out in a huff. "You are the most demanding and imperious female."

"Comes with being queen," I say in my queen voice. Because I own that shit. "Spill."

With a smooth decisive flourish, he reverses his magic sword and lays it lengthwise across the foot of my bed. Then he plants his hands on his narrow hips (which only draws my attention to the fact that his breeches are half-laced and sliding down so low I can see the moss-green lick of his happy trail).

OMG, yum.

My dragon queen purrs with interest and slips an X-rated visual into my mind.

Steady there, showgirl. We are definitely not unlacing his pants with our teeth.

And I'm really glad this Fae doesn't appear to be telepathic.

"Fortunately for you," he mutters, "I'm extremely well accustomed to dealing with demanding and imperious royal females."

Guess he's talking about that mom of his. That dowager queen, who I probably ought to meet, except apparently she wants me tortured and dismembered. I drag my gaze from that alluring glimpse of forbidden terrain down below to his irritated face.

"Well, that's lucky," I drawl. But I'm not getting sidetracked here. "So spill."

Temper floods his olive skin with a flush. "To enhance my magical energies and maximize my potential for breaking the curse, I have been… celibate… for some years. This circumstance makes my physical relationships… complicated."

That bombshell blows open the door to insights about him and his relationship with Ash I've been struggling with all night. Suddenly, I'm seeing Zephyr's need to restrain his lover, to keep his distance, to control every iota of what goes down between them, in a whole new light.

Self-censorship isn't my strong suit, so the words just burst out.

I uncurl my knees from my chest and lean forward. "Is *that* why you chain Ash up in your dungeon to play? Why you won't let him touch you?"

He lowers his head and eyes my barely decent body with an intensity that makes my clit tingle. You know, thanks to this mating heat.

It's not like I'm reacting to him or anything.

"Ash is not always restrained. He is permitted to lie with others." Zephyr's gaze goes predatory. "At times, I like to watch."

"Yeah, no kidding. I kinda figured that much out on my own." All of a sudden, I'm fighting back a blush. The way he's looking at me, like he's remembering how I looked and sounded when I climaxed, the way I fucked his boyfriend, the way we all got off, makes waves of heat pulse low in my core.

Hell. Just that look of his is making me wet.

If this guy's been celibate for years, when he finally relaxes his grip and loosens all that ironclad restraint, he's gonna go off like dynamite.

I swallow hard. "Let's talk more about Ash. Where does he fit into your hypothetical marriage scenario?"

He answers right away, so I know he's already thought about it. "I will take Ash as my consort. Now that I have seen how well you suit each other, how well you… please each other…"

For some reason, I'm holding my breath.

"After the ritual is complete," he whispers, "if you choose to stay? It can be all three of us."

In a flash, the lightbulb of an idea flares in my brain. If I'm wearing two crowns—one in the witching world and one here—what if I could actually have two harems?

I must look kinda thunderstruck, because he huffs out a short laugh. "Surely, given your own circumstances, this proposal cannot shock you. I have already said Fae royals are polyamorous. Ash will never wear the Seelie crown, which passes through the matrilineal line from mother to daughter. Still, he is a prince among his people." He hesitates. "As you can see, I am not unwilling to negotiate the particulars of our union."

"Well, you shoulda led with that," I point out forcefully. "Your so-called *willingness to negotiate.* Instead of just kidnapping me."

His sinewy shoulders ripple in a shrug. "If I had sought to negotiate, you could very well have refused. Then, with the ritual looming, would I have lost the element of surprise. That was a risk I could not afford to take."

I don't want to admit he's kinda making sense, given that curse he's dealing with. And I'm still fighting to wrap my head around the whole concept of two separate harems when a door slams in the distance.

That sound is notable because it's been pretty quiet around here. I've been figuring these two guys live alone together in this bachelor pad-slash-castle.

Now Zephyr lifts his head and calls without breaking my gaze. "Ash? In here, if you will."

He's not exactly asking, but Ash puts up with it. Boots clump across the floor till the Seelie's spiky pewter-gray head pokes around the lintel. His alert silver gaze goes straight to Zephyr looming over my bed, then me sitting up in my nightie.

When our eyes meet, Ash's crinkle in a lazy grin.

"Morning, princess," he drawls. "How's our girl?"

The flush of warmth that spreads through my chest is all kinds of alarming. I'm *not* their girl, and I'm not gonna get all distracted thinking about how that whole being-their-girl scenario could work. The last thing

I need, as in the very last, with all the unresolved issues percolating in my polycule, is some complicated Fae ménage on the side with these two.

"I'm hungry and uncaffeinated," I say dryly. "Any chance I can get someone to make a latte run?"

"The Fae drink herbal tea." Ash chuckles at my horrified look. "Lucky for you, I was raised on your side of the portal. I'm a java guy myself. How about I hook you up with a cuppa joe and a breakfast tray, soon as I unload this getup?"

His massive frame ambles fully into view, dressed like he was when we first met, in the sleeveless Conan tunic and leather pants and fur-lined boots (complete with knives) that show off the bloody thorns and ivy inked around his thick biceps. Under one arm, he's gripping a leather sack that I eye with suspicion.

Zephyr's gaze zeroes in on the mystery parcel. "May I conclude you fetched what I require?"

"Yup." Unoffended by the guy's peremptory tone, Ash strolls in and moseys over to stand at his boyfriend's side (though now I notice how carefully the two of them don't touch).

Still, the space between them trembles with all that longing they're both holding at bay. Side by side, they loom over my bed and smolder down at me. The Dark Fae King and the Light Fae Prince.

Yowsa.

I clear my throat. "So what's in the sack? If that's a flogger of any kind, I'm outtie."

For the second time in one morning, the corner of Zephyr's lips curls up. "Why don't you show her what you've brought for her, Ash."

This Dark Fae King doesn't smile, like, at all. Anyone who loves him (if there is anyone beyond Ash) must really work for those tiny hidden grins. Aaaand this whole captor-captive dependency situation must really be getting to me, because I almost feel a sense of accomplishment for wringing this one grin out of him.

Then Ash opens the sack and upends the contents onto my bed. I glimpse the first alluring glitter of vivid green dragonscale and what can I say?

I'm a girly-girl. I like pretty shit.

I scramble forward and swarm all over the cool AF Avenger suit Ash just laid at my feet like tribute. This outfit's like the one Zephyr was wearing yesterday on dragonback, but I can already see it's tailored to fit my curves. I gather it up, all light and flexible. The scales are sleek and supple in my hands.

"It's a catsuit?" Somehow I manage to sound simultaneously excited and borderline suspicious. Because that's pretty much how I feel. Isn't there some fairytale warning about never accepting gifts from a Fae?

Even if there isn't, nothing comes free in any world.

"Behold, 'tis dragonscale armor, impervious to cold, heat, and dragonfire." Now Zephyr looks and sounds inscrutable as hell, which shoves my suspicion needle right into the red. "In Avalon, only Dark Fae royals are dragonriders. As my future queen, you're entitled to the honor."

Ash gives the sack another helpful shake. A pair of green leather gauntlets and green platform boots tumble out next.

By this point, I'm dying to try the whole thing on. Still, I gotta be smart here. This entire setup's about way more than Zephyr giving me presents.

I shoot the Dark Fae a careful look. He's close enough to touch (I mean, if I wanted). Close enough to slide my hand down his sleek bare chest over those washboard abs, under the unlaced breeches barely clinging to his hips, to cup that prominent bulge shoved up against the silk.

Not that I'm gonna be doing anything like that.

"It's your color, right?" I say softly. "This mossy green? I'd be wearing your color?"

"Wearing that color tells all of Avalon you are mine," Zephyr murmurs in a tone that makes me shiver. "That is a protection you will require to survive the Academy."

I scrunch up my forehead and kneel so our heights are equal. "Um, hello? I'm already surviving the Academy, even if the last queen-in-waiting didn't. I mean, I survived the queen killer. Then I shacked up with the biggest bully at Icarus, that's Vasili, and he's major." To put it mildly. "Sure, our residential college has a rival house, they've got assholes there who've caused problems in the past. But I'm doing totally fine on my own—"

"I am not speaking of the Icarus Academy." Zephyr's cool voice slices through my monologue like a silver blade. "As a royal, you are expected to attend the Avalon Academy for Promising Royals of the Court."

Cheese on toast.

There's, what, another dark witch academy on this side of the curtain? Like a rival academy?

I blink and shove that fact into my interesting-but-not-currently-relevant file to check out later. "Yeah, fine, but I'm not *staying*, remember? I'm already enrolled in a magical academy back home."

"Dark Fae elemental witchcraft cannot be taught." Zephyr shrugs and looks superior as fuck. "Either one is born with it, or one is not. You, clearly, are not. Students at the Avalon Academy study deportment, language, literature, and the performing arts."

"Which all sounds like stuff I'd hate." Looking for an ally to back me up, I glance hopefully from Zephyr's unyielding face to Ash, who's a good foot taller.

The Light Fae gives me a sympathetic grimace but doesn't say a damn thing. Guess he's firmly on his boyfriend's side on this one. Which totally shouldn't surprise or disappoint me.

Even though it does.

Zephyr betrays a twitch of impatience. "Your sentiments are duly noted. As it stands, my mother—the dowager queen—is the Avalon Academy's principal patron. She also styles herself the institution's headmistress. She's demanded to see you. As you will shortly learn, 'tis generally best that her demands are not disobeyed."

I plant my hands on my hips and scowl at him. "Now look here—"

"Don the dragonscale or wear that nightgown as you prefer." Clipped and curt, Zephyr snatches up his sword and strides for the door. (Well, conversation over, I guess.) "But harbor no illusion that I'm offering you any choice. Immediately after breakfast, you will attend my royal mother at the Avalon Academy."

Chapter Twenty-Five
Zephyr

"Just so you know, I'm doing this under protest."

The Gemini queen's forceful voice reaches me in the lair, over the high pure whistle of the morning wind. I'm twisted under Xhevith's considerable bulk to cinch the dragon saddle under his scaly belly. This is a vulnerable placement for a dragon, one Xhev will tolerate only from me—his trusted rider.

Needless to say, this sudden invasion of our ledge by the violent young witch who nearly stabbed him through the heart with cold iron is not well received by my dragon.

Xhev sidles away from the sound of Zara Gemini's voice with a snort of alarm. His girth nearly crushes me, like a bug smeared against the floor under a careless boot.

I hiss a warning to my beast and scramble out from underneath. Simmering with annoyance, I whirl toward my troublesome houseguest. "Let me offer a word of advice regarding your presence and my dragon…"

The words dry up in my throat.

For several breaths, I'm unable to think clearly at all. When my startled brain finally lurches into motion, my first thought is nonsensical.

Clearly, Ash has misjudged her size.

That dragon armor he acquired for the Gemini queen on my command encases her lush curves so tightly the entire effect is indecent.

Quite possibly, knowing Ash, he's deliberately sized her armor to achieve this effect.

The supple green dragonscale clings to her full breasts and tiny waist and pert derrière like a corset (which happens to be an item of lingerie I appreciate). She's donned the high boots and leather gauntlets and twisted her hair in a thick teal braid that swings over one shoulder. Her periwinkle eyes are boldly rimmed in cobalt. Her soft lips are slicked in bubblegum pink so bright it's nearly neon.

Her skin is flushed, her braid is floating, and her entire demeanor crackles with defiance.

Somehow, the shiny travel mug of coffee she's gripping—a personal item Ash smuggled over with his possessions from the mortal world when I claimed him—only heightens the entire outrageous effect.

Apparently, she's planning to consume her third cup of that vile mortal beverage (not that I've been watching her closely enough to count, while she and Ash enjoyed their cozy breakfast as I paced and muttered over the delay) on dragonback.

In brief, this girl looks nothing at all like the deceptively delicate hothouse beauties who attend my mother's studies at the Avalon Academy. I harbor no doubt that poisonous nest of scorpions will despise Zara Gemini on sight.

Throwing this mouthy, reckless, impertinent witch into that vicious scrabble for power and influence with my mother's venomous creatures can only lead to disaster.

In passing, I absorb the fact that Ash (who clearly has a soft spot for this girl) must have supplied her with the cosmetics she's applied so boldly. This largesse is an anomaly that gives me pause, since my lover's attentions to his paramours do not typically outlast their brief sexual dalliance.

It seems Zara Gemini has captured his wandering eye.

Just as she has captured mine.

Under my stare, which is perhaps too sustained to be courteous, the Gemini queen cocks her head, plants one hand on her hip, and taps her booted toes.

"Well?" she demands. "Don't keep me in suspense. What do you wanna tell me about you and… Xhevith, isn't it?"

Recognizing the sound of his name, my dragon chuffs in surprise.

Zara's turquoise eyes study my beast, then narrow on that new scar he's bearing—a souvenir from his violent encounter with her iron poker.

Something flickers in her vividly expressive face that one could almost mistake for guilt.

"That's some healing potion you got there. He looks just about patched up," she says to me over a swallow of coffee. The scorched scent of Ash's wickedly caffeinated mortal beverage pollutes the crisp air.

"Moon magic," I say briefly. "Ash's, to be precise. Healing is a Seelie gift. As for that warning I was attempting to administer, 'tis best you keep your distance from my dragon. He may be healing, but he remembers who attacked him. He is not the forgiving sort."

The mere memory of my dragon's terror and agony, which I suffered in full measure through the empathic rapport that binds a Dark Fae royal to his beast, still makes me furious.

My voice hardens. "For that matter, neither am I. Consider yourself warned."

Zara's stubborn chin firms and her dangerous eyes narrow. "Yeah, well, I got a bad habit of attacking guys who try to kill one of my mates and then kidnap me. Next time you wanna propose to me and then fuck me, try sending me flowers first. Or at least, you know, an email?"

I sneer at her annoying attempt to be clever. Thanks to the energy interference of the magical wards that guard our realms, neither her world in Icarus nor mine in Avalon is connected to the mortal Internet.

My world is not even electrified in the harsh and glaring mortal fashion. We rely upon our witchlight crystals, mined from the volcano's fiery heart, for their gentle light and heat.

"I shall take your preference under advisement." I spin away from this infuriating Gemini and busy myself gathering the reins I use to direct my beast when we're aloft.

Otherwise, I'm liable to shake that girl until she spills her foul-smelling coffee.

How can she possibly jest at such a time? Can she truly not understand why I've taken her? Doesn't she realize the survival of my entire race is hanging by a thread?

If she grasps nothing else during her upcoming visit to the Avalon Academy, I trust she will come to comprehend the grim imperatives that drive me to these desperate measures.

In plain truth, this wild queen will be fortunate to survive her audience with my moon-fucked mother.

With swift movements designed to conceal my unease, I knot my reins around Xhev's pommel. "Let me also extend a word of warning regarding your coming interview with my royal parent."

Apparently undaunted by any of my warnings, the infuriating girl saunters into my line of sight, which places her within striking distance of Xhevith.

He rumbles deep in his chest and eyes her with suspicion.

"You just settle down," she says (presumably to my dragon). Still, her voice is far gentler than anything I've heard from her to date. "I'm not gonna hurt you, long as you keep away from my mates and the people I love, okay?"

"He doesn't understand spoken speech," I mutter. "For the most part. A Dark Fae communicates with his dragon through emotions and images via telepathic rapport."

"Huh. So you do have some telepathy, at least with your dragon." Calmly she sips her coffee and studies my dragon. "Him and me, we understand each other fine. Don't we, Xhevith?"

My dragon chuffs out a skeptical breath and snakes his head slowly toward her. Clearly, if she attacks him again, he's poised to respond in full measure.

"Careful," I warn both of them, tightening my grip on his reins.

Her armor may be impervious to dragonfire, which should afford her some protection from our feral and highly aggressive fire-breathing blacks. But no armor ever crafted can ward against a green dragon's scalding acid.

Feral greens are typically skittish, but Xhevith is both the largest and the fiercest of his breed.

I'll say this much in her favor. This Gemini queen does not lack courage. She stands very still and waits, with a patience I never imagined this wild girl would possess, while my dragon's massive fanged muzzle looms closer. Xhev pulls in a long sniff of her scent.

Zara voices a dragonish chirp that must rise from her own shackled inner dragon.

Xhev whuffs out a snort of surprise. His head snakes lower to draw in another lungful of her complicated scent, cream and roses laced with dragon mating heat.

She sips her coffee and waits him out.

Gently his muzzle bumps her pelvis, where that musky perfume from her heat is strongest.

His ripples of interest pulse through our rapport.

"She isn't for you, sweeting," I murmur to him, scratching his crest with my gauntlet, reinforcing my words with the stream of mental images and wordless emotions he understands best. "She is mine. Mine and Ash's. You must help me to protect her from all others who seek to claim her or hurt her."

Not the least of those being my mother.

He's still breathing her in, his wings flaring wide with curiosity. Whereas the girl herself, well familiar with dragonish anatomy for all the obvious reasons, bends to peer boldly under his heavy girth at the barbed organ between his legs.

"Been a while for him, huh?" she says dryly. "Doesn't he get to sow any wild oats, like, with the female dragons?"

I swallow a sigh as this ignorant girl unerringly pinpoints another of the damnable complications of a Dark Fae royal's life in my troubled realm.

"When a dragon queen rises in her mating flight, all interested males are free to rise. But Xhevith cares not for the ferals. Moreover, this city's dominant queen is my royal mother's mount, Yersinia." My throat tightens. "For whom Xhevith harbors an active dislike. You would do well to approach my mother with a similar caution."

"If she's anything like you, I'm sure we're gonna hit it right off," she mutters. "She above you in the pecking order or something?"

Pivoting away from my dragon, I swing the scabbard that holds my two swords into place so the blades cross behind my back and the hilts jut over my shoulders. "We rule as co-equals. Formally, neither of us can issue any ruling or render any judgment without the other. Informally, each of us possesses considerable autonomy."

She cocks her head. "You mind spelling that out in plain language for slow learners like me, buddy?"

"It means I devote significant effort to remaining far from her notice and, especially, her presence." I position myself beside the saddle and extend a hand to propel the girl aloft.

When the Gemini queen merely eyes my extended hand with one teal brow lifted, I wiggle my fingers impatiently. At this rate, surely, we'll be late. Lateness is one of the many shortcomings my mother does not tolerate.

My dragon, who is still rather more interested in this shifter queen than I expect, overcomes his caution sufficiently to extend her a helpful foreleg.

"Okay then, let's do this." Pointedly Zara deposits her travel mug into my impatient hand, then scrambles up Xhevith's extended foreleg without my assistance and throws her booted leg over the saddle.

As I gaze up at her wordlessly, she bends to retrieve her coffee from my astonished grip. "Will I be your co-equal too? I mean, if I ever agreed to this whole crazy scheme?"

"If you are crowned." I bestir myself and toss the flying harness across her thighs. "Until then, you're merely my bride. Your coronation would be one of those matters upon which Her Moonstruck Magnificence and I must first agree."

Nor have I been planning to broach the matter with Maeve anytime soon. This wild Gemini is nowhere near suited to navigate the subtle perils of the Dark Fae court.

But that is hardly the only reason for my restraint.

Zara's bubblegum lips move silently as she repeats my mother's mouthful of a title with her smooth brow puckered. She watches me buckle the first strap around her thigh, quick eyes taking note of the essentials.

When I duck under Xhevith to grasp the opposite strap and approach her with purpose, this bewildering girl says, "Hold up there, flyboy."

Twitching with impatience, I glance toward the climbing sun, now framed in the mouth of the lair. "Believe me when I say 'tis truly for the best not to keep my mother waiting any long—"

"If you strap me into this thing," she speaks right over me, damn this girl for her impertinence, "what's gonna protect you?"

I glare up at her while she calmly sips that revolting beverage. With extreme difficulty, I cling to my patience.

"Xhevith and I have flown together since we were both juveniles," I inform her stiffly. "I rather believe I can contrive to stay aloft during one short flight."

"Just a puddle jumper, huh?" She nods. "Well, that isn't the way this whole thing works. I don't need to be coddled and protected just because I'm queen. See, the way I look at things, it's my job to protect you. I mean, if I ever agreed to mate you."

This notion is so extraordinary that I find myself momentarily stricken speechless. Except for Ash (and, at one time, Ronin), no one ever protects me.

In truth, flying without my fighting straps *is* risky. As their numbers swell and the ranks of my royal kin suited to tame the beasts dwindle, feral dragon attacks are becoming increasingly common. But my dragon saddle was not designed to carry two. This untutored girl, herself unfamiliar with riding on dragonback, surely requires the precautionary harness more than I.

Meeting my perplexed stare, Zara puffs out a sigh. "Okay, listen up. Here's how this works. I get one strap, you get the other, and we both watch out for each other in the air."

This proposal stings my admittedly touchy pride like a bee. "For moon's sake, I'm a Dark Fae warrior. No one 'watches out for me in the air.'"

"Not even Ash?"

"Ash… does not fly on dragonback." My gaze avoids her curious stare.

My love's complicated Seelie secrets are his to share with this new mate of ours.

Or not, just as he chooses.

"Huh." She sips her coffee and licks foam from her upper lip with a slow swipe of her tongue that heats my blood. "Well, Your Radiance, day's not getting any younger, is it? You want me in the air or not?"

"I want you over my knee," I mutter.

But I say it softly enough that she can pretend not to hear.

Without further ado, I scramble up Xhevith's side and swing myself into the saddle behind her. My thighs close around the hourglass swell of her hips. Her sassy derrière tucks up against my groin.

This intimate arrangement introduces a new complexity that even I, with my intricate web of plots and secrets, have failed to foresee. My sex-starved body responds to her. I respond to the blaze of intimate contact with this girl for whom I'm harboring a highly unsettling but swiftly growing attraction.

Instant heat rushes to my groin. My cock swells with a powerful jolt of need.

Suddenly I burn with the savage drive to grip her tiny waist, bury my face in her exposed throat, and rut into her sweet ass until she melts. I crave the right to peel her out of her armor, unbuckle my codpiece, and bury my desperate shaft in her tight pucker until she screams and shatters in ecstasy.

Of course, it will need to be her fertile pussy rather than her rear passage that I claim tonight. Since, after all, we are casting a fertility spell to shatter the curse.

But I've never lain with a woman.

Thus, my imagination dives for the familiar.

If I'm going to shove Zara Gemini forward over the pommel of my dragon saddle and fuck her while my dragon shares our mating through empathic rapport, the way I once longed to do with Ronin, then my fantasy of claiming my Gemini queen's naughty ass seems most expedient.

By the moon, I'm dizzy. I'm spinning in the sucking swirl of this powerful vortex of fantasies. The creamy sweetness of this girl's perfume twines from her soft skin and vivid hair to seep through my senses like a hallucinogen.

Zara squirms against my cock in a manner that considerably worsens my plight. "Hey, you okay back there?"

Thankfully, my codpiece guards my secret from her keen shifter senses. I pull in an unsteady breath, will my erection into abeyance as I've grown so drearily accustomed to doing (but not for much longer!) and buckle around my thigh the lone fighting strap Zara herself has spurned.

Then, being exceedingly careful not to inflame matters any further by touching her, I reach around Zara to gather the reins.

"Hold tight to that revolting beverage. Or you shall shortly find yourself wearing it," I say gruffly.

With my hands and mind, I launch Xhevith into the skies.

The crisp burning cold of an Avalon morning, acrid with sulfur from our wrathful volcano, slaps my skin and sends tingling warmth rushing into my face. Under my seat, Xhev's vast wings beat and his mighty body labors. My fur-lined cloak snaps and billows in my wake. The austere lines of my city spread below, streets exposed and empty in the dazzling light, my fragile domain trapped between the fiery mountain and the endless sea.

But the lion's share of my interest stays firmly fixed on *her*.

This untamed, untamable, impossible queen.

This wild Gemini who will shortly become my bride.

Despite all her braggadocio and swagger, Zara's armored body is tense and wary in my arms. No doubt she'd prefer to be in command of her own flight. Clearly, this is a queen who's meant to rule.

But those cuffs beneath her gauntlets that prevent her dragon from rising are meant to do more than prolong her captivity.

They are meant to ensure her survival.

At least one of my wary suspicions about the likely dangers to her person here on Avalon has already been confirmed by my dragon's unusual interest in this girl and her heat. If her dragon rises in such a state, while she's fertile and needing, she'll have Xhev and half the ferals on this island wanting to fly her.

Dragons are savage when they mate. Even if this shifter girl desires such an encounter (which I cannot possibly imagine she does), she would never survive the mating.

Preoccupied as I am with the imperatives of Zara Gemini's survival, my royal mother poses the more immediate threat.

I lean forward until my lips are nearly touching the girl's ear, rimmed with a half-moon crescent of silver piercings. "As I was saying. Let me extend a word of caution concerning the dowager queen."

A tremor runs through her, triggered by my words, or perhaps my closeness. Still, she keeps her voice casual. "Lay it on me."

In truth, there is much I could say, but I limit myself to the essentials Zara will require to survive the looming ordeal. "Our queens have symbolic and magical value to the entire race, just as yours do. Their strength, fertility, and selfless devotion to the welfare of our people are central to our survival. Queen Maeve has ruled Avalon, pampered and indulged, since she was a student at the Academy herself. She is addressed as Her Moonstruck Magnificence, and her commands are to be acknowledged—however unreasonable or excessive they may appear—with a respectful curtsey."

Zara pulls in a long breath and replies in a level voice. "So here's Thing One. I didn't ask to be here, so I'm not in the mood to grovel. Then there's Thing Two. You didn't dress me in this catsuit to curtsey. You dressed me to rule, right?"

Without waiting for me to voice the astonished reply that's rising to my lips, she twists in the saddle to lock onto my alarmed gaze. "And Thing Three? I'm not the curtseying type."

Her turquoise eyes blaze into mine. Her bubblegum lips hover inches away. These reckless words she utters so calmly fill my heart with agitation.

But the fearless light that animates her face seizes me with a violent impulse to kiss some sense into this unconventional queen. Giving in to that impulse to touch her before the ritual would be disastrous.

For one thing, I'm torqued far too tightly with repressed sexual tension to trust myself to stop.

Instead, I forge ahead with my next warning.

"Queen Maeve becomes more temperamental and less predictable with every passing year. She demands absolute and unquestioning obedience. I strongly suggest that you give her what she desires. That tactic is essential to surviving her interest. Her glare can shatter glass and her screams can shatter steel. Her dragon is an abomination whose very breath carries pestilence." My fists clench around the reins. "In short, the Unseelie Queen is quick to anger and slow to forgive. Believe me when I say you would not survive her rage."

"You just said you're co-equals, and your people need me to survive." She takes a thoughtful sip of her coffee. Thoroughly undaunted, damn the girl. "Is she really gonna jeopardize all that just because I don't curtsey and kiss her royal ass?"

"My mother is among those who question my choice of bride. She is prepared to tolerate you because we are co-equals and I insist upon it," I say forcefully. "But our accord in this matter is… fragile. Her resolve will not hold if you try her patience."

"Not into sharing power much, is she? Probably not too thrilled to add another ass to the royal throne." She tilts back her teal head to meet my gaze. "I mean, once I'm crowned?"

The tiny muscles in my throat squeeze shut. I cannot answer directly without lying. There is no plan to crown Zara Gemini.

My mother is not the only Unseelie royal who dislikes sharing power.

Deftly I shift the current of our conversation into an unobstructed channel. "Without a crown, you are powerless. This is the most important truth for you to grasp."

I lean close to whisper the warning before the cruel Avalon wind can snatch it away. My lips graze the soft shell of her ear. Her flowery scent invades my senses. Sharing my saddle in this intimate fashion, we two are so intertwined I can feel her shiver. Almost embracing, I tighten my hold on her tensile body. She is softness and strength, sheathed in dragonscale and afire with purpose.

Wearing my own proud color, she is glorious.

Truly, this dragon shifter queen is so… unexpected. Forthright and passionate, she's perfectly suited to Ash, whose warm nature and generous heart have been so starved by my cold and violent affections. My dragon is clearly fascinated by her, even after she tried her damnedest to slay him.

As for myself—

"Not exactly what I asked, is it?" she says softly. My wandering mind jolts back on course. All too clearly, she knows better than to take anything I say at face value. This ungovernable girl may be impulsive, but she's nobody's fool. "And I'm not exactly powerless. How about you take these cuffs off and give me a fighting chance?"

"No." Under my dragonscale armor, my gut knots and clenches in protest. If only I dared to trust her. "Not a chance of it. I'll not risk losing you. Wearing those cuffs in my mother's presence may very well be your best and only chance for surviving the encounter."

Her breath hisses in alarm. "This isn't gonna go well, Zephyr. Next time I'm not asking. Cuffs. Off."

"For moon's sake." Irritation spikes my pulse and turns my words to ice. "I'm not one of your amorous warlocks to be ordered hither and yon, scrambling to indulge your every reckless impulse. I am a true king, Zara Gemini, unlike any other in your harem who plays at crowns and titles. I was born and bred to rule."

"Any other, huh?" All too clearly, this upstart queen is unimpressed. She positively bristles in my arms. "Zephyr, let's get one thing straight. You. Are *not*. In my harem."

Moon take the girl.

I may not desire to share her mettlesome mates. But, beyond any doubt, I'm in the damn harem whether she wants me there or not.

My dragon dips beneath us and angles his flight in a downward sweep. My conflicted gaze veers from Zara's stubbornly determined face to the sharp shining spires that skewer the sky.

We are well and truly out of time for warning. What little I have told her must somehow suffice.

"The Avalon Academy lies yonder." I sigh. "Her Moonstruck Magnificence awaits. In truth, I caution you to be on your very best behavior. If caution is even possible for such a queen as you."

Chapter Twenty-Six
Lucius

Ordinarily, for me, the hurried scratch of pens and pencils on paper as my students race against the clock to complete their History of Witchcraft exam before the bell would be a soothing sound.

Today, the sound of that frenzied scribble scrapes against my overstretched nerves like sandpaper against a rash.

For the hundredth time, my gaze drifts to the mechanical clock ticking away on my desk. This time, I barely bite back a growl. Curse that antiquated trinket with its ceaseless ticking. The tiny metal arms are crawling around that innocent oval face at an abominably glacial pace.

I must contrive to fill more than an hour of empty time until that damnable Messalina's plane touches down on the island airstrip.

Somehow.

An hour or more to kill before I've been ordered by my irate Dean to meet our Aquarius queen on the tarmac and inform her that my precious charge, the bride she seeks to barter, is missing. Once I weather that cringeworthy ordeal, I must next inform our celebrity Senator Mercury (who's also aboard) that his favorite son, my star pupil, has likewise disappeared.

I must manage all this without the formidable bulwark of Vasili at my back.

My alpha, my colleague, my student, my lover. In truth, his presence is rarely comfortable.

But he's a powerful ally.

Now that he's gone flying off to the standing stones, my heart positively aches with missing him—

"Aah-CHOO!"

Near the back of my orderly classroom, a student voices an explosive sneeze. Half my students, well attuned to my tightly strung nerves, jump in their seats and drop their pencils. Inside my skin, my wolf twitches and snarls. My startled gaze snaps to the back row, where Mallory McSnicker is mopping her red nose with a tissue.

She meets my irritated frown with an apologetic grimace and mouths, *"Sorry!"*

While I glare, she tucks away her tissue and huddles meekly over her exam once more.

Apparently, rushing around in the rain last night in that inadequate mackintosh and galoshes has given the girl the sniffles. For fairness' sake, I rein in my irritation. After all, that hapless McSnicker incurred her head cold while she was trying to help Zara.

Next my gaze roams over the row of bent heads until I meet Ronin's smoldering topaz stare.

Merciful Christ, my mate isn't even pretending to work.

He's slouching in his seat, arms folded across his broad chest, all golden skin and midnight hair, looking so broody and so blatantly sexual in his schoolboy blazer and smartly knotted tie that he's indecent.

Without any warning whatsoever, my skin tingles and my cock tightens.

You nipped out of bed before we could say a proper good morning, Ronin murmurs in my mind. Since we're linked in this way, I'm briefly reassured that at least he's left that accursed medallion behind. *Not too late to remedy that, is it, love?*

The reason I "nipped out of bed" early was to ensure Vasili took more than his Louis Vuitton luggage with him while he's off hunting Fae in Avalon. If only my wolf and I could fly, I'd never allow my alpha to leave me behind.

Actually, it's Ronin *and* I who are left behind. Mine is a situation with which I'm wearily familiar, the responsible adult left behind to teach class and keep house while the others are away—but Ronin is not. Clearly this mate of mine is feeling a trifle forlorn.

Admittedly, I'm feeling a trifle forlorn myself.

Still, no matter how we both feel, having Ronin Pendragon lurking in my classroom in an amorous mood is never a wise notion. Discreetly I loosen my buttoned-tight collar.

Ronin's amber gaze turns positively wicked. *What's the matter then? Feeling a trifle warm down below, are we?*

I frown and shake my head in subtle warning. *Kindly focus on your essay, Mr. Pendragon. I won't issue you brownie points while I'm grading this exam just because you, er, polish my apple.*

From her seat in the front row, Dez gives a little hiccup that sounds like a giggle. I meet a flash of her mischievous olive eyes before her ponytailed head bends diligently over her essay. Abruptly recalling that Ronin isn't the only Valyrian telepath in my classroom, a flustered heat floods into my face.

I'm doing my damnedest to ignore Ronin's knowing grin and manage the inconvenient situation in my trousers when the gong of the church bell in the belfry thankfully signals the end of this interminable hour.

Chairs scrape and papers rustle. Liberated students leap to their feet and lunge for their backpacks.

Without rising, I pitch my voice to carry over the clatter. "Kindly leave your essays on my desk. For tomorrow's lecture, read chapter thirty-three in your textbook on the history of the Dark Fae exodus."

Typically, Faerie lore is covered in Agrippina's Witching World Lit class sophomore year. However, in light of current events, I've deemed it prudent to alter my syllabus to include the highlights of that Shakespearean drama in my History of Witchcraft curriculum for all students.

If indeed the Dark Fae are returning, the witching world must be prepared.

My students toss their essays onto my desk and stampede for the door like wildebeest in the Great Migration. The Schedule A's are headed for early lunch in the commons, while the Schedule B's have Genetics of Witchcraft with Agrippina.

Racetrack drops her essay on my desk and lingers while she shrugs into her battered motorcycle jacket. That jacket is a blatant dress code violation I choose to ignore.

With all these young rebels in my charge, I choose my battles wisely.

"Need any backup out there on the tarmac, Teach?" she asks gruffly. "My moms are major donors for Senator Mercury's campaign, and

Messalina knows better than to fuck with an old witching family like us Prynnes."

Clutching her schoolbooks to her chest, Dez lingers beside her girlfriend and looks attentive.

Despite my reluctance to deliver my unwelcome news to our arriving VIPs, my worried heart softens. These two girls might not be part of my harem, but they're very much a part of my cohort.

That makes them a part of my family.

"Thank you very much for the offer, Racetrack," I say gravely, because this girl hasn't answered voluntarily to *Ms. Prynne* or, worse, her Christian name of Abigail since the day she arrived at this Academy. "That's very kind of you. Neither the queen nor the senator are likely to be very happy, but they're political creatures, not assassins—and the Aries clan wields its own considerable clout. Professionally, I expect to emerge from this entire affair with nothing worse than another letter of reprimand for my faculty file. Now you and Ms. Maali had best run along before you're late for Genetics."

Racetrack scrubs a hand through her bristly blond hair and subjects me to a sober scrutiny that is entirely adult. "You sure about that? Might not hurt to have some Mogadon muscle in your corner. Just for insurance. If that royal twat Messalina pitches a fit, I can teleport you right outta that whole sitch—"

"Thank you very much indeed, but no." Still, I find myself unexpectedly moved by her loyalty.

But fair is fair. None of this mess is Racetrack's fault. If anyone is to be rebuked for failing to protect our future queen, that person should rightly be myself.

"Told you he'd say that, didn't I, cobber?" Dez gives me a rueful look. No doubt her precognitive abilities are hard at work. That magical gift must be an uncomfortable one to manage, but this girl handles her tricky witchcraft and the ethical dilemmas it poses with such grace she makes it all seem effortless.

I manage to maintain my composure until Racetrack links her hand with Dez's and tromps off, with RT's combat boots ringing loud against the weathered floorboards of my classroom.

In fact, I'm so touched by this display of support from my students that I fail entirely to notice I'm not alone until Ronin closes my classroom door and turns the lock to seal us both inside.

I shoot to my feet in instant protest.

With one look at his darkly purposeful expression as he prowls toward my desk, I know perfectly well what manner of trouble this mischievous mate of mine is up to.

Even before he begins loosening his tie.

"Ronin, my dear one," I begin resolutely, because it's useless calling him by his surname when he's in this sort of mood. He'll only sneer at the pretense of propriety I insist upon maintaining between us in the classroom. "I'm due at the airstrip in an hour—"

"Plenty of time for what I've got in mind." He unknots his tie with deliberate intent, a slow tease he couples with a sinuous roll of his lean hips that makes my wolf growl in anticipation.

"I won't allow you to distract me. Not this time." Firmly I grip my briefcase and plant it upright between us on my desk in an unsubtle declaration of intent. "You know quite well how I feel about maintaining decorum in the classroom—"

"Here's what I know. I know you've never gotten us both off harder than the time you gave me a proper shagging facedown over your desk and made me spill all over your gradebook." Ronin circles my desk like a stalking panther. "Rather fancied that little indiscretion, didn't we?"

"That was… an abominable moment of weakness on my part." With both hands, I clutch my briefcase to my chest. "Besides, that misdemeanor occurred in my office in the crypt, where at least I could ensure our privacy—"

"Bollocks, you made out with Neo right up against this bloody chalkboard." Ronin looks indignant at my feeble evasion. "He blushed like blazes when he told me."

This allegation is (to my embarrassment) quite true. I grit my teeth around another protest and settle for a stubborn headshake.

Ronin eyes my desperate stance. "For shit's sake, Lucius, stop clutching that briefcase like a tourist on the London Tube who's afraid of some bloke snatching your purse. You're wound so tight you're going to shatter if you don't get off. Just let me take the edge off, all right?"

My wolf is emphatically on board with this scandalous notion. But, dear heaven, half the students in my *domus* are missing. I've *lost* our queen-in-waiting. I've already weathered a stinging reproach from the Dean for this disgraceful imbroglio—

"Devil take the Dean." Following my thoughts without effort, Ronin wrenches my briefcase brutally from my grip and tosses it on my desk.

A growl of mingled protest and hunger rises from my chest before I can stop it. My tortured gaze darts to the locked door. Trapped behind my zipper, my traitorous shaft swells with need.

Ronin's lidded stare drops to my crotch and his sultry grin widens.

Dear God, I'm lost.

Of course, he knows I'm lost.

"I'll punish you for this indiscretion later," I say thickly, fangs descending from my palate.

"You can punish me now." He drops to a crouch with tigerish grace and starts unbuckling my belt. "I want you to fuck my face till I choke."

This time my growl is all wolf.

While he unbuckles and unbuttons and unzips me, I stroke both hands over his sleek black hair, swept into a regulation ponytail that bares the cruel lines of his face. He's the first mate I've ever bitten, the first student I've ever fucked, the first everything for me. I broke all the rules in the Academy Codex to claim him, which made it easier to break them again when I claimed Zara. Then, of course, there was Vasili, who decided to inflict upon me his irresistibly addictive mating bite and never allowed me an ounce of choice…

Ronin dips a hand into the slit of my boxers and wraps his fingers around my shaft. I snarl and punch my turgid length into his fist.

"Paisley silk," he mutters, pulling me free from my boxers. "I swear to fuck, Lucius, you make me mental."

"My choice of unmentionables seems to have a similar effect on Vasili," I murmur. "For some reason."

"Do you honestly not know?" He barks a short chuckle that sends a gust of hot breath over the sensitized head of my cock. "It's that mannerly Old World gent lurking behind those carnivore fangs of yours. Bloody wrecks us—Zara too. Makes us wild to see you all messy and undone."

I'm still attempting to comprehend how my old-fashioned European manners (the product of a rather fusty and aristocratic upbringing by my Hungarian wolf shifter grandsire) could possibly be perceived by anyone as alluring, when Ronin guides my shaft to his lips and licks a long hot stripe from my balls to my tip.

That languid swipe of his wicked tongue makes every coherent thought in my head dissolve.

Especially when he burrows his face into my boxers to mouth the swollen sac of my balls.

"Jesus Christ," I whisper.

By the rigid tenets of my Roman Catholic faith, taking the Lord's name in vain is a mortal sin.

But considering what else is currently taking place in my trousers, my cursing is the distinct lesser of two evils.

Ronin chuckles into my crotch and burrows deeper to suck one of my balls into his sinful mouth. I grip his head desperately in one hand and grope blindly behind me for something to hold me up. His hands glide up the backs of my thighs and ease me against the blackboard. In a frenzy of need, I grip the chalk tray behind me and send an eraser tumbling to the floor. The dry puff of chalk dust mingles with my mate's dark ambergris spice.

"Easy, love," Ronin whispers against my balls. "I've got you."

This complicated arrangement must be awkward as hell for him. It would be far simpler to push my trousers and boxers down my hips.

But damn if I'm going to interrupt what he's doing.

He mouths his way back up my shaft, teasing and testing my patience with every slow sucking kiss. Abruptly my wolf surges to the fore and lunges against my skin.

We haven't climaxed, my wolf and I, since the night we emptied ourselves inside Zara and then jealously guarded her deliciously fertile quim all night from any other male's penetration. My wolf wants her pregnant and rounded with our pups—a poignant longing that adds a particularly keen edge to my desperate worry for her safety.

But even though we cannot procreate, Ronin too triggers my mating instinct.

All at once, I can wait no longer.

With a snarl that rises straight from my wolfish heart, I grip Ronin's head in both hands and sheathe my full length in the exquisite sucking heat of his mouth.

My wolf is scarcely courteous about the matter, he wants our mate stuffed and mastered, and Ronin gags a bit to find my cock suddenly nudging the back of his throat. But I'm relentless, hips driving forward, fingers clenching in his hair, talons descending from my fingertips to add an extra edge.

Ronin chokes on my length, then swallows me down like a champion.

As I watch every inch of my ruddy swollen shaft vanish between his gorgeous lips, the delicious clench and ripple of his throat around my length rips from my chest another guttural growl.

My mate grips my hips to anchor both of us and starts working me, backing off to let inches of my cock slide into view, all shiny with his saliva and veiny with my need, before he envelops me again and swallows me back down. His skillful tongue strokes the tender ridge on the underside of my member while his cheeks hollow to give me the powerful suction that wrenches a wolfish whine from my throat.

"Oh Christ," I gasp through my fangs, all raspy with need. *"Ronin."*

His chuckle vibrates against my length as he pulls me in deeper, swallowing me down and down until every oversensitized inch of me can feel every pulse and ripple of him. His amber eyes lift to find me staring down at him. My eyes must be red and my face half-shifted, because his pupils blow wide and his entire body shivers.

The unavoidable truth is this. I'm a monster from a fairytale. My mannerly Dr. Jekyll persona barely reaches skin deep.

Now my secret Mr. Hyde is rising.

I bare my fangs and growl, "Faster. Deeper. Take all of me."

My luscious mate grins around my shaft and picks up the pace, plunging down my length and sucking his way back up, clutching my hips like he's drowning on my dick. His head bobs along my member, earnest as a penitent schoolgirl, until my taloned hands lock around his head and I fuck his face like he's asking for, the way he damned well deserves for tempting me past my resolve like this.

Snarls rip out of me with every savage thrust.

I'd never be this brutal with my precious queen Zara or my sweet boy Neo. Truly, even with Ronin, the crudeness of my needs is unforgivable.

But Ronin can take me at my worst.

Suddenly his brow furrows and his eyes widen. His sharp strangled cry quivers around my dick. The musky scent of semen drenches the air.

By using him like this, I've made him spill in his own trousers, which I don't imagine he intended, but which I know he doesn't mind (to put it mildly).

He loves when I make him filthy.

Pleasure coils at the base of my spine and clenches my balls and rushes down my shaft in an explosion of violent ecstasy. I arch into his mouth and fling my head back and howl like the beast I am. My hips pump into his willing mouth in blatant abuse until my world goes gray and my knees go weak.

Finally I sag against him, my perfect mate, both of us spent and shaking and drenched with sweat. My wolfish mating scent lurks thick in my nostrils and drenches every cell and pore of Ronin's slumped and trembling body.

"My dear one," I whisper, tender and broken. "Oh, God. I…"

His bowed head snaps up and his eyes blaze fire. "Don't you dare apologize. You needed this, Lucius. You needed *me*."

In my emotionally pulverized state, his ferocity catches me on the raw. My brow furrows and my jaw clenches. "But my needs are monstrous. I—I hardly expect you to—"

"That's what it bloody well means to be in love then, isn't it?" Ronin shoves to his feet and locks onto my tortured stare.

I'm not a small man, yet he manages to loom over me as I fumble to tuck away my spent member and restore order to my attire. Merciful Christ. I've sweated through my shirt. And the queen's expecting me on the tarmac in less than an hour. Given my mates' determination to ambush me sexually at all hours in the crypt and the classroom and the library, it's fortunate I keep a freshly laundered and ironed shirt in my office for precisely this sort of situation…

Then my sex-stunned brain trips over the words Ronin just said. Slowly my fangs recede into my palate.

In love.

He's in love.

With *me*?

"You're… in love with me?" I ask hesitantly.

God knows, we say it all the time to Zara and Neo. Vasili, my alpha, whispers the words to me in private and destroys me every time he says it.

But, somehow, I've never said those miniscule but incredibly momentous words to Ronin.

Ronin sweeps a hand over his disheveled hair and stares at me blankly. "For fuck's sake, Lucius, what do you think we're doing in this blooming harem? You and your professorial sense of propriety and your bloody-minded Catholic conscience make me mental—but, yeah, I love you."

I gaze at him. My student. My mate. The relentless object of my filthiest sexual obsessions.

And now, it seems, my love.

I'm overwhelmed by a sense of gratitude so powerful it makes my eyes burn. With his movie-star looks and his rock-star charisma, this mate of mine could have anyone at Icarus (and, truly, he *had* everyone before I came along). But the unattainable idol formerly known across this Academy as Sir One and Done has finally chosen… me. Us. All five of us.

If he hadn't, I'd be alone in this entire ordeal.

Without him, I'd be so alone.

I lunge at him like the wolf I am and drag his mouth to mine in a desperate, clumsy kiss that's sticky with my own musky essence. The fact that he tastes like my spunk and he's drenched in my scent (mingled with my alpha's, because Vasili too came buried inside him last night) fills me to the brim with a ferocious swell of satisfaction.

Ours, my wolf growls with contentment. *Lucius, he is ours. He is ours for always.*

"Too right I am," Ronin mumbles against my lips between kisses. Then his husky tone hardens with resolve. "You're mine for always too, love. That's why you're not doing any of this alone. Whatever happens in Avalon with Zara, Vasili and Max and Neo can help her handle. I'm bloody well staying here with you."

Chapter Twenty-Seven
Zara

We've barely landed in the dragon's lair when the fuckery starts.

The Avalon Academy's like a twisted version of Cinderella's Castle, but with a *Game of Thrones* spin. Here's what I mean. This spiky, swirly, shiny castle on the cliff above the sea looks like it's carved from the spun-sugar frosting on a wedding cake. But this joint's rocking a cave-like dragonlair that's the size of an aircraft hangar.

Turns out inside there's only one dragon allowed.

The second Xhevith touches down on the ledge, that resident dragon comes exploding out of lurk in a glitter of ice-white scales and snarling jaws that shoves my heart right into my throat.

Vasili's slender snake of a dragon is silver, but I know right away this isn't my warlock. Those claw-tipped wings beating in my face are way too massive.

Not to mention the pustulent yellow cast to that glaring gaze is pure evil.

While Xhevith lets loose one of his nails-on-chalkboard screams and backwings so hard we almost tumble off the ledge, my gut heaves with an aversion to this corpse-colored monster that's so intense I feel like hurling.

When my arms sweep up to summon lightning, my travel mug goes flying. In my throat, the lightning voice coils and hums. But all that happens is my gauntlets start crisping.

Because, of course, I'm still wearing these goddamn handcuffs.

"Cheese on toast!" I yell to the Fae behind me. "You wanna get us killed? Get these things off me. *Now!*"

But Zephyr's already in motion, and it's not to take off my cuffs. Transferring the reins deftly to one fist, he sweeps an arm overhead in a circle and flings a fistful of air toward the snarling dragon.

That thing's jaws are just opening to breathe… whatever it breathes… when a violent gust of wind sends the white dragon skidding backward, clawing at the stone and slavering, deep into the lair. Gobbets of greenish saliva that look like pus drip from those gnashing teeth to spatter the ledge.

That pus-like drool is seriously disgusting.

But I can't help feeling (reluctantly) impressed by Zephyr and that Dark Fae witchcraft he's rocking.

Elemental magic. Isn't that what he called it? I guess the Dark Fae King's element is wind.

Whatever it is, he's badass.

"Now, Yersinia, where are your manners?" Zephyr says tightly to the thrashing monster. "We come at Maeve's express bidding."

Those seem to be the magic words, or I guess it's words plus images for their kind of telepathy. Because Yersinia stops thrashing and subsides from losing her shit into a malignant but not actively attacking glare.

Xhevith isn't so quick to unwind. The green's still trembling between my knees.

I think maybe he's trembling with rage.

Of course, his rider senses what's going down. The Fae leans over my back (that's a searing second of full body contact I don't totally mind) and gives Xhevith's scaly shoulder a reassuring thump.

"Be at ease, sweeting," he murmurs. "Let's give the queen's dragon her space."

I'm definitely not the one he's addressing.

But.

I also can't help noticing when he croons endearments like that, with that voice of his like water running over rock, some of the tension that's knotting my gut and clenching my shoulders unwinds.

Fuck. That's fucked up. This Dark Fae tyrant's the only reason I'm even in danger.

Xhevith grumbles into stillness and perches warily on the ledge. Zephyr unbuckles his harness and jumps down with a lightness that reminds me of the sparrow Ash likes to call him.

For the first time, I kinda get why Ash calls him that.

Zephyr leaves me to manage my own buckles (so I guess he's learning about me too, because I definitely don't like being fussed over) and knots his reins around the dragon saddle. I free myself from the harness and hop down under my own steam.

Ash's travel mug has definitely gone bye-bye, so I'm gonna owe him one. And I already miss the rest of my latte.

Damn it.

I'm undercaffeinated.

We've barely stepped clear of the saddle before Xhevith launches into open air and drops from the ledge. Wherever he's going to roost, can't say I blame him for not loving the company up here.

I shoot a dubious look at the corpse-white Yersinia, now crouched and coiled half a hangar away, hissing softly through her fangs and eyeing us with a baleful stare.

My own inner dragon recognizes a rival and hisses right back. But I manage not to voice that shit.

"Come," Zephyr says briefly, striding across the lair toward a high arched door that's set in the stone. "We're already late. And keep clear of the pus. It's infectious."

Eeeew.

My gaze shoots to the puddles of yellow-green goop on the floor. I give that yuck factor *and* the hissing dragon a major berth and head across the cavern after him.

"I thought Fae and humans couldn't swap diseases? That we're, like, a different subspecies?" I aim the question at the back of Zephyr's green head. "I mean, that's what Ash was saying about STDs."

The Fae spares me a narrow look over one shoulder from his good eye that manages to appear offended. "STDs? What do you take him for? Ash is not diseased."

"I'm just saying, sounds like he plays the field. Not that I'm judging or anything, God knows." Okay, we're definitely getting sidetracked here. "But about the pus?"

"A dragon is a magical creature," he says curtly, keeping one eye (since he's only got one) on the subject of our discussion as we scurry past. "Yersinia's magical gift is pestilence. Once her spittle touches flesh, all living beings decay into slow corruption and putrid rot. How do you think the mortal plague spread so swiftly in ancient times?"

Wow. That's one hell of a witchcraft.

And I thought hurling lightning was lethal?

At least the guy's answering me now, but he definitely sounds distracted. Despite the fact that we're apparently in such a rush, Zephyr pauses before that arched door to settle his crossed swords more securely over his shoulders.

I take advantage of the breather to give the hangar bay a longer look. "These digs are definitely spacious. Why aren't there more dragons in here?"

His ruthless mouth tightens and his jade-green eye turns guarded. "There are too few Dark Fae royals left to tame and fly the beasts. In these times, most of the dragons on Avalon are feral."

Silently, I slot that fact away in the *Reasons Avalon's in Trouble* folder.

But Zephyr's still talking. "Besides, a Dark Fae's dragon is far more than a cuddly pet or a glorified carriage. Our dragons serve as weapons. Her Moonstruck Magnificence will tolerate no such threat in her vicinity."

"She's that twitchy, huh?" I fiddle with the cuffs around my wrists, but I'm done asking for my freedom.

Clearly, I'm just gonna have to take it back myself.

"Zara." His somber tone (not to mention the fact that he's using my name and I don't totally hate how that sounds) captures my full attention like the crack of a whip. "Be of care. Queen Maeve and I are oathsworn, each to raise no hand in violence or bloodshed against the other. If you ignite her wrath, truly, there is little I can do to aid you."

Well, all righty then.

"Uh, thanks for the warning?" I mutter. "Just one more reason this howdy-doody isn't gonna go so well."

On that sobering note, he gives me another sharp look, then wrenches open the heavy door and ducks into the cool blue glow. I suck in a steadying breath and follow him. The door swings shut behind us and seals us in with a shuddery boom.

That audio effect is pretty atmospheric.

But at least, you know, we're shutting out that plague-breathing dragon.

So there's that.

Then it's all twists and turns and spirals through curvy halls and corkscrew stairs lit with more of those witchy blue-white crystals set in the walls like torches. This whole setup seems solely designed to confuse. I'm talking a whole lotta blind corners, dead ends, steep stairs soaring up or plunging down, blank walls, empty air, empty rooms.

What I'm not seeing? Yep. Not seeing any other Fae.

I definitely get the sense it's been a while since they've had much enrollment at this Academy.

Kinda like Icarus back home.

Which just gets me thinking again about how this world and the witching world are linked. Like distorted reflections, each one seems to mirror the other.

If that's right, maybe I can't really save the witching world on its own.

Maybe I've gotta save this one first.

I huff out a breath of major frustration and wish I could talk to Lucius. He'd help me sort through this mess. Without him and the rest of my guys, my thoughts just spin like kaleidoscopes and lead me in circles going nowhere like this labyrinth.

Zephyr runs lightly up a steep corkscrew coil of stairs, then stops so abruptly I almost run into the back of him. I manage to stay on my feet and peer over his green-scaled shoulder, because I'm actually a little taller than he is. Clearly, we're at the top of one of those towers I saw outside. We're standing in front of a pair of arched double doors carved from twisty driftwood with a swirly Art Nouveau motif.

Through that door eddies the low trickle of a voice like glacial melt that sets my teeth on edge.

"Welcome to the Avalon Academy," Zephyr murmurs. "This is the queen's lecture kiva. I'd advise you to adhere strictly to royal protocol and wait to be acknowledged before you speak."

Suddenly I'm wrestling with a whole lot of misgiving that bottles up the questions in my throat. Not the least being protocol of any kind and me, we don't really go together. I'm reaching for his arm to slow him down when Zephyr opens the door quietly and slips inside, his green cloak whispering at his heels.

Suddenly this whole scenario's moving way too fast.

Gritting my teeth, I adjust my utility belt over my Avenger suit and march in there.

I don't know what I expected, but this joint's nothing like Lucius' classroom. This lecture hall on top of a tower is more of a round kiva like Zephyr said, with narrow keyhole windows slitted in the wall all around, under a massive oculus skylight that lets in plenty of cold winter sun. Stone benches set in the floor circle a sunken center. In the middle, under the oculus, lit by a spill of natural sunlight and a round hearth dancing with pale witchfire that does nothing to heat the icebox chill, a tall slim woman soars like a stalagmite with her back to us. She's sheathed in a gown of glittering silver scales, with ice-blue hair piled high above her pointed ears.

She's the one speaking in that voice like glacial melt, saying something complicated about composition and perspective in ancient Avalon cave art.

I'm not kidding, this crap's dysfunctional.

Sweet Jesus. With their whole Dark Fae existence hanging by a thread, this is the stuff they're studying?

No wonder Zephyr needs help here. They all do, all the Dark Fae.

Clearly, they're not getting the help they need from her.

Maybe I really am their best shot to break this curse.

Still, honestly speaking, I'm too distracted by this whole scene to take in much of what this icicle queen is saying.

Maybe a dozen students are scattered around the circle, which isn't a lot in a room that was made to hold more, and it proves that point Zephyr was making about these being the last Dark Fae to be born before the curse. They're mostly female, with skin ranging from cream to honey to olive, hair in fantastic shades like pink and mint and lavender spilling down their backs (for the guys) or piled atop their heads (for the girls) to expose their pointed ears. The girls are all wearing long pale gowns with high waists and elbow gloves and silk stockings and ballet slippers that look totally unsuited to the dragon riding and the arctic climate.

Huh. I guess that's the school uni at this Academy?

Tell you the truth, given this racial extinction scenario, the whole setup's ridiculous. These Fae should be learning survival skills from their queen, not deportment and painting.

The schoolgirls look like ladies in a Regency-set historical romance. They're actually poking at delicate scraps of needlework while they listen to the lecture, like actual lace and embroidery and shit, while the guys lounge around like pashas in cream silk waistcoats and gray riding breeches.

The entire effect is like high tea in a Jane Austen novel.

Of course, that all changes when the students facing the door get a glimpse of Zephyr and me.

Then the refined atmosphere of elegant ease cracks and shatters like a dropped plate.

Students straighten and nudge their neighbors and start to whisper. Awareness ripples around the circle. Heads turn and eyes widen.

They're beautiful the way Zephyr's beautiful, yet they're weird, alien, *other*, their swift sudden movements firing with the feral birdlike grace of velociraptors.

When these Fae with all their chilly beauty stare at Zephyr, hunger and avarice burn in that circle of perfect faces. Everyone in this classroom wants a piece of him, whether it's his power at their command or his head on a spike or his cock stuffing their favorite orifice.

Honestly, with subjects like these, I feel for the guy.

While that glittering tower of a woman lectures away in her icy voice with her back to us, Zephyr links his hands behind his own back and paces near the door like a caged cheetah. Subdued light glitters on emerald dragonscale. Moss-colored hair swirls down his rigid spine.

Looking every inch a king.

For maybe the first time, I wrap my head around one of those warnings he was trying to give me. All the guys in my harem, my Gemini kings, they're powerful warlocks. Every one of my guys is a scion of their witching world clan, just like I am for the Geminis. Still, under witching world law, the lion's share of their political status comes from being mated to me, the future queen of the witching world.

Over here in Avalon? Zephyr was born and bred to be the Dark Fae King. He isn't beholden to me for his power.

If I ever mate this guy?

I'll be beholden to him for mine.

I'm still working my way through that dynamic and the ramifications of what it means when that circle of pale faces swings away from their king to study me. I meet those stares head on, like a flight of arrows hissing toward me to ping off my dragonscale (and yep, definitely noticing that I'm out of uniform here). Their nose-in-the-air disapproval ricochets off my who-gives-a-fuck attitude.

Then I watch all that hunger and avarice curdle and sour into jealousy.

I'm not their kind of telepath, but they're not hard to read. Without even trying, I've got what they want.

Their king in my bed.

Or so they all think.

"Your Moon-Dazzled Radiance," a voice says coldly, like a spill of ice cascading down my spine. (Jesus, these monickers they use.) "My son, you were expected with this one before first bell."

Nice. Clearly I'm not a queen here. I'm totally powerless. That's what she wants me to know.

I'm not even Zara. I'm just *this one*.

Plus I haven't even been here five minutes and I'm already gonna get thrown in detention for tardiness.

I lift my chin, pop my hip, and nail that bitch with my Zara look. If I had gum, I'd blow a bubble.

But she's not even looking at me. The White Witch of Narnia over there's only got eyes for Zephyr. Her flawless, ageless, emotionless Tilda Swinton face is too cold and remote to be pretty. But I can definitely see where my Fae—I mean, *the* Fae, the one who nabbed me—gets all that lord-of-the-manor arctic arrogance.

"Your Moonstruck Magnificence." Zephyr inclines his haughty chin a fraction in, like, the world's most miniscule bow. Still, it *is* a bow, and I file that factoid away under the *Dark Fae Power Dynamics* subfolder in my noggin. "I could not deny my intended bride the unparalleled opportunity to observe your instruction."

That's my cue to look appreciative without moving too far from the door, in case we have to make a run for it.

"Behold the Gemini queen." Still not looking at me but clearly playing to her audience, the Faerie Queen gestures in my general direction, like I'm some exotic animal on loan at the city zoo. "Zarina. Selene. Gemini. For you see, a mortal witch protects not her true name, but shouts it from the rooftops."

The sound of my full name jolts through me like that Compulsion spell I learned in Lucius' Common Magics class. Names are power, especially for these Fae, where the power of names seems supercharged. That's why I'm on a first-name-only basis with Zephyr and Ash. They haven't told me the rest of theirs.

And here's mine spraypainted on the lecture kiva wall of this

Academy. Hell, just to make sure no one misses it, that icicle queen with her megaphone might as well hire a blimp.

Guess that puts me at a disadvantage.

I fold my arms across my chest, ignore the hostile glares of my so-called classmates, and lock right onto the queen bee. I stare at that bitch till she's got no choice but to look back. Otherwise she'll risk coming off as weak, like she's afraid to meet my eyes.

Slowly her stately head turns till our gazes lock. Her eyes are long and lidded and glimmering with secrets.

Maeve.

Queen of the Dark Fae.

That's my title. The knowledge falls like a raindrop and plinks against my skin, fallen from God knows where. *I'm the queen they need here. That's my title and she knows it.*

I can't read her mind, can't read much of anything behind the cold porcelain perfection of that Venetian mask of a face. But she doesn't look like that's any kinda power she's planning to share.

Not with me. Not with Zephyr. Not with anyone.

If this bitchy witch gets her way, as long as she's breathing, no other woman will ever wear that crown. As long as she does, these cursed Dark Fae will just keep dying.

Her eyes, blue and deadly as pilot lights in a gas leak, flicker over my unorthodox attire. But she doesn't give me the power of an acknowledgment.

Instead, she jabs her remark at Zephyr like a spear. "Your intended bride is improperly attired to observe my instruction. In the main, she appears singularly unsuited to join this cohort. Or, for that matter, to join this court."

"Yeah, well I'm not staying." Sensing Zephyr's alarmed stare veering toward me, I tack on hastily, "Your Moonstruck Magnificence. I'm just here to get a look at the place. I mean, you're in trouble here, obvi."

The already uncomfortable silence in this classroom congeals and thickens to ice. The queen's eyes harden to steel.

From the keyhole slit of glass behind me, the staccato crack of a brittle break makes me twitch.

I sneak a peek over one shoulder to find a web of fine cracks raying across the cloudy glass.

Maybe the looming extinction of their race is something I'm not supposed to talk about. But come on, that curse is definitely the elephant in this half-empty room. How are they supposed to break it if they can't even talk about it?

I give an apologetic shrug for not knowing the protocol, but now I'm on a roll, so I just keep going. "I mean, no offense or anything, I'm not saying I won't help you out, we gotta talk about this shit. But I'm not staying. I'm already enrolled at the Icarus Academy." I pause, but there's no reaction. "Maybe you've heard of it?"

"The Icarus Academy." Finally, the queen's delicate mouth tightens in distaste. "Ah yes. That pathetic establishment of mongrels and misfits and half-breeds whose geriatric Dean fancies herself my rival."

I barely know the Dean. She's a million years old and she's kinda this enigma. I've never even been in the Dean's Tower, and she hardly ever comes out.

But I'm already bristling in defense of my school. I mean, who uses the word *half-breed* in this day and age?

I tap my booted toes against the floor and try to hold onto my patience. "Look, about the Dean, it's not like we're besties, but listen—"

"You are that wolf's pupil." Okay, so clearly she's not in a listening mood. And the way she says it makes me rear up in instant defense on Lucius' behalf. She says it like he's vermin, and I am not amused.

"For your information," I say shortly, *"that wolf* is the Aries scion, he's smart as fuck, he devotes his whole life to putting every single other person's well-being before himself—and he's also my mate, so I'm gonna ask you to give him some respect. You feel me?"

Clearly *not* feeling me, her pale eyes shift to Zephyr. "And you, my son, would appear surprisingly well prepared to accept that four-legged animal's soiled leavings."

Yep, that tears it. The gloves are coming off.

"Hey." I plant my hands on my hips and scowl at her. "I thought you're supposed to be all about the manners at this Academy? You're not exactly the Avalon equivalent of Emily Post, are you? Your Magnificence," I tack on.

"By the moon, my queen, we appear to have disrupted your lecture." Smoothly Zephyr steps between her and me, and he's all casual, but I'm not deceived. His voice carries an edge to make anyone nervous. "Such was never our intent. After all, ancient Faerie cave art is a topic far too paramount to disrupt. My intended bride and I will await your leisure after class in the Headmistress's Bower—"

"Why, my son, how now?" his mom murmurs in a voice like silk spread over ice, with so much lurking spite she's giving me major willies. "We all comprehend the central significance of the woman who wears the Unseelie crown. Upon her strength, her worth, her witchcraft, her fertility, hinges the entire future of our race. We wished to assess the suitability of this mongrel witch, with her salad of bloodlines and her well-trafficked bed, to fill the role of your future queen, did we not?"

"I agreed to an interview, not a public inquisition." Crisply Zephyr pivots on his heel and ushers my belligerent body toward the door. "I now discern it may have been a mistake bringing my intended to this Academy at all—"

The sharp crack of breaking glass gives me barely enough warning to leap away from the shower of tiny shards that fly from the nearest keyhole window.

That's what happens when glass shatters.

"Oh fuck," I mutter.

Zephyr locks a hand around my arm to propel me forcefully from the cracked window toward the door, and he isn't being gentle. But I can already see we're way too late for a graceful exit. All too clearly, his bitch of a mom doesn't want me here. And she definitely doesn't want me sitting on her throne. She's spoiling for this fight. (And why do my warlocks always need to have such horrible parents anyway? I thought Max's mom was bad. Now here's this piece of work.)

"The ritual begins at moonrise, my son." Maeve's voice coils and snaps through the riveted silence. "When better than the present moment to test your so-called queen's mettle?"

Oh hell to the yeah.

Let's test that shit.

I shake off Zephyr's insistent grip and ignore his hissed warning. Slowly I swing around to confront her.

The queen's looming in front of the witchfire like she's chiseled from stone. But her students are rising from their seats and scrambling out of harm's way, their faces firing with anticipation and alarm.

"You really wanna see what I can do, huh?" Deliberately, one by one, I peel off my dragonscale gauntlets and let them drop. "How about you get these cuffs off me and I'll show you?"

"That is a singularly ill-advised notion." Zephyr skewers me with a look of complete exasperation (but honestly, what did he expect to happen when he dragged me in here?) then whirls back toward his mom with a lot more patience than he's showing me. "Your Moonstruck Magnificence—"

Whoops. Too late.

The queen's long arms spread, scaly sleeves dripping from her wrists to slither and hiss like snakes against the floor. She closes her eyes, tilts back her regal head, and…

Screams.

Her students yell and cover their ears. My scalp crawls and my skin cringes and my ears practically start bleeding.

Geez, the lungs on this woman.

Under that ungodly racket, Zephyr bites off a single resigned-sounding curse, crosses both arms over his shoulders, and unsheathes his twin swords in a smooth sweep that's gorgeous to see (partly because *he's* gorgeous, he really is. And partly because clearly he's doing it in my defense, like he's been trying to warn and guide and defend me since the minute we walked into this insane asylum.)

Then, as the queen screams, the charmed silver cuffs soldered around my wrists start glowing. While I watch in mingled dread and anticipation, the silver softens and starts to melt.

If I wasn't wearing this dragonscale armor, I'd be dealing with third degree burns, thanks to this lunatic. But due to this fireproof Avenger suit my two Fae have me wearing, those gobbets of molten silver drip right off me to puddle on the floor.

I can hardly believe this crazy witch is dumb enough to free me. In fact, there's probably more to this apparent largesse than meets the eye, because Zephyr nails me with a burning stare and grits a command through his teeth in a voice like bedrock.

"Do. Not. Shift."

"Yeah, good luck with that." Already the lightning's lurking in my voice.

I give in to a wild laugh myself (because these Fae don't have a monopoly on crazy, there's plenty of crazy to go around in this place).

The dizzying rush of my witchcraft crackles and surges through me. My hair uncoils from my braid and swirls around my shoulders. The shadows turn purple as psi fire spills from my eyes.

Fuck. Me. Sideways.

That head-spinning hit of power, as all my bottled-up witchcraft breaks free, feels freaking amazing.

Across the kiva, Maeve meets my wild stare and bares her teeth in a savage smile. For some reason, I'm getting the sense she actually *wants* me to use my witchcraft. Which is definitely weird, and a part of me— the part Lucius is teaching not to fear my own magic—wants me to think through this stunt before I act. But I've been fucking kidnapped. Held captive. Made to feel helpless.

And now I'm being threatened.

I fling my arms over my head, release all my pent-up rage in a howl of raw fury, and summon the lightning.

A jagged purple fork of electric whoop-ass shatters the oculus skylight in a shower of jagged glass.

Big shards plummet down and students scatter screaming in all directions. A knife-like stalactite drops toward Zephyr, who tucks and dives and rolls clear of the danger.

Then Maeve adds her voice to mine (which is fucking deafening, believe me). Those falling shards pulverize in a glittering cloud of harmless dust.

My gaze shoots from the queen's deadly form to the empty circle of open sky.

That circle of sky means freedom.

My inner dragon lets loose with a trumpeting bugle and bates her wings. *Zara! We rise!*

Whoa. She's, like, not asking.

Like me, she's been chained up in this place way too long.

I barely have time to unbuckle my utility belt and drag down the zipper of my dragonscale before the tingling heat of the shift sweeps through me. With desperate haste, I peel everything down my torso and kick free of my boots till I'm all nakey.

Across the room, Maeve watches the naked Zara show and laughs like a loon. All around us, the cloudy glass in the keyhole windows cracks and shatters with explosive force. Icy wind rushes into the room and flying shards slice across my unprotected arms and torso in a dozen places. Sharp pain streaks through my lacerated skin and makes me yell.

That yell isn't anything human.

It's the deep brassy bellow of my dragon.

"Zara!" Zephyr snaps in a voice that commands attention from halfway across the kiva. His lithe armored frame sprints toward me through the bedlam, green hair streaming behind him. Under the narrow stripe of his eyepatch, his face is white as milk. "Don't you *dare* rise!"

As if I can stop it? My head swings up toward that circle of sky. My body ripples and pulses with a surge of fiery heat.

Mating heat.

Zephyr's mom just keeps on screaming. I swear to fuck, that psycho's shredding my eardrums. Waves of shattered glass explode inward from window after window. Zephyr twists through that deadly sea of flying glass like a green eel, swords slicing through the shrapnel, flinging currents of air with every stroke that divert the deadly shards away from both of us.

Yeah, I appreciate the assist. But the guy's clearly got an agenda. He's not attacking his mom, and she's not attacking him, I guess because they've both sworn not to. When he reaches me, he's gonna bring *me* down. And I just bet he's got some slippery Dark Fae trick up his sleeve that he thinks is gonna hold me.

Yeah, no, not happening.

I launch into a dead run that carries me away from him, push off my back leg, and hurl myself naked into the air. A blinding flash of light turns my world a dazzling white. My mouth opens in a scream that ends in a roar.

I explode through the oculus in dragon form and take half the tower roof with me when I spread my wings. Chunks of concrete fall away behind me. Lashing my tail and winging hard to gain altitude, I twist my long neck to see if I can catch a glimpse of Zephyr down there.

Because, you know, crushing the guy to death in the rubble really isn't part of my game plan.

I don't wanna kill him. Not anymore.

I might even wanna help him.

But it's gotta be on my own terms.

Fuck, it's no use. I can't see shit down there, just a cloud of rock dust floating over what's left of the oculus tower. Now, as I climb, the spires and turrets of Cinderella's Castle fall away beneath me. I bellow with rage and triumph and tilt into a spiral that swings me over the vast blue sea till I can spot the smoking volcano looming against the horizon.

That volcano's my compass.

It points the way home.

Home to Icarus and all my guys.

I trumpet at the sky, just because my dragon's feeling frisky, then angle my flight over the city toward the mountain. I'm wasting no time, because I'm definitely expecting to be pursued. No way Zephyr's gonna let me get away with this *Escape from Avalon* caper, mere hours before his best shot at breaking the Dark Fae curse.

Under the adrenaline rush of exhilaration and exertion, my mating heat throbs and pulses low and fierce in my belly like a beating heart.

Fuck. I need Max.

Right now.

Once I vamoose through that portal and hook up with my dragon king back at Icarus, I'm not even sure I'm gonna shift back. My dragon queen's not gonna be a juvenile much longer. I mean, she's definitely hit puberty. She's been wanting this with him—wanting it with Vasili in his flying serpent form too—for a good solid while. Vasili's twisted enough to go for it, especially if I ask, and I already know Max would be more than into it. He probably figures it's the quickest way to get me pregnant with his dragonets.

But shifty sex is a lot to wrap my head around.

So I've been hanging back.

Here, now, in this condition, all my human hesitation is melting away.

I'm winging for that mountain with everything I've got when my attention is snared by the glitter of sunlight on scales. My neck twists toward the sparkle of blue and brown and black that's issuing from a spatter of tiny caves in the mountain's flank. That scattered sparkle whirls and rises to dot the horizon, growing steadily more distinct as the whole shebang bears down on me.

Dragons. Ferals. A whole freaking flight of them.

Trepidation unfurls in my tummy and my six-chambered heart beats harder. My brain shoots straight to that funny moment at the lair this morning when Xhevith was nosing my pelvis, his wings flared wide with extreme interest.

Then that wry murmur when Zephyr told his dragon I wasn't for Xhevith.

Finally, to tie the whole montage together and wrap it in a pretty bow, there was that flash of stark intensity firing in the Dark Fae's face just now.

When he shouted at me that desperate demand not to shift.

My nostrils flare and my eyes telescope. A sharp dart of realization shoots through the chaotic jumble in my head and hits home with a ping.

I'm not much for gambling, because I was raised in a Gemini casino, and I know the house always wins. But I'd pay real money those feral dragons winging toward me from those caverns in the volcano's flank are male.

To be real precise, they're feral males, drawn into rut by the irresistible scent of my dragon queen's mating heat.

No matter how hard I fly, I'm nowhere close to finding my way outta this place. I'm never gonna reach the stone circle or its Avalon equivalent (even assuming it's easy to find) before that flight of males reaches me. And shifty sex I might choose to have voluntarily with my shifty mates is one thing, but non-consensual rutting with some random mindless dragon—or maybe a whole flight of them, I don't know if they fight or share here—that's something totally different.

I mean, I don't have to spell this out for anyone.

Sweet Jesus.

Right now I've got a more immediate issue to deal with than hauling my ass back to Icarus before my outraged would-be bridegroom on Xhevith—or his hellacious mom on that plague-breathing Yersinia—hunts me down and claps me back in cuffs (or worse).

Thanks to this mating heat my dragon and I are rocking, I'm suddenly confronting a whole new crisis that's pretty fucking urgent.

Chapter Twenty-Eight
Maxim

I have hunted for Neo and fed him and we are aloft and winging for the shining city near the sea. That is when my mating bond explodes with the unmistakable electric hum of my sovereign.

Zara.

The familiar jolt of my mate's determination and desperation sizzles through every synapse in my dragon body. In mid-flight, I fling back my head and bellow.

Zara! My queen! I am here!

My deep sonorous roar, as a fully mature black dragon, makes ice and snow cascade from the volcano's steep sides. I wing past an avalanche of tumbling snow with my head swiveling to search the mountain's pitted flanks for any glimpse of my queen. Gamely clinging to my back in his harness, Neo hammers at my crest for attention and voices a thin cry of excitement I can barely hear under my own roar.

Clearly he has sensed his own waking bond with his fated mate.

An adrenaline rush floods my limbs and makes my mighty heart thunder in the vast cavern of my chest. That surge of emotion is not mine alone.

It is hers. Zara's.

My mate is in danger. She is fighting. She is in need!

My muzzle curls back to bare my fangs in a vicious snarl.

Desperately I search the skies, where is she, where? Why can I not see her? This clear morning, once so promising for our search, is filling with thick banks of fog and cumulus. Curse this weather. Another winter storm is brewing. Already fat wet flakes drift past my intent gaze to spatter my scaly face.

I roar like blazes. Where is my mate!

I swear I will hunt until I find her.

"Max!" Neo's faint cry barely reaches my ears before the wind snatches his voice away.

I crane my neck to peer back at his tiny form clinging to my back and waving madly for my attention. Thankfully he is managing better in the air than yesterday, but our constrained communication in this form is far from ideal.

If only I had bitten him as I yearn to do, we would not require human speech. We too would have a mating bond.

That is a degree of restraint I now regret.

I chuff out a disgruntled snort.

"Max!" Neo yells faintly. "She's behind us. *Behind us!* Turn… around!"

Of course. Behind and above is the blind spot for a dragon. If not for Neo, there I too would be blind.

I bank away from the mountain in a tight soaring turn, eyes searching through tendrils of the thickening fog. Powerful waves of my queen's pain and distress and alarm batter me through our mating bond.

She is too pressed to answer my frantic bugles, but surely she knows I am coming.

My queen! It is I, Maxim! We will never stop hunting until we find—

Another thin cry from Neo, so tightly bound to his fated mate, brings my head snaking up to scan the volcano's heights. Through thick eddies of cloud and snow, I glimpse flashes of brown and green and black. Over the howling wind, my keen ears pick out the shrill screams of feral dragons. A full flight of the creatures wheels overhead in wild agitation. Now they dive after some fleeing scrap of doomed prey—

Through the fog, I spy the distinctive glitter of turquoise. The skies split around the resonant bellow of my queen's lightning voice. The heavy clouds glow with a purple fork of electrical energy.

I part my jaws wide enough to swallow a house and trumpet for my mate.

ZARA! My sovereign, I am here!

These feral dragons are wretched, they are half my size, scarred and starved by their hardscrabble existence in this harsh land. Still, the nearest of these creatures are wise enough to screech and scramble away from the enraged bellow of a monster like me. In dragon form, I am this population's dominant male.

And I am vicious.

To protect my mate, I will slaughter them all.

I breathe in deep. Carried on the biting wind, the dark rich spice of Zara's mating heat floods through me. My dragon cock stiffens and my barb flares wide.

Curse this Avalon moon. The full moon has brought on her superheat.

She is mine!

Of course, I will share her delicious heat with Neo, who is also mine (even if he does not know it). But no one else!

A dragon queen's superheat is sufficient to trigger an entire population of dragons into rut. The outcome is a biological certainty.

These feral males will kill to breed her.

Now I too am in rut.

Blind with lust and fury, I roar out a warning to all my rivals. But my mate is too hard-pressed to answer my heartfelt bellow. She is fighting for her very life. She screams with the lightning voice. The skies come alive with dancing forks and flickers and flashes of energy. The tinny tang of electricity burns my tongue and sparks along my scales.

Vicious with purpose, I tuck my wings tight and arrow toward my nearest rival, who is too mad with rut to flee.

The rusty brown dragon howls and turns on me with a disemboweling swipe of wicked sword-length talons.

I swerve to avoid the attack, barrel into the beast like a locomotive, and bury my jaws in his scarred throat to rend and savage. Scales part, flesh tears, and the salty heat of blood explodes in my mouth. I lock my jaws around that vulnerable column and shake the wretched creature like a rat until I snap his neck with a violent *crack!*

Roaring in triumph, I fling him aside, already dying, in a spatter of falling blood.

Neo thumps on my hide in alarm. Raw instinct flares to life.

I dive barely in time to avoid a wild rut-fueled charge by a skinny black dragon who is in no way my equal. I twist in a tight spin that wrings a despairing wail out of poor Neo, cinched tightly to my back, then soar up flaming.

I paint the heavens with a sheet of dragonfire. Ferals fall from the sky, burned and screaming, like a shower of fiery comets.

Safely beyond range of my deadly rage, Zara's teal queen bellows in welcome. Her scales glow neon with sexual vitality and her eyes flame like suns in her crafty dragon face. Now that I finally have her attention, I trumpet my triumphant arrival and my absolute possession of her—my mate, my love, my sovereign, mine—to this entire benighted realm.

My queen's streamlined body twists and dives toward me.

A foolish blue dragon blunders between us, clumsy with lust. But Zara coughs out a fork of lightning that sends the witless beast fluttering off with a howl. A feral green, mindless with rut, soars toward me from underneath with deadly acid dripping from his jaws. My hide throbs with remembered agony. Snarling and slavering, I whirl away from the fiery acid and sweep my rival from the sky with a swipe of my massive tail that sends the creature tumbling.

"Max, you big galoot, will you *listen*?" Neo's exasperated yell finally seizes my attention. "Look where we are!"

I drag my gaze away from the riveting sight of my mate fighting her way toward me and twist to find Neo gesturing madly toward the looming volcano.

Our erratic flight has carried us near the place we started, the small safe cave where we sheltered last night. Zara herself is soaring toward it, very likely because Neo can speak to her through their mating bond in ways I cannot while I am bestial with bloodlust.

Clearly, Neo has told her where to find shelter.

I growl in acknowledgment and wing in a tight circle to guard my mate from above, where she is vulnerable, to protect her blind side. All around us, feral dragons who survived my initial attack wheel and scream in sexual frenzy. Their bodies appear and vanish in gusts of thickening snow, but I am vigilant. I keep Zara well in my sight. When a frustrated brown strays too close, I rumble up a gout of warning fire to keep my sovereign safe.

Zara's glittering teal dragon arrows to the cave and alights on the ledge in a blinding flash of light that dazzles my eyes.

When my vision clears, she is gone.

It's okay, big guy. Before I can panic, her beloved voice streaks through our mating bond. *I'm inside. Pretty nifty setup you've got in here.*

Still strapped to my back, Neo laughs in giddy relief.

I bugle my triumph to the heavens and warn away any rival male who would dare to challenge my claim. Then I dive toward the ledge myself. Neo is already loosening the harness, not even waiting for me to land before he scrambles fearlessly from my back and leaps to the ledge. I barely give him time to duck inside, which he does at a dead run, before I myself alight.

The tingling heat of the shift sweeps over me. My scales melt away, my tail dwindles and vanishes, my body rises upright to stand on two legs. The blinding light of my transformation dazzles my eyes.

With the dark musk of my fertile queen thick and luscious in my human nostrils, I am savage with rut.

Every inch of my naked and fully aroused body throbs with violent need.

Blindly I race into the cave, safely guarded from any rival, to find the two that I love—my precious queen and her fated mate—wrapped tight in each other's arms.

Chapter Twenty-Nine
Zara

I barely have time to brace for impact before Neo gallops across this chilly cave where I've taken shelter from my obsessed dragon suitors and hurls himself into my arms.

The warm muscled strength of my fated mate's body envelops me. In the dim gray light streaming through the entry, he's wearing plaid pajama pants and an Academy sweater with loafers, which is just so Neo, and his magenta curls are all windblown and his glasses are steaming with excitement and sliding down his nose. His clean soapy scent of sage and lavender seeps through me.

God, he smells like home.

That familiar scent makes my eyes flood with tears. I wrap my arms tight around his waist, bury my face in his broad chest, and whisper, "Hi, baby."

"Oh, babe." His voice trembles as he pulls me hard against his body (which definitely makes my superheat sit up and take notice). His warm arms close around my flight-chilled and very naked body, while his big hands cradle my head and stroke my back. "Thank God you're okay. Lord, it was awful waking up and you not being there."

Hearing his earnest tone, I hide a wobbly smile in his sweater. "Yeah, sorry about that. I was planning to be back before breakfast."

Shit, I've missed him. I've really, really missed him.

My fated mate, the easiest to love of all my mates, the one who asks the least and gives the most. Of course, he'd be the one to come after me. Of course, he'd refuse to be left behind.

Even if I was shocked as fuck to glimpse him and not Ronin strapped to Max's back.

Because as far as I know, Neo hates flying.

Our teary reunion gets interrupted when Max erupts into the cave, naked and wrathful. Which is another whole emotional moment. Typically I can take care of myself, no problem, but I'll admit I was in over my head out there today. When I glimpsed my dragon king bearing down on all those ferals and heard his tyrannosaur bellow, I was never so relieved to see anyone in my life.

Neo might not blame me for taking off, but my alpha dragon is a whole other story. Max storms across the cave, all six feet of sexy, with his buttery blond hair streaming around his shoulders and his slitted eyes flaming gold and eight-plus inches of barbed dragon cock jutting straight out in a blatant declaration of intent.

Apparently my out-of-cycle superheat has thrown every male dragon in sniffing range into rut.

Including this one I'm actually mated to.

I lift my head from Neo's shoulder and step gently free of him so I can say hi to Max as he charges toward me. "Hey, big guy—"

"Never," he grates out in a voice like gravel. "Do that. Again."

The leather-and-brimstone scent of angry dragon precedes him. One hit of my dragon king's head-spinning mating scent kicks my superheat into overdrive and triggers a flood of my own Mogadon pheromones.

If I'm not careful, that biochemical cocktail's gonna set us all off.

(And, you know, I'm hardly ever careful.)

Sure, I figured my alphas would be pissed. But they can't possibly think this shit's my fault.

I prop a hand on my naked hip and cock my head. "Well, it's not like I asked to be kidnapped—"

For the second time in as many minutes, I absorb a full-body impact with one of my mates. Max's rough hands close around my waist, sweep me off my feet, and shove me against the vivid painted dragons that fly and wheel and claw across the wall. His hot hard body collides with mine in a scorching kiss.

Oh hell to the yeah.

My sex-starved body responds to this cavalier treatment exactly the way you'd expect. I open to the slick lick of his tongue and his burnt cinnamon taste. I snake my arms around his lean waist to grip a double fistful of tight dragon ass and drag his pelvis against mine. The coarse wall scrapes my back and the sandpaper rasp of his unshaven face abrades my cheeks and I don't give a single flaming fuck about any of it, I really don't. Not with my nipples tingling and hard as cherry pits and my cunt slick and dripping and his barbed dragon cock shoving roughly between my thighs to probe my soaked slit.

Right before his dick drives in deep to claim my drenched pussy with a single vicious thrust.

"Fuck!" I gasp into his mouth. "Fuck, Max."

"That is the general idea." His gold dragon eyes flame into mine as he recoils, then snaps his hips hard in a second savage strike. "To fuck."

My dripping cunt stretches to fit around all those inches of his complicated dick. Then his barb shoots out and plinks into my pussy to lock me. I yelp with surprise. My dragon queen keens with pleasure.

Neo's worried face appears at his shoulder. "Wow, Max, I really don't think you should—"

Max breaks off our tongue-sparring tournament with a growl, wraps a hand around Neo's curly head, and drags him into a hard claiming kiss.

Whoa.

My spinning brain trips over that visual like a skipped record.

Sure, Max and Neo have been eyeing each other from a distance since my dragon joined the team, but Vasili's so possessive over our bookworm he never lets Max anywhere near him (to Neo's obvious frustration).

Now here's Max kissing our bookworm like my dragon feels good and entitled to it.

And check out Neo, fiery-blushing and fumbling with his glasses, just softening and yielding so sweetly to Max's testosterone-fueled lip lock.

I lick my own tingling lips, already swelling from Max's brutal kiss. My hoochie definitely likes what we're seeing, because she ripples in response and clenches around my dragon king's thick dick.

I've only been gone a couple days, but geez, I'm getting the definite feeling a lot has gone down in my absence.

Even before I've gotten around to explaining to the guys how I've claimed this whole new warlock and he's a Light Fae prince named Ash and somehow we've gotta figure out how to accommodate—

Clearly sensing that I'm a little distracted, Max snarls and drives into me harder. Hard enough that I see stars.

My disjointed attempt at thinking shatters like a thrown glass.

"Yesssss," my dragon queen hisses (in *my* fucking voice). She's done being shackled and held back, and so am I. "Fuck me. Claim me. Both of you."

"Oh, Lord," Neo mumbles. He surfaces from Max's kiss and turns toward me blinking. "Were you, um, still wanting to save your pussy for Lucius?"

So much has happened that it actually takes me a sec to remember the way Lucius went full alpha and wolfed out over my pussy that last night on Icarus.

Anyway, that whole saving-my-pussy-for-Lucius moment ended the exact moment I fucked Ash.

Max's own alpha dragon doesn't like hearing about me saving my pussy for anyone. He pins me harder between the wall and his pistoning hips and just rails me. Savage grunts rip out of him with every vicious thrust.

"That was—a one-time thing," I gasp around the punishing rhythm of Max's dick. "Just to accommodate—his wolf. Lucius wants pups— like crazy."

"I want dragonets." Max bares his shifty fangs (which is hot as fuck, I love when he goes full alpha like this) and pounds into me. "But it will be your choice. Neo Mercury, take off your pants."

My eyes telescope wide and shoot to my fated mate. Man, hearing Max give Neo orders like that, in his sexy alpha growl, is so hot I'm melting.

And check this out.

"Okay." My fated mate is already shucking his clothes at warp speed. His sweater goes flying one way and his pants go spinning another. "I, um, don't know if there's room…"

"There is room." Max's gravelly voice gives me shivers. "Behind her. Quickly. She needs both our cocks inside her, filling her with our seed, to shatter her superheat."

Sweet Jesus.

That's what I'm talking about.

Neo gulps and his leaf-green eyes get big and round behind his glasses. He's pretty much the resident bottom in our polycule, he's actually really into that, and God knows my guys can't get enough of him. But he's tapped my ass before. When he's in the right mood, he loves that. He's gonna need the face-to-face connection of fucking my pussy for reassurance pretty soon too, and I totally want to give that to him. I'm his alpha the same way Max is mine.

But there's nothing Neo won't do for me.

Sure enough, my bookworm licks his lips and nods. "Okay. That works for me."

"Yes." With a vicious snarl, Max drags me off the wall, supports my full weight on his hands clamped under my ass, and shoves my back into Neo's front.

My bookworm's barely had time to get out of his briefs, but he catches me like a champ and plants his own back against the rough wall to anchor all three of us. Because my fated mate's good like that.

Max is still supporting my weight, sinews standing out in his sun-bronzed shoulders, but this new arrangement lets me wrap my legs around my dragon's wiry hips, which spreads my ass and exposes my puckered rose back there for Neo to plunder. We don't have any lube, but Neo's not First Boy on the Dean's List for nothing.

He's an inventive guy, you know what I mean?

Neo wraps a big hand around my tit and snakes the other between my legs from underneath to get a palmful of slick from my juices and Max's, which are dripping out of me with every thrust.

Him copping a feel gives Max some extra friction too, and Neo lingers to enjoy the experience. Clearly he can feel Max's cock sliding in and out of me, drenched in both our juices.

Oh my God, that's hot.

My mating bond hums with arousal and my dragon queen purrs with approval. Max's slitted pupils blow wide and his gaze drills into mine.

"What have—the two of you been—up to?" I gasp between downstrokes of Max's ruthless dick.

"I had my first superheat," Neo pipes up happily while he lubes his dick with our slick. "It had to get broken, and there was no one else. Max, uh, took one for the team."

"Ohmygod," I moan on a long exhale. Because now Neo's lubing up my pucker, and I'm super-sensitive back there, with every nerve in my body firing and tingling with mating heat. I want him inside me bigtime. "You telling me I missed it?"

"Next time, you will not rush off into danger without us." While he ruts into me with demonic fury, Max spies Lucius' fresh mating bite in my neck. That bite hasn't been healing too well without an alpha to tend it. Max's lips skin back from his fangs and he glares at the bite like he wants to set me on fire with his eyes.

Like I'm personally responsible for this whole shitshow. Even though I didn't exactly ask Lucius to bite me again (but it's not like I minded).

And I definitely didn't ask to be kidnapped.

Then Max dives in and starts tonguing my tender bite with long sweeps of his hot tongue. The biochemicals in his shifty saliva deliver instant relief to the inflamed flesh. I breathe out another moan. I love it when my guys do this to me and each other. When they tend each other's bites, it's the sweetest fucking thing they do in my harem.

Hearing me moan over that stimulation's enough to inspire Neo to start probing my back door with his monster dick. Max's hard thrusts drive Neo's fat cockhead through the tight ring of muscle back there on an adrenaline rush that rips out of my lungs a cry of mingled pain and triumph.

"Whoa, hold up, she needs time, Max." Neo grips my hips and tries to take it easy on me. But every time Max's pelvis slams into mine, my ass takes another inch of Neo's thick girth.

"What she *needs*..." Max's head swings up to reveal his flaming eyes and shifty fangs, and I just about climax on the spot, "...is cock. Filling every hole in our queen's sweet body. Spilling out of her from every orifice. Until she swears never again to leave us."

Oh fuck yeah. That's what I need all right.

Especially when Max punctuates his words with a series of hammering thrusts that bury Neo balls deep in my ass.

"Not my fault," I remind them both breathlessly, squirming on all that cock filling both my holes in a way that makes both my guys groan. "But if me running off means I missed the two of you fucking, then next time I'll definitely think twice."

Plastered against my back, Neo breaks into a sweat and rocks into me in short desperate strokes. He feels apologetic in our mating bond, he doesn't want to hurt me, but he can't help himself, because he too is experiencing a superheat.

I shouldn't ask, I should give them their space, but with all three of us fucking, the question just slips out.

"Any chance of a repeat?" I blink into Max's carnivorous stare. "With the two of you?"

"No," Neo bursts out. Our mating bond floods with his chagrined embarrassment.

At the exact same moment, Max growls, *"Yes."*

"Whoa." Now I'm battered by the predatory aggression of Max's possessive alpha. Jesus, the communication between these two is a mess.

But this shit is hot. As. Fuck.

Neo squirms against my back and his gentle rocking stutters. "Gosh, no. No repeat. I mean, Zara—he isn't even into me. Obviously. He was just doing me a solid—"

"Neo Mercury, you are the most vexing creature." Max's nostrils flare wide and his stare burns over my shoulder into my fated mate. "You are mine and I am yours and I will fuck you again repeatedly."

Oh hell yeah.

My inner dragon and I are both on board with the idea of these two fucking repeatedly. In fact, we're so on board with that whole concept that my pussy clenches around Max and my ass clenches around Neo and my first magic moment races through me in a tingling rush. Skewered and filled in the best of ways, I writhe against their cocks. My head falls back against Neo's chest and a sharp breathless cry spirals out of me.

Max's grip on my ass tightens and his back arches. The first hot flood of his potent shifter seed spurts against my inner walls. His ruthless face convulses in a spasm of pleasure.

"Oh gosh, babe," Neo moans and whimpers. His cock swells to stuff me. "Wow… that's intense. Lordy, you're tight. But… Max… you don't have to."

Max's head lowers and he scowls at my fated mate.

"I will fuck you again, Neo Mercury," he says like it's a threat. "Very soon. And when I do, you will enjoy it. As will I, *kotyonok*. You are mine."

Well, dayum.

That dark sexy growl of his makes Neo shiver against my back. I bite my lower lip around a grin.

No doubt Vasili's gonna be an issue, he's one of Neo's alphas, and he's possessive as fuck over Neo right now. And my Goblin King definitely gets a say, that's how shit works in our polycule—but he doesn't get to decide. These two mates of mine have their own relationship now. And I, for one, plan to enjoy it.

"Hey, babe?" Neo whispers in my ear. "You're into this, right? The idea of me with him? It feels to me like you're into it."

"Baby, I'm so into it. But that's also because *you* are." I clench my thighs around Max's hips and pull him deeper, because feeling me submit to having my basement flooded with dragon jizz is part of what's gonna make Max's barb finally retract. "The two of you are gonna be so good for each other."

Neo whimpers and grips my hips to steady all three of us and reams my ass with his monster cock while Max drives into my pussy. They're both filling me so good, I'm drum tight squeezing and spasming around all that cock, and they're feeling each other too through the thin membrane that separates those two dicks inside me. We're all slick and sweating. The dark spicy hit of my pheromones and Max's mating scent is so thick in this confined space it's making all three of us loopy.

And I'm pinned between my guys and wrapped in their arms, all three of us panting and moaning in unison over the wet sucking sounds of sex.

I'm just so happy. So happy to be with them again, and so happy they've finally found their way to each other.

Now I just gotta coax Vasili to be okay with this whole new normal, and help Vasili and Max over their bullshit who's-on-top stalemate that's sending spiderweb fissures all through our harem, then help Lucius overcome his overdeveloped Catholic conscience enough to fuck one more of his students (Max), because I know he kinda wants to. Oh, and get everyone to be okay with the whole idea of Ash.

Plus there's still the elephant in the room.

All this unresolved baggage, like major baggage, between me and the Dark Fae King.

Plus the even more major unresolved baggage between the Dark Fae King and Ronin.

Neo wraps both hands around my tits to tug and twist my nipple rings the exact way I adore. The way that makes me gasp and shiver with pleasure that's right on the edge of pain.

Then he buries his face in my neck and whispers against my skin, "Babe, take a breath. You're thinking so hard you're gonna give yourself a migraine."

With Neo nuzzling my neck on one side and Max licking my bite on the other, with their two cocks filling my two holes and our three linked bodies falling into a rhythm of alternating downstrokes that fucking ruins me, all my worries spin away.

By this point, Max has already spilled like three times inside me, his spunk's dripping out of my cunt with every recoil to seep down my thighs. But he's in full rut, his barb's lodged good and tight, and he's getting really close to spilling again. While Neo's been having little pulses of microheat inside me since he started.

I'm so full of warlock jizz that I squish with every downstroke.

I'm perched right on the edge of the big avalanche of an O that's gonna finish me off for good. But I don't want this feeling of the three of us together to end.

I don't wanna face what I'm gonna need to face when the three of us aren't fucking.

Max lifts his head from my mating bite to give me a suspicious look. He knows I'm holding back. He feels it through our bond.

And he's having none of it.

"Kotyonok." He growls that new Russian nickname he's got for Neo. "Play with her clit. Make her come for us until she screams."

Oh yeah. That'll definitely do it.

Neo moans in my ear and works a hand between me and Max to find the hard swollen nub of my clit. He knows I don't need much to push me over the edge, not when I'm already so sensitive from stimulation and superheat that I'm creaming and clenching all over Max's dick. When Neo starts working that nodule of throbbing heat, my back arches and my head falls back and my hips shove into Neo's firm grip in desperate demand.

"Come for us, my mate." Max is guttural with need and his dragon is rising and his eyes are flaming like the dragon king he is. "Let me feel you come all over my cock. We will make you filthy."

Cheese on toast, my dragon king knows what to say to get me off. That tingling rush of urgency pools between my legs and pulses through my clit and ohmygod, ohmygod, ohmygod—

My cunt fists Max's dick and the pleasure hammers through me in surge after surge of raw need. Max bellows and Neo moans and both of them lose it inside me in gouts of spurting heat. I scream with pleasure in the lightning voice. Electric light flashes and crackles beyond the cave.

I think I might be floating too (shit). But they're both anchoring me safely to the ground.

When I'm limp and boneless and sagging between them, Max lowers my feet gently to the floor. The three of us lean into each other and pant.

"Wow," Neo whispers dreamily between breaths. "Superheat."

I huff out a giggle into Max's neck. "Uh huh. We really oughta get you in that hot spring, baby. So you can unwind and clean up. That's what my alphas do for me when they break my heat."

"No," Max growls. "Not you, my queen. You must not yet bathe. We must protect my seed inside you until I fuck you again."

Oh right, his breeding thing.

I'm not into that (am I?) I'm overdue at this point for a shot. But I'm not supposed to get pregnant while I'm in Avalon either, I mean, unless I drink moon tea… am I? My reactions to the whole thought of mating right now are all kinked and twisted in, like, the world's biggest knot.

I pull in a breath to say what I always say. The words that reject Max's claim on my uterus. The words that push him away and hurt him and piss him right off.

But I let my breath spill out without saying them.

"Let's just hold each other," Neo suggests meekly. That's my bookworm, always the peacekeeper.

Okay, I'm into that.

Anyway, I just don't feel ready to wash the two of them out of me or their mingled scents off my body. And it's not because my dragon queen wants eggs and dragonets either… even though she kinda *does*…

"Thinking too hard again, babe," Neo mumbles against my back.

That's Max's signal to shift the three of us from the wall to the pile of furs on the floor. A pile of furs that already smells like both of them, like Neo's soap and Max's brimstone. Which makes my already boneless body relax even more.

I snuggle down in the warm furs between my guys, with my head pillowed on Neo's shoulder and Max lazily licking my mating bite, which is already less inflamed under his care. Max reaches across me to grasp Neo's hand. Now my warlocks are holding hands across my tummy.

Which is honestly just so cute.

Neo seems flustered but pleased by how firmly Max is claiming him. I love that Max is so sure. That dragon's never had any problem knowing what he wants.

Must be nice, right?

My road's never been a straight one. Like, right now, it's twisted as fuck.

Beyond the cave mouth, it's snowing pretty heavily, fat flakes drifting down to blanket the ledge in white. I don't think Zephyr and Xhevith can track me in this mess (though I don't doubt for a sec they're trying). But that snow's gonna mask the scent of my heat. As for me and my guys, we aren't gonna be much good flying in these conditions either. Not over this strange terrain in a blinding blizzard.

Looks like no one's going anywhere right now.

But I'm running out of time.

"Time for what?" Neo says sleepily into my hair.

"Time to make up my mind," I say softly. "But I kinda think I already have."

Max's head lifts sharply, nostrils flaring, but he doesn't say a word. Because he already knows what I'm about to say. And he knows there's gonna be no talking me out of it.

Still, I say that shit anyway.

Just to make it real.

"I'm going back to him," I whisper. "Back to Zephyr."

Max's eyes narrow to dangerous slits. His dragon gives a warning rumble. "Zara…"

My dragon queen croons to soothe him. I turn my head to nuzzle his raspy jaw and breathe in the smoky tang of his mating scent.

"Just for tonight," I promise, lips gentle against his skin. "Just for the moon ritual, so we can break the curse." I hesitate. "And to figure out what to do about Ash. But I am definitely going back. And I'm gonna need the two of you to help me."

Chapter Thirty
Ash

When Zephyr blows into our digs on Xhev without Zara, I already know what kinda bullshit must've gone down during our girl's admission interview with the goddamn queen.

It was me that forged charmed silver strong enough to chain a lightning witch's magic. So when Maeve gave a howl and shattered my spell, I felt that shit.

I felt it all the way across town.

"Lit outta here, didn't she?" I grip Xhev's reins and give his scaly shoulder a hard rub to settle down that dragon, who's all excited with his crest bristling and his eyes spinning like pinwheels.

Xhev says howdy back with an over-enthusiastic bump from his muzzle that almost knocks me over.

"Easy there, fella. Anyway." I shift my gaze back to Sparrow. "We always figured that was a risk."

"A risk?" My guy won't even hop down. Pale with fury under his eyepatch, he glares down at me from the saddle with his pupil blown so wide there's barely any green showing around the rim. "*Ash.* If she flees Avalon, she'll doom this entire realm and all its subjects to certain extinction. By the time the next full moon coincides with a spring equinox and the conditions are correct for the ritual, the entire Unseelie race will be dead."

"Take it easy, kid. We'll find her." Kinda taking a chance, I shift my hand from Xhev's shoulder to Sparrow's thigh. I reckon it's safe enough to touch my guy this once, when he's zipped into his dragonscale and strapped to his saddle.

Still, the supple flex of his thigh under my palm heats my blood.

I've wanted him for so long.

Since way back when he was my student, tell you true, I've wanted him. And I'm never allowed to touch him except when I'm chained to his goddamn ceiling. I want him so much I let him string me up like a slab of beef just so I can feel him. So I can get him off the only way he'll let me.

That messed-up setup was supposed to be history after the ritual.

If there is no ritual due to our girl getting spooked, guess he'll just have to keep chaining me to the ceiling.

Hell. Now I'm the one who needs a rubdown.

"We'll find her," I repeat, good and firm, for both our sakes. "Even if that ain't exactly what Maeve wants us to do, true?"

"I'm well aware my moon-fucked mother freed Zara from your spell in the full expectation that my intended bride would flee. My mother does not believe Zara strong enough to shatter the curse." Sparrow's gaze sweeps the lair like he expects to find our girl hiding out with Xhev's spare fighting gear. "I take it she hasn't returned."

"Nope. No sign of our gal. And I've been here grading all morning." I'm the Potions prof at the Avalon Academy, it's my side hustle. Which gives me something to do with myself other than cook Sparrow's meals and mope around over this whole forced celibacy sitch. "Any rate, this isn't where she'd come, is it? She's gonna be headed for the standing stones."

"For moon's sake." He twists in the saddle to eye the landing ledge, where a good film of fat white flakes is already building up. "She can't possibly mean to attempt that sort of flight in this storm. Not to mention, both she and her dragon are in heat."

While Sparrow scowls at the storm, I sneak a peek under the dragon's kilt (so to speak) and find the big fella's all worked up.

God knows, I sympathize.

Bet his rider's in the same state under that codpiece.

With that empathic bond they share, both Xhev and his rider are horny as hell.

All on its own, my hand drifts up Sparrow's thigh, all wiry and corded with muscle under his dragonscale. If he'd just let me get him off like this, only to clear everyone's head, it'd be the best thing for him.

"Sparrow," I say softly. Shoot. My voice is thick with longing.

"Ash." A muscle flexes in his hard jaw. For a tick, his gloved hand closes over mine. That's the only way he'll ever touch me when I'm unchained.

With all his armor between us.

Fuck, if that's all I can get, I'll take it. My cock aches and my chest burns with everything I want from him. I suck in a breath and ease my hand up his thigh.

His fingers clench around mine to pin me in place. His face tightens in warning. "Don't. You know my limits."

"Yeah, sure, kid," I mutter. "I'm starting to wonder if you know mine."

Without even looking at me, he gently dislodges my roaming hand. "Moon and stars, Ash. If we don't find her…"

I swallow down my disappointment, salted with bitter frustration, the way I'm used to. Then I dig down deep for my patience. "We will. We'll find her. Any rate, I don't take our princess for one to back down from a fight. Want me to come with you to the stones?"

I don't like flying in heavy snow like this. But I'll do it for him.

And I'll do it for her. She's mine now too.

What I have, I know damn well how to keep.

"You hate flying in foul weather." A grim smile crimps one corner of Zephyr's lips. "Stay here. And keep *her* here—in case our wild Gemini returns to her senses and seeks shelter, of her own accord, once the ferals start hunting her. Xhevith can't track her scent in the snow, but we can find our way to the stones far more easily than she. I'll wait for her there."

He's already reining Xhev in a tight circle to face the open air. I sidestep outta the way and give my bare arms a brisk rub to stay warm. Light Fae like me, we're built to survive the elements when we fly. But I'm not gonna lie, this extreme Avalon weather's a real challenge. And the climate's getting worse.

If we all cook when that volcano blows, seems sometimes like that'll be a blessing.

Just to be warm again.

"If you see our princess, you just give her a chance to come to you on her own, okay?" I eye the militant set of his shoulders under the fall of his green hair with real misgiving. With the stakes this high, my guy's strung pretty tight. "You hear me?"

"We haven't time to woo a temperamental schoolgirl. The ritual is hours away." Irritably he gathers the reins, and Xhev's muzzle swings around attentively. "If I see her—*when* I see her—I fully intend to act accordingly."

Well, fuck. That's what I'm afraid of.

"Now hold on a sec—" I swallow down the words with a muttered curse, because Xhev and Sparrow are already in the air.

The green beats his wings in a powerful downstroke that propels those two high above the spiky rooftops and well outta earshot before you can say Peter Pan.

"Aw, crap." Feeling horny and all outta sorts, I schlep back inside and head for the great room. As I clump down the spiral stairs, I gotta wonder if I'm fooling myself about the princess and what I thought I felt growing between us.

The start of something real with her and me and Sparrow.

Heck, I'm probably just a lonely old guy who's been out here on his own with blue balls and an empty bed, hankering after somebody he can't have, for way too long.

When I shoulder the door open and trudge glumly into the great room, it takes me a sec to wrap my head around what I'm seeing. That funny little anomaly that's so outta place in the familiar tidy order Sparrow likes, to keep our digs all ship-shape.

Propped on the floor, right in front of the witchfire burning in the big hearth, there's a piece of trendy men's luggage.

That's a goddamn Louis Vuitton suitcase.

I blink at the thing for a tick before I breathe in an unexpected hit of Mogadon pheromones. That odor's unfamiliar, but so thick with murderous aggression I can practically see the miasma. The hit of aggression smells like caramel and vetiver.

That right there's the scent of a powerful warlock. One who's pissed as all fuck.

That's what that is.

A heartbeat later, I'm staring right at the head of a Fae-killing spear. The shaft's polished ash, tipped with a deadly barb of cold iron. I swear to God, it came at me outta nowhere.

Now that thing's pointed right at my chest.

My alarmed gaze skids up the shaft to find the guy holding it as he floats down gently from the ceiling to the floor. He's got one arm extended in a spill of white lace under a sparkly coat like the Goblin King in that old Jim Henson Muppets flick. He's wicked tall, especially in those heeled boots and britches he's rocking. And he's slim and stropped as a goddamn razor, with a mop of gilded hair tousled around his sharp face and pale eyes rimmed in a pop diva's smoky makeup, frigid as Greenland glaciers.

But he's pretty. He's real pretty.

He'd be sexy as hell, for real, if he wasn't so clearly psychotic.

I just hope the man ain't feeling too stabby.

"Well, darling," he says coldly into the sudden silence, in a tone so lethal it raises every hair on my neck. "You can't possibly have imagined your wretched little realm would escape my notice forever."

"Uh, well, the thing is, I probably ain't who you think." I raise a cautious hand—slow, real slow, so this pretty escapee from the glam rock '80s doesn't skewer me with his Fae-killing spear—and rub the back of my neck. "But I can take a wild-ass guess who you are. You gotta be one of Zara's—"

"Asher Apollo Aurelius, Eagle of the Air, Prince of the Light-Born Fae." The unleashed power of my true name, my hidden name, crackles through the air and snakes around me like a bullwhip. "There. Will. Be. *Silence.*"

Aw, shoot.

This psycho's just triggered one heck of a Compulsion spell. Clearly this dude's an honest-to-God potent-ass warlock.

Plus he knows my true name.

He knows my true name, *and* he just Compelled me to silence. My throat locks up tighter than a casino vault in Vegas.

I don't like getting ambushed, so I twitch with aggression, natch. But, all of a sudden, there's nowhere to take that. Because the guy lifts his free hand and curls his fingers in a fist. The air turns thick and dense as concrete, congeals around my limbs, and cements my feet to the floor. Even with the sharp tip of that iron spear lodged against my naked throat, now I can't move a goddamn muscle in my own defense.

Guess our drop-in guest can do more than levitate and play with common magics. Clearly, he's one of those Mogadon telekinetics. These days, they're rare as fuck in the witching world.

But lucky me, I got one in my living room.

"Now that we're civil." The warlock's deadly eyes narrow in satisfaction and he hisses his sibilants like a cobra. That's when I notice, between those glossy pink lips, he's got fangs like an actual viper. "You and your vile trespassing cyclops of a boyfriend have taken something that belongs to me. I'm here to take her back."

Chapter Thirty-One
Zara

When I wing back in dragon form to Zephyr's palace at sunset, the storm's dwindling, and I've got Max and Neo to guard my six. My superheat's tamped down for now. But as long as the Avalon moon is full, my hormones are still definitely a thing.

However.

Max is twice the size of any feral on Avalon, his mating scent's all over me, and those scrawny feral runts are way too intimidated to challenge him.

Xhevith *is* big enough to challenge him, and I'm kinda worried about what might happen when he and Max cross paths.

But I'll have to back-burner that particular worry. When we arrive, Xhevith's lair is dark and quiet and empty.

Ugh. I guess Xhev and Zephyr are still out in the storm.

Looking for me.

But my nifty green Avenger suit, last seen abandoned on the Academy floor when I shifted, is now hanging on the wall. Which means those two have already been here looking for me.

Not gonna lie. I'm happy to see that suit.

I hustle right into it (so I'm not cold and nakey), shove my feet into the boots, then strut and preen a little so my guys can admire the effect. Neo oohs and aahs, while Max is suspicious and grumbly that I'm wearing clothing provided by a rival male.

Really, it's Xhevith's scent that's setting him off. The scent of a rival dragon.

That's pure instinct, so there's no reasoning with that shit.

Me, I don't even mind (that much) that I'm wearing Zephyr's color and smelling like Zephyr's dragon. Given what I'm about to do with the Dark Fae King, I'm okay letting him be a tiny bit possessive.

You know, just for tonight.

So I send Max back up into the air, with him protesting and balking but finally reluctantly going (because I don't want one of my super-aggressive alphas lurking in the lair when Zephyr gets back). This whole hi-honey-I'm-home situation with Zephyr's gonna be tricky enough to manage without Max going full alpha in the lair.

Then Neo and I head inside to look for Ash.

As the two of us hustle down the spiral stairs toward the great room, Neo's already bursting with clever observations and probing questions about the witchlight and the witchfire and the curse and the ritual. Most of which I have no idea how to answer. But I love that he's putting his sharp First Boy brain to work slotting in pieces of the puzzle of this place.

God, I missed him.

"I mean, an erupting volcano and a worsening Ice Age *and* an infertility curse. That's, like, a lot," my fated mate ventures as he trots along behind me. "Do you have any idea how you're actually going to break the curse and save the Fae? I mean, how the whole thing's supposed to work?"

"Nope," I say wryly. "I'm leaving that part to Zephyr."

What I don't say is that, ever since the exact moment I decided I'm coming back here, that I'm not gonna just abandon Zephyr and his Dark Fae to face their fate alone, I've felt this vast spreading sense of… certainty.

Like I'm doing what I'm meant to do.

I'm queening it.

And that royal bitch Maeve? She had her chance. She better just stay out of my way.

So I'm feeling more confident than I probably should when Neo and I tumble through the door into the great room.

Which is… empty.

The cold flicker of witchfire throws spooky shadows against the wall. Darkness gathers in the corners. The twisty scatter of Art Nouveau furniture coils in wait like a den of basilisks. Cold fingers of foreboding skitter down my spine.

I clear my throat and give a hesitant holler. "Hey, Ash? You here?"

I get a big fat nada. Just the hollow echo of my voice against the walls. Through the row of arched windows, the red sun sinks over the darkening sea.

A twinge of anxiety plucks at my nerves. Under my Avenger suit, my chest gets tight. Which I guess means I'd suck as an actual Avenger.

Here's the thing. With that ritual scheduled to start at moonrise, we really don't have a whole lotta time to file a missing persons report.

"Crap," I mutter. "Where is everyone?"

"Maybe in the shower?" Neo offers helpfully.

My superheat likes the sound of that (a lot) but my instincts are already whispering that we're alone in this joint. King or no king, Zephyr really doesn't have any live-in servants. He seems to like his privacy, and he doesn't seem much into trust.

Ash is nowhere to be found. Neo and I do a quick search (almost on tiptoe, though I give the requisite hollers) through the shadowy bedrooms and the ominous-looking library and the innocent cooking hearth out back where Ash made me breakfast.

Even the dungeon-slash-playroom in the basement, whose impressive collection of immaculately displayed chains and cuffs and floggers makes Neo's eyes go round as dinner plates.

No Ash.

That sense of dread is congealing in my chest. But I try to keep a lid on my misgivings.

Back in the great room, I plant a hand on my waist and tilt my head. "You don't suppose they left for the ritual without me, do you?"

"Babe, you're kinda the guest of honor. They can't *do* the ritual without you." Picking up on my worry through our bond, Neo snuggles into my side with a hug.

I slip my arm around his waist and give him the alpha reassurance he needs. But there's no hiding the fact I'm worried. I don't even know where the ritual's supposed to go down (because I was so focused on opposing the whole thing that I never asked any practical questions about it).

We're still standing in the great room, eyeing the setting sun and wondering what the hell we're supposed to do now, when my shifty senses pick up the light quick patter of Zephyr's footsteps racing down the spiral stairs.

My heartbeat kicks up, my breath hitches in my throat, and an explosion of tiny butterflies flutters through my tummy.

It suddenly occurs to me that I'm nervous.

I'm, like, really nervous.

Zephyr's gonna be worried and annoyed as hell and probably downright pissed over my little disappearing act. That control freak inside him's gonna be wigging out over the fact that he can't control *me*. Of course, I'm hoping his overwhelming relief at finding me alive and kicking, not to mention actually cooperating, in the nick of time to perform the ritual will outweigh all that.

But beyond that, I want him to be happy. I want him to be happy to see me.

The fact that I even care if he's happy, I care how he's feeling toward me as a person? That's an actual revelation.

"Oh, wow," Neo whispers, big eyes shining behind his spectacles. "Babe, that's so great. You're falling in love with him."

My mouth pops open in shock. "No way! That's not why I'm doing this. I'm doing it to save the Fae and break the curse and, you know, save the witching world. Because I think these two worlds are linked."

Neo pushes a hand through his magenta curls and gives me a patient look.

"Baby, no, I mean it." I shake my head wildly. "You and me and Max, we talked about this. Zephyr and me, we don't even get along. We're gonna be a one-night stand."

Even to my own ears, I sound less than convincing.

Cheese on toast.

There is not room in my life to fall in love with the Dark Fae King. Even without all that fucked-up history he's toting around with Ronin.

No, really. There isn't.

Even if, as queen, I'm allowed—even encouraged—to take more mates.

And even if I always fall fast. I know what I want when I see it.

Shit.

I suck in a breath and wrench free from the swirling vortex of that major distraction, because Zephyr is definitely coming.

Urgently I whisper, "I don't wanna overwhelm him, he's kinda temperamental. Go hide in the bedroom, baby. Just for this first part."

Neo looks dubious about the wisdom of that plan, but by now, he too can hear that Zephyr's almost on top of us. My fated mate kinda rolls his eyes at me (I love that he's getting so cute and snarky now that our whole polycule's so into him) and darts into Ash's bedroom just in time.

Neo's pulling the bedroom door almost closed (so he can eavesdrop) when the stairwell door flies open.

Zephyr bursts into the room at a full run, with his hair flying behind him and his face stark and desperate.

Then he catches sight of me and twists to a catlike stop.

His wild gaze locks on mine with his pupil dilated. His lips part so his sharp little fangs are showing.

"Hey," I say softly into the breathless silence. "I, uh, came back. For the ritual."

Because I still can't bring myself to accept or admit the rest.

That I also came back for him.

Zephyr blinks hard, like he's fighting to wrap his head around the fact that I'm really here.

Well, that makes two of us.

His silence is starting to freak me out. Like maybe he's found an understudy to play my part in tonight's performance and now he's just gotta find a way to tell me.

Feeling awkward as fuck and also worried (because what if he did replace me? And why do I feel so bleak at the thought?) I pop my hip like a runway model and scare up some Gemini attitude. "I mean, assuming that's still what you want—"

"Zarina. Selene. Gemini." His hoarse whisper stops my voice in its tracks. "You are never to do anything like that again."

"Like what exactly?" I slant him a suspicious look. "Like shifting into dragon form when I'm in heat? Or like fighting with that queen bitch of a mom you're stuck with, who's doing literally nothing to solve your problem? Or—?"

"Like leaving Ash and me." His whiplash voice slices my snark to ribbons. "You are never again to do anything like that."

Now it's my turn to blink.

In fact, I'm still trying to wrap my head around that explosive statement and every single disruptive impact a demand like that would create in all our lives when the Dark Fae King closes the distance between us in three swift strides, snaps a hard arm around my waist, and drags me up on tiptoe against his lean body. Then he strains up on tiptoe himself (because I'm taller than him) and captures my breathless mouth in a blazing kiss.

The urgency of that kiss sears through me like a bolt of lightning.

His lips are hard and hungry, his tiny fangs are needle-sharp, and his tongue is a lick of sin. He tastes like cloves and desperation. I grapple to drag him closer (which he allows) and take control of the kiss (which he doesn't). He growls and my dragon queen hisses under the distant trumpet of Xhevith's triumphant roar.

Our armored bodies crash together and struggle and meld. I can't feel enough of him. His codpiece is in the way. I slick my hands down his whipcord frame to grip the flex of his ass.

He's lithe and twisting and almost frantic in my arms. His hand burrows into the loose fall of my hair and fists the heavy mass hard enough to pull. Our desperate lips fuse together around his gasp and my moan. Our mouths melt and cling in an atomic flash of need.

I wonder how long it's been since he's allowed himself to kiss anyone who isn't chained to his ceiling.

Because he's kissing me like he's drowning.

And I'm the only woman in his world who can save him.

My whole body lights up with exhilaration and craving. My hair rises and swirls around my shoulders. Sparks hiss from my fingers to sputter and skitter over his dragonscale. Heat snakes through me and pools between my thighs. I cradle his head between my hands, silky ribbons of hair spilling between my fingers, my dangerous touch gliding over the tips of his pointed ears. He gasps and trembles and I smile against his desperate kiss.

Guess those pointy ears are an erogenous zone for a Dark Fae King.

I wonder what other sensitive spots he's hiding. Tonight's my chance to find out.

"Never again," he breathes in a shower of kisses like falling stars, with that voice like water rushing over stone. "You must never again leave us. Swear this to me now."

"Um…" My thoughts flash straight to the Icarus Academy, to Lucius and Ronin and Vasili. Then Neo and Max, who belong there too. Honestly speaking, so do I.

Yet, somehow, there's another part of me that belongs here in Avalon.

Here. Queening it. With Ash and Zephyr.

Apparently, we really are enacting some twisted Hades-Persephone fairytale. Apparently, I really am falling for the guy who kidnapped me. I don't even know how or when this happened. Though I think Zephyr putting his whole self on the line to save his dying people, starving himself of all sex or intimacy literally for years, making Ash and me come on command, then fighting like hell to protect me from his batshit mom, maybe all that had something to do with it.

Under all this Dark Fae energy, my bond with my fated mate is humming with excitement. Still hiding obediently in Ash's bedroom, Neo's hugging himself and beaming.

He's happy when I'm happy.

For Neo, happiness really is that simple.

"Zara." My Fae wrenches free from our burning kiss, chest heaving for air, and licks his lips. His eye smolders jade with fire and temper. Guess he doesn't care for my silence. "So you will not swear never to leave us? It seems I am asking too much from my intended bride."

"No." I drag my head together. "I mean, maybe? I don't know. Vows like that mean something, especially in this place. But… ritual first." I seize on this imperative with relief. "Right? You and me and Ash and all my guys, we've all gotta talk the rest through later. Ritual first."

His gaze shoots past me to the windows and the setting sun. His face hardens with purpose. "Yes, this I will not challenge. Ritual first."

Before I'm totally ready for him to stop kissing me, he's already gripping my arm in an urgent hand and dragging me toward the guest room. "There's a gown for the ceremony in your wardrobe. And I too have ceremonial attire to don. But we must hurry—"

I dig in my heels and balk, because despite the passing time, it suddenly feels like we're moving way too fast. I mean, sure, I'm definitely on board to fuck the guy (you know, for the ritual). But I'm not ready right this instant to marry him.

At the bare minimum, I can't do anything like that without the rest of my warlocks. I'm not marrying just him.

Zephyr jerks to a halt and waits. But his entire body quivers with impatience.

"Okay, so before all that." I bite my lip and glance toward Ash's bedroom. "There's someone you should probably meet. And I don't want you freaking out about this, okay?" I could call through our bond, but I use my voice instead to give everyone a little heads-up. "C'mon out of there, baby."

Looking all flushed and breathless with excitement, Neo emerges shyly from the bedroom.

Clearly my fated mate's put his time in there to good use, because he's replaced his plaid pajama pants and Academy sweater (which were both looking kinda travel-worn) with one of Ash's primal *Conan the Barbarian* ensembles. To be specific, he's wearing one of Ash's sleeveless leather vests laced over his broad chest and a pair of Ash's fur-trimmed leather boots pulled over snug buckskin breeches. Ash is taller than Neo and broader through the shoulders, but those rawhide laces are adjustable, plus my fated mate's big enough and built enough to pull the whole look off. The vest shows off his impressively bare biceps. And the breeches cling to his bubble butt in a way that's practically indecent.

Still, with his bookworm spectacles and shining eyes and soft magenta curls, he's just so Neo. His eager face turns toward Zephyr's riveted frame.

"Hi, Zephyr." My bookworm gives my Dark Fae a tentative smile. "I'm Neo. Neo Mercury?"

"One of the mates in her famous harem, I presume." Zephyr sounds a bit dour, but at least he isn't losing his shit the way I worried he might. Of course, Neo's so harmless-looking and so darn appealing it definitely helps.

Zephyr arches a skeptical green brow. "The senator's son, if I'm not mistaken?"

"Uh huh, that's me. Plus I'm Zara's fated mate." Neo walks right over to us with his hand extended for a shake. "And wow, you're the actual Dark Fae King, right? I've read, like, really a lot about you."

"I pray you don't believe everything you read," Zephyr says wryly, but actually shakes his hand (such is my bookworm's appeal), though the Fae looks a little awkward doing it and it's probably not an Unseelie custom. "You are welcome in Avalon. Harm none in this realm, and you may claim my royal protection."

He's saying all the right words, but his gaze sneaks over Neo's luscious body in those leathers in a way that makes my bookworm color up and duck his head and bite his lip. I can practically feel Zephyr's dominant side sit up and take notice.

This is going way better than I dared to hope.

Of course, it's Max and not Neo who's gonna be the real problem. My dragon king's circling and hovering over the city, all growly and broody, and I have to keep reassuring him and reminding him through our bond to stay the hell away from Xhevith.

"That's a nice look on you, baby." I pull Neo into my free side for a hug. He snuggles up happily against me and we both look expectantly at Zephyr.

"Very well then." Zephyr reaches impatiently for my arm in that proprietary way of his, but I take his slender hand instead and lace our fingers together with a smile. His hand is no bigger than mine, but his grip is hard and capable, honed by years in the dragon saddle and callused from taking care of Xhevith.

We've all got a lot to learn about each other. But this right here—the two of us holding hands and all three of us daisy-chained together—that's a start.

"Your gown." Zephyr tows us all urgently toward the guest room. "My attire. You, ah, Neo, are suitably attired for the ritual—"

Zephyr jerks to a halt so sharply we all stumble. His green head lifts alertly and his nostrils flare wide in alarm. Then his narrowed gaze arrows straight to me.

"Where in moon's sake is Ash?"

Chapter Thirty-Two
Vasili

You don't get a second chance to make a first impression.

That's what I tell myself as I float gently to the ground, with my sparkly long rock-star coat swirling around me, my Fae-killing spear in hand, and my nicely compliant Seelie Prince Asher leashed and collared like a dog at my heels, just inside the open-air coliseum at the Avalon Academy where this unholy moon ritual is supposed to occur.

Dear fuck.

Is that an actual bed, clearly exposed for public viewing, on the high platform at center stage?

Truly, it is.

A four-poster bed large enough to rival Zara's big medieval bed back home, with a mountain of silver cushions and filmy curtains tied back for display. Tall lamps, lit with glowing crystals, soar at each corner. In the gathering dark, they bathe this impromptu fuck palace in merciless light.

Only the fact that no one is actually fucking in it (yet), because the bed is currently empty, preserves the elite audience in the imperial viewing box, perched directly over the promised spectacle, from my imminent wrath.

This coliseum can accommodate thousands, yet its wide wings barely contain a few dozen scattered Fae, huddled far apart in little groups on the benches for warmth or, possibly, reassurance. The Seelie Prince—Asher—has explained to me why they're so skittish.

And so few.

Well, darling, cry me a river, to the accompaniment of the world's tiniest violin.

As far as I'm concerned, this entire Unseelie island can sink into the sea like lost Atlantis. My Zara's not going anywhere near that fucking bed. (Well, unless she's willing, of course.) With a queen like her, one who thrives on impulse and unpredictability, one should never make assumptions.

Still, it does seem safe to assume she may very well *not* be willing. And the Dark Fae King doesn't seem like one to take no for an answer.

Too bad for him.

Although I do enjoy a showy entrance, I've timed my arrival tonight for stealth. A putrid pus-colored nightmare of a dragon is winging down from the skies to deposit the apparent ruler of this infernal realm—a pale Goliath of a woman in silver armor, wearing a spiky crown that looks lethal—near the viewing box. Under the cover of this distraction, Asher and I alight simultaneously in the shadows. I'm careful to keep my distance from the hissing wing of saddled dragons squabbling and snapping in the arena sands, whose ranks this putrid monstrosity now joins.

Those dragons are distinctly not shifters. Trust me to know.

Apparently these Unseelie—or at least their royals—are a race of dragonriders.

"Queen Maeve, I presume?" I give the leash of my handsome captive a ruthless tug to drag him under the shadow of an empty viewing box. Safely concealed from casual discovery, we coil in the darkness like two snakes in a den.

Or rather, we lurk like one snake and one very disgruntled eagle.

"Yup, that's her. Maeve. Zephyr's mom." The Eagle of the Air scowls and straightens his drool-worthy leather clothing, disheveled after our entertaining little flight (a tidying I allow, as I've only Compelled him to obey my commands and do me no harm). Now he gives the tall glittering figure climbing the stairs to the viewing box a measured look. "Along with her lickspittle courtiers and a few looky-loos from your world."

"Hmmm." Of course, I recognize my own reigning queen, Messalina Aquarius—looking positively haggard, the poor dear—under her distinctive pile of copper ringlets and the ceremonial witching world crown my Zara should be wearing herself. The Aquarius queen has never seemed strong enough to wear that crown, and that weakness has nothing to do with physical frailty. As an ardent anti-monarchist myself (at least until Zara came along), I'm utterly convinced Messalina and her uninspiring Aquarius predecessors are the underlying reason my own world is struggling.

Among the throng of witching world sycophants dancing attendance on the Aquarius queen, I likewise recognize the celebrity senator holding court at her side in his designer suit, with his pompadour hair and megawatt smile, as Theo Mercury.

Neo's daddy.

Rumor has it Daddy's a bit chagrined that I've deflowered his favorite son (even though it was Ronin, not I, who popped that particular cherry, since Neo and I were deadly rivals at the time).

I know. Despicable me. I'm always blamed for everything. God knows why.

Oh. Could it be my reputation?

Mercury Senior's brought his own press corps, now swarming the box to immortalize Maeve's grand entrance on film. Thanks to that WNN news crew, the secret island of Avalon will shortly be exposed. Splashed across the witching world airwaves back home.

And here I am, about to make a televised appearance without my cosmetics case.

I pat disconsolately at my windblown hair and sulk.

Lurking behind Messalina, the trashy-looking ginger with the flashy bling and the Vegas suit makes my eyes ache. Sweet fuck, surely that fashion disaster can't be Zara's very own daddy dearest—Mick Gemini, the casino czar? Surely taking a front row seat for his kidnapped daughter's ritual fucking would be considered an act in rather poor taste?

Well, apparently not for him.

My sharpened shifter senses detect others lurking in the back of that viewing box. Foremost among them—barely visible in the twilight—are a tall man in a narrow suit and, clinging to his arm, a model-slim rake of a woman with a spill of merlot hair.

The others in the rear are mere shadows.

But with the paparazzi and their portable lights now focused on that glittering icicle of an Unseelie Queen, plus Senator Mercury chewing up the scenery, glad-handing like the politician he is and grinning for the cameras, I can't see well enough to identify properly those lurkers in the back.

Still, something about one of those faceless spectators—the tall man in the narrow suit—tugs at my sleeve for attention.

Under my pretty coat, the back of my neck tightens. I grip my Fae-killing spear (a gift from Lucius, purloined from the Academy Vault. Truly, he gives me the sweetest gifts.) Then I inventory the hidden brace of knives secreted about my glamorous self until I've dispelled any discomfort.

"It appears the players are assembled," I murmur. "Except for the guest star of tonight's performance."

"Told ya she's missing," my captive prince says shortly. At the moment, it appears, I'm *not* his favorite person. "Zara's on the wind. And my guy won't show for this shindig without a prom date. Not much point, you feel me?"

It doesn't take much discernment to detect that my handsome abductee hasn't exactly taken a fancy to me and my highhanded treatment.

Oh well. Perhaps I'll grow on him.

Of course, I'll be relieved (in a way) if my darling girl's a no-show, spared this ritual rogering that her Dark Fae abductor fondly imagines he's going to give her.

Still, Zara's complete disappearance in this nasty place will make finding her all the more imperative.

"I'd advise you to pray to whatever gods you worship that our little queen hasn't so much as chipped a nail," I say to my captive with silky menace. "For your sake, Seelie. Or I'll make you and your Prince Charming both earnestly wish you'd never been born."

"She got many more like you at home?" Asher Aurelius gives my fashionable form a distinctly unimpressed once-over I find deeply offensive. "Just so I know what I'm getting into."

I sweep aside a wind-tossed ribbon of hair that's clinging to my mascara-enhanced lashes and preen for him. "Darling, there is no one like me."

He dares to snort.

I pout and give his leash a vicious twist that drags him hard to his knees. Bespelled into compliance, this luscious hunk of meat gives me *such* a ferocious scowl. Under his spiky pewter hair, his silver eyes blaze up at me with an intensity that makes every alpha nerve and synapse in my body quiver like a plucked guitar string.

My. Oh. My.

This Seelie royal might despise me for collaring and leashing him like a dog I've brought to heel. But my captive prince has a submissive side that likes being on his knees for me.

That submissive side likes what I'm doing to him. Indeed, he likes it quite a bit.

Hmmm. My eyes narrow and I allow myself a little smirk, then coil his leash tight enough to make his beefcake body strain for me. His gaze drops to my mouth and color rises along his chiseled cheekbones.

"You wanna play games like that?" he says, low and husky. "A kid like you, with a guy like me, you're gonna have to earn it. I don't bend for just anyone."

I practically purr with anticipation.

Well, darling, what can I say?

I can resist anything except a challenge.

Nor have I missed for a moment the unmistakable roses-and-cream essence of Zara's mating scent, and the heady hit of her Mogadon pheromones, all over this dreamboat Fae.

It seems my little queen has been busy making friends here in Avalon.

Not to say that I blame her, to be sure, with this one. He does possess a certain scowly, yummy, tattooed tough guy, silver fox appeal that must have proven difficult to resist. Despite the obvious age gap between them, my girl herself projects plenty of alpha (even though she submits to me).

This massive male, for all his muscle and his years, was born to submit.

Just as I was born to dominate.

A dragonish snarl from the arena sands, where the pus-colored queen dragon is lunging at a randy male who's dared to venture too close, snaps my wandering wits back to the current crisis. I let enough leash spill from my fingers for my kneeling prince to take my cue. He rises (obediently) and looms over me.

"Well then, perhaps later," I murmur, turning away. "If you ask me nicely."

Behind me, he voices a growl of frustration. For the moment, I pay him no heed. He'll have to work quite a bit harder for my attention.

A kid, am I? We'll see about that.

My own mating bond with my girl is humming. I'm no telepath, except in direct proximity with mates I've bitten and bonded, but I can sense she's close. Neo too, because I'm both their alpha. Inconveniently, I can't sense Maxim, because I haven't allowed that brute of a dragon to deliver the mating bite he's been begging to give me. (As if.)

But I know he too must be close.

Protecting both our mates.

"Where are you, little queen?" I whisper. "The moon is rising, but they can't start without you. You're the star of this show."

A vast shadow sweeps over the coliseum.

Still looming behind me, Asher quivers on his leash and mutters a curse of relief.

My gaze narrows on the powerful dragon body, sheathed in scales green as venom, that soars overhead and circles before winging to land before the royal box. My breath hisses through my lips and I bare my fangs.

That dragon is an absolute brute. In fact, he's very likely the same brute who scalded poor Max with acid, judging by that slender armored figure in the horned helmet perched high on this dragon's crested back.

But I barely spare that horned Hades in the dragon saddle a glance.

My entire world narrows and zooms into focus. Nestled before that Fae in the saddle, apparently quite comfortable in his arms, there's no mistaking my petite teal-haired darling, confidently straddling that dragon's back, with her lush curves encased in glittering green armor and violet fire spilling from her eyes.

That's no shrinking violet of a Persephone.

That's my Zara.

Bold and brash and reckless as a lioness.

The breath rushes from my lungs in a gasp of sheer relief. The fist of tension that's been clenching my chest for days unknots.

This reaction is a moment of despicable weakness on my part. One that I pray my collared captive doesn't notice.

In truth, I haven't allowed myself to linger on my carefully hidden feelings since the moment my darling girl went missing, because what would be the point. There's simply no use fretting myself to a frizzle.

Now that my worst fears—Zara imprisoned, tortured, violated, murdered—have been assuaged, I'm positively giddy with relief.

I'm still lightheaded when the green dragon glares across the sands at the Unseelie Queen's pus-colored atrocity and roars with defiance. In unison, Zara lifts her exquisite face to the darkening skies and cries out in the lightning voice. The skies light up in a sheet of purple lightning.

Merciful fuck.

Our little queen certainly knows how to make an entrance.

"Nicely done, darling," I whisper.

In the royal box, a minor sensation ensues. Messalina leaps to her feet, her pinched features lighting in a blaze of triumph. (Apparently, I wasn't the only one who was worried.) Her courtiers burst into relieved applause (the fools) and flutter about. Theo Mercury stands too, his famous megawatt smile gone dim, clearly searching the skies and the sands for his missing boy—who's still nowhere to be seen. Nearly invisible in the gloom, the runway model with the merlot hair clings to her shadowy male, who supports her with a distracted air. My senses give a ping of recognition.

Truly, there is something damnably familiar about that man.

Queen Maeve remains in her throne and skewers my girl with an icepick glare.

My, my. *Someone's* not very happy to see my Gemini queen hurl lightning.

Now the horned dragonrider hoists off his helm. A spill of moss-green hair tumbles around his pointed ears and the crossed swords sheathed against his spine. Presumably, this savage-looking creature is Ronin's ex.

Zephyr.

I'm not close enough to see much, here in the nosebleed section, so I lean my spear against the viewing box and drift closer to listen.

In the breathless silence, a trickle of voice like running water spills into my ears.

"Your Moonstruck Magnificence," the dragonrider cries, "I present to you and all here assembled my royal bride. Zara the Moon-Blessed, Queen of Dragons, Lady of Lightning." He pauses for effect. "Behold the Gemini queen."

Well. Against my will, I'm impressed.

Clearly, names matter to these Unseelie. Knowing their true names gives you control. This is precisely how I've brought my current pet to heel. This Dark Fae King has just deftly managed to avoid shouting Zara's full name from the rooftops, while also giving Zara the political stature she needs to stand toe-to-toe with her assembled enemies.

For that clever little trick, I don't (entirely) loathe him.

Perhaps I'll slay him quickly instead of slowly with my Fae-killing spear.

There's simply no denying the icicle queen Maeve in the viewing box appears displeased. Perhaps she was hoping Zara would be a no-show.

Undaunted, Messalina Aquarius steps into the media spotlight and gestures toward Zara's commanding figure in her dragon saddle like the ringmaster at the Cirque du Soleil.

"Your Moonstruck Magnificence, my bargain with you is fulfilled." Even without a microphone, Messalina knows how to project. "A queen for a queen. This royal queen-in-waiting to preserve your realm, in exchange for my own royal daughter's freedom." Her smile falters and her voice sinks nearly to a whisper. "Which was purchased at so dear a price."

"Yeah, about that." Zara swings a leg over the green dragon's back and hops down to the sands. The dragon swings his head around, with apparent affection, to nose her. She loops one arm around his neck and plants the other on her cocky hip. "I'll do the ritual and all. These people got a real mess on their hands—which is apparently your fault, Messalina, right? Because of the way you took your half-Fae kid and vamoosed? Not that I'm judging or anything."

She pauses to give Messalina the space to respond with effusive thanks for Zara's more than generous offer of assistance. If I'm not mistaken (and I'm never mistaken), my girl has just offered to fuck the Dark Fae King.

My own inner dragon hisses with menace. He too is alpha—that flying serpent I am when I shift—and he isn't much for sharing.

Disappointingly, the Aquarius queen says nothing. Although at least she's stopped her ridiculous gesturing.

"Anyway," my darling Zara resumes, "I'm okay helping Zephyr clean up your mess and fix this shit. I think it's a win-win for everyone. I'll do your ritual, so everyone chill, okay? But there's not gonna be any wedding."

Still leashed at my side and watching this spectacle unfold as intently as I am, Asher grunts in surprise.

Still, the last Aquarius queen isn't queen for nothing. Messalina gives my girl's don't-fuck-with-me attitude a level look, then pivots toward Maeve with a lofty shrug. "You certainly can't deny I've upheld my part of our arrangement. You have your queen to replace the one I took. She'll solve your race's problem."

Queen Maeve's royal ass remains in her throne—the seat of power in that viewing box—but her gauntlets clench around the armrests.

"That remains to be seen," Maeve says coldly. "You've always been rash, Messalina Aquarius, driven by fiery emotion rather than intellect. That aspect of your character appears unaltered by the passing years."

Oh, snap.

Messalina's voice acquires a brittle edge. "You're a schemer and a plotter. I'm a woman of action. That's a character trait your brother Oberon never seemed to mind."

Hearing that name invoked, as Messalina has now done so deliberately, a visible ripple runs through the assembled Fae. Not being immersed in Avalon history myself, I'd be entirely at sea—if not for the tutorial I coaxed out of Asher as we flew.

Oberon was the last Dark Fae King. When Messalina was a student herself at the Icarus Academy, Oberon stole her away to Avalon for his bride. To hear Asher tell the tale, the royal marriage was (surprisingly) a love match. But Messalina had barely given birth to their daughter and heir when Oberon died—by poison, possibly at his own sister's hand. When Messalina fled home through the portal, she stole her daughter back from Avalon.

Apparently, the theft of the heir is what triggered the curse.

Now Maeve leans forward in her throne and bites off the words. "My brother Oberon was ever as rash and selfish as you are. He chose you as his bride for pure narcissism—a mate who mirrored his own reckless folly and endless ego in full measure."

"Speaking of mates, whatever became of that pretty songbird *you* married?" Then Messalina feigns a parody of surprise so broadly even I long to slap her. "Oh, that's right. He died. By poison. Just like Oberon."

"Dear fuck. This is better than Shakespeare," I murmur.

"Kid, you don't know the half of it," Asher mutters back. "For real."

By now, Maeve is bristling like a porcupine. Her putrid dragon is stretching her neck toward the box and hissing. The green dragon twists his head around and bares his fangy teeth at the menacing queen. The Dark Fae King, alert and wary, sits straight and still in his saddle. I have the sudden sense that he's guarding Zara, who's so deceptively tiny as she stands with booted legs spread, watching this Shakespearean drama unfold.

"My mate died as he lived!" Maeve all but screams, in a pitch that nearly makes my ears bleed. "Drunk and rutting between some whore's thighs!"

"Oh dear," I say to Asher. "Did she murder her own husband too?"

"She's maybe a little homicidal." Asher rubs a big palm over the back of his neck, where the tips of those lovely feathered wings tattoo his skin. "Doesn't like being challenged. Curse or no curse, that's why we got problems here, you feel me?"

Maeve's courtiers exchange nervous glances and begin sidling away from their incensed sovereign.

But Messalina Aquarius, either quite brave or quite foolish, gives her furious hostess a dismissive look. "Look, Maeve, this is all ancient history, isn't it? Since my heir appears willing to conduct the moon ritual with yours, why not seize your chance and take what she's offering?" She gestures toward the open sky. "After all, time seems to be of the essence."

That's the director's cue for all heads in the chorus to turn in unison toward the silver glow against the coliseum's eastern rim.

That glow is the full moon rising. Within mere minutes, that moon will be within view. It's the rare night of the spring equinox under a full moon. Asher has been very clear that, in order to be effective, the moon ritual must occur during this particular moonrise.

Apparently, the threat of the rising moon galvanizes the Dark Fae King. Still astride his dragon, he gathers his reins with a decisive snap.

But Zara lifts an arm and immobilizes the entire arena, merely by snapping her fingers. Violet sparks flare at her fingertips.

"Before we seize anything," my girl drawls in the sudden silence, "I wanna know what my dear old dad's doing with your crew up there. Because the last time he and I shared airspace, he was trying to shove me off a roof."

Now all eyes turn to Mick Gemini.

"Aw, shite, Zara." The casino czar sprawls in his seat and shoves his hands in his pockets with a good-natured grin. "Sure and ye'll not be holding me to blame for that old mischief, will ye now? And me here to walk me only daughter down the aisle."

My darling girl snorts at his Irish mob boss blarney. (She warned me once that he actually talks like that. Sadly, I didn't believe her at the time.)

"Yeah, no, that's not happening." Zara folds her arms across her chest. "Not without all the rest of my guys. We've got some shite of our own to work through in this harem before anyone starts shopping for wedding clothes."

That remark gives Senator Mercury an opening to pursue his interests, which he steps into like the politician he is. His face is congenial, but his voice is cordite. "Speaking of your harem, Ms. Gemini, I spoke with your headmaster Lucius Aries at the Icarus Academy. He informed me that my son is missing. I'd surely appreciate if you'll direct me toward my boy."

That's when the sound I've been waiting for—the unmistakable throaty purr of my queen—finally echoes through our mating bond.

Neo, baby, your dad misses you. But you and the big guy stay put a little bit longer just in case, okay?

Our bond lights up with Neo's earnest voice. *Okay, babe, we'll wait. Even though Max really isn't very happy up here.*

My own relief to hear his voice is an actual thing, because Neo (and Max) have been missing as long as Zara. Once I get the three of them tucked up safe in our bed back home, I swear, I'll make them all suffer for nearly giving Lucius and Ronin and me a damn heart attack.

Why on earth did they ever leave the *domus* without us?

Still, my own instinct for stealth and caution runs deep. This is why I don't pipe up and insert myself into our mating bond, but lurk in the shadows like the viper I am.

"Neo'll be along," Zara says out loud, casual as fuck, clearly not giving two shits (or shites) about putting off Senator Mercury. "You don't need to worry. Plus I've got a few more things to say to you people myself. But before that, like Messalina said, Zephyr and I have this moon ritual to finish."

Without waiting for anyone's permission, my darling girl scrambles up the green dragon's foreleg into the saddle. The Dark Fae King wraps an arm around her waist and settles her between his sinewy thighs with a distinctly possessive air I've learned to recognize in the males who comprise her harem.

And my sweet girl lets him do it.

Well.

Clearly, Asher Apollo Aurelius, Eagle of the Air, isn't the only royal Fae in Avalon whose heart our little queen has sunk her pretty claws into.

I'm so busy absorbing this latest big reveal and watching while the green dragon soars the short hop to the bed on the platform, then while my girl and her Unseelie jump down and immediately start untying the curtains to conceal their fuck palace from the eyes of both their parents, that I don't pay any heed to the drama unfolding in the viewing box.

It's only when Messalina drops back into her chair, crosses her legs in her elegant red evening gown, and calls for someone to mix her a champagne cocktail, that my gaze flickers back to the royal mess my girl's left behind.

Clearly those paparazzi want to follow the action in the mating bed, they'd love nothing more than to shove their mics and their news cams right through the damn curtains. But that green dragon coils menacingly on the sands between them and the focus of their obsession.

So no one's getting very close.

Instead, the press start to interview the big names in the viewing box. Mercury Senior is giving interviews left and right, while Mick Gemini blathers amiably to Messalina—who isn't nearly as relaxed as she's projecting for the news crews.

That Aquarius queen of ours is up to something. Some deep scheme that revolves around Zara, the heir foisted upon her by the Senate, whom Messalina has always held at arms' length. She's up to something.

I'd bet my Louis Vuitton luggage on it.

When the curtains fall closed around the fuck palace on the platform, sealing Zara and her Unseelie inside, the statuesque model with the merlot hair steps forward in the viewing box, intent on the action behind those curtains she can no longer see.

The movement brings the woman with the merlot hair into the light. A jolt of recognition arcs through me. Because, wicked fuck, I *know* that woman.

She's none other than the Ferrari girl.

My father's former protégée at the Arcane Investigative Bureau—which is the witching world equivalent of the CIA.

I learned from Max only recently that my father is far more than the obscure (if well-paid) bureaucrat for the AIB that I always imagined. In actual truth, my father runs the entire Bureau. He's Messalina's spymaster. Which means that my father's protégée too must be more significant in the AIB hierarchy than I ever believed when she'd turn up periodically to see him, for hush-hush meetings to which I was never privy, amid the joyless luxury of our family yacht in the Seychelles or the lonely Romanov dacha on the Black Sea coast.

And if *she's* here…

I feel as though I'm falling backward into endless darkness, the light receding before me while the world dims, in a smothering silence that steals my breath.

Then, inevitably, the tall man in the narrow suit steps into the light, his hand placed far more intimately on the Ferrari girl's shoulder than any contact he ever allowed me to glimpse between them when she'd visit.

Because, of course, the man with the Ferrari girl in the viewing box is none other than he.

Nikolai Romanov.

The same man who threw me out of his home and his family and his life like yesterday's trash, the very moment he discovered his only son likes dick.

Christ.

That's my fucking father.

Chapter Thirty-Three
Zara

"I legit can't believe we're actually doing this," I admit to Zephyr, the second the last curtain falls into place around the bed, enclosing us in some semblance of privacy. "I can't believe I'm actually fucking you—like, this was never the plan?"

That's putting it mildly, but what can I say? The guy's persuasive.

"I mean…" I wave a disgruntled arm in the general direction of the viewing box. "I can't believe we're fucking in front of both our parents and a goddamn news crew from WNN."

"There is only the moon to see. She's the only witness we require to shatter the curse." Zephyr darts a worried glance at the square of open sky above our heads. "In theory."

I might be all hormones and mating heat right now, but Zephyr's all business. He's already stripping off his gauntlets and scrambling around the curtained area in a controlled frenzy. His scaly armor ripples and glitters, green as emeralds, around the supple flex of his body.

In the shadowy starlight inside our space, I watch him compulsively adjust the precise placement of the bespelled chunks of purple crystal guarding the four corners of our bed (check), the cloudy silver mirror that looks and feels like a magical artifact propped against the headboard (check), the silver pitcher and goblet standing near the foot (check).

"In theory, huh?" I pace around the bed to work off my own jitters.

This whole ritual is fucking theory.

Because of course no one's ever broken an infertility curse of this magnitude (that we know of).

But, hell, I apparently deactivated the whole island's birth control back home and made half the female population of the Icarus Academy pregnant, just by instigating an orgy at Mallory McSnicker's birthday bash.

Orgy instigation and fertility spells. Those are apparently my Gemini queen superpowers.

If anyone can break this curse by fucking the shit out of the Dark Fae King—the guy who's been ritually celibate and denying himself for years to store up the magical power to save his doomed subjects—that person would be me.

"The ritual will succeed. It *must* succeed. But we must hurry." Hastily Zephyr splashes a torrent of something dark and rich from the pitcher into the goblet. The fruity bite of fermentation curls through the night air and hits my nostrils.

Without ceremony, he thrusts the goblet in my general direction. "Drink."

Despite being all in on the concept of this curse-breaking fuck—a concept that's had me hot and bothered and breathless since I agreed to do it, because A) I'm still having my superheat, and B) this twisted Dark Fae is hot as fuck and I want him inside me pronto—I eye that goblet with sudden suspicion.

"Uh, that's not moon tea, is it?" I ask.

Although he's staring worriedly up at the square of sky framed by our curtained bed, where unfamiliar stars emerge pale and twinkling in the night, I manage to snare his impatient gaze.

"What?" He spares me a distracted frown.

"I'm asking if this is the moon tea that makes everyone pregnant," I repeat doggedly. I get that he's distracted, but this is important. "Because I'm definitely up for a fuck. But if you want some little Unseelie in a playpen outta this whole operation, you're gonna have to stand in line. There's, like, multiple guys in my harem ahead of you, wanting to get me pregnant."

Despite both of us being in an obvious rush, the worried clench of his jaw loosens. His tight mouth curls in a subtle grin. "By the moon. Was that an admission that I am now a member of your harem?"

"Was that an admission that you'd like to be?" I counter. "I'm kinda thinking you and Ash are gonna be more like my ménage on the side. At least till we figure this whole thing out."

He crawls onto the big cushiony bed like a cheetah and eyes me under a spill of green hair.

"You need not keep us on the side." His voice deepens to a growl.

"If they are all like your Neo Mercury, these others in your harem, and if it… pleases you… I am prepared to indulge your penchant for multiple males in our bed."

Before I can wrap my head around that extremely interesting concept, he's lifting the goblet to his own lips for a long deep swallow. I watch his throat ripple under that smooth olive skin while his jade-green eye never strays from my cautious face.

"This is moon wine," he says quietly, lowering the cup. "Moon-blessed and pressed by harvest under the light of a full moon. Moon wine is meant to nourish new beginnings and dilute old magics that no longer serve, such as our curse. The moon tea ritual that will open your womb for conception is similar, but separate."

He offers the goblet to me. "Drink and no harm will come to you. You have my word upon it."

Well, that's one thing about the Fae not being able to lie.

When he speaks plainly like that, with none of his twisty evasions, I trust him.

Besides, I've already been eating his food and drinking his wine. If this really is some Hades-Persephone myth we're re-enacting, I've already made my choice.

I'm choosing him.

Especially since he gets the fact that I've also chosen others.

"Okay then. Down the hatch." I grab the goblet he's offering and take a healthy swig.

Sweet Jesus, that shit's potent. The tart sweetness of pomegranates and figs and currants rushes over my tongue and hits the back of my throat like a shot of Tennessee moonshine.

But the real reason I cough (because I'm no new recruit in the alcohol department) is because Zephyr's just unslung his crossed swords from his back, hung his blades over the headboard, and unzipped his dragonscale in a smooth pull from the throat to the navel.

Whoa.

In the midst of all this curse-breaking and political drama and parental shit, it would be easy to lose sight of the guy who's at the center of all this.

But you don't lose sight of a force of nature like the Dark Fae King. I haven't lost sight for a second of Zephyr.

Or the fact that I'm adding him to my bed, and he's adding me to his.

There's a lot we still need to talk about—really a lot. I haven't even consulted Lucius or Vasili yet about adding a fixer-upper like Zephyr (not to mention Ash, who's not exactly issue-free himself) to the harem. And I'm really afraid Ronin's gonna lose his shit if I just pop up at the *domus* without warning, bringing his ex (not to mention his ex's massive Light Fae boyfriend, who hates Ronin's guts) home with me.

But the moon.

There's no time.

Beyond the filmy draperies that enclose our bed, the Avalon night is silver with moonrise.

And here's this guy at the center of everything. Just a guy, under the dragonscale and the eyepatch and the crown and the heartbreak and the legend. A guy with a missing eye and a twisted heart and a shitty mom. A guy who's been struggling alone with the tragedy of his dying race and his lonely nights for way too long.

God. Neo was right.

When it comes to me and what I need deep down, Neo's always right.

I fall in love fast. I know what I want.

Now I'm falling in love with Zephyr.

The fact that this living legend's so beautiful and noble on the outside, yet so dark and tortured on the inside, that's the exact reason I'm falling for him. He's like me, carting around the weight of saving a whole world he never asked for, but doesn't dare drop.

Plus, you know, he's Zephyr.

Control freak. Wounded warrior. Dragonrider from another world, with terrifying powers and a hidden heartbreak that's never stopped hurting.

He needs saving too.

My gaze drifts from my guy's wide, worried, suddenly vulnerable stare over his parted lips and his tiny fangs, down the naked vee of olive skin framed by his open armor, over the plane of his hard chest and tight abs.

My heat pulses like an ember in my clit. My pussy clenches in a rush of slick. Under my skin, my dragon queen uncoils.

Yesssss, Zara, claim him, my inner dragon whispers. *He is ours.*

I gulp another long swallow of wine, which shoots straight to my head and makes me dizzy. I swallow and swallow till I've drained that cup dry. Then I set the empty cup aside.

Wow.

My whole world is dancing. A glittering dust of snowflakes drifts down from the starlit sky and makes the air sparkle. The curtains sway and ripple in an eddy of wind.

Holding my guy's gaze, I crawl on the bed and rise unsteadily to my knees. I fumble to find the zipper at my throat and ease it down in a slow pull, all the way to my belly button. I unzip till my Avenger suit barely contains my tits. (Because underneath, as usual, I'm nakey.)

It's bitter cold in Avalon. But somehow, here, our secret space is balmy.

Zephyr watches me on hands and knees, so still he barely seems to breathe, through a silky spill of hair.

"Okay, Your Radiance," I whisper. My tongue darts out to taste the tart wine that clings to my lips. "You ready for me?"

Before the words are even out of my mouth, he pounces.

I've been sorta wondering how much I'll need to ease him into this, after however many years of self-enforced celibacy. As far as I can tell, he's rigorously conditioned himself to avoid being touched in any sort of sexual way. That kind of conditioning can fuck with a person's head.

Or it can lead to a pent-up demand situation, with years of restraint and bottled-up sexual frustration exploding at a touch.

Clearly Zephyr's in that second category.

I barely have time to suck in a breath before he's on me, arm snaking around my waist, hand fisting in my hair, bending me backward as our mouths fuse together with a flash of electric heat. His hot tongue surges in to plunder and twine around mine. The taste of nutmeg and moon wine swirls through my senses, with the sweet chiffonade of cloves like a grace note at the finish.

Beyond the curtains, Xhevith trumpets a roar of sexual triumph and bates his wings so hard the curtains billow.

That's when I appreciate, in a whole new way, how closely those two—Zephyr and his dragon—are linked. Xhev is part of this.

At least, that dragon's definitely following along.

All of a sudden, my mating bond is full of jealous alpha dragon. Because Max is circling possessively over the coliseum, with Neo strapped to his back. Abruptly faced with a situation where my heat is spiking and another dragon wants a piece, Max wants down, and he wants *in*.

Hey, no, you stay put up there a little longer for me, big guy, I whisper through our bond. *This dynamic's pretty volatile. And we don't have a lotta time.*

I will not wait long, my sovereign, Max says darkly through our bond, all rumbly and warped with rut. *I will suffer no other dragon to claim what is mine!*

Cheese on toast. My dragon king's a flying landmine.

I fight to project a firm but soothing vibe. *No other dragon's gonna take your place, Max, I promise. But this is really not the time to introduce Zephyr to one of my alphas, okay?*

I kinda broadcast that message on all frequencies, because I keep getting flashes of sly slinking malice through that bond that really remind me of Vasili. Even though, in my understanding, my Goblin King's supposed to be light years away at Icarus.

But, you know, I wouldn't put it past my snake to slither through the portal and surprise me.

A distant roar blasts through the curtains. That's definitely Max, it's the roar of a frustrated dragon in full rut. In reply, Xhevith bellows his own full-throated challenge.

Shit.

I really hope my baby Neo's able to exert some influence of his own to keep our alpha dragon in line, because I've kinda got my hands full down here.

Still on my knees and upright (but barely, because I'm swaying in heat and dizzy as fuck), I wrap my body around Zephyr while we grapple to peel each other out of our dragonscale. Up close and personal, he's lithe and sinewy and fierce, all hot skin stretched over tight muscle. He's the smallest of my guys, but he's the most feral. Right now he's kissing me like he's starving for kisses. Like he's gonna crawl down my throat and devour me from the inside. He's bending me back over his arm till he's all that's holding me up, my hips pressed against the bulge of his codpiece, my hands peeling his dragonscale down his torso so I can explore the sleek plane of his chest and the tight nubs of his nipples.

He's so hypersensitive, so starved for any touch, that he gasps at the first graze of contact against those tiny peaks.

He's quivering like a teakettle before the whistle goes off.

"It's okay," I mumble between hot desperate kisses that steal my breath and make me forget there's a whole arena of people out there waiting for whatever goes down between us. Now I stroke his hair and his pointy ears till he moans in my mouth. "Zephyr, it's gonna be okay. I've got you now. You're mine. You got that? You. Are. *Mine.*"

He surfaces from my mouth with a gasp and kisses his way down my neck, all scorching lips and hungry tongue and the prick of teeth that make me shiver. My hair spills down my back and floats around our twined bodies and my fingertips glow purple with power.

I snake my hands under his dragonscale and cup a flexing double fistful of hot silky ass. He moans into my neck and shivers all over.

"By the moon," he breathes, half-smothered in my skin. "I… don't think… I can do this anymore. I can no longer be… alone."

"It's okay, sweetie." Suddenly, for no reason, my throat is thick and aching. "You don't have to be alone. Not anymore."

Panting into my neck, he wrestles my dragonscale off my shoulders and down my arms. His desperate body crushes up against my naked tits.

Face buried in my neck, he stiffens in sudden stillness. The sound of his rapid breath scrapes harsh against the silence.

We're not bonded yet, I can't read his mind till I bite him.

But I experience a lightning flash of intuition.

"God. It's your first time, isn't it?" I breathe. "I mean, your first time with a girl?"

Because who knows how far he and Ash took things, back when he lost his eye and Ash nursed him back to health? Those two males are deeply bonded.

"Not Ash," he whispers into my skin, soft as breath, so I can barely hear. "Ronin. He's the only one. I never meant to. He's mortal. But he was… impossible to resist."

The ache in his voice opens an ache in my chest. Ash might've healed him physically, and in other ways too. But the business that went down between Zephyr and Ronin damaged both my guys in ways I'm just starting to appreciate.

Well, I'm gonna fix that too.

Right now, we've just gotta get through this ritual. And Zephyr's more than capable. I know when a guy's hot for me, and this one's filmed in a fine sheen of glittering sweat, he's strung tight as a steel cable. But he's been reining himself in for a really long time.

He's just gotta get out of his head. And let go.

"No worries, Your Radiance," I sigh into his hair. "I'm gonna be easy for you to fuck."

I capture his hard hands in mine and fit them over my breasts.

His breath hitches in his lungs. Slowly his calloused palms spread to explore my curves and slide over my skin. His careful fingertips find my pierced nipples and glide over my little rings. His head lifts so he can watch what he's doing. That reverent touch of his makes my tits tingle and my nipples pucker. My heat pulses and lights me up all over like Fourth of July fireworks.

"Yeah, like that." My voice is all husky with love and lightning, but I give him the reassurance he needs right now. Gently I work his dragonscale down his hips. He's definitely going commando, and that first lick of moss-green pubic hair makes me pant a little myself.

"You are… very unlike a man," he observes softly. "You are soft and small and lovely. A man could break you in two with his bare hands. Yet you are fierce and mighty."

I bite my lip to hold back a grin.

I don't feel mighty. I'm making this shit up as I go along.

But I like how he sees me.

Anyway, me not being like a man doesn't seem to faze him. He's staring at my body like he can't tear his gaze away, at his hands dark against the creamy swell of my tits. I tug at his hips to bring him closer.

With a sudden surge of violence, he pushes me back hard on that mountain of silky cushions and crawls on top of me.

Oh hell to the yeah. Now we're getting somewhere.

He cups my tit and his mouth finds my nipple, a lightning flicker of tongue and scrape of teeth. Pleasure zings through me like a bolt of lightning. I moan and part my legs and pull him closer, my knees coming up to cradle him, though we're both half-wearing our armor.

I slide a hand under his dragonscale, down the taut plane of his abs, over the silky roughness of his pubes. My fingers graze the hot tensile length of his cock, already standing straight up for me, his tip smeared with precum.

A strangled cry rips out of him. But he likes it.

Sweet Mother of God. So do I.

Over his shoulder, framed against the sky, the massive wedge-shaped shadow of Xhevith's head looms against the stars. His flaming golden orbs gaze fiercely down at us.

He's guarding us. From all the fuckery out there.

And he's part of this, he is, even if my dragon queen and his never touch (which I'm pretty sure Max would never tolerate, even if I was willing to go there). We're both Xhev's riders now, Zephyr and me, both tangled in our matching armor, his green hair mingling with my teal locks, both of us sprawled and writhing under his dragon's fiercely possessive stare.

We belong together. All of us.

I gaze into the dragon's glowing eyes. Xhev croons with approval. My dragon queen purrs back.

I toe off my boots while I jack Zephyr's dick, long and hard and ropy in my fist. That steady friction drives him wild. My Dark Fae King is already dripping for me, rutting into my grip and writhing between my thighs while deep broken moans spill out of him. I hook my toes into his dragonscale and peel the armor and the sewn-in codpiece down his hips.

His cock springs free, swollen and flushed an urgent violet with need. I knead his hot length under my palm and stroke down his shaft all that precum he's pumping out, finding an audible rhythm that's sexy as hell. He fucks into my fist in a frenzy that's barely restrained.

I figure he needs to come inside me, this first time, for the ritual to work.

"Yes, that is how it works," he moans, guttural with pleasure. "The first time. I will pay my devotion at your Altar of Venus and fill you with my pleasure until I spill out of you."

Yowsa.

Okay then. I'm a Valyrian telepath even if he isn't. I'm clearly projecting. We're enough in synch that he's hearing me.

I tighten my fingers around his hard length and quicken my stroke. "You're gonna fuck me deep and hard with this, aren't you, Your Radiance?"

His head swings up to find my gaze, his pupil wide with need. *"Yes."*

"And then what?" I add a twist at the end of the upstroke that drags my palm over his glans. His brow furrows and his jaw clenches.

"Later," he says in a dark frenzy, "I will spill my seed again and again over your gorgeous breasts and your luscious cunt. Until you are soaked and slick and dripping with my tribute."

"God, yes." All on its own, my thighs spread and my body arches in a way that puts out the welcome mat. "Sign me up for that."

He bares his tiny fangs in a savage grin, then dives back down to tongue and suck my nipples and twist my rings between his teeth. For a guy who's never been with a girl, he's definitely getting the hang of that.

Quick study, that's what he is.

While I gasp and moan beneath him, he pushes my armor down my legs. I'm bare underneath, already slick and clenching for him, hardly able to wait for his touch.

We're both still tangled in our dragonscale when I grab his hand and push his palm hard into the pulsing heat of my pussy. Pleasure explodes through me. I grind my aching clit into the heel of his hand and arch into his touch. His finger slides through the slick heat of my cleft and crooks into my core. My pussy weeps for him.

"Oh, sweet moon," he groans. "You're wet. So gloriously wet. For me."

"That's right, Your Radiance," I pant. "This is all for you. This pussy is yours to fuck."

Maxim's primal jealousy stalks and lurks along the edges of our mating bond, laced with Neo's sweet earnest warmth. Jesus, my bookworm's all that's keeping my alpha dragon sane as he circles up there.

A sly cunning intellect slithers through the shadows with a hiss. That's gotta be Vasili.

Somehow.

But I can't focus on my alphas right now. The one who needs me is Zephyr.

While I grind into his hand and pant, chasing that first peak, he works a second finger into my tightness. My first little O surges up and breaks over me. I tighten my fist around his slick dick and ignite under him, rippling and clenching around his fingers and fucking into his hand. The creamy spice of Mogadon pheromones and mating scent floods the air.

I'm claiming him.

Looming over us, Xhev flares his nostrils and snarls with satisfaction.

"Zara." My Fae's simultaneously rutting into my grip and struggling to fit himself between my legs. His desperation is lighting a fire inside me that's going to burn me to cinders if it's not quenched.

I need to feel him inside me.

Filling me.

Claiming me.

Beyond Xhevith's horned head, the full moon is rising.

Hurry.

I fumble to fit Zephyr's slick dick at the right angle against my hungry snatch, with him already pushing into me and panting and not giving a shit about the angle. Yeah, it's awkward, this is a whole new thing for him, but we're both so desperate for this that nothing else matters. And, yeah, it's about the ritual and saving people. But it's also about us.

Me and him.

I love the whole idea of being his first. Ronin and me both, which makes me feel a little bit like Ronin's here with us too in spirit, the way I wish he could be in person. God, I love that so much—

Zephyr's thick cockhead nudges into ground zero, where I'm already spread wide for him and creaming. I arch up and he surges down and his shaft slides deep into me, aaaaall the way in, like we were always meant to.

Like we're destiny.

A hoarse cry rips out of him. I groan long and low as he fills me to the max, all those slick hot inches seating deep inside me, till his cock nudges my cervix. With all the action I get down there, you'd think there'd be plenty of room for one dick. But my greedy pussy's a snug fit.

I clench and pulse around all those inches with a gasp of triumph.

Buried balls-deep inside me, he goes still. Just absorbing the experience of our bodies locked together, his cock sunk to the hilt, balls snugged against my ass, tits pressed against his chest, my knees gripping his hips. He's trembling all over with desperate restraint, shaky breaths spilling from his parted lips, his wide eye locked on mine through the spill of his hair.

"Hi," I whisper, my own lips curling in a smile. "You're doing great. You like this?"

His cock pulses with need.

"Like it?" he growls. His sharp feral face ignites with hunger. "I'm afraid if I move, I shall spill. Too soon. Before I please you."

"Pleasing me isn't gonna take long, believe me." I gasp out a chuckle, wrap my hands around his tight yummy ass, and hump into him like the bitch in heat I am.

My legs snake around his calves (which is as far as I can go with both our feet still tangled in dragonscale). He braces his arms beside my head and fucks into me, a few slow careful strokes at first, building to short hard thrusts as he learns the rhythm. Every pump hits my sweet spot. The way I've got my hips tilted, every downstroke gives my clit friction and clenches my cunt around his delicious dick.

"Oh fuck," I whimper. "Fuck, Zephyr."

He swoops in to fuse our breathless mouths together, his wine-drenched tongue plunging deep, his breath harsh against my skin. I moan into his mouth as he pounds into me, him grunting with every determined thrust, his lean thighs pushing hard against mine to spread me wider and pin me to the mattress.

His sheathed swords thud against the headboard and the curtains sway. Which pretty much means every Fae in Avalon must know (if they didn't already) how hard I'm getting fucked in here. Fucked by the guy every Fae of any gender at this Academy (as far as I can tell from my classroom visit today) is jonesing to shag.

Looming overhead with his big fanged muzzle hanging right over our bed, Xhevith watches us fuck with lidded eyes.

My whole body's humming with electric charge. Violet shadows dance against the swaying curtains from the witchy light that's spilling from my eyes. Zephyr's pelvis pistons mine and my magic moment surges closer to the surface with every sizzling stroke of his cock against my soaked channel.

I grip the sheets in both fists and whine with need.

"Zara. My queen. My goddess." My Fae pins my fists to the sheets and punctuates every sentence with a ruthless pump. "Come for your king. Come for me. Come *now*."

Sweet Jesus, that does it.

I fling back my head and come on his fucking command. Just like I did the last time. Shit.

He plays my body like a goddamn fiddle.

I writhe against him and scream in the lightning voice and drench his cock while thunder crashes. The sky lights up with purple. I come so freaking hard I almost wet the bed.

Zephyr arches his back, cords standing out in his neck and shoulders, and unleashes a savage shout that claws up from his chest and erupts with a bellow. It's a shout that's been building in his belly for years. His cock kicks and spurts and floods my basement with jet after jet of hot jizz.

Xhevith raises his muzzle to the sky and releases a deafening roar of triumph. (And, fuck, I'm pretty sure that dragon's also coming.)

The full moon glows down on us and bathes our bed and our entwined bodies in a sea of silver light.

Zephyr fucks me through a corkscrew rollercoaster of a climax that rockets me up to the stratosphere, then brings me screaming back down, with my head spinning and my hair wild and my throat hoarse from hollering. He wrings every last spurt and spasm of climax out of both of us till I'm dishrag-limp beneath him. When he finally collapses on top of me, shaking and drenched in sweat, his release and mine flow between our sticky thighs like the Mississippi in flood.

Beyond the curtains, a distant chorus of moans and cries rises and falls on the night air.

So yeah. Everyone's fucking out there. Just like they did at Icarus the night I accidentally/on purpose triggered that orgy at Mallory's party.

Like I said. Gemini superpower.

I'm pretty sure that power has something to do with how I'll save all of us.

I don't really wanna think about my dad in the viewing box and who he might be fucking. But it could be relevant. Messalina didn't look like she was buying his Irish casino czar blarney, like, at all. Maybe he's doing it with Zephyr's mom. (And if they did, with Zephyr and me also hooking up, would that be like incest?) Anyway, those two parents of ours would totally deserve each other.

Zephyr turns his head to listen too, then heaves a deep sigh into my hair. That's a sigh of soul-deep satisfaction.

It's a sigh of letting go of all that weight he's been carrying.

The mild air is actually balmy against my sweat-slicked skin. The tinny tang of snow has softened to a floral sweetness like night-blooming jasmine. I pull in a long breath of spring and nuzzle my Fae's pointed ear, which makes him purr and snuggle into me like a contented kitten.

"So…?" I whisper, hardly daring to hope. "Mission accomplished?"

"Yes." He rubs his face affectionately against mine, and my relieved breath spills out in a sigh. "Time will tell, but our mission feels well accomplished indeed, my bride."

My happy post-coital glow dims just a little.

Because I don't wanna mislead him about what comes next.

"Um, well, not your bride yet." I think about my circling dragon and my lurking snake and my patient bookworm, plus my wolf and Ronin, left behind at Icarus. "We gotta ease you and Ash into the polycule, so my other guys can all have a say and get used to the whole idea. Especially my alphas. They're gonna need time."

Not to mention Ronin. Him I don't need to mention, because he's a complication of which Zephyr is already extremely aware.

"Zarina Selene Gemini, Queen of Dragons, Lady of Lightning." He dips his head to whisper in my ear. "Gemini queen. You mated me with magic under the light of a full moon with my dragon's blessing. By moon magic and Unseelie lore, we are most decidedly wedded."

Wedded?

The soft warm remnants of my afterglow unravel and shred into tatters. My indignant head pops up from the pillow.

"Oh hell to the no." I try to wrap my brain around that hand grenade he's just lobbed at me so I can contain the flying shrapnel. "What the actual fuck? We've literally been all through this—"

"Trouble in paradise already, darling?" The acidic bite of an alarmingly familiar voice, in a timbre that unspools like gray silk, has me shooting up to sit. "My, my."

My eyes fly wide and my pulse starts galloping. My heart lodges in my throat so hard I can't breathe past it.

I swear to fuck, Vasili's never looked more like the Goblin King than he does right now, standing just inside the curtain with his tall elegant frame draped in a sparkly ice-white coat over a gossamer shirt and gray suede breeches, with those heeled boots that make his legs go on for miles and his gilded hair teased into a shaggy punk-rock mop that adds even more inches to his height. In the cold porcelain beauty of his David Bowie face, his smoky eyes glitter with a viper's temper and his glossy lips compress with rage. He's gripping an iron-tipped spear with a casual air that doesn't mislead me for a second.

Because a heartless schemer like Vasili doesn't do casual.

The air is thick with the vetiver musk of pissed-off warlock and Mogadon aggression.

I press a discreet hand over my chest to calm my rioting heart and try to focus on the overwhelming relief I'm feeling to see him.

And not my overwhelming terror of how the most unpredictable and dangerous alpha in my whole harem's about to react at finding a strange cock roosting in his own personal henhouse (a.k.a. my magic snatch).

Or how Zephyr, the Dark Fae King, and his now thoroughly mated dragon are certain to react when they're challenged.

Chapter Thirty-Four
Maxim

I will slaughter that rival dragon.

This I swear.

I swear it.

I swear it to myself repeatedly, in a mantra like the rigid Orthodox prayers of my strict and loveless youth, while I wing in vast sweeping circles over the open-air coliseum of the Avalon Academy.

I will slaughter that rival dragon.

Somewhere beneath me, hidden in that curtained bed and concealed from my incensed sight by the looming green bulk of that enemy dragon, my mate is writhing with pleasure under the weight of a rival male.

The rival male is that dragon's rider. So I will slaughter him too.

It is her right as queen to take many mates. I did not always wish to share her. But I have made my peace with it.

Mostly.

I have even begun to love (secretly) those mates in her bed that I too am fucking.

But the psychic pulse of my queen's pleasure, rippling hot through our mating bond, coupled with the dark musky reek of a rival dragon's spilled seed?

This is too much.

It is a provocation beyond anything any self-respecting dragon should ever be expected to endure.

That rival dragon is watching them fuck. And her pleasure is making him climax.

I will slaughter that rival dragon.

Winging over the cold spires of this alien city under the full moon, I roar my frustration to the night.

My full-throated roar makes that wing of tame dragons, saddled and penned like livestock on the arena sands, cringe and whimper as I soar overhead. I am a fully mature, fire-breathing, alpha black dragon—the largest dragon I have seen in this unholy place. I am the dominant male of this population. They do well to fear me.

Except for that rival green, who is nearly as large as I am.

He was likely the dominant male before I came along. Now he uncoils his serpentine neck and bates his wings and bellows his hatred and his rage that I am here, circling just beyond reach, challenging his dominion over his dragons and his claim over my mate.

"Take it easy there, Max." A thin voice floats to my ears on the wind. A small hand rubs the scales on my back in a soothing rhythm. "He's protecting Zara just like we are. He needs her—I mean, his rider needs her—more than we do tonight. Okay?"

Neo, who is also my mate, is trying to talk me through this crisis.

If not for the imperative to protect Neo, who is strapped to my back and stubbornly refusing my every offer to set him down (even though he hates flying), I would swoop down breathing fire on that rival dragon and I would slaughter him. I would disembowel him with my claws and my teeth. I would rend his flesh to ribbons and feast on his guts and light him on fire before I kill him.

With my queen's mating scent so beguiling in my nostrils, with the hot drive of my own rut beating in my blood and pounding through my cock, in truth, I am so aroused by her superheat I can barely think. I can hardly string two words together in my jumbled thoughts. In this form, while I am in rut, I am a creature of instinct and impulse and *need need need*.

But I am bound by my oath. I must obey my sovereign.

I swore I would always obey her command. And Maxim Rasputin does not lie.

So I will not dishonor my vow.

But it is hard to remember this—my oath, my scruples, my honor—when I am my dragon, and in such a state.

Besides, there is another dragon below worth watching.

That other dragon worth watching is the enemy dragon queen. The pustulent white with the hateful glare whose stink of rot and disease and putrescence hovers, thick and sickening, on the night air. While her rider Maeve (whom I will never call queen) is rutting with half the VIPs of all genders in the viewing box, that pus-colored dragon of hers is eyeing the enemy green across the arena sands.

While the green is coiled around the curtained bed, fully consumed with enjoying his own rider (and my mate!), that putrid white is creeping slowly toward him, crouched low and slinking, across the vast sands.

It appears that this vile enemy and I share a common foe.

It is the Romans, cited in the antique books I hoard with many other treasures in my dragonlair in the Russian tundra, who were the first to say it.

The enemy of my enemy is my friend.

Chapter Thirty-Five
Zara

"Good to see you, Goblin King," I say cautiously, sitting up in bed and eyeing that spear he's holding. Because it's pretty obvi my snake of an alpha's in one of his moods. "I missed you like crazy, for real. Did you, ah, bum a ride through the portal with Neo's—?"

"What is that fusty old-fashioned phrase? Marry in haste, repent at leisure?" Vasili slices through my overture in a tone that's edged in danger. He gives a vicious wrench that parts the curtains and suddenly…

There's Ash.

Being brutally dragged inside to join us on some kind of… leash.

Zephyr's twisting in bed next to me, working his dragonscale desperately over his hips (the better to deal with Vasili and his Fae-killing spear, I guess). Now, with Ash in the room, Zephyr pulls in a sharp inhale and knifes up to sit.

"Ash!" I blurt out. "There you are. God, we were looking all over for you. We wanted you here for this. We couldn't find you."

"Howdy, princess." The massive male, leashed and collared like a dog, looms scowling at the Goblin King's side. "You can bet I woulda been here if not for this piece of work. Claims he's one of your alphas."

"Darling, I'm the dominant alpha in her harem," Vasili says coldly. But his dangerous stare never veers from me. "Our Eagle of the Air informs me that—due to your ritual fucking, little queen—you're now a married woman."

Oh geez, he's pissed. At me.

For getting kidnapped (not my fault). And then for fucking the guy who nabbed me (maybe my fault?)

"Yeah, well, that's debatable," I mutter. "Look, I know you're annoyed. You think I just vamoosed without telling you, but—"

Vasili talks right over me. "My felicitations on the joyous occasion. Remind me to send my winged companion here to open a wedding registry for the happy couple at Harrods."

Well, shit.

He's definitely in a mood.

I sneak a wary glance at Ash, who's apparently the winged companion my snake's referring to, though his vest is currently covering the feathered wings tattooed on his back. Ash's broad chest and biceps look so yummy he's lickable in a creamy ivory version of his sleeveless Conan vest and leathers. The color matches his pewter hair and darkens his silver eyes to slate.

Then there's that collar and leash my Goblin King has the poor guy wearing.

Despite my concern over how badly Vasili's clearly taking all this, I'm relieved as fuck to see both of them.

Vasili's still holding both the leash and the spear in a deceptively casual grip, but no one's under any illusion that my Goblin King isn't the most dangerous person in this joint. So Ash doesn't challenge the grip. He's actually riveted on the disheveled tangle of the bed, where Zephyr and I sprawl all sweaty, with me buck naked and the remnants of my dragonscale still twisted around my feet.

Hell, Zephyr never even took his boots off.

"Ash." Zephyr's voice is husky with sex, less guarded around his boyfriend than I've ever heard him. Even though he just explosively came inside me, and his copious spend is still dripping down my thighs, there's an intensity in his tone that gives me goosebumps.

I mean, the nice kind.

"Well, shoot. Guess you did it, Sparrowhawk, didn't ya? You and the princess? Whole kit and kaboodle out there's still fucking—including the royals and the VIPs—and it's gotta be thirty degrees warmer. You broke the curse." Ash's eyes crinkle in a smile.

But he's guarded. He's holding back. He's waiting.

Xhevith's head swings lazily into view above us, his fiery eyes half-closed in satisfaction. That dragon looks positively sex-drunk. He's practically smoking a post-fuck cigarette.

I figure that's how Vasili got past him.

Or, more likely, Vasili got past him because Xhev doesn't perceive Ash or anyone with him as a threat.

"Yes, we seem to have broken the curse, but time will tell." Zephyr's quizzical gaze shifts to Vasili and his head tilts. "May I presume this dramatic apparition to be another of your notorious mates, my bride?"

"Not your bride," I repeat. "But yeah, uh, that's Vasili." I wave a hand. "Vasili, this is Zephyr. He's had a hard day. Be nice."

"Nice." The Goblin King's eyes narrow dangerously. He twirls the end of Ash's leash in a lazy loop and gives the Dark Fae King the patented look of disdain we all refer to as the Romanov eyebrow.

Sweet Jesus. When my snake wears that look on his face, even I wanna slap him.

Although I gotta admit, I'm not totally opposed to the concept of Ash on a leash, as long as it's consensual.

Vasili's smoky lids drop over his icy stare. His gaze wanders slowly over Zephyr's bare chest and taut abs in a smoldering perusal that makes my inner dragon (fucked into a boneless stupor) lift her head in sudden interest.

"Hmmmm," Vasili says in a throaty purr. "Shall I be… nice to you, Zephyr? For the little queen's sake?"

Oh fuck yeah.

That sex-drenched purr, coming from my dominant alpha (which he is, I'll give him that, just not when Max is present) is enough to kick the engine of my superheat, still idling in the background, into high gear. Chances are my snake wants, first and foremost, to establish his dominance over Zephyr. But, hell, if he's actually willing to allow the concept of Zephyr (and Ash) joining our polycule any kind of chance…

Zephyr gives the Goblin King's tall body a slow once-over that takes in everything from the mouthwatering bulge jutting against Vasili's breeches (because I'm definitely still in heat and my alpha smells it on me) to that spear he's still gripping in casual threat and the humming tension between him and Ash.

"I'm properly addressed as Your Radiance," Zephyr says softly, in that voice like running water. "Or, if we're being formal, Your Moon-Dazzled Radiance."

Ugh.

He's not kissing the ring.

The cold light of challenge glitters in Vasili's gaze. His pretty lips curl in a small cruel smile. "Well, darling, I'm the Scorpio scion of the witching world. That's how *I'm* properly addressed. However, given this particular set of… circumstances…" His gaze flickers over me sprawled naked between them "…*do* let's not be overly formal. At the Academy, I'm known as Master Romanov. But *you* can simply call me… Master."

Oh fuck.

He's not kissing the ring either.

Zephyr's nostrils flare, which is literally the only indication in his perfectly still body that he's wrathful. With a deliberate hand, he sweeps back a tangle of green hair (because I've disheveled him pretty thoroughly, so yeah, he looks totally well-fucked).

Then Zephyr leans over me and licks a slow hot swipe up my bare shoulder.

While he's staring at Vasili and smoldering.

The.

Whole.

Time.

As clearly as if he's written it across the Avalon sky in a royal proclamation, that long slow lick from the Dark Fae King says *Mine*.

Yikes.

Vasili's casting hand gives a warning twitch.

I'm already so hot for all three of these males, Zephyr might as well have licked that fiery stripe right down my pussy. I shiver and breathe out a little moan. I shift my hips and part my knees, the shiny slick of his come and my cream coating my inner thighs. Then I swipe a slow hand up my thigh through the mess in a way that rivets every male eye in the room.

Even Xhevith lowers his fangy head to get a better look.

Be nice to him, Goblin King, I whisper through our bond. *And I'll be nice to you.*

So softly you'd need shifty senses like mine to hear, my snake's breath hisses through his teeth.

"Ash," Zephyr murmurs, low and languid, "come over here and

greet your king properly. If anyone shall restrain you on a leash, it should be my royal bride and I."

"Not your bride," I murmur in my own sex voice. "Not yet."

Vasili smiles coldly and plays the leash between his fingers. "Oh, I'm not certain I'm done with him."

"What if I said you could put that collar on me instead?" I blurt out.

Which pretty much spikes the temp inside these curtains a good twenty degrees hotter.

Vasili's sexy fangs, which are totally hidden under normal circumstances because he's super sensitive about them, slip into view and sink into his lower lip.

"Do you promise to behave?" my Goblin King breathes. "To be my good girl?"

Oh hell to the fucking yeah. I'll promise that shit.

"If you promise to share," I counter, grinning like a cat with canary feathers clinging to my whiskers. "With Ash *and* Zephyr."

"Hmmm." Vasili props his spear against the headboard (hallelujah) and swirls one finger in an airy circle, giving Ash his cue to turn.

Obediently Ash pivots to give Vasili his back. Deftly my snake unbuckles the collar, revealing the tips of those feathered wings tattooed on the nape of Ash's neck. Vasili lurks very close behind him— dangerously close—and rests one hand lightly on Ash's leather-clad waist.

Ash stands totally still, his spiky head bowed slightly, that massive body of his completely obedient to a single light touch.

Such is the power of my Goblin King.

I don't even think he's using his telekinesis.

"You and I…" Vasili whispers against the back of Ash's neck "…will talk later."

Except I don't really think it's talking that Vasili intends to do with him. And with all that tension simmering between them, Ash definitely knows it.

"Maybe," Ash says thickly. "Gotta earn it first, kid."

"Go and greet your king," Vasili breathes in his pointy ear, just grazing the tip with his glossy lips. Ash quivers under his kiss. "No touching her unless I allow it. Which will only occur, under strictly defined parameters dictated by me, if both of you behave."

Just the idea of my Goblin King deciding who gets to touch me and how squeezes my thighs together around a sudden ache of need.

Who died and put him in charge of this whole encounter is a question I'm not gonna ask. Zephyr and he are both wary as fuck, and Max has gone darkly silent in our mating bond in a way that's deeply worrying. But there's no way Zephyr's ready to deal with another of my alphas yet either. This dynamic is already too volatile.

So, with Max and his silence, I decide to let sleeping dragons lie.

"You ain't the boss of me, beautiful," Ash says to Vasili.

"We'll see." Vasili gives him a sexy smirk.

Ash shifts into gear and climbs purposefully on the bed. The mattress sinks under his monumental weight. I lick my lips and part my thighs hopefully, but that Seelie's got his marching orders. He crawls over the tangled mess of dragonscale and draperies and beelines straight to Zephyr.

Zephyr sits very still beside me, so still he's barely breathing. Ash pulls up short, on hands and knees, and eyes his guy under furrowed brow.

Because, hell, he's not in chains. And that's the only way Zephyr ever lets them touch.

"The curse is broken," Zephyr says softly. "There is no further need for restraint. That is… if you still… desire me."

Ash mutters an explosive curse and lunges at him. Zephyr dives forward to meet him halfway. Despite the difference in their sizes, they're two equal forces crashing together with cosmic need, Ash's arms wrapping around Zephyr like the big male's afraid of breaking him, Zephyr gripping Ash's head between his hands and dragging him into a desperate kiss.

As their mouths come together, Ash groans and Zephyr voices a harsh sound like a sob. Ash's big hand comes up to cradle his head in comfort.

My eyes sting and blur with a sudden rush of tears.

"Little queen," Vasili hisses in my ear.

I tear my gaze away from the heart-wrenching scene going down right next to me and meet the hot silk of my snake's deadly kiss. His cool lips find mine and his cruel grip traps my jaw. The sleek dip of his tongue parts my lips. His scent of caramel and musk floods my senses and his mouth ravages mine in a punishing kiss.

God, I've missed him. My whole body aches with missing him. I moan into his mouth and tongue his fangs and grip his sparkly coat in my fists to pull him into the bed.

But he resists.

And he's stronger than he looks.

I'm still chasing his kiss and gripping his coat and so totally focused on getting him into this bed ASAP that I completely forget what I've promised.

That's when the warm fur-lined collar buckles into place around my neck.

I lift my fingers to feel it. Solid and heavy, it's in pristine condition like all Zephyr's toys, a bit too big for my little neck, and clearly meant for Ash. I've never worn one before. I stare up at the warlock who's holding my leash—the most ruthless and downright cruel of all my warlocks—and wonder with a sudden qualm if I might've rushed into this BDSM arrangement a little too hastily.

Guess there's a reason Lucius always says I'm reckless.

Vasili spools the leash around his hand and drags me roughly to my knees.

Kneeling naked on the bed, with Zephyr's sweat still cooling on my body and his come still oozing down my thighs, my body tingles under the probe of those unsparing Goblin King eyes. My nipples peak. My face heats. My cunt throbs to be filled and reamed and ridden.

Slowly his gaze crawls over me. Vasili's sexy-pretty face is a heartless mask I can never read. And, God, I'm a mess. I'm the only woman he's ever wanted, the only one he's ever been with, he's normally into guys and only guys.

He thought he was gay till I came along.

What if he doesn't want me like this? I mean, with a strange guy's spunk dripping out of me and that guy's strange dragon looming possessively over me like a Godzilla-sized bodyguard? (I swear, between what's going down with Vasili and me, plus that kiss for the ages happening between Ash and Zephyr behind me that's like a *Princess Bride* level of romance, that dragon's hovering so close he'd be in this bed with us if he could fit.)

Anyway, the thing is, I'm all gross and messy and I probably need a shower.

And, God, this superheat. It's intense.

Like, the strongest one I've ever had.

All on their own, my hands glide down my body, over my full tits and aching nipples, down my tummy toward the messy pussy splayed between my thighs. My clit's so swollen and hard I swear I'm gonna come at the first—

"No touching, you naughty girl." Vasili tightens the leash and brings my head up with a gasp. "That succulent little cunt of yours belongs to me. I'll decide if and when you touch it."

"Cheese on toast, Goblin King." My situation here's so desperate I'm not sure whether to cry or laugh. "Have you seen that goddamn moon?"

"Yes, I know you're in heat, darling," he purrs. "I know what you need. I know you need cock. I'm going to fill your every orifice with so much alpha shifter spunk I'll be dripping out of you for days. You're going to squish when you walk, darling. Everyone who sees you will know."

Well, all righty. That'll work.

I lick my lips and look at him expectantly. Because I'm sure he'll tell me where he—

"But not yet." He chuckles like a demon at my obvious disappointment. "First I want you on your knees with your naughty schoolgirl mouth filled with your alpha's cock."

Now this I can get behind.

Besides, the quicker I prime his pump, the quicker he'll fill me like a fuck toy, right?

I scramble off the bed and drop to my knees, seizing the chance to finally pull my dragonscale all the way off (thank you God) and wad it under my knees for padding. While I unlace his breeches—which inevitably takes a while, even when I'm rushing—I sneak a few peeks toward the Ash-Zephyr reunion that's unfolding in the bed next door.

Ash already has Zephyr peeled totally out of his armor. All that smooth olive skin stretched over lean bones and taut sinew and that moss-green lick of pubes, it's all gorgeous, and Ash handles the guy's body in a way that's both worshipful and hungry. Like Zephyr's a precious treasure and Ash is afraid his big hands will break the guy. I mean, Ash hasn't been allowed to touch him unless he's chained up since, like, forever.

Now it's Zephyr who's reassuring him with every tender touch.

As I watch, Zephyr slips the last button on Ash's vest and pushes it gently from those powerful shoulders. The pewter-gray wings tattooed across the big male's back almost seem to flutter in the moonlight.

I finally manage to get Vasili's breeches unlaced. Underneath, he's wearing the prettiest scrap of hot pink lace panties you ever saw. I sigh with pleasure and glide the tips of my fingers over the hard bulge beneath, then press my lips gently to the lace in a kiss.

"I missed you," I whisper to my Goblin King's gorgeous cock.

That makes Vasili laugh, which he hardly ever does, before he remembers that he's mad at me.

"No more delays." He uses the leash to drag me closer, so I have to grip his thighs for balance. For him, that's being gentle. "Suck me off, darling. This is the faculty talking. Put that sassy schoolgirl mouth of yours to work. You have three minutes to make me come down your throat. If I'm not drained dry, I'll make you suffer."

That's Vasili's love language, I mean threatening me like that. And he actually is provisionally on the faculty at Icarus, he teaches Mogadon Magics, though I pity his poor students.

My skin tightens in a shiver. I skim his panties down his slender hips till his dick springs free, all long and slim and pretty, flushed pink with need and so hard for me his shaft is twitching. His balls are a deeper violet, swollen with seed and drawn tight to his body. I cup his hot sac in one hand and grip his base in the other and lick a slow circle around his tip with my tongue. A tiny spurt of salty release hits my palate and makes me smile.

He strokes my hair from my face and clenches it in his fist so he can watch. "Two and a half minutes."

"Are you literally *timing* me, you asshole?" I grumble, pausing long enough to glare up at him. "Do you even have a watch?"

"Two minutes twenty-five seconds," he says like a goddamn sociopath. "And no more talking."

Beyond his expectant body, Ash is kneeling on the bed and watching me mouth Vasili's dick with eyes like molten lead. Zephyr's working Ash out of his leather pants and kissing his way down the guy's six-pack, lingering over every kiss, in a way I'd really like to watch.

But, apparently, I'm being *timed*.

I roll my eyes at Ash in a bid for sympathy and his eyes crinkle in a sexy grin. Then I dive into a sloppy blow job for the Goblin King, because finesse takes time I evidently don't have.

I dunno if you've ever tried giving head on the clock. But elegant… it's not.

The wet rhythmic suck of my mouth gliding up and down Vasili's dick is interspersed with messy slurping sounds as I try to deal with my spit and his precum. Despite my best efforts, moisture's seeping out of my mouth and rolling down my chin. I use the flat of my tongue against his underside and the sensitive spot right under his glans while I play with his balls and try to slip a finger up his ass—but he jerks my leash hard to put a stop to that.

Because this fucker's holding out on me, like he wants me to fail so he can inflict one of his sadistic punishments for things he's all pissed about that aren't even my fault.

But I'm determined, damn it. And I'm talented.

Ronin and I take turns giving our alphas head back home, because he loves dick as much as I do. It almost feels like Ronin's here with me now, wrapped around the back of me, cupping my tits and finger-fucking my cunt and mouthing my neck and whispering his wicked suggestions in my ear.

Sweet Jesus. Ronin. He's a little bit psycho. When he's in the mood, he can be an actual bully.

But he's my bully. I miss him.

I deep-throat Vasili like Ronin loves to do, fighting my gag reflex when my Goblin King's trouser snake hits the back of my throat, swallowing him down so the ripple of my throat muscles clenches his cock, then backing off with plenty of tongue till he's almost out of my mouth before I take him in deeper. My head's bobbing up and down his dick like a cheerleader with the captain of the football team (an analogy that would make Vasili shudder).

That magic mirror from the ritual is propped up at an angle, and the round glass is mostly cloudy and swirly and not like a typical mirror at all. But I do get a few glimpses of the two of us that are pretty pornographic (not super flattering, but weirdly hot). My snake's slick dick plunging between my lips, my cheeks hollowed to give him plenty of suction, my face brick-red, gag-induced tears streaking my cheeks, tendrils of my teal hair spilling from Vasili's ruthless fist.

In fact, he's getting even more ruthless.

Like I said, my snake's been holding back, but me deep-throating him like a porn star is finally breaking him down. First he starts fucking into my mouth, short hard thrusts coupled with soft gasps and grunts that mean his control is slipping, but he's still holding on.

Pretty quick, he grips my hair in both fists and starts fucking my mouth like you read about, totally controlling the pace and the depth, his breath getting harsh and raw moans ripping out of him. He hates losing control and he's punishing me for that, but God, he's into me. He's into what I'm doing to him.

I sneak another peek at the mirror so I can check us out myself—and catch the flash of a familiar tawny face with golden eyes, framed in a spill of raven hair. Sweet fuck, is that…

Ronin?

I'm so startled I totally lose my tempo. Vasili snarls and tightens his grip till my scalp burns.

"Look at me," he snaps.

My gaze shoots up to find his vicious eyes pinned on me, brow furrowed, lips parted, fangs fully exposed and hissing like the hooded cobra he is. I moan around his dick and grip his pistoning hips to stay upright and just hold on for the ride.

"Never. Leave. Me. Again."

He punctuates his every word with a vicious snap of his pelvis that drives his dick farther down my throat. I guess this is gonna be a theme with every one of my warlocks after me getting kidnapped. But, on top of all that, Vasili has major abandonment issues from his dickhead dad.

Which means Vasili's taking this the worst.

I can't even nod around the violent pounding he's giving me, but I hold his gaze and whisper through our bond, *I won't leave you, bad boy. I'll never leave you. Not ever. I love you.*

His face convulses and his eyes squeeze shut. His whole body arches with the force of his climax. His cock kicks in my mouth. He spurts down my throat. A long tortured groan rips out of him like he's in agony.

Out of all my guys, he's the one.

The one who always comes when any of us says we love him.

I swallow him down and keep the suction going through spurt after spurt of release. When his cock finally spends and he sorta sways into me with a last soft moan, I back away to lick his jizz from my lips, then lean my forehead against his thigh.

His fist loosens and he strokes my hair.

"Good girl," he whispers. "Such a very good girl. Tell me. What do good girls receive?"

I'm afraid to answer when he's the one asking. But I lift my head and climb to my feet (because surely I've earned that much) and suggest, "Presents?"

He flashes a grin of sheer devilry. "Cunnilingus."

That word shoots straight to my head like a hit of high-octane booze on an empty stomach. Partly because Vasili, for whom the pussy was *terra incognita* till I came along, is still new to going down in my Dixie. And he's really self-conscious about his technique, though he has absolutely no reason to be, so he only ever does it when we're alone—

Swift as a snake, he bends and twists. Even I, who am combat-trained but kinda distracted, don't see the move coming till I'm sailing backward through the air. I shriek in exhilaration and land on my back on the mattress so hard the whole bed bounces.

I catch a wild glimpse of Ash straddling Zephyr, who's flat on his back with both of them buck naked, wide-eyed faces turned toward me. Still looming over all of us, Xhevith snorts in surprise.

Then Vasili seizes my ankles in his ruthless hands and drags me toward him till he's rearing between my knees like the hooded cobra he is.

"Or perhaps I mean yummilingus?" my snake says with a wicked gleam. "Lip service for your divine pussy?"

I grin up at him, because making him spill down my throat has definitely improved his temper. Though I can still hardly believe he actually intends to do this act he's so self-conscious about performing in front of an audience.

Not to mention, my hooch is still dripping with Zephyr's cum.

"You in the mood to play in my sandbox, bad boy?" I breathe, hardly daring to hope.

One after the other, my snake drapes my legs over his shoulders. "Darling, I'm going to worship at your altar until you speak in tongues."

I barely have time to suck in my breath before he spreads my thighs, pins my pelvis to the mattress like a butterfly in my high school biology class, and swoops in.

I'm expecting, I dunno, kind of a gradual approach, which is how he normally eases into going down on me.

But with me in superheat and already writhing beneath him, he dives straight in to drag his tongue down my soaked and messy cunt. Straight from my throbbing clit to my dripping hole. When his tongue dips inside me, my pussy flutters and tightens around his tongue.

"Wicked hell, Goblin King," I moan.

Between my thighs, his head lifts. His tongue sweeps over his glistening lips and his smoky stare darts straight from me to Zephyr.

"Well, darling, *you're* tasty," my Goblin King purrs at him.

My neglected clit demands attention, but I tilt my head back to see how Zephyr's taking this. My Dark Fae King looks… riveted. His face blazes with a flash of possessive male heat that makes my needy pussy even hotter.

Of course, part of the reason has to be Ash straddling my Dark Fae's hips, his big hand stroking Zephyr's erect cock with a purposeful rhythm, while Zephyr pants and moans beneath him. Ohmygod, I think Ash is getting ready to climb on top of that Dark Fae cock and ride him till they both see stars—

"Eyes on me, little queen," my snake murmurs, venomous with warning. "That is, if you want your reward."

"Shit, yeah, I want it." I flop back down with a breathless laugh. "But, God, the three of you…"

He spreads my pussy wide between his thumbs and I lose track of whatever I was planning to say. I mean, the words just float out of my head like smoke. The Goblin King starts going down on me like it's an Olympic sport (not like curling or something, more like biathlon, a sport that requires both stamina and precision). And he's in it to win it. He just parks all that performance anxiety on the back bench and sets out to fucking ruin me.

Let me put it this way.

It's not the tongue fucking I deserve, but it's the tongue fucking I need.

I come on his long talented tongue, thrusting deep inside my greedy pussy, then lapping my juices and Zephyr's residual cum with the flat of his tongue, a good three times before Vasili starts tonguing my clit for real.

Of course, like the sadist he is, he won't let me reach that final peak. Even when I break down and beg.

Which is something he usually likes.

In fact, he's torquing me so tight that I keep trying to slip a few fingers down there myself and lend him a hand (so to speak). But every time I try, he hisses a warning and pins my hands to the mattress.

He's sucking on my clit like a lollypop and I'm getting hoarse from yelling when Ash finally finishes lubing Zephyr's length (like a scout, that Seelie Prince came prepared). Then Ash sinks down on Zephyr's cock, one slow inch after the next of Unseelie boner vanishing in Ash's ass, which lets me savor the look of wide-eyed wonder on Zephyr's face while he feels his lover's body engulf him and accept him for the first time. I get to thrill over the way Ash stares into Zephyr's gaze the whole time, with the Seelie Prince's weathered brow furrowed and his silver eyes blazing and his whole heart written all over his craggy face.

They're in love with each other. It's *so* obvious. And they've been waiting years to share this moment and probably fearing this special time might never happen for them.

Suddenly the sublime suction of Vasili's mouth disappears from my clit.

"Darling, you're terribly distracted." The Goblin King's voice goes evil with intent.

My alarmed head pops up in protest. "No, God, Vasili, you feel amazing, I mean, you're totally a cunning linguist—"

Of course, I already know my hasty reassurance is too little, too late.

"Hmmm. It seems I'll have to resort to far more extreme measures if I intend to hold your interest." Before I can even tense in protest, that pit viper I'm mated to dives in and sinks his fangs into my inner thigh, just below my pussy, in a fucking mating bite.

Another one.

Goddamn it.

I've already been bitten by him and Lucius and Max, all three of my alphas. Lucius' last bite just barely finished healing.

And every bite makes my superheats more intense.

I howl with indignation and pain, because that shit hurts, and you're supposed to ask first.

But fuck if that sharp spike of pain and the hot trickle of blood, coupled with the delicate swipe of his diabolical tongue over the wound and the hit of his biochemically enhanced shifty saliva, doesn't push me over the peak of my superheat.

I come so hard for Vasili Romanov, while he's simultaneously tonguing my bite and finger-fucking my pussy, that I bellow his name in the lightning voice.

Which, of course, summons lightning.

Although, thankfully, that ultraviolet flash of voltage doesn't strike the bed. At least I've learned that much control over my power from Lucius' lessons in the Icarus Academy belfry.

But that flare of lightning illuminates the shadowy bed and my two fucking Fae bright as day. Zephyr's really reaming him, just gripping Ash's hips and pounding up into him, his tiny fangs bared in a snarl that rips out of him with every upward thrust.

And Ash.

Wow.

He's got… wings.

I mean, real ones.

They're a shimmery pewter gray, all feathery and massive like an angel's, sprouting from where the tattoo used to spread across his mighty shoulders. Those wings fan wide behind him, protecting him and his lover beneath him, beating gently with every thrust.

I take all that in with a glance, because Vasili's got my attention now, just the way he intended. My Goblin King gives my new bite just enough tongue play to stop the bleeding before he skims his breeches down his hips and sheathes his long pretty dick in my soaked and pulsing snatch.

My body floats off the mattress beneath him, that weird new power I'm manifesting is trying to rise. But Vasili, who looks a little startled but not shocked (because after all, he too is a Mogadon who levitates), just pins my floaty body to the bed and gives me the merciless railing I know he's been burning to deliver since the morning he woke to find me missing.

Down is up. Up is down. I'm fucking my snake's coiling body in a frenzy of blind need, he's vicious as a goddamn adder, but somehow I'm fucking all of them.

Ash, my Seelie Prince, my Eagle of the Air, so patient and strong and true, who's reaping the spoils of his long sexual bondage at last, losing every molecule of his mind in explosive gouts and ribbons of semen, drenching Zephyr's abs and chest with a soul-deep passion too long denied.

Zephyr the Dark Fae King, who's endured, lonely and alone, for endless years. Zephyr who still manages to wait for his lover's pleasure before he casts aside all that iron restraint. Zephyr who finally lets go, buried deep in Ash's body, with a hoarse shout that's echoed by a jubilant bellow from one very excited dragon (because Xhevith is clearly having the night of his life out there).

Ronin, my growly bully, my wicked telepath, the first mate I ever fucked, the one who started all this with me months ago, grudging and scheming at a penthouse party for a Hong Kong triad boss in Singapore. Ronin who feels so oddly present with us tonight, whose face I'm pretty sure I saw in that magic mirror's cloudy surface which is catching all this X-rated action.

Neo, my fated mate, whose sweet warm essence wraps around me through our mating bond with the clean wholesome scent of soap, while he eases our restless alpha dragon shifter by finally telling him we're landing now, it's okay, Zara says everyone's ready to meet another of her alphas.

Max, my broody dragon king, whose dark presence I sense winging purposefully toward us through the night, whose frustrated vigil I intend to reward with sooooo much love and praise and attention he'll never want to get out of this bed with me again.

Lucius, who's always held close in my heart. My anchor, my teacher, my guiding star. The quiet sun around whose steady heat all our turbulent planets and erratic comets revolve. They all think I'm the center, but they're wrong. Lucius is the force that brings order to our chaos. He's the reason we're more than a polycule. He's the reason we're a family.

And Vasili, my terrible snake, this most difficult and gifted and complicated of all my alphas, the one who never planned to love a woman but fell for me anyway, who's finally slaked his viperish rage over my disappearance and wreaked his horrible revenge on my sex-ruined body.

Vasili shatters in a million pieces and comes buried deep inside me, wrecked and shuddering and totally lost, when I whisper in his pretty ear that I love him.

I'm still trying to come down from that sexual high we're all riding, my senses spinning and my consciousness floating somewhere like six feet above the bed, when the skies split around the berserker roar of an outraged dragon.

Attacking.

Chapter Thirty-Six
Xherith

I am lost in the peak of my beloved Zephyr's passion for the winged one, that cherished mate he has finally claimed, when the dragon queen Yersinia attacks.

The Scourge of Pestilence, as she is known among dragons, swoops down on me from behind, where I am blind and vulnerable. Her talons rake across my body as she wings past. My crest and scales protect my back, but my wings are very fragile. Knowing this—for the Scourge is a canny and seasoned killer, the victor of many battles—her slashing attack targets me where I am weakest.

Searing pain slices my wings with ribbons of burning fire. I bellow in shock and fury.

As she hammers past, Yersinia screams with hatred.

Still bellowing, I snake my head up to track this new threat. My deadly acid simmers and bubbles in my lungs.

I barely recall in time that I must not spray blinding acid over my beloved rider and his lovers, who shelter beneath my bulk in their bridal bed.

No.

I must protect my beloved and the winged one and the young queen in her heat, so they may love and breed and spawn many dragonets.

Above the coliseum, where a tangle of mating dragons—locked in their own frenzy—humps and writhes on the sands, the putrid Scourge of Pestilence I have always despised banks and wheels for another attack.

Clearly, I can expect no aid from my fellow dragons or their riders. This entire coliseum (if not this entire island) is lost in mating rut.

I must take to the skies and destroy my enemy.

I rise on my back legs and bate my wings. But blinding pain tears through my slashed limbs. Hissing with distress, I twist to eye the damage. Both wings are badly torn, and one hangs askew from my wing-joint. Green ichor dapples my tattered wings and drips in gobbets to the sands.

In such a state, I cannot fly.

And a flightless dragon? He is vulnerable.

Already the Scourge is sweeping toward me, low and lethal, for another pass.

I lunge to plant the bulk of my damaged body between this threat and the bed that holds my loved ones. I rise high on my haunches, spreading my injured wings and roaring with rage. I do not understand why Yersinia is attacking, but that dragon who belongs to the elder queen is barely sane. This is a dragon who needs no logical reason to murder.

She kills for punishment.

She kills for spite.

She even kills for pleasure.

I must protect my beloved rider and our mates.

With me roaring and rearing before her, at least this Scourge cannot spray my beloved and our young queen with her pestilential breath. Already I hear shouts of alarm and command rising from the curtained bed. My stand will give Zephyr and the winged one the time they require to arm themselves and protect our young queen.

Even if this sacrifice exposes my vulnerable underbelly to Yersinia's rage.

The Scourge of Pestilence hammers toward me with teeth bared and forelegs extended for a vicious disemboweling strike. Yes, I am in danger, but she too will pay a price. As the distance between us closes, I rumble up a spray of scalding acid in the back of my throat and brace to endure her attack.

My enemy is all but upon me when a mighty black dragon hurtles down from the skies, golden eyes flaming, death written in every deadly line. A tiny white-faced rider clings to his back, magenta curls streaming in the wind.

I am paralyzed by the chill of pure cold terror. That black dragon is my rival. When the young queen returned to us today, she reeked with the musk of his passion.

Now my two enemies have joined forces to destroy me. My militant spirits spiral into despair. Against Yersinia and this rival male together, I cannot hope to survive.

Not while I am disabled and cannot fly.

Still, I will buy time for my beloved and our others to escape. Even if I buy it with my life.

I trumpet my defiance at both my enemies.

A breath before impact, the black's mighty jaws yawn in a deafening roar. Crimson fire spews from his throat and boils across Yersinia's unprotected back and wings.

Astonishment rivets me where I stand. Bugling with surprise, I watch the massive black dragon thunder past. Without turning that horrible flame on me.

He has spared me.

Burning and smoking, Yersinia screams and flails and tumbles through the sky.

In the eyeblink of time I have to react, I know I can now evade her. But then her burning body will crash into the bed, from which my beloved rider is only now emerging.

As Yersinia hurtles toward me, I spray her screaming face with a lungful of blinding acid, while she howls and twists to evade. Then I hurtle my flightless body into the air to deflect her deadly approach.

Our bodies crash together with a cataclysmic force that shatters teeth and breaks bones.

My world flashes white with agony.

Yet with the scrap of thought that remains as we tumble through the air, I see the illuminated island of the bed flash past. I snarl in satisfaction. I have deflected the mighty Scourge from her deadly trajectory.

We crash to the ground in a tangle of snapped bones and torn wings and flaming cinders and blind anguish.

The shock of impact flings our bodies apart.

I lie, bent and burnt and broken, on the arena sands. Inside me, something vital has shattered and torn. Blood bubbles with every labored breath. I am all but senseless. I can do no more.

Yersinia too is burnt and broken. Yet she is fueled by madness.

Her own madness. And the pure screaming madness of the elder queen, her rider, who is now stumbling toward us across the sands, with her glittering dragonscale armor gaping open and her ice-blue hair streaming loose.

The elder queen is screaming at a pitch that makes blood burst in my eardrums and trickle from my battered nostrils.

The elder queen, under normal circumstances, is coldly sane. But her dragon is dying, and she shares the beast's anguish. Too, she shares Yersinia's thirst for vengeance.

I writhe on the sands and whimper in helpless torment.

Blackened and smoking, half-blinded by my acid, Yersinia struggles to her feet, her evil white gaze narrowed on the tiny figure of the young queen, racing toward me across the sands with purple light spilling from her eyes and lightning crackling from her fingers.

"Xhevith!" That is my name. My young queen is screaming it in a voice choked with tears. *"Xhevith!"*

I am finished. I am spent. I have spent my life to save her.

She must not spend hers to save me.

Yersinia parts her terrible, plague-breathing jaws. I wail in desperate warning.

But it is the black dragon, the rival male, who swoops from the skies with a rumbling cough of crimson fire. That deadly inferno pours gout after gout of vengeance over Yersinia's snarling, coiling menace.

Until that terrible Scourge who has terrorized so many ignites in scarlet sheets of flame.

My world is turning dim and dark, my rib-punctured lungs are filling with blood, my end is coming. But, beyond any doubt, Yersinia is burning. Without her dragon, the elder queen will not survive. That rider's fate, I must entrust to my beloved Zephyr.

I have spent my life for a worthy cause.

I am content now to die.

Yet I fear, before I do, the soul-splitting screams of the elder queen will cleave my skull in twain. Hers is a scream that drives men and beasts mad. And her dragon's agony, in her death throes, is driving the elder queen beyond all restraint.

My eyelids are heavy, yet I prise them open one last time. I find the young teal-haired queen now kneeling at my side, tears streaking her tortured face, blood trickling from her ears.

Yet she is not helpless, not she.

My young queen hums to summon the lightning.

With a sweep of her arm, she hurls it to end Yersinia's suffering. At her command, a jagged bolt of ultraviolet zags from the heavens to deal the stroke of mercy.

When the deafening crash of thunder falls silent, so too does the white dragon.

Yersinia, the Scourge of Pestilence, lies blackened and dead.

The elder queen stands beside her dragon—unharmed, for magical lightning cannot kill the Fae—with head flung back and arms plunged skyward. Now the elder queen's body arches in a scream that makes the stone walls of the coliseum crack and crumble. In her anguish, she will bring this entire arena down in rubble on our heads.

She will bring death to all our people.

Here where we are gathered for the ritual.

Through the gathering darkness of my failing sight, a tall male draped in a pale glittering coat streaks across the sky toward the maddened queen. Dark blood streams from his ears to darken his mane of gilded hair. In his graceful hand, he grips a spear tipped with cold iron.

In a sudden vicious thrust, he drives the spear through her. The bloody tip splits her sternum and emerges through her back.

Blessedly, mercifully, that ear-shredding scream chokes into silence.

The elder queen sways and topples.

By all that is good, she is dead.

A labored sigh slips from my battered body. That sigh is my dying breath.

But I am content.

Now my beloved Zephyr is standing over me, sword in hand, a ribbon of blood trickling from one nostril, his face stark and stricken. His grief and horror for my fate pulse through our bond. My eyes are closing. But I am grateful, so grateful, for the familiar warmth of my rider's hand, so gentle on my cooling muzzle.

"Ash!" Parched and blasted with grief, the voice of my beloved rider drifts to my dying ears. "By the moon. For all that is blessed—and— merciful. *Heal. Him.*"

Chapter Thirty-Seven
Zara

That dragon is snoring again. But I'm sure as shit not complaining.

It's good to hear him, for real.

Good to hear Xhevith breathe without effort. Especially good after that first awful night when we were all terrified he wouldn't breathe again, like, ever.

I'm propped up against the sun-warmed curve of Xhevith's massive tail. We're all sprawled on the black sand below the goblin city, with the scent of salt and seaweed thick in our noses, a summery breeze teasing our hair, and the Avalon sea crashing and foaming with Hawaiian surfer intensity against this little crescent cove. Neo's curled up next to me with his glasses sliding down his nose, looking sexy but cute in a set of Ash's sleeveless leathers. He's cramming furiously for his Honors Alchemy midterm.

Because he has to fly home for midterms.

Tomorrow.

We all do.

Maxim's sprawled on my other side, wearing Ronin's leather pants (I *really* like my guys in leather) and a billowy white shirt he's borrowed from Zephyr. Max is supposed to be studying for his Genetics of Witchcraft midterm, that's a really hard subject for him. But he's an indifferent student (to Lucius' despair), so his textbook lies face down and abandoned across his long legs. Arm bent comfortably behind his head, hand planted squarely on my knee in his territorial alpha way, he's another dragon who's sound asleep—and also another dragon who's snoring.

Me?

I've got a notebook propped against my own bent knees, because I'm supposed to be writing a History of Witchcraft essay on the Dark Fae exodus to Avalon. It's overdue, but I want to make it a good one, to make Lucius happy. He's been *so* patient about the three of us sticking around here a little longer, while Zephyr settles into ruling and cleaning up the mess his mom left behind, and Xhevith recovers after that whopping dose of healing spells and moon potions and overall moon magic Ash whipped together that barely saved that dragon's life.

Anyway.

The point is, Xhev's still healing. More than any of my guys, right now Zephyr needs me. And the three of us—Neo, Max, and me—doing our coursework by correspondence? That's the only way Lucius could convince the Dean to excuse our absence.

Now even that much patience on the Dean's part seems to be all used up.

Which is really okay, as I keep reassuring everyone, especially myself.

Zephyr's doing better because Xhev's doing better. So my warlocks and me, we wanna go home.

Home to Icarus and Lucius and Ronin.

I miss those guys like crazy. Especially Ronin, who's kinda gone dark since I hooked up with Zephyr.

It's just… I keep hoping against hope for some out-of-the-box solution that'll keep Zephyr and Ash with us too.

A shadow falls between me and the sun. I shade my eyes with my hand and watch a tall slim figure float lightly to the sands. I breathe out a sigh of appreciation.

Along with real relief.

Vasili's wearing his Academy uniform (the royal blue, so it must be Tuesday) with his narrow blazer and trousers all spiffed up with French cuffs and cobalt combat boots, his tie in a stylish twist. Against the sun's glare, he's added a pair of fashionable rock-star spectacles with rose-colored lenses. Framed by those glasses and his tousled pale hair, blue mascara makes his eyes pop like a runway model's.

The effortless way he throws it all together and keeps it together, even after he's been levitating, is part of what I appreciate.

And the reason I'm (secretly) so relieved? That's because he's been leaving Avalon more often, and staying away longer, since Xhev turned the corner health-wise. Even though Xhev isn't flying yet, it's been weeks, and the immediate crisis has definitely passed. This whole time, my normally temperamental and erratic alpha's been the responsible conduit for our correspondence with Lucius and the Academy.

But every time Vasili flies off, I'm more afraid he's not coming back.

To say my dominant alpha hasn't exactly hit it off with Zephyr (and, by extension, Ash)?

Major understatement.

Not to mention the Goblin King's been really quiet since the night of the moon ritual. I've got a bad feeling something might've happened that night, maybe before I saw him—but he absolutely won't discuss it. When I asked, all his prickly barriers went shooting up. Which means I gotta respect his privacy.

Even when I don't like it.

"My, my, aren't the three of you a sight?" My snake's sharp gaze passes over our entwined and mostly non-studying bodies. "The very essence of academic rigor. Lucius will be *so* pleased to hear."

"Hi, bad boy." I hand my notebook and pen to Neo so I can scramble up and welcome Vasili properly. I need him to know he's loved. "Long time, Goblin King."

But I've scarcely gotten my bare feet under me before the vise of Vasili's telekinesis closes around me and drags me toward him. My feet leave furrows in the warm sand.

"Hey, don't be such a Neanderthal," I complain (though I'm also grinning) because you can't let him get away with shit like this.

Plus I'm just so happy to see him. It's been, like, three days since he flew off.

"Don't *you* be such a dawdler." He drags me right up against his tall elegant body (totally without using his hands) and holds me there while he smirks down at me through his smoky lids.

My whole body starts tingling like I'm electrified.

Because that's what happens when your goddamn alpha gives you *two* mating bites (both without asking, but that's Vasili for you).

"Nice shades. I like." I grin up at him, pluck the specs off his pretty face, and perch his trendy accessory on my own nose.

His lips part with appreciation to give me a glimpse of his snaky fangs. I'm already shivering even before he dips down into a lingering lick of a kiss that tastes like tart cherry lip gloss and goblin and totally makes me moan.

"Hmmm." Humming with approval, he takes his sweet time surfacing from that kiss. Which means I'm left all warm and achy and wanting a whole lot more. "I do believe you're reacquiring your delicious Malibu suntan. And, surely, this island isn't getting warmer?"

I'm about to agree that it is, the snow's all melted, even the nights here are balmy and drenched with tropical sweetness (which really seems to encourage all the fucking these Fae are doing since the ritual). And, yep, we're already hearing some are pregnant. When they get knocked up, apparently the Fae know right away.

Maxim wraps himself around both of us with a dragonish rumble.

"Sweetheart." Max loops a possessive arm around Vasili's narrow shoulders and rubs his tawny stubbled jaw into V's neck to scent him. "You are a vision."

I hold my breath, because that's a pretty alpha way for Max to greet our prickly snake.

But Vasili only preens at the compliment and condescends to let Max pull him into a possessive kiss that makes my inner dragon purr with interest.

I can't figure these two out, with all their alphahole jockeying. That chemistry simmering between them is, like, dragon fire levels of hot.

Alpha or no alpha, those two are lusting.

"Darling, you're all sandy. Whatever *have* you been doing? Rolling in it?" Vasili pouts at him and extricates himself deftly from that uber-possessive kiss he's just totally tolerated. He brushes sand off his blazer with a little moue of annoyance.

Max rakes back his long blond hair against the ocean breeze and eyes Vasili with a smolder like he's totally ready to drop trou and shove the guy face down over the curve of Xhevith's tail. A tail which (as I can personally attest) happens to be the perfect height to support a vigorous reaming by one of my alphas.

Neo joins our group grope and snuggles up happily between Max and me, so Vasili can engulf him in a growly alpha kiss that makes our bookworm shiver and blush. We all tuck around Neo so it's the four of us together, totally included, with no one left out.

Except for Zephyr, who's at the Avalon Academy, trying to figure out how to pivot the Unseelie educational system to something that's actually useful.

And Ash, who teaches at the school himself, and who hasn't left Zephyr's side since Xhev got hurt.

Watching those two Fae, finally together after all these years apart, makes my throat swell and my chest ache. The fact that I'm falling hard and fast for both of them—but now I'm gonna have to leave them?

That looming separation is killing me.

Heartbreak city, dead ahead.

There's a definite reason I'm dwelling on all this now. It has to do with what I'm picking up from my snake through our mating bond.

Shit.

"We have to go back," I whisper, hugging Neo hard against my side and leaning my forehead on Vasili's chest. "Don't we?"

The dark spice of V's mating scent mingles with the briny ocean air and the leathery musk of dragon, because Xhev has uncoiled his sunbaked body to nose us drowsily with his muzzle.

"Tomorrow," Neo agrees softly. "Just in time for midterms. But it's not like we won't ever come back, Zara. The portal between Avalon and Icarus is open now."

"Actually, darlings," Vasili murmurs. "Lucius is truly hoping we'll return today."

"Today?" My head pops up from his chest. My body floods with a rush of anticipation—because I really miss my wolf and, God, I know Ronin needs me. This whole idea of adding Zephyr to the harem is gonna be a truckload of fuckery for Ronin to process, and I won't do it without him on board.

Yet the thought of leaving my two Fae behind, along with our sweet Xhevith who's still healing, makes me crazy.

To my surprise, my territorial dragon shifter is the Lone Ranger who rides to the rescue. Max wraps a protective arm around my waist. "Zara cannot just leave. Not without saying goodbye to Ash and Zephyr."

"Yeah, we can't just take off and leave them, not even with a note or something," Neo agrees firmly.

Vasili's pale gaze kindles with malice. "Oh, why? She's done it before."

That's him still not happy over getting left behind the last time.

"Yeah, but I try to learn from my mistakes, Goblin King," I say.

Vasili's tone slices like a scalpel. "Do you really?"

"Hey, guys, no fighting." Neo, always the peacemaker, pushes his glasses up his nose with a determined frown. "Anyway, why the big rush?"

Vasili reapplies his lip gloss, delicately tracing his lips with the little wand. Finally, he snaps shut his silver compact and eyes me with a discontented pout.

"Well, little queen, you're *really* not going to like this." My snake sighs. "Of course Lucius, our incurable optimist when it comes to that horrid Aquarius monarchy, claims it's a positive development. Admittedly, I don't particularly like it myself."

"Like *what*?" I push away from all of them to stand on my own, arms folded and feet spread in a power pose. "What about the monarchy? C'mon, Goblin King. You're making us all nuts. Spill."

He assesses my belligerent stance and deploys the Romanov eyebrow. "Well, of course the problem is Messalina. Again. It seems our reigning monarch is planning *quite* the public celebration for your twenty-first birthday, little Gemini. And she's inviting the *entire* witching world. Lucius thinks she might actually be planning a coronation."

"A coronation?" I stare at him blankly. "You don't mean, like, mine?"

"No, I mean Racetrack's." He rolls his pretty eyes and snatches the glasses off my nose in a fit of pique. He parks them on his own perfect nose and scowls at me. "Darling, pull your carnally obsessed mind out of that green-haired Faerie's skintight trousers for five minutes, *do,* and try to keep up."

Damn. I liked those specs.

Even if I also really like them on him.

I tap my sandy toes against the sand. "Well, stop dripping out the deets like an asshole and just gimme the whole story."

"I have." He offers an airy shrug that makes me want to shake the truth out of him. "The rest is window dressing. Messalina's sailing the Aquarius yacht, in all its aristocratic glory, to Icarus Island. That's where she's summoning you, along with every other scion in the witching world. We're all invited to celebrate your birthday with a splash. Ronin,

Lucius, Racetrack, and I have already received our invites, and Dez is shopping for a party frock. Max's envelope and Neo's and yours are waiting."

(Because, yeah, I have pretty much surrounded myself with half the scions—the heirs to the twelve great witching clans. If you're a witch or a warlock, Icarus is your only higher educational option.)

But I'm delaying, because I don't like the ping I'm getting from my erratic Valyrian foresight.

"Well, it's about time Messalina gets to know you," Neo pipes up. "I mean, now that you saved Avalon for her and cleaned up her mess and everything. Especially since she took off with her whole entourage right after Xhev got hurt and never even thanked you."

"Yeah, that was weird as fuck," I agree. "Not that I'm complaining."

Honestly, we were all really distracted trying to save Xhevith and dealing with the fallout from Vasili killing Maeve (a crime punishable by death that required an immediate royal pardon by a super-distracted Zephyr).

I never even noticed till the next day that Messalina and all her crew—including my obnoxious ass-kissing dad—vamoosed in that totally rude and disrespectful way.

Vasili thinks she's up to something.

And I have to wonder if he's right.

Sensing my thoughts, Neo cuddles right up against my side. "Babe, it's okay. You don't have to go to her party if you don't want to."

Vasili eyes me sharply over his glasses. "I *am* rather hoping you'll at least consent to leave the enchanted isle and come home today, darling. Truly. Ronin claims he's fine with you fucking, if not outright marrying, that little green-haired tyrant who broke his heart. But I have my suspicions."

"Not married," I mutter, just like I say every day. "I never said 'I do.' And Zephyr's not a tyrant."

"Tell that to the tyrant," my snake counters.

I bite my lip and wrap my arms around my tummy, while Xhev noses my back for comfort. Since the start of this whole thing, I've been aching for Ronin. Clearly, right now, *he's* the mate who needs me most.

My snake's pretty much just said the exact right thing to get me packing.

(Not that I have anything to pack.)

"Yeah, I hear you. I don't give a shit about Messalina, but Ronin's a whole other story. Plus we all miss the hell out of Lucius." I straighten and eye my expectant mates. "We'll go today. Just let me find Ash and Zephyr—"

Xhevith stops nosing me to give a happy bugle. That's the sound he makes when he senses his rider.

Despite my preoccupation with my guys back at Icarus, my heart gets all floaty with the endorphin rush of seeing my two Fae.

They arrive kinda dramatically.

When I glimpse Zephyr, he's scrambling down the cliff face—and despite his sparrow-like grace, that path's wicked steep.

Xhevith shifts around like he's getting ready to fly up there, but Ash hasn't cleared him for flying yet, so I tug on that dragon's ear to remind him he's grounded.

My Dark Fae's still up pretty high when Ash sweeps into view over the cliff, his gunmetal-gray wings fully extended against the eggshell sky. His muscled frame descends in a lazy spiral. Turns out all Seelie are winged (which has to be hard to hide back home, where they live among the normals like regular joes. I mean, your neighbor could literally be one.) That's one reason the Light Fae, unlike their dark cousins, don't ride dragons.

They have their own wings.

He's a thing of grace and power and beauty, my Eagle of the Air, to watch in flight.

Especially when he swoops in dramatically to pluck Zephyr from the cliff, then wings down like the eagle in *Lord of the Rings* with the Unseelie King clutched in his talons… I mean arms… and alights on the beach, running a few steps to bleed speed and stick the landing.

Ash lowers Zephyr to the ground and folds his wings. Those wings blur out of sight (because magic) and revert to their tattooed form under Ash's sleeveless tunic. That's why he wears that kinda thing all the time.

The leather is cut narrow across his shoulders to let him spread his wings.

"Hey guys!" Drawn to those two like they're a fridge and I'm a magnet, I shoot over there and launch myself at Zephyr first, because he's been dealing with a lot, and I haven't seen either of them all day.

My Unseelie looks a little disgruntled at being swept off his feet like that in front of us, because he's a stickler for his royal dignity. His lean body is encased in a velvety green-and-gold doublet, worn with his dragonscale breeches and boots, and he still looks totally like a dragonrider. Even with his green locks held back by a narrow braid around his head, his pointed ears peeking out, and the barely-there silver circlet he prefers to his mom's spiky crown, those trappings of civility don't make him look any more civilized.

He still looks totally feral.

Especially when he gives me a savage grin that bares his tiny fangs and swoops in to ravage me with a devouring kiss.

Sweet Jesus. That's what I'm talking about.

His dragonish scent surrounds me. I wrap my arms around his neck and lick into the cloves-and-nutmeg sweetness of his enchanted kiss. My body thrums with craving.

"Take it easy with the princess, Sparrow." Ash is laughing as he slings one brawny arm around me and one around Zephyr and pulls us both into his warm hard body. "Xhev's keeping her outta trouble. How's the schoolwork comin' along? Anything I can help ya with?"

He directs that question over my head in a way that includes Neo (whom everyone likes, that's honestly my fated mate's superpower) and Max (who's earned major cred with both my Fae because of the way Max defended Xhevith).

But I'm also totally noticing that Ash doesn't acknowledge Vasili, even though V's been gone three whole days.

Even Zephyr only gives my Goblin King a regal nod.

That question about Ash offering to help with our schoolwork hangs awkwardly in the air.

I'm opening my mouth to answer when Vasili (who's enough of a predator to pick up the tension) sneers into the silence, "They don't need lessons in deportment or embroidery from the Avalon Academy. Besides, we're all leaving."

Aaaaand that would be why both my Fae are wary as fuck about my snake.

"Thanks for that, Goblin King," I mutter.

Vasili's been horrible, just his most horrid bully self, toward Zephyr ever since he figured out the way my Dark Fae ghosted Ronin for years.

And the way Ronin self-hated and grieved and suffered all these years, thinking he killed the guy?

Vasili puts that on Zephyr.

Which in turn makes Ash all protective over his mate.

The thing is, they've both grieved and suffered. Ronin and Zephyr. They both need grace and forgiveness and healing.

And I'm determined to help.

"You're leaving?" Zephyr's brittle tone snaps my gaze back to him. His hands fall away from my waist and he takes a step back.

Empty air opens between us.

"Just temporarily, but yeah." I sigh. "We talked about this, remember? We've got midterms, and there's a lot going down with Messalina back home."

Behind the eyepatch and the kingly demeanor, my Unseelie can be pretty inscrutable. Sure, we fuck like alley cats in permanent heat, and he showers me with impractical and occasionally bloody Dark Fae gifts (I might've mentioned he's feral?) and calls me his bride (which I always deny) and heavily hints that maybe he loves me.

But he's not actually human.

In so many ways, he's still a mystery.

Now, seeing his guarded expression, watching the way Ash steps in solidly beside him and throws an arm over his slim shoulders to support him, I can't stand it.

I rush forward to close this awful distance between us and wrap myself around both of them.

"C'mon, you're the headmaster of the Avalon Academy now, right?" I tease, because Zephyr inherited that title too when that queen bitch Maeve bit the bullet. "And you're the Potions prof, right, Ash? You gotta appreciate the value of a good education."

"Sure, we appreciate it." Reliable Ash wraps an easy arm around my waist. "Sparrow and me, we've been talking. I reckon maybe we can work out some kinda student exchange program with the Dean at Icarus. Our kids need more practical training than they're getting here, and we still got a volcano that's gonna blow someday, so the whole race needs a Plan B. Besides, now that portal's open, your classmates need to learn about us Fae."

I bubble right up with enthusiasm for that idea. And with gratitude for Ash, my Seelie Prince, who's clearly been giving our whole situation a lot of thought.

"That's literally the best idea I've ever heard." I tighten my grip around both of them. "We can do faculty swaps too. I bet Lucius would love the chance to come here and study the history of this place, like those cave paintings and shit. And that means you two can spend time at Icarus."

"Sure, if they need a Potions prof or a healer," Ash says easily. "There's more Seelie blood in the witching world than most folks realize. Betcha got Light Fae you don't know about right now at Icarus."

Zephyr doesn't answer in words, but he finally unbends enough to open up a space between him and Ash, which I promptly step into and spin around.

Shoulder to shoulder, me with an arm looped around both their waists, I give my Icarus warlocks a hopeful grin.

Vasili still looks pissy as hell (even while he's eye-fucking Ash in his leathers), but Maxim's wrapped protectively around my snake from behind, totally taking advantage of the distraction. My dragon king's arms circle the Goblin King's slim waist and his slitted golden eyes turn thoughtful.

My bookworm Neo hovers between us, all excited over the idea of an academic exchange program that he'll obviously be the first one chosen for. He's always so easy to read through our bond. He's not sure where to be right now or who needs him most, he's missing Lucius and Ronin like fuck, he's intimidated by Ash's size and wings, he's attracted to Zephyr but shy about it. And he always wants to be with me, but Vasili's being all complicated, so—

My Goblin King resolves that dilemma when his hand snakes out to claim Neo. Our bookworm laces his fingers with Vasili's, leans into him for comfort, and gives me a hopeful smile.

Which lets Max wrap a claiming arm around Neo too and loom over our bookworm in his possessive alpha way. That whole Maxim-Neo situation's definitely taken some major doing to get Vasili on board with. (But that's like a separate story for another time.)

So that's us right now.

Me sandwiched solidly between my two royal Fae, one of whom I might or might not have accidentally married, but both of whom I'm definitely falling hard for and fucking.

My three Icarus warlocks locked together for comfort and support, Max and V sharing Neo, sharing me, sharing the absent Ronin, and pretty goddamn close to working through their rival alpha bullshit and finally sharing each other.

My wolf king Lucius waiting patiently at home, the anchor for all of us, whose steady arms I'll sleep in tonight (you know, after he lets his wolf out and fucks me into a literal sex coma).

My broody bully Ronin, so gifted and so gorgeous and so fucking tortured. Sure, Zephyr and Ronin have a trust issue right now (bigtime). But I don't think Zephyr's ever stopped loving him.

Ash thinks he hates him—but he's never met Ronin.

Ronin literally makes straight guys crave dick. He'd make the Pope curious. When it comes to Ronin, no one's immune to his hotness. That's *his* superpower. (I mean, along with psi fire and telepathy and all his mad warlock skills.)

But I can't help noticing the way we've gathered in two separate groups, with the Fae and me on one side, Vasili and my Icarus warlocks on the other, all of us eyeing each other across the gap that's opened between us.

Suddenly I have to wonder if that's how it's destined to be back home.

I wonder if, by bringing these two Fae into the Gemini harem, I might be swinging the blade that splits our polycule right down the center.

But I shut that shit right down. Because I'm just not gonna let that happen.

Not ever.

"Sounds like we're all going to Icarus," I announce firmly in my queen voice, tipping my head to look up at Xhevith. The green dragon gives a happy roar and spreads his almost fully healed wings. "As soon as Xhev can fly through the portal, okay?"

"Tell your Lucius to change the sheets in the guest chamber, my bride," Zephyr murmurs in my ear, in that velvety sex voice that always makes me shiver. "A king has exacting tastes."

Oh hell to the yeah.

That's my Dark Fae King, all lurky and indulgent, climbing right on board with that plan.

"Screw the guest chamber." Feeling that little clump of tension dissolve and trickle away, I relax and grin into my Unseelie's jade-green gaze. "Anyway, we don't have one. Pretty sure you and Ash are gonna be bunking down with the rest of us in my digs."

That's definitely the goal for all seven of my guys and me.

Even if the Devil's lurking in the details.

THANK YOU!

Hey, witchlet! Thank you sooooo much for reading *Gemini Wild*! What did you think of Zara's latest adventure??? I write to bring joy to readers like you—you're my "why" for this crazy author life!—so I'm dying to hear from you. If you loved spending time with Zara, Zephyr, Ash, Xhevith, and all Zara's sword-crossing warlocks in their sexy secret world, please consider leaving a review. Just a few words make a huge difference! Your feedback is so important to me. It helps readers like you give writers like me a chance. **Here's the link to leave feedback for** *Gemini Wild* **on Amazon** (https://www.amazon.com/dp/B0CG3X4LYY)**, the Goodreads link** (https://www.goodreads.com/book/show/197300414-gemini-wild)**, and the BookBub link** (https://www.bookbub.com/books/gemini-wild-a-dark-witch-academy-paranormal-romance-by-laura-navarre)**, if that's your thing!**

**Want more Zara & her sexy sword-crossing warlocks
without having to wait?**

*You're in luck, because you can keep reading
what happens next right now!!
You want access to spicy bonus Gemini content
you can't find anywhere else?*

How about <u>five spicy secret bonus chapters of</u> **Gemini Wild**
*that reveal how Vasili discovers that hidden Maxim-Neo
relationship… and the hot-as-fuck MMMF hookup that
persuades our snake to play nice (for now)?
Free follow me here in the Witching World
for some sexy bonus chapters!
(https://reamstories.com/witchingworld/public)*

You want access to the next Gemini novel right now, months before everyone else?

You want eyes on an exclusive, extra-steamy Zara-Vasili-Neo MMF novella about Neo's first heat that's only available to tempt and tantalize you in one super-secret place?
You ready to get whisked away from your day-to-day?
Then you're ready to join Common Magics 101!
(https://reamstories.com/witchingworld/public)

From Academy outsider to witchy insider, this intimate reader community whisks you through the magical wards that hide the Icarus Academy from the average reader to inhabit the sexy secret world of Zara Gemini and her sword-crossing warlocks.
Join the Witching World, my reader community, here!
(https://reamstories.com/witchingworld/public)

READ THE COMPLETE DARK WITCH ACADEMY SERIES

Gemini Queen (Book 1)
(https://www.amazon.com/dp/B09V1PQRPB)
Available on Kindle Unlimited and in print.

Experience **Gemini Queen**
(https://books2read.com/geminiqueenaudiobook/)
a whole new way—in audio!

Gemini Kings (Book 2)
(https://www.amazon.com/dp/B0BF952NCH)

Gemini Wild (Book 3)
(https://www.amazon.com/dp/B0CG3X4LYY)

Gemini Wicked (Book 4)
(https://www.amazon.com/dp/B0CMCCCLXR)

AUTHOR'S NOTE

This book's for you… yes, you! For wonderful you and all my incredible friends and readers who keep loving Zara & her warlocks and wanting me to continue their story! If you ARC read for me, if you review, if you download and read, if you follow me on the Witching World or subscribe to my newsletter or like and comment when I post on Facebook, all those things you do matter! I write to bring joy to readers like you.

I especially want to thank my brilliant editor and career coach Angela James, my frighteningly competent formatter and hand-holder Judi Fennell at Formatting4U, my faithful PA Clare Harrison, my talented cover artist Kim Killion, my insightful beta readers Taylor and Kara, my incomparable alpha reader and cosmic mate Steven, author advocate Michael Evans and the Ream Team, and all the members of the Witching World—my amazing reader community of first joiners in Common Magics 101 and Zara's Belfry on Ream. Here you are on the Dean's List, you amazing first joiners! Thanks for hanging out with me in the Witching World!

THE WITCHING WORLD DEAN'S LIST

Heather	Samantha	Kristy	Ariel
Katrin	Amarie	Kayla	Keri
Penelope	Melissa	Nadia	Cheryl
Amber	Serena	Serafina	Sharon
Rachel	Lisa	Nikki	Melly
Katelyn	Mali	Jenna	Jana
	Haylee	Turtledove	Persephone

You ready to get whisked away from your day-to-day with an extra spicy out-of-this-world why-choose adventure series that's complete and free in KU? Keep scrolling down for a sexy sneak peek at my paranormal **Hunger Games** *in space why-choose romance* **RENEGADE ANGEL,** *available for free in Kindle Unlimited and now in print, along with the complete MMMF Astral Heat Romance Series!*

RENEGADE ANGEL:
An Astral Heat Romance #2
By Laura Navarre

Chapter One
The Duel

As a notorious scourge-of-the-galaxy space pirate, Zorin had survived a lifetime of guys trying to kill him. He'd even survived having interstellar war declared on his ass by Dex Draven, First Indomitable of the Mogadon Empire.

The guy who was Zorin's ultimate nemesis, his mouthwatering obsession, and the galaxy's premier military power.

But after four-plus decades of nick-of-time near misses, it turned out what was gonna kill him was the girl. The girl he'd fallen for harder than an asteroid collision. The girl whose bed he'd laid his life on the line to compete for, against five hundred ambitious, aggressive, testosterone-fueled yahoos, in the galactic mating contest called the Tombola.

To be real specific, what would kill him—or at least paralyze him, pretty much permanently—was the nerve gun his opponent in the fighting pit was pointing at Zorin's chest.

And Dex Draven, in his role as referee and master emcee, was gonna see it happen. Maybe once he did, he'd finally find his way past that whole butchering-Dex's-psychopath-dad-in-cold-blood incident that had gotten Zorin exiled from Mogadon, back in his prior-to-being-a-pirate days. Back when Zorin was First Indomitable himself.

Maybe.

But Zorin didn't plan to stand here, dead in space like a stalled starship, and let it all go down. Not when his girl was counting on him to survive.

And counting on him to win.

Ten cubits away in the blood-spattered clay of the fighting pit, ringed by tiers of screaming spectators, his opponent grinned at him. The guy was half his size—hard-faced, sorrel-skinned, lean and wiry under the colorful robes and battle-scarf of a Kryllian bloodletter. Which was how the bastard had smuggled an illegal weapon into the pit for what was supposed to be strictly an unarmed throwdown.

A stricture that should've ruled out the microfiber steel net the Kryll had just flung over Zorin's sorry carcass to pin him down.

That net was complicating the heck out of Zorin's survival odds.

Well, shoot.

Kaia of Kryll had been crystal clear from the get-go. Being tamely auctioned off to any joe in the show by her tyrannical dad was never part of her game plan. The fact that Zorin, out of all five hundred wannabe consorts in this galactic shindig, ended up being the guy who turned her crank?

He was one lucky sonofabitch.

And he wasn't gonna let his girl down. His rebel princess, his prize, his Prime Class cyber samurai.

Too bad all his struggles only tightened the net.

A guy could escape an unbreakable steel net in one of two ways. He could pick his way free with time. Or he could cut his way free with a blowtorch.

Zorin, right then and there, didn't even have a match.

"Come on, you big galoot," he muttered to himself. "Think it through."

Meanwhile, the Kryll was taking his sweet time lining up the kill shot with his contraband nerve gun. A gun that was outlawed across the galaxy due to that whole permanent paralysis issue.

Above him in the viewing box, Kaia was leaping to her booted feet—a breath away from drawing her cyber saber and flinging her furious body into the fray in his defense. In his periphery, Dex was charging into the pit, shouting rules and prohibitions despite the fact no one in this madhouse gave a single flaming shit. Because it turned out this hootenanny wasn't a ritual contest. Not anymore.

It was a hit job.

And the *only* reason that Kryll would be aiming a disqualifying nerve gun at Zorin's ugly hide was because someone had paid the guy to do it.

All around him in the arena's humid heat, his competitors were on their feet howling for his blood. Zorin's Syndax pirates—his best boys, brought aboard Dex's battleship to cover his six as they shot through space—were drawing their blasters and converging on the pit. Too bad for Zorin they were all moving way too slow.

The gamy scent of Mogadon pheromones flooded the air. That head-spinning hit of his own aggression gave him a biochemical kick in the pants, just the way Mogadon genetics intended. Adrenaline spiked his pulse and roughened his breath.

Danger streaking through his senses like a meteor shower, rage spurting through his veins like liquid nitrogen, he watched the Kryll's finger tighten on the trigger.

Way too close to miss.

Trapped in that goddamn net like a Solarian sardine, Zorin did pretty much the only thing he could.

He dove.

Directly into the Kryll with the nerve gun.

#

The nerve gun discharged—a shrill *bzzzzt* that pierced her eardrum like a drill. The combatants crashed to the dirt in a single thrashing knot.

"Let *go* of me, damn you!" Twenty cubits above the fighting pit in the viewing box, Kaia raged and writhed in her lifemate's grip like a harpooned eel. "I'll flipping kill you for this!"

"Not on your life," Ben Nero ground in her ear. "You're not going anywhere near that nerve gun. Let Dex deal with it."

"But he hates Zorin!"

"Give Dex some credit, Kaia. He'll handle it."

Chains and dreadlocks streaming, Syndax pirates were hurtling into the pit. But they couldn't fire without risking Zorin, their leader. Responding with precision to his steely orders, Dex's elite praetorian guard wheeled into motion, training stun rifles on the seething mob— barely holding off a full-scale riot. Only Dex's incandescent glare kept the agitated Syndax at bay. Someone was shouting for a blowtorch.

Over the chaos, the struggling knot of limbs and net erupted in a scream. A scream that cut short with jarring sharpness.

The entangled figures went fatally still.

Kaia, too, went slack, heaving for air in Nero's arms. He held her tight against his lean length, eyes glued on the scene in the fighting pit.

None of it remotely appropriate according to the Tombola ritual's sacred dictates. Not the nerve gun, not her ex-boyfriend's hands all over her, not her obvious favor for the Syndax pirate.

And she cared not a nanoparticle. Her entire being was riveted on the deadly drama like a rocket. Sure, she'd only just met Zorin when the contest launched. But she'd known from the start he was the only one of those five hundred candidates she wanted in her bed.

Because Dex and Nero, the only other guys she'd ever wanted, couldn't even bid. Dex Draven was her Tombola master, bound by a treaty with her father that Dex couldn't break, committed to deliver her fiercely resistant body to the winning candidate. And Ben Nero, her psychic lifemate and the galaxy's most powerful telepath, was oathsworn to guarantee it all went down the way her godlike father demanded.

Formidable and stern in his black uniform, Dex closed in on the combatants with a blowtorch, blue flame spitting from the nozzle. Swiftly he peeled back the steel net.

"I think…" Nero whispered. Clearly relying on his telepathic Valyrian senses to tell him what his eyes couldn't.

"You think *what*?"

Because Kaia, a half-Valyrian hybrid and unreliable telepath herself, was way too agitated to think or feel anything but sheer screaming panic.

"I'd say 'Nobody panic,'" Zorin announced dryly, untangling himself from the net. His Kryll opponent lay poleaxed at his feet. "But somehow I got a feeling it's a little late."

The bristling Syndax were first to react, jubilant fists shooting skyward, shouts of triumph ripping from a dozen throats. Dex was already in motion, seizing the contraband weapon and flipping back the Kryll's battle-scarf.

The would-be assassin lay sprawled at a nauseating angle, head violently wrenched to one side.

"Snapped like a wishbone," Kaia whispered, shaking with a violent surge of satisfaction. "He won't be saying a word. We'll have to interrogate his brothers to sniff out who hired them. They're Kryllian bloodletters, trained assassins—so they won't be easy informants. Promise me you'll do it yourself."

Because no one breathing can lie to you.

"If his brothers aren't long gone by now." Gently Nero released her and stepped back. "Those two probably had a getaway shuttle in the hangar bay on standby. Looks like Dex is battening down the hatches."

Dex was muttering into his wrist unit, nerve gun secure in his belt. His grim cobalt gaze sliced from the raucous Syndax and the agitated mob to Zorin's monumental frame looming over the dead Kryll. Jaw clenched with steely necessity, light flashing on platinum epaulets, Dex strode to his side and raised Zorin's mailed arm briefly overhead.

"The Syndax will advance," Dex clipped out. "The Kryllian brothers are disqualified."

The pirates roared in rowdy acclaim, echoed this time by the rest of the hoi polloi. Around Kaia, the rattle and flash of creds changed hands. Zorin had won himself more than a few allies with that impressive maneuver. Huddled in anxious pockets around the viewing stand, an array of less murderous candidates for her bed muttered and shifted in unease.

Fervently she wished Dex could disqualify them all.

From the pit, one fist raised high in victory, Zorin lifted his head and looked straight at Kaia—the rugged lines of his face etched with anticipation and triumph. Despite the physical distance that yawned between them, the smoking heat in his aquamarine eyes seared through her like an electrical charge. Beneath the bronze silk of her cybersuit, her breasts felt swollen and her knees felt weak.

Damn it to the moon and back. He'd just nearly *died*.

And in that raw moment of naked knowledge, when fragile life had never felt more vital, she knew on a visceral level exactly what he needed.

"Ready room," she whispered, shaping the thought with her lips. Somehow knowing he'd hear her, even though non-telepaths often couldn't. "I'll find you."

Zorin held her gaze while heat pooled and pulsed between her legs, making her slick and wet.

Even while Dex dropped his arm like Zorin was garbage and pivoted to confront his volatile viewers.

"The names of the two hundred finalists will be broadcast over interstellar news at midnight." Dex pitched his voice to carry above the ripple of anticipation. "The contest resumes for the finalists tomorrow. Transport from this battleship for the rest of you departs for the nearest spaceport at oh-one-hundred. I'd firmly advise each of you *not* to be late."

"In a rush to get rid of them, isn't he?" Nero turned to find Kaia halfway to the stairs. "Gods of Solaris, Kaia, wait!"

"Try to keep up—if you must." Without slowing, she swung energetically over the rail and scrambled down the stairs. "Because I definitely don't need a babysitter."

"Why the hells are you always running away?" he muttered, glowering at avid suitors to keep them at bay as Kaia powered past. "Drives me insane to be always chasing you."

"Feel free to stop anytime." She edged sideways to slip between the scrum of Syndax bunched outside the ready room with knives and blasters bristling. "I meant what I said last night."

"I assure you, so did I."

The harum-scarum horde eased readily aside for Kaia, appre-ciation gleaming in their wolfish eyes. But they closed ranks tight before Nero.

"Not you, pretty boy," one tattooed titan said with a sneer. "Zorin only wants *her*."

As tall as the Syndax but far less wide, Nero smoothed back a sleek curtain of raven hair from his sculpted face. And eyed the obstruction with interest. "I'm the Valyrian Precursor. The galaxy's ranking telepath. Which means I can pull your brains through your ears with a passing thought. Out of curiosity, how precisely do you propose to stop me?"

"Good gods, Ben! Don't you think we've seen enough slaughter for one day?" Impatience simmered in Kaia's blood, laced with an agitation she seemed helpless to control. "Do you honestly think Zorin would let anything happen to me?"

"Comets! You know you're not supposed to be alone with the candidates. Dex has been more than clear—"

"Dex isn't my father. And neither are you, Ben Nero."

"Let me put it this way." Over the pirate's chrome-studded shoulder, Nero's violet eyes smoldered hot with promise. "If you're about to give that Syndax a congratulatory kiss, I definitely want to watch. Maybe he'll even appreciate a private demonstration from the galaxy's leading expert on how to blow your circuits."

An alchemical sizzle of heat seared through her. An instinctive response to the arrogant accolade she reluctantly acknowledged he'd more than earned after the way he scorched her synapses when they'd finally come together last night—all without violating her no-penetration edict.

The problem was, after abandoning her and letting her believe he was dead in the biowar for eight flipping *years*, she'd rather swallow her own tongue than admit the way Ben Nero still made her feel.

"Blast it, Ben! I assure you I have zero intent—" She eyed the titillated pirates soaking up every syllable and finished coolly, "Why don't you make yourself useful and interrogate those Kryll for me. Because I can't stand the sight of them."

Spinning away before he could lob another sexually incendiary innuendo, she shrugged the curtain aside and escaped into the ready room.

Zorin stood in solitude, etched against the battleship's viewport, towering frame and shoulders blotting out the stars. His craggy profile snapped toward her with an alacrity that told her she wasn't the only one with fight-or-flight adrenaline still sparking through her circuits.

Not to mention sexual stimulation bubbling in her blood.

Shyness was an impulse she'd outgrown years ago. Because shyness wasn't any help at all for a circus acrobat or a runaway samurai with a vengeful god on her tail.

Now a powerfully inconvenient surge of shyness reared up and hammered her feet to the floor. Tongue-tied, hot-faced, she could only stand and stare. Knowing if she said a word, she'd stammer like a Prime Class simpleton.

Confronted with her dumbstruck silence, Zorin's scarred brow hitched. He even nodded like she'd said something he understood.

"It's real now, isn't it?" His deep voice rumbled through the starlit shadows.

Her tight throat unlocked to release a careful breath. "What's real?"

"You and me." One corner of his mouth lifted in a wry smile. "This is new to me too. It's okay to be afraid."

"I'm not afraid," she shot back by instinct.

But that was a lie, wasn't it? She'd barricaded herself from every man she'd ever met behind an unbreachable battlement. That vow of abstinence she'd made before she was old enough to know what it meant, soldered in place by the crisis of Ben Nero's betrayal, had become the armor she hid behind to keep anyone from getting too close.

Ever.

Now she was going to venture out of that protective shell for him. The guy standing before her. The guy who'd just killed a man to clear his path to her bed.

The guy she still barely knew.

"I'm not afraid," she repeated, to make herself believe it. "You're the one. The one I'll fly away with on the *Relentless* five days from now. Together we'll end this whole monstrous farce."

"Cuz I'm the only guy with a snowball's chance in a sun storm of taking on Dex." His tone was easy, but his eyes were wary. "Dex with his fleet and his nukes and his badass arsenal. You figure I'm your best bet to stop that galactic germ war he's threatening."

"Yeah." She leaped headlong for that face-saving logic. "That's pretty much why. I'm half Valyrian. One biowar was more than enough."

Enough to eradicate eighty-eight percent of the Valyrian race.

Even if the last war was his dad's fault, Maximus Draven's been dead for years. So the next one's all on Dex.

Carefully she cleared her throat. "That's why I wanted you… at first. To stop Dex and prevent the war. But… it's not the only reason."

His eyes never left her face.

Like he was waiting for something he didn't want to miss.

Her tongue traced her dry lips. "Do you even realize you're the only candidate in this Tombola who's offered me *freedom*? As in—the only one. I've read five hundred bids over the past two days. And yours is the only one that doesn't turn my stomach."

"Well, it's an honest offer. I want you willing and eager or not at all." A subtle tension threaded his voice. "But I'm not the only choice you got, am I. You don't think Dex would hand you the Mogadon moons or anything else in the universe you ever wanted? Just to keep you with him?"

"Dex?" Her bubbling agitation erupted. An eruption far too long suppressed. "Why are you asking me about Dex? He's my Tombola master. You know he's not an option!"

"It's a fair ask, Kaia. The kid and me—we go way back. I was Dex's mentor back on Mogadon. I'm the one who taught him to fight. The one who taught him to kill." His steely eyes hardened. "And I can smell his mating scent on you all the way over here. Long story short? He doesn't act like a guy who's planning to let you go."

"It's not up to him. He can't bid!" Her volume spiraled until she was all but shouting. "And that's a choice he made all on his own."

"A choice he made before he met you."

"A choice he can't revoke." She planted hands on hips and scowled.

"Even if he wanted to—" *even if I wanted him to* "—he can't! He signed a binding treaty with my father. An ironclad pact for Kryll's merchant fleet to supply his battlefront. In exchange for Dex's service as arbiter and enforcer of this whole farking contest. If Dex voids the contest now by claiming me himself, he'll lose his war, his command, and probably his life."

Because my flipping father will declare a kill edict on his Indomitable head. And Kryll's faithful fanatics—men like those bloodletters—will carry it out.

"That might be a risk Dex is willing to take." Before her obstinate stance, Zorin's hard face softened. "Look. I might not know you the way I'd like. But he's a compelling guy, sweetheart, and I think he's caught your eye."

An uncomfortable heat climbed in her face. A heat she knew in her heart there was no point denying. Because the scourge of the galaxy was nobody's fool. And every word he said was true.

Shifting on her feet, she glanced aside. "I don't get it. Why are you arguing against your own interests?"

"Cuz I'm not so sure it's in my interest taking a consort who wants me solely for my military prowess and because I won't make her wear chains in my bed. Not to mention a consort who's already half in love with somebody else. Like a lotta folks, I've had consorts before. Everyone wants it to last forever, but it hardly ever does. This time's the real deal. Trust me to know what it takes to make this work."

Unable to meet his level gaze, she paced the shadowy confines of the ready room. "You make a fair point. You really do. Even though I'm not in love with him." *Why is this so farking hard to say?* "Anyway, um, I haven't been totally straight with you. Those aren't the only reasons I— I wanted you."

"No?" As solid and settled as she was jittery and jumpy, he leaned one armored hip against the wall and crossed his bulging arms. Starlight brought out the silver in his sandy hair.

"You know it's not," she whispered. She couldn't look at him. *Angels and asteroids, is he really going to make me say it?* "I want you because… I just… want you."

In the history of confessions, this wasn't much of one. But the heat of making it scorched through her until she thought her cybersuit would burst into flames. Slowly her gaze lifted to find him.

An outlaw. A space pirate. A wolf in blast armor.

Too smart to trick. Too strong to overpower. And probably too old for her to boot.

But the thought of climbing out of her armor and stripping him out of his and giving him everything he wanted from her—access she'd never given another man, had in fact been saving all her life just for him—made her weak with wanting.

"It's true," she said, throaty with the fever burning in her blood. "You say you want a woman who's eager for your bed? Trust me when I tell you that's not going to be a problem."

He hooked his big hands in his utility belt and lowered his head to eye her. "You got Dex's smell all over you. But Ben Nero says you spend your nights in *his* bed. The way I see it, you maybe got a thing for all three of us. That's a pretty big chance for an old guy like me to take, Kaia."

"I know. It's mixed up. It's just—I'm trying to figure things out." Her eyes pleaded for understanding. "I feel the way I feel. That's why I'm choosing you. What more do you want me to tell you?"

"Tell me?" His rough rasp sent shivers shooting down her spine. "Not a goddamn thing. Why don't you shimmy on over here and show me?"

Kaia's heart thundered like a war drum and every synapse in her body thrummed in a symphony of nerves. Tingling with tension, she prowled across the expanse of ready room floor that was all that stood between her and this Syndax pirate she'd chosen to mate.

Steady on, samurai. This isn't your mating night. There's zero reason to be nervous.

Even if he is watching you like he's finally letting himself imagine what you're going to look like naked.

He'd kept himself so carefully in check since the moment they'd met. When she didn't know who he was, when he let her do all the talking, when she fell toes over tailpipe for this interstellar menace until nothing else mattered except finding some way to be his.

He was always letting her take the lead.

Just so she wouldn't run away.

He'd kept whatever he felt himself so thoroughly under wraps that the raw hunger animating his war-hardened face right now felt as intimate as the slide of a hand down her naked spine.

Tonight was different. Because tonight he'd almost died. He'd snapped a man's neck with his bare hands to clear his path to her bed. And those genetic Mogadon instincts that still drove him even in exile were driving him now to claim her.

The prize he'd killed for.

The woman his most primitive self now saw as his exclusive property to protect and possess.

That image alone, that bare whisper from her erratic psychic senses of the primal imperatives that drove him, made her breath hitch and her pulse pitch. Beneath her cybersuit, she was slick with her own passion, her clit a swollen nub that chafed against her cybersilk with every step.

He was done waiting.

He wanted her.

And her entire body ached to give him everything he wanted.

Her eyes slid slowly up his frame, all size and strength and raw physical power encased in the starmetal mesh of his armor. Battle-scarred space boots and thickly muscled thighs spread to claim the space around him, biceps bulging in the arms folded across his chest, broad shoulders blotting out the stars.

She wanted to drop to her knees and wrap her mouth around his cock. She wanted to climb him like a tree and wrap her legs around him and let him sink deep inside her the way no other man had ever done. She wanted him to ride her until she forgot her own name.

She wanted to feel him come inside her.

She wanted him to sire the son the prophecy said she had in her.

"Mars," he breathed, raw and ragged with wanting. "A guy could get used to the way you look at me. Better warn you I'm about six ticks away from tossing you over my shoulder and taking you back with me to the *Relentless*. And to hell with the auction. You're mine."

She added an extra sway to her hips and watched his eyes darken to navy. "That doesn't sound very civilized."

"I'm a space pirate, sweetheart. I don't do civilized all that well. Never have." One tawny brow hitched. "Neither do you, by the way."

"To everyone's dismay." She laughed, but it held a bitter edge.

"Not mine," he fired back, gruff with anticipation. "I know what I'm getting. And I wouldn't change a goddamn thing."

"Right back at you," she whispered, low in her throat.

Two cubits away, she tilted her head and looked up at him. He was way too tall for what she had in mind.

She put her back to the viewport and hopped lithely to the ledge, using her acrobat's strength to swing her bottom up to sit. He was still taller than she wanted.

But not by much.

Booted legs dangling, gaze never leaving his, she spread her knees wide in invitation and hooked a hand in his belt to pull him close.

A growl rose from his cavernous chest. He planted one big hand on either side of her hips and moved into her space. She ducked her head to study his hands, her slim fingers sliding over scarred knuckles and calloused skin, and heard the harsh husk of his breath.

Plenty of women would find him brutal. Even terrifying. All that size and unapologetic violence.

But not her.

She wanted it—wanted *him*—wanted the threat and the promise of everything he wanted with an intensity that made her entire body throb.

Leaving her hands over his—a silent plea for restraint she didn't know if he'd heed—she let her eyes rise over his mighty chest and muscled neck and the strong line of his jaw. The golden glitter of day's-end stubble tempted her to touch. And his eyes, locked on hers like heat-seeking missiles, were so intense she couldn't sustain his stare.

Keeping her hands where they were, she leaned in carefully and touched her lips to the rough bristle of his cheek. His sharp exhale rushed out. He'd been holding his breath. The sudden scent of steel and predator rose dark and hot from his skin.

The intoxicating essence of mating scent.

"I know I barely know you," she whispered in his ear. "But I really, really like you."

"Show me how much—" His voice broke as her tongue traced his ear. His hands tensed beneath her palms and a groan rumbled from his throat.

"You like this, don't you?" She licked the hot salty skin under his ear and felt his pulse jump. "And this?"

"Your mouth on me anywhere, answer's gonna be yes." He sounded strangled with the effort of restraint.

Tingling with the energy that leaped between them, she backed away just a little and leaned in to kiss his other cheek, stubble abrading her tender skin.

"I like your strength," she breathed in his ear, just to feel him shiver. "I like your restraint and I like your patience. I like when you're brutal and savage like you were in the pit. I like the way you feel safe and the way you feel dangerous—all at the same time."

She pulled back and leaned close, his lips a breath away. "But most of all, Zorin the pirate, I like the way you make me feel. Like there's no part of me you aren't going to own."

With a harsh sound, he leaned in and kissed her. Fusing them together with his mouth on hers, tongue meeting tongue, hot and fierce with need. Demanding the response she'd been born to give. He tasted like sex and violence held barely in check. And just the feel of his mouth on hers ignited the dormant volcano of craving deep inside and made her burn with an aching caldera of need.

Gods, I need you. Need you inside me. You're going to be the one. And I don't think I can wait.

She moaned and leaned into him, arms wrapping around his neck, hands threading through the short rough spikes of his hair. His hands closed over her thighs and dragged her hard against his bulk. Her legs wound around his hips and his armored cock nudged her clit.

"Please," she panted, rocking into his heat, hardly knowing what she was begging for. Just knowing she needed more than she was getting. "Please—I need—*more*. I need more of you."

"I'll conquer worlds and lay them at your feet. Every star system my army claims is another realm for you to rule." He leaned his brow against hers while they both fought for breath and her body begged him to ride her. "Just let me look at you. Let me at least do that much. I've been imagining you in my bed since the moment we met. I'm gonna lose my mind if I can't see the real you. *All* of you."

She closed her eyes against the molten metal of his stare and whispered, "Yes."

At that point, she would've said yes to anything if he was the one asking.

And she trusted him not to abuse the privilege.

His hands spanned her waist and eased up to find the tender fullness of her breasts. She arched her back to push into his touch, head falling back, stars swimming in her eyes. She heard the buzz of a zipper, felt her bodice release, shivered when the frigid cold of space through the viewport licked along her naked spine.

He muttered something rough and reverent in a language she didn't know.

Then his palms chafed her naked nipples. Twin jets of tingling pleasure shot through her. Straight to the pounding need between her thighs. The sudden musk of her own juices, hot and slick and pumping, mingled with the wolfish whiff of his mating scent.

He breathed her in deep and growled like the apex predator he was. His hands slid her cybersuit to her waist. Her wrists tangled in her sleeves' tight fabric, snared in her Valyrian torques. That paralyzing pleasure immobilized her—exposed and helpless as a harem slave. Hard fingers cradled her breasts and tweaked her nipples. He was different from Ben, his touch less polished and a lot more rough. His pace less thoroughbred and a lot more draft horse.

Her hips thrust against him with panting need. Desperate for the starmetal friction of his cock.

"Jumpin' Jupiter," he said hoarsely, "you like that, don't you? Being tied up while I work you."

"Seems so," she gasped, head falling back to give him more access. *Who'd have thought?* "Gods, Zorin. I never even… knew I wanted…"

"To be restrained? Sometimes what turns us on is what scares us. And you like it a little rough too, don'tcha?" His growl sent a shiver skidding down her spine that answered him without her having to say a word. "We can do this any way you want. You can't hurt me. And it makes me crazy that you smell like Dex. You're *mine*."

One solid arm slid around her back to close off her escape, but she only pressed harder into his heat. One deft pull of his hand, hard enough to sting, released the knot that held her hair. It slid down her back like a silk curtain. His mouth seared her breast, hard lips closing over one tingling nipple—the scrape of teeth over sensitized skin, the pulse of pleasure between her legs. She cried out and clamped her legs around him, booted heels digging urgently into the hard bulge of his ass.

That dark savage scent poured from his skin and made her head reel.

With an oath he lifted her, mouth finding hers in a scorching kiss— more certain, less restrained, more dominant now he knew how much she liked it—and staggered to the couch. Beneath her back, the sleek leather sank under their weight.

Gasping for oxygen, she forced her eyes open. "We can't, um, do everything. Not until the mating ritual…"

"Kaia." He straddled her hips without crushing her, one hand fisting in her hair, the other finding her breast. "Gimme some credit, will ya?

I've been waiting for you my whole life. You're gonna be my consort and the mother of my sons. You'll rule the Syndax horde at my side. I'm not about to do this in the ready room of a fighting pit with a dozen of my boys listening in."

His voice deepened. "But damn if I'm not tempted."

The hard pinch of his fingers on her nipple rolled her hips and made her writhe. He caught her aching cry with a kiss that claimed her like a brand and made her even hotter.

One big hand freed her arms from her sleeves, then engulfed her wrists and pinned them overhead. Her eyes flew open to find his rough-hewn face looming over her, starlight gleaming silver in the spikes of his hair, eyes burning platinum with arousal, full mouth ruthless with intent. She tugged against his confining hand and his grip tightened.

And the hot rush of pleasure that rolled through her nearly made her climax on the spot.

"Angels of Anaxos," she panted, legs twining around his hips to pull him closer. "Zorin… I need…"

"Maybe this is what you need?"

Trapping her wide-eyed gaze with his, he eased a hand down her bare tummy under her open cybersuit to find the slick folds of her pussy.

And Kaia, who could count on one hand with fingers left over the number of guys she'd ever trusted enough to permit the privilege, let her thighs drift open and her body arch into his touch.

Feeling her arousal drench his fingers, his jaw clenched and his eyes darkened to lapis. Heat surged into her face. Suddenly way too conscious of just how much she wanted him—how close to the ragged edge of total surrender she was riding—she turned her hot cheek into the cool leather cushion.

"I'm right here, sweetheart," he said, thick with passion. "Look at me so I can see if you like this."

If he so much as grazed her clit, he was going to ring her bell. When he eased one careful finger into her slick heat instead, she clenched and pulsed around him.

A low savage cry rolled through her. Blind with need, her eyes found his and let him look straight into her soul.

"Gods, you're so wet for me, aren't you?" He eased back and her hips rose to meet him. With a groan, he slid deeper, hand cupping her soaked flesh, and she moaned in unison. "So wet and so tight and so darn perfect, I'm about a whisker away from losing my mother-loving mind. Guess the rumors were right. You're a virgin, ain't ya?"

"Story of my life. Does that… turn you off?" *Please, gods, don't let it turn him off.*

"Pretty much the opposite. I'm dying here, Kaia." He gasped out a laugh. Which sent a vibration through the careful rhythm of his thick finger inside her.

A vibration that pushed her hard over the edge.

With the force of a star imploding, a sonic wave of orgasm shot down her thighs and curled her toes. Her head fell back and comets streaked against her closed lids. Her mouth opened on a scream that he caught with a savage openmouthed kiss.

She cried out her climax into his mouth, barely caring if he managed to muffle the sound.

When her head cleared, her entire body was still rippling with gentle pulses of bliss. And he was still braced above her, sparing her his formidable weight, with the cataclysmic strain of sexual restraint engraved in his granite features and the galaxy's most monumental erection jutting between her thighs.

A flood of contrition scorched through her. "Ohmygods, I'm so sorry! I, um, wasn't actually planning on having that happen."

"Don't you dare apologize. I loved every bit of what just went down. Good to know I can rock your world, sweetheart. We're gonna need that."

With meticulous care, he disengaged and rolled off her replete and satiated body to sprawl on the floor beside her with a labored groan. "Shindig or no shindig, I'd take you to bed right now if I could. But scuttlebutt says you sleep in Draven's quarters."

His gaze swerved toward her. "It's true, ain't it?"

"He's very… protective," she managed to mumble, knowing the admission only validated every dark suspicion he was already harboring about Dex.

And Dex's fixation on me isn't exactly unrequited. Which I'm pretty sure you've also figured out.

This Syndax she'd chosen wasn't a telepath and couldn't transmit, but he seemed to have no trouble at all receiving. At least from her.

His measured curse rang heavy with frustration.

"You and Dex, huh?" He scrubbed a big hand against the back of his neck. "What in tarnation am I gonna do about you and Dex?"

Without a flicker of warning, one electrifying option sizzled through her. A visual of what would happen if he took her to her quarters and Dex found him in her bed. A sudden searing image of Zorin's big hand in Dex's burnished hair, the rough consuming hunger of mouth on mouth, a flash of tongue meeting tongue as these two fiercely dominant men came together above her. In her runaway imagination, while the two of them went at it, her hand slid under her soaked panties to finger her swollen clit.

Asteroids. She could come just watching the two of them kiss.

"Neptune's knickers," Zorin said from the heart. "What a visual. Is *that* what you want?"

"I, uh, think I might… want both of you," she admitted in a whisper. "Both of you together."

Breathless not only because the mere thought had her perched again on the naked edge of climax—but because she was reeling under the sudden, searing, completely unexpected impact the image was having on Zorin.

"Gods of my father, Zorin. You want him too… don't you? You've wanted him forever. You can barely even remember a time when you didn't want him."

Grappling to get her head around that revelation, she suffered through his complicated silence.

"I can see having a telepath for a consort's gonna take some getting used to," he said wryly, bowing his head against her bare shoulder. "This is a lotta excitement for an old guy like me. Gimme a tick to catch my breath, will ya?"

That's not a denial, she thought, skin tingling. *You don't need to catch your breath. And you're not old.*

But she knew better than to press. The first rule of courtesy any telepath learned was never to intrude without an invite.

Even when she was suddenly tingling under the rush of a shining, unlikely, utterly novel notion. The notion of becoming the bridge that finally brought these two galactic rivals together.

The way they were meant to be.

Against her skin, Zorin pulled in a long inhale. When he raised his head, his face blazed with masculine satisfaction. "Now you smell like *me*. And I damn well intend to keep it that way. No matter what it does to Dex. If he doesn't intend to claim you himself, he needs to stay outta my way."

"I smell like both of you." The deep ripple of sexual pleasure that rolled through her nearly derailed her train of thought—but not quite. "I'm into both of you. And I think both of you need to talk."

"And I think that particular parley's gonna have to wait," he said lightly, letting her read nothing in his face. "Cuz if Dex ever found me making love to you in his bed, you better believe joining in would be the last thing on his mind. He'd probably declare interstellar war on the spot. Oh, wait, he's already done that."

"Or it might be just what the two of you need," she murmured, wiggling regretfully back into her cybersuit. Because as much fun as she was having with Zorin on that couch, he wasn't her consort yet and she knew they needed to stop.

He lounged on the floor beside her and watched her with aqua eyes whose lidded heat made her shiver.

"Meaning?" he rumbled.

"Meaning I heard what you told him about his father—and I believe you." She pushed up to sit. "You killed Max Draven all those years ago because someone had to. You went into exile so you wouldn't have to kill Dex. He was your student. You were his mentor. And I don't think the two of you should be enemies."

"I happen to agree. But Dex isn't exactly on the same page, is he? And even if someday we buried the hatchet, it doesn't follow like two plus two that we'd end up in the sack. Anyway, I gave up that sorta thing years ago."

She made a neutral noise.

But Dex still turns you on. She gave him her back and swept up her hair so he could join her on the couch and zip her up. *Even if you've just spent years convincing yourself he doesn't. The bare fantasy of you kissing him, and him kissing you back, was just about enough to spank your monkey.*

And the thought of him alone in his space-cold quarters on that rusting hulk with his hand wrapped around his cock and Dex's name on his lips was just about enough to make *her* come.

Again.

Suddenly, with the certainty she associated with her inherited and unpredictable dash of Valyrian foresight, she wanted to see the two of them together. Wanted it so bad she could taste it. And the thought of both of them looming over her, pushing her flat, one bucking into her mouth to hit the back of her throat with every thrust, while the other spread her wide and rode her hard and fast—

"Kaia, I'm begging for mercy here." Half laughing, Zorin eased up her zipper. "Dex and I are not about to fall swooning in each other's arms, believe me. We're at war, in case you haven't noticed. And the one and only time he and I got a little too cozy—at my initiative, by the way— the bastard up and shot me."

She absorbed the inflammatory memory playing through his mind of Zorin's legendary escape from Mogadon. Which certainly gave her oodles to think about. Including the fact that Dex might've shot his former mentor for kissing him—but that didn't mean Dex hadn't liked it.

In fact, maybe it meant the opposite.

Clearly reading the speculation scrolling across her face, Zorin chuffed out a wry chuckle. "Aw, come on. If he walked in here right now and I laid one on him the way you want, I guarantee he'd haul off and sock me in the face. And that's if I'm lucky."

Would he?

She wondered.

His hands squeezed her shoulders, then firmly put distance between them. "Now pay attention, sweetheart. I gotta mosey on back to the *Relentless* for some shut-eye. Before I do that, I got something for you."

"A Tombola gift?" A happy sense of anticipation bubbled through her. She scooted around on the couch to face him and bundled her wine-red hair in a twist. "Because you haven't given me anything yet."

"Just my heart on a plate with a carving knife." He eyed her efforts to tidy up. "Leave it down. It suits you. And right now I want every guy on this ship to know I've been all over you."

"If they did, there'd be a riot." Apparently Dex wasn't the only Mogadon male who got possessive with his woman. She pressed her thighs together to suppress another wicked pulse of need. "What did you bring me?"

"Like presents, do ya?" Grinning at her enthusiasm, he dug from his utility belt a flat steel box the size of an antique postage stamp. "Gotta remember that. So I can spoil you, sweetheart. You'll find I'm a pretty indulgent lover."

"I like the sound of that." With a delighted little bounce that made him grin, she accepted the box and snicked it open. Eagerly she leaned in to check out the flat glittering object, no bigger than her pinkie nail, on its bed of velvet.

"A cyber chip!" Her astonished eyes flew up in surprise.

"Figured it was a fitting gift for a cyber samurai." He leaned forward and tapped the cyberport at her temple. "Was I right?"

"It's perfect." She lifted the chip to study it with a professional eye. "This is gorgeous work. How's it programmed?"

He looked pleased by her appreciation. "Well, it's really just a prototype. Ginned up by a cyber wiz who followed me from Mogadon into exile. It's a transcription chip."

Her mouth fell open. "A *transcription* chip? I thought they were an urban myth."

"They were." His big shoulders lifted in a self-deprecating shrug. "Jules—my man Julius—managed to make it work. I'm no samurai, but I've used it myself. Believe me, if it wasn't safe, I wouldn't be letting you anywhere near it."

"Never mind if it's safe. It works!" Excitement sharpened her voice and spiked her pulse. "Where did you go with it?"

"Ever wonder how I powered from the Omega Sector the night Dex declared war—the night I ambushed his patrol in deep space—onto the *Relentless* six clicks later to coast into Mogadon airspace for your auction?"

"I didn't think you commanded that ambush yourself. It takes weeks at hyperspeed to fly that distance."

"Yep." He grinned. "With that transcription chip, I plugged into a full-body cyberport and ported from the Omega Sector to the *Relentless* in less than a click. You need a working port at each end, dead accurate coordinates programmed into the chip, a decent level of skill to navigate the cyberverse—and titanium balls. I'm not gonna lie about that. Cuz once you commit, you can't back out. The only way out is through."

"No kidding!" She stared at the chip in fascination. Totally jonesing to try it. "Everyone who's ever tried to transport their physical body through cyberspace from one geospatial location to another has flipping *died*. Or else disappeared permanently trying it."

"Except Jules and me. And pretty soon you, if you're game to give it a whirl. That chip's programmed to navigate to the cyberport on the *Relentless*—where I'm at. With your chops in the cyberverse, you can program it to go anywhere in the galaxy, long as you have working coordinates to a full-body cyberport at the other end."

Her brain raced to juggle the implications. "If you can mass-produce these chips—and if the tech holds up—it's a game changer. Whoever holds the galactic patent will earn billions!"

"Spoken like a true Kryll," he murmured. "Fact is, that patent's the main act in my Tombola bid for your Pops."

"Who'll definitely appreciate the value. He may be a god, but he's also a merchant. Just don't call him 'Pops' when you bid. He strongly prefers 'Your Holiness.'" For the first time since she'd landed in this whole mess, she dared to feel hopeful. "All we need to do now is make sure you make the final ten."

Then hope like hell my father chooses you.

"And you'll leave that to me," he said firmly, unfolding to tower over her with his colossal height. "This entire gig's a bomb rigged to blow. You're supposed to be neutral, sweetheart. And after what just went down in the pit, you better believe every joe in the show knows I'm your guy. That's despite watching gorgeous Ben Nero with his hands all over you. By now, every poor schmuck on this ship either wants to fight him or fuck him."

"That's Ben for you," she murmured, studying the chip cradled in her hands. "He specializes in inspiring that effect. I keep telling him we're done. To go back to his telepath breeding program and his pedigreed stable."

"With the way he looks at you? And the way you look at him every boot-scootin' time he touches you? Doesn't look like you're done to me—not even close. And I guarantee you he's not buying it."

He held up a patient hand to fend off her flustered protests. "Not to mention whatever the heck's going down between him and Dex. Then there's the First Indomitable himself going hardcore Mogadon and threatening to rip the head off anyone who touches you with his bare hands. Long story short? Your shindig has this entire ship on edge. And two thousand Mogadon with twitchy trigger fingers packed on this nuclear-armed battle bus… well, it's enough to make a Syndax war dog like me a little twitchy myself."

Infected by the warning that threaded through his words, Kaia pushed to her feet and started to pace. "I know this Tombola isn't going the way it should. Dex took a knife for me today, and you almost died yourself. Obviously, I know it's dangerous. What do you think we should do?"

Zorin checked the blaster at his hip. "Play the game, samurai. Play it out like a champion to the last blasted move. That's what Dex is doing—shipping these wannabes off his ship by the boatload before they spark a mutiny. And preferably before he gets spaced by some political rival who's even more ruthless than he is."

Violently she shivered and chafed her arms to ward off the deep-space chill that tiptoed down her spine. She didn't like thinking about just how much danger Dex was putting himself in.

And she liked even less hearing Zorin treat the same danger so casually.

Once he cared about Dex so much he fled into exile to protect him. Maybe I'd even say he loved him. Surely all that emotion doesn't just disappear?

Feeling Zorin's thoughtful gaze, she shot him a pensive look. "What happens then?"

"Easy-peasy. When we're down to the last ten yahoos, that's when you tell Pops I'm your guy." One side of his mouth tipped up in a rueful smile. "Then we let the strength of my bid and my natural charm do the rest."

His plan was simple and solid. It made eminent tactical sense. Except for the lurking sense of dread she couldn't seem to shake that his easy-peasy plan wouldn't go down the way they both wanted.

Wanna read the rest of this steamy PNR why-choose MMMF adventure? Renegade Angel is available free in KU and now in print! Read RENEGADE ANGEL now!

Other Laura Navarre Adventures Now Available from Ascendant Press:
Anticipated Angel: An Astral Heat MM New Adult Novella Prequel
Interstellar Angel: An Astral Heat Romance #1
Renegade Angel: An Astral Heat Romance #2
Atomic Angel: An Astral Heat Romance #3

Or binge the complete series with The Astral Heat Romance Box Set

About The Author

Amazon category bestselling author Laura Navarre (she/her) whisks you away from your day-to-day with extra spicy, extra shifty, wild & witchy why-choose romance starring hot bi heroes and the confident women who love them. Laura's paranormal adult academy why-choose series delivers intense and steamy out-of-this world adventure with powerful heroines who never have to choose, passionate prose that packs a punch, and enough heat to set your Academy uniform on fire.

A long time ago in a galaxy far away, Laura wrote dark fantasy romance for Harlequin, while her sinister twin Nikki Navarre wrote sexy spy romance. Now, with seventeen sexy stories released worldwide, this Washington, DC-based nomad writes erotic paranormal adult academy why-choose romance featuring bi heroes, badass heroines, sweet poly love, and extreme poly steam.

Laura is a cat lover, globetrotter, wine addict, PhD candidate, and president of Ascendant Press. When she isn't conjuring witchy worlds, she's a professional diplomat with a professional background in weapons of mass destruction and an MFA in writing popular fiction from the University of Southern Maine. She's won the 2023 New England Readers' Choice Award, the 2023 Virginia Romance Writers Holt Medallion Award for Best Book by a Virginia author, finalled in the 2023 RWA Fantasy, Futuristic, and Paranormal Chapter's PRISM contest, and is a former Golden Heart finalist. She's also relentlessly obsessive, alarmingly efficient, and a recovering perfectionist. She's deeply suspicious of the Oxford comma, but she's never met an em dash she doesn't love.

Stalk Laura across the galaxy like the queen killer stalks Zara at the Icarus Academy! Her adventures across the witching world are trackable by witches, warlocks, humans, and aliens alike at:

http://reamstories.com/witchingworld (best way to reach me and grab steamy free reads)
http://www.LauraNavarreSciFi.com (go here to join my newsletter)
https://amzn.to/3FrX5t7 (follow me on Amazon to be alerted to new releases)
http://www.goodreads.com/LauraNavarre
https://www.bookbub.com/authors/laura-navarre
https://www.facebook.com/LauraNavarreAuthor
https://www.tiktok.com/@LauraNavarreAuthor
http://www.instagram.com/LauraNavarreAuthor